On cue, Aunt Ginny hit the sound effect on my iPhone and a boom of thunder came through the Bluetooth speakers, followed by the peal of Toccata and Fugue in D minor—Dracula's pipe organ. The theme song of every haunted house. A power surge from the speaker overloaded the weak electrical system. The lights flickered and everything went black.

Owen Rodney whimpered. "Oh no. Figaro was trying to warn us."

Joanne hollered from the kitchen, "I got it!"

She must have flipped the breaker in the mudroom, because the lights came back on to reveal Dr. Simon Beck lying facedown in his tiramisu.

Gladys Philippot tapped her cell phone and snapped off a couple pictures. "Whoa. That'll go on the front page."

His wife reached out to nudge him. "Very funny, Simon. Joke's over."

His head flopped over to the side, and she pulled back her hand shaking it like it was covered in fire ants.

I said a prayer and put my finger on Simon's neck to check for a pulse. I looked to Aunt Ginny and shook my head. "He's dead."

Dracula's pipe organ gave out a repeat of its earlier cry and Aunt Ginny gasped. "I wonder if he saw that coming . . ."

Mischief Nights
Are
MURDER

LIBBY KLEIN

Kensington Publishing Corp.
www.kensingtonbooks.com

To Linda
Who is a good sport both on and off the page.

And to Bob
You finally got that dream to be called, Kenny Love.

CHAPTER 1

"**I** can't promise you won't be murdered." I held the phone away from my mouth and made a face to my boyfriend across the peach-colored kitchen. "I also can't promise that you'll have a ghost sighting, the police will investigate, or that anyone in residence will receive a death threat during your stay."

I could promise they'd find an inordinate amount of Figaro's hair on their clothes, but I don't think that's the kind of pledge they're looking for. I reached out and removed the smooshy-faced Persian from his forbidden perch on the counter next to my espresso machine. "Lots of people stay here and go home just fine."

The caller on the other end of the phone rolled through several stages of irritation, but at least they hadn't asked about the viral interview from a few months ago that someone had remixed to music. The phone went dead, and I shoved it back in my pocket. "Well, we can add requests for survival guarantees to the list of red flags when vetting prospective guests."

My new house cleaner, Kenny Love—who kept begging me to call him my manservant despite my constant refusals—puffed the air out of his cheeks. "Well, did they mention the dinner tour?"

"No. But they hit our reviews on Facebook, Tripadvisor, and Yelp—the trifecta of doom. They want to think about it and get back to us."

My onetime high school bully now reluctant assistant, Joanne, threw her head back. "Pass!"

Kenny's orange eyebrows took a plummet. "Cripes, what do we have to do to attract some guests who aren't flakes? I was sure being on the tour circuit would at least help bring in a higher quality of weirdos."

Gia flashed me a grin over his coffee cup. He was my calm in the eye of the storm.

Joanne took a cookie sheet from the cabinet and slammed it on the counter next to Kenny's hand. "Don't act like you're all fed up. You've been here for fifteen minutes."

Joanne Junk was pushy in high school. Twenty-six years later she had taken it to another level. I wished she'd go back to working out her aggression in field hockey and be nicer to the rest of us. She'd been working here as a favor to Aunt Ginny for six months now. Six very long months.

Kenny had recently taken over the B&B guest room cleaning duties when Victory's visa expired at the end of the summer. She'd returned to Ukraine to attend university for the fall semester. Aunt Ginny and I still missed her. We also had our fingers crossed that *World News* wouldn't mention Victory's name along with the words "meltdown" or "nuclear winter" on their nightly broadcast.

Her replacement was about my height, with flaming hair and a long face like Dr. Bunsen Honeydew's assistant, Beaker. Kenny was the most enthusiastic applicant I'd ever interviewed, even though I worried that three redheads in the house was the hair color equivalent of summoning Beetlejuice. He shot a dagger of spite at Joanne that she masterfully deflected with her shield of scorn.

She had taken an instant disliking to him much in the same way she had a seething dislike towards me. One day I hoped to find out just what that reason was.

The timer on the copper double oven dinged and Kenny snatched the potholders from their hook. "Now come sit down for lunch. You are going to love this! My mother's shepherd's pie with mashed buttery rutabaga. If you love it like I think you will, we can add it to the menu for the gourmet tour dinners next week."

Figaro's eyes popped open like tiny suns, and he trotted over to call dibs with some strategically placed figure eights around Kenny's ankles.

Joanne snorted. "People don't want shepherd's pie for a fancy do."

"They'll want mine," Kenny shot back.

The front door slammed, and Aunt Ginny rolled down the hall in a grumble. Two yellow leaves stuck out of her spiky red hair. "That jack-o'-lantern is possessed."

I grabbed four plates from the cabinet and handed one to Gia. "Oh, it is not. I told you that's your imagination."

The eighty-year-old dropped her purse on a loaf of bread next to the commercial refrigerator and pulled off her navy scarf. "It was smiling this morning. Now it looks like it wants to kill me."

Gia snickered. "Maybe it is rotting."

She ripped the leaves out of her hair and, with a glare in the Italian's direction, crushed them to powder over the trash can. "We just put it out a couple days ago. I think the kids have started warming up for Mischief Night a week early."

Mischief Night was prank night. And it happened the night before Halloween. Audacious kids got their egg-throwing, pumpkin-smashing trickery out of the way, then returned the next night to brazenly demand candy while dressed as Wonder Woman or Harry Potter. "I doubt they've started early. Have you seen how much toilet paper costs now?"

Kenny set my eggplant-colored Le Creuset Dutch oven on a trivet in the middle of the table. "I almost forgot the secret ingredient. Be right back." He threw the potholders down and disappeared into the pantry to go up the secret back stairs to his room on the third floor.

Aunt Ginny inched over to give it a sniff. "What is that?"

Joanne frowned at the browned casserole. "He calls it shepherd's pie. It looks like slop. You're not going to eat that, are you?"

I took a serving spoon from the drawer. "Of course we are. Why don't you try it?"

Joanne turned her back to the offending dish. "I wouldn't touch it. It's supposed to be made from an old sheep."

Gia turned wide eyes to me and there was concern in those baby blues.

I shook my head. "It's not sheep." *I don't think.*

Kenny burst through the pantry door holding a little red bottle. "Eww. I heard that. It is not an old sheep. It's ground beef and a little ground lamb. Where do you think we are, Wuthering Heights?"

Joanne muttered, testily, "Well, if you'd made it right, it's supposed to be mutton. That's why they call it shepherd's pie."

Kenny ignored her and placed the red bottle on the table. "I had my mother send me this hot sauce from home. Wait till you taste it. Now, who's ready?"

Figaro answered the invitation by jumping on the table next to the casserole and Gia shooed him away. The black smoke Persian gave him a swat on the hand in retort.

Aunt Ginny grabbed a plate and passed it over. "I'll give it a whirl."

Joanne, having lost her last ally, sucked in a breath and stomped from the room.

The rest of us took seats at the kitchen table to try Kenny's newest masterpiece. He'd been making special lunches for us since he started. Some of them were good. Joanne had yet to try any that we knew of.

Aunt Ginny held up a forkful of the topping. "What kind of taters is this?"

Kenny drizzled hot sauce over his shepherd's pie. "Rutabaga. On account that Poppy can't have potatoes."

Aunt Ginny glared at me like I was somehow responsible for ruining all her dreams and begrudgingly took the bite.

Gia nodded while he chewed. "Is very good, but hot."

Kenny eyed me expectantly while I tasted the savory dish. I definitely picked up on the rosemary and thyme. I also picked up on the butter and wondered how many Weight Watchers points this meal would cost me. Then I was hit with the heat. *Wow. That's a lot of something.* I reached for my water glass at the same time Gia reached for his.

Aunt Ginny started to fan herself. "Sweet Jesus."

Joanne peeked through the crack in the door from the dining room, but I pretended I didn't see her. "It's delicious. I think this would be perfect for an Irish-themed weekend, but we may need something fancier to serve on the gourmet tour. You can make this for the four of us anytime." I grabbed my water and took another gulp. I was starting to sweat through my leggings.

The door shut and Joanne's disapproval could be heard by the china clattering in the hutch as she stomped through the dining room.

Kenny grinned. "Maybe you can convince Mr. Hansen to put a good word in with the East Lynne Theater Company to let me audition again? You know they're doing that Sherlock Holmes production all month."

Aunt Ginny surgically deconstructed her casserole into three piles to remove the corn from the middle. "Royce will be here later to watch *Psych*. You can ask him yourself."

Gia laid his arm across my shoulders and mopped his brow with my napkin. "I thought your audition was last week."

Kenny's checks flamed.

Aunt Ginny put another pat of butter and a hefty shake of salt on her mashed rutabaga. "What happened this time? And why is this hotter than the Devil's backside?"

"Is it?" Kenny doused his plate with more hot sauce. "There was a theater mishap. I might have improvised something that was mistakenly applied to the director's wife."

I held back a laugh. Kenny gave worse auditions than I'd had in the ninth grade, and I only got to sing one line of "I Feel Pretty" before the director gave me the cut sign.

Kenny glanced at me for just a moment. "Well, how was I supposed to know she wore a girdle? I was just trying to freestyle some lyrics with the music."

Gia snorted and I gave him a playful jab in the ribs.

Joanne waltzed back in the kitchen with her chin in the air and clanged together the aluminum mixing bowls like she was playing cymbals for the New York Philharmonic.

Kenny ignored her and raised his voice over the passive-aggressive symphony. "I don't think he really banned me from the theater until *Sugar Babies* gets a revival. That's probably just an expression."

Aunt Ginny had that look in her eye that told me she had a zinger prepped and ready to launch, so I knew I'd better change the subject quick to save Kenny's feelings. "I'm going to call Linda at the Inn of Cape May to discuss next week's dinner tour. I think there's been some confusion about our part in the event."

Aunt Ginny pushed her plate to the side. "What confusion? We're making fancy dinners for a week of tour groups. What's to discuss?"

Figaro's ears slowly rose behind the abandoned plate, then his eyes and his flat nose. His whiskers twitched in the direction of the gravy. He slowly descended back under the table.

I took a breath. "The event on the tour website says a little more than that. In addition to the five-course gourmet dinners every night . . ."

Joanne rhythmically smacked the metal sifter against the mixing bowl and raised her voice. "Gourmet dinners that *I'm* making."

"That you're *helping with*," I corrected. "Well, it seems that we're supposed to entertain the guests with stories."

Kenny shook his head and shrugged. "Okay. Stories about what?"

I steeled myself. "Um. Our ghosts."

Aunt Ginny gave me a droll look. "You said I couldn't do that anymore. That I was taking money under false pretenses."

I squirmed in my seat. "I told Linda we don't have ghosts." *I didn't mention that we may not believe in them.*

Gia pulled up the tour website on his phone while I talked. He cocked his head to look at me. "Bella, their website says this is a Halloween Week Package including a paranormal breakfast, a nighttime scavenger hunt, and a week of Haunted Dinner Tours. Why did the Inn ask you to be a part of that?"

I picked up my glass of iced tea and tried to drown myself through my answer. The room got very quiet.

Aunt Ginny wouldn't let me off the hook. "I'm

sorry, what was that?" She eyed me so hard I thought she was going to pull out a gooseneck lamp for an interrogation.

I swallowed. "They're calling us the murder house."

After a moment, Joanne started laughing so hard that she had to cross her legs. "The murder house. Oh, that's awesome!"

Figaro took advantage of the distraction, and a gray paw appeared to swipe at Aunt Ginny's plate and got a pawful of rutabaga. He licked it, spit it out, shook off his paw, then went in for swipe number two to try it again.

If it were possible, Kenny's chin slid even lower. "I thought you said no one was murdered here."

I nudged Figaro off the bench seat to the floor before he could go in for swipe number three. "They weren't. And I told Linda just that. Right after I found these on The Hotel Macomber's front desk when I delivered those gluten-free muffins." I pulled two tickets for the Cape May Haunted Dinner Tour out of my pocket. "The manager tried to hide them under a box of mints, but I'd already seen them. I told her I wasn't aware of the haunted part of the dinner tour, but she insisted we're just a fun new stop they've added to their annual Halloween event. She said it's all in good fun."

Gia's new iPhone vibrated. He looked at the screen and turned it over. He squeezed my shoulder. "Do you want to back out?"

Aunt Ginny snatched the tickets from my hand. "Back out? No way. If anything, we need to ask for a bigger share of the pot. Don't you give me that look, Missy. Those tour organizers knew what they were doing when they got you to put the Butterfly Wings on the route. People are fascinated by the fact that you keep finding murder victims. No wonder the week sold out so fast."

I gave Gia a pitiful look. "I thought it was because of my baking."

Joanne muttered, "Well, that shepherd's pie will put a stop to that. Maybe you should serve it after all."

Kenny got up from the table and banged the lid onto the Dutch oven. "If you're so offended by my mother's comfort food you can stop drooling over it like the Wasp Woman."

Gia's iPhone vibrated again. He picked it up and frowned.

"What's the matter?"

It continued to buzz while he shook his head. "Nothing that cannot wait. Your baking is delicious. I think it is time we put a sign in La Dolce Vita that the gluten-free pastries come from the Butterfly Wings. You could get more business."

Aunt Ginny looked as though she was about to hyperventilate. "Are you going to answer that?"

Gia's phone went silent, and he smirked. "Answer what, signora?"

My cell phone rang from across the room, and I looked at him. "I think someone is determined to find you." I walked across the kitchen and dug it out of my purse. "Hello? . . . Yeah, he's right here. Hold on."

I held Gia's eyes as I walked to him and handed him my phone. "They found you."

He took it with a sigh. "I am not free. I will call you back when I am ready." The blood drained from his face. "Are you sure? . . . Do not lie to me, Daniela. . . . Okay. I am on my way." He handed me my phone. "Daniela says Momma had a fall. Ambulance is taking her to hospital."

Like the real hospital? Or like she's watching General Hospital *and faking it again?*

Aunt Ginny put her hand on Gia's arm. "The poor thing. Let us know if there's anything we can do."

Gia took my hand. "What do you think?"

"It's been three months since she's faked an emergency. And your sister Daniela doesn't usually do your mother's bidding. That's more Teresa's MO. I think you should take it seriously."

He rolled up the sleeves of his black dress shirt. "I am not so sure. But they have left us alone for weeks."

I grinned. "Well, you didn't give anyone but Karla your new number after you destroyed your phone."

Gia smiled. "*Sì.* I will check. This better not be a fake."

"Do you want me to come with you?" *Or I could eat a cactus instead?*

Joanne choked. "Are you trying to kill her? The woman hates you."

She's not wrong.

Gia waved me off. "No. You do not need to worry. I am sure it is nothing."

He pulled me against him, and Aunt Ginny and Joanne groaned and made *uck* noises. "I will come back soon." He ignored them and kissed me slowly. *"Ti amo, cara mia."*

Bells were ringing, and bluebirds flew around my head as they often did when Gia kissed me, and I had to watch him leave.

"Oh, fer Pete's sake. Snap out of it!" Aunt Ginny was standing next to me holding out the kitchen phone. "I called Linda at the Inn of Cape May for you. She says they've had an unprecedented number of bookings for the tour, so they decided to add a few nights. Our first dinner isn't next week. It's in two days."

CHAPTER 2

"You can't just commit me to a five-course dinner in forty-eight hours, Linda."

The gravelly voice coming through the phone balked like I was turning down a free vacation to Tahiti. "I don't know what the big deal is, honey. I'm doin' you a favor so you can make some money before the off-season. You don't exactly have the best reviews in town."

I paced the library while Figaro chased the dangling belt on my sweater.

"You know those reviews are fake. And once you get one bad review people love to pile on. I literally just found out about the ghost stories this morning. I have no idea what I'm doing on this tour. We're not haunted."

Linda softened her voice. "It's no big deal. Ya just make a little dinner, tell some stories, and give a little house tour—easy peasy."

I stopped short and a ball of gray fur flopped at my feet. "What do you mean, give a house tour? I didn't agree to that."

"Sure, you did, hon. When you agreed to be part of the Haunted Homes Tour."

"I didn't agree to be part of the Haunted Homes Tour. I only agreed to a week of gourmet dinners."

I heard someone in the background talking and Linda put her hand over the mouthpiece. She said something I couldn't make out over the muffle. When she returned, her voice was all sweetness and light. "Huneee. It's no big deal. You just walk them around and show off that beautiful house of yours. And while you're at it, tell them about Siobhan. We've all heard the rumors. It was on that lady's blog who stayed with you. Being haunted's nothing to be embarrassed about."

Oh, my Lord. Elaine Grabstein is still plucking my nerves two months after checkout. "I'm not embarrassed because it isn't real. That guest had a very vivid imagination." And I suspected day drinking, but I kept that thought to myself.

"Look, we could have asked any number of bed and breakfasts who would jump at the chance to be on this tour for the promotional opportunity, but we asked you—to help you out for your first season. We already got the Victorian hearse lined up. Everything is a go."

"What in God's name is the Victorian hearse?"

"One of the carriage tours is going to do transportation for us. They got a pair of black stallions pulling the tour groups in the wagonette draped in black bunting to each of the locations. Didn't you read the contract I gave you two weeks ago? It outlines all your duties including your agreement to pay for a fifth of the advertising costs."

That shepherd's pie was about to make an encore appearance right there in the library. I ran to my desk in the hall to see if there was a contract I had missed. "What advertising? I haven't approved anything. And how much is a fifth?"

"Don't worry, it will be taken off the top before you get your cut from the ticket sales." Her voice turned a little threatening. Much like Aunt Ginny trying to playfully tell you not to touch her whiskey truffles at Christmas. "Unless you back out. If you back out or do anything to publicly make the tour look bad, you'll pay a penalty to offset our cancellations."

I moved the candy corn–scented candle and flipped through the disheveled stack of papers on my desk. I didn't come across anything that looked like a contract. "I'm not trying to back out; I just don't want to lie to people."

"Honey, with everything that's happened to you in the past year, you will have plenty of stories to entertain the guests without having to tell one lie. Trust me."

Aunt Ginny's copy of *Garden & Gun* magazine peeked out from under a crossword puzzle, and I moved it out of the way. A fat white envelope with the Inn's green logo fell from the center. My heart rate started heading up the on-ramp of the panic freeway.

"Tell you what, hon. The tour starts here tomorrow night. We have a phenomenal chef, so adding days was no problem for us."

I was only half listening to Linda at this point. The envelope had already been ripped open. I slid out the folded document and Figaro jumped on the desk and swatted it like it had a feather and a bell. I unfurled the paper and scanned it for the signature line.

"Why don't you come to the Inn and see how we

run our tour? Maybe you'll be more comfortable for Saturday night after you see how it's done."

Aunt Ginny came around the corner from the kitchen drinking an iced coffee, took one look at the contract in my hands and the look on my face, and did a one-eighty back to the kitchen. *Ginny Frankowski* was clearly scrawled on the dotted line.

"I'll take you up on that. By any chance did you receive the signed copy of the contract from us?"

"I got it right here. Ginny signed it while I waited."

I narrowed my eyes in the direction of the kitchen. "Oh good. Well, I'll see you tomorrow night then."

I stood under the archway leading from the hall to the kitchen. Aunt Ginny was seated on the banquette hunched over her glass, a striped pink straw caught in her mouth. Her eyes darted back and forth from Joanne to Kenny. Neither of whom would make eye contact with her or me.

I took a step into the room. "I don't suppose there's anything you forgot to tell me?"

Her face was as passive as Lake Lily on a still day. "The Inn of Cape May sent over a tour contract. I took care of it for you."

Kenny slowly sucked air in through his teeth and emitted a low whistle.

"Did you happen to read it before you signed it?"

Aunt Ginny gave me a one-shoulder shrug. "Boilerplate stuff."

"Like the part where we agree to give guests a paranormal house tour? Or how the Inn can extend the event dates all the way to Christmas without warning? Or maybe the penalty we pay if we cancel for any reason?"

Joanne blew out a breath and focused on her pan of maple bars.

Aunt Ginny gave me a weak smile. She looked like she was just about to apologize when the doorbell rang. "You'd better get that. It's probably Dr. Rodney here to check in."

I gave her one last look of exasperation before I headed to the front door. Figaro had beaten me down the hall and was in pre-flop position. "At least let me get it open before you hit the floor, Fig."

My pinecone wreath clattered against the front door in a burst of cinnamon. A delicate-looking man with a pale complexion and a ten-dollar haircut stood on the front stoop holding a weathered brown suitcase. He was wearing frumpled Dockers and a baggy yellow sweater that had seen better days.

"You must be Dr. Rodney. Welcome."

He pulled at the neck of his sweater, nervously. "Oh dear. You have a cat."

If he's allergic, Figaro will never leave him alone. "We're a pet-friendly B&B. I hope that's okay. It is mentioned in your contract." My face flamed at the hypocrisy of the situation.

He put his suitcase down and took off square-rimmed black glasses. He searched his clothing for some corner with which to clean them, found only his fuzzy sweater, and disappointedly returned them to his face. "I'm not allergic."

Did I say that out loud?

"I was just hoping for some quiet this week."

I held the door open wider to reveal Sir Figaro Newton, the picture of decorum, with one leg in the air, tidying his nether regions. "This is Figaro." *In all his glory.* "He's a very quiet cat."

Figaro peered under his leg at Owen Rodney. His eyes grew twice their size and then he sprang up and did a weird sideways double hop down the hall.

What in the world was that?

"Oh dear. I'm afraid he is very uncomfortable with my visit."

I looked down the hall where one ear and an eye poked out from around the corner in the sunroom. "I'm sure he's fine. Fig is used to guests. He won't trouble you any." *I guess the lying starts now.*

Dr. Rodney picked up his suitcase and took a tentative step into the marble foyer. He took his time examining the chandelier and sniffing the spider plant on the foyer table. "Do you have any other guests staying this week?"

"We do. We aren't fully booked, but—"

He pulled at the neck of his sweater and cut me off. "Are they aggressive?"

Aggressive? "We don't allow aggressive pets. We only . . ."

Dr. Rodney pushed his glasses back on his face. "I mean are the human guests aggressive."

"No. I don't believe so." *They tend to be sleepwalking, snack-hoarding portrait thieves—but not aggressive.*

He sniffed the coatrack. "I know there are no other animals in the house. I don't like to be around a lot of people."

I sniffed to see what he was picking up on. *Do I need to change the air freshener?* "So, far, there is only one other lady who has checked in. She's a retired librarian who collects teapots. She seems very sweet."

He squatted down and looked under the sofa in the sitting room.

I followed suit and squatted down to see what he was looking at. "She has the room across the hall from you, but she's out for a stroll. You'll probably meet her at breakfast. Shall I show you to your room and get you checked in?"

He picked up his suitcase and looked down the hall. Figaro's ear disappeared around the corner. I led Dr. Rodney up to the Adonis Suite and he touched every rosette on the banister as he walked up the stairs.

"Are you here for the ghost tour, Dr. Rodney?" I held my breath waiting for his reply.

He stared at the framed painting of Hughes Street on the landing. "Call me Owen, please. And no. I have no interest in ghosts or any of that weird stuff. I'm just a regular guy, and I want a quiet week, away from the voices."

CHAPTER 3

"Where did you get that Owen Rodney guy from?" I came down the stairs from taking our new visitor to his room.

Joanne was setting out the tray of maple bars and hot cocoa on the library coffee table for the guests. She fanned orange and black napkins into a graceful arc. "Ginny booked him."

Aunt Ginny reclined on the sofa, conveniently close to the afternoon snacks. "He passed all the tests. Why? What's wrong with him?"

Where do I start? "Did you ask him how he heard about us?"

Aunt Ginny nodded. "I followed your script exactly."

Joanne rolled her eyes. "Why you always so uptight, Buttface?"

Probably because of this hostile work environment.

Aunt Ginny took a maple bar. "He said he found us on the Internet."

That could mean anything. We could be on a website

called murder houses dot com. "Did he say anything else?"

Aunt Ginny shrugged. "He didn't mention my interview from last summer. And he didn't have any accounts on social media for me to check what bizarre groups he belongs to. Why?"

I pointed to Figaro, who was peeking out from under the cherry cabinet where we kept the board games. "The cat is freaked out by him for one. And he seems like someone familiar with taking a psych eval."

Aunt Ginny brushed a crumb from her lap. "You're too suspicious. He's a doctor. I'm sure he's harmless."

"He sniffed the room key."

Aunt Ginny paused. "Maybe he's a psychologist. They're always crazy."

Joanne stuffed her hands in the pockets of her pink camo fatigues. "You said you wanted to talk to me before I went home today. Can we get this over with? I have a life."

Oh good. Time for my daily argument. I glanced at Aunt Ginny, who was pouring herself a cup of hot cocoa and settling in, then back to Joanne. "Why don't we go in the sitting room?"

I stalled for a few minutes and stoked the fireplace. Then I fluffed the fuzzy pumpkin pillows. I couldn't find anything else to fuss with, so I sat on the edge of the wing chair opposite Joanne and drummed my fingers against the stack of acorn coasters on the side table.

Joanne crossed her arms over her belly and scowled in preemptive disgust.

I took a breath and dove in. "I wanted to thank

you for all you've done to help me these past few months. I could never have gotten through the summer without you."

Joanne snorted. "You couldn't have gotten through the tea party without me."

"True. But I also don't want to keep you here when I know you were only doing us a favor to begin with."

"I was doing Ginny a favor."

"Right. You've said. Many times. But now that Kenny is here, you don't have to stay any longer. He can help me with the breakfast and baking duties before he cleans the guest rooms. Plus, since room and board is part of his salary, he has extra responsibilities."

Joanne's eyes narrowed to slits. "Are you firing me?"

"What? No. You've reminded me every day that your being here was only supposed to be temporary. I'm just saying, we're good now. You're free to go."

A wave of anger rolled off of her and crackled. "Whatever. It's not like I care. This was only charity."

Why is this a problem? I thought she'd be dancing on the ceiling right now. "I know. That's my point. And you were amazing while I had to do the baking for three different businesses. I mean, except for your attitude. You're really mean. I can't imagine how that works for you in a normal job situation. Like, maybe try to be nicer when you get an actual boss. But now you're free to do something you'd really enjoy instead of being stuck at my house every day."

Joanne stared at my forehead like she wanted to light me on fire. I couldn't understand what she was so mad about. *We're on the same side, Joanne.* I took a little sniff to make sure I didn't smell smoke coming from my hair. "Take your time, and when you find something you really like, let me know and I'll give you a great reference."

Joanne stood with her fists balled at her sides. "You can keep your reference. My work speaks for itself. This favor to Ginny has gone on about six months too long. Kenny will only ruin the reputation I've worked so hard to make for this place, but you wouldn't know anything about that. You're on your own—I'm outta here."

She stormed out of the room and slammed the front door behind her.

Aunt Ginny toddled across the hall dabbing a cocoa mustache from her lip. "What happened?"

"I have no idea."

"What'd you say to her?"

"I told her we didn't need her help anymore now that Kenny is here full time."

Aunt Ginny's eyes doubled in size. "You fired her?"

"No! Why would you both say that?" I swung my arm out in a fan. "I released her."

"Released her? Like throwing a toddler into the deep end of the pool?"

"No. Like opening a cage and letting a trapped sparrow go free." I fanned my arm again. "I thought it was what she wanted."

Aunt Ginny snorted.

"What? She was only here because you begged her to help me through the summer."

Aunt Ginny quirked an eyebrow. "Uh-huh."

"And she let me know every single day that she hated it. I was starting to think my name was actually Buttface. She said I was the reason there were directions on the box of Eggos."

I was forming another argument in my defense

when my pocket buzzed. I pulled out my phone and checked the text. "It's Gia's sister Karla. He's on his way back to the coffee shop and they want to talk to me."

"Uh-oh. I'll get my purse."

"Why are you going?"

"'Cause I don't trust you to give me the full scoop. You can't even read the signals with Joanne."

Gia paced the length of the polished espresso bar like a sleek Italian panther. "Momma has broken her hip. She will be out of the restaurant for weeks."

His baby sister, Karla, leaned against the counter in the back and followed her brother with her eyes. The only concern she showed was the occasional glance to her cuticles. Their other sister Daniela sat at one of the dark wood tables and gently bounced five-month-old Violetta on her knee while Gia took another lap.

"I should have answered my phone. *Stupido.*"

Karla sighed and snapped a dish towel. "Giampaolo! She's the boy who cried wolf. This is not your fault."

Gia shook his head but didn't step off pace. "She is just old lady. I should have known better."

Aunt Ginny and I waited quietly for him to calm down. Well, I waited quietly. Aunt Ginny wanted to know if he was going to make us coffee since we came all the way over here.

He stopped and stared at her, absently. "Mia Famiglia will have to close. Momma cannot finish the season."

Daniela lifted Violetta over her head and gave her a little wiggle. "Marco can take over for the rest of the year. The restaurant's closed New Year's through Valentine's Day anyway."

Gia shook his head and his dark hair curled over his collar. "Marco is only sous chef. He can do dinner and pasta, but only Momma does *il pane* and *dolce.*"

Karla tightened the apron around her tiny waist. "We can't afford to close. We need the shoulder season to pay the bills before it gets really slow for the winter. Especially now that we lost certain exclusive contracts." She shot me a look behind her brother's back.

Don't blame me. I didn't blow the whistle.

Gia stopped pacing and pressed his palms against the counter. "Poor Momma is only allowed to go home, church, and Mia Famiglia to work."

Poor Momma? She's on house arrest. Not a prisoner of war.

Daniela looked my way. "I guess we can now add the hospital to the list."

The muscles in Gia's jaw clenched and released. He stared into the empty dining room.

I wanted to do anything to make it better. My mouth did not consult my brain before offering up suggestions—as was my custom. "Why don't I make the desserts until she's back on her feet? I can bake in the middle of the day after the breakfast shift and before the dinner tour."

Karla pointed one of her long orange fingernails at me and nodded. "Yes. I bet Poppy can bake bread too."

"Bella, no. You have enough with the ghost stories about fake ghosts and the murders."

Daniela stopped wiggling Violetta to look over the baby's bald head at Aunt Ginny. "The what?"

Aunt Ginny put her hands out for the baby. "Psh. I'll tell you later."

Gia took my hands in his and kissed them. "Momma has not been kind to you. You owe us nothing. I will take care of it."

Daniela passed Violetta to Aunt Ginny. "Now, wait a minute. The money from the restaurant also helps pay for Karla's apartment, and Violetta's diapers, which are outrageously expensive. We've already had to make cuts."

Karla piped in, "If you start paying for all our expenses, how will you pay for Henry's preschool? He has another year until he can go to kindergarten."

I grinned to myself. The little guy just turned five last month. He missed the cutoff for kindergarten by ten days, and he had a lot to say about it.

Gia sighed, walked behind the bar, and turned on the espresso machine.

Aunt Ginny nudged me in the ribs. "Now we're talking."

He took out the coconut almond milk. "No. Is not enough. Marco cannot do it all by himself."

Karla handed Gia the frothing pitcher. "He's not by himself. He has Esteban and Frankie."

Gia shook his head, unconvinced.

Aunt Ginny wanted to help, likely because she wanted a free coffee. "Poppy could make lasagna and manicotti, and you could make me a latte."

I hissed, "Aunt Ginny."

"What?" She shrugged like she had no idea what I was talking about.

Gia pulled a shot of espresso and dumped it in the hot milk. "Momma will never allow it."

Daniela threw her arms up in exasperation. "Then

don't tell her. It's not like she'll be able to walk to the restaurant and check on things."

Aunt Ginny gave Gia's younger sister a fist bump and a nod.

Gia handed me my latte. "Do you really think you can do this for us?"

I lowered my voice. "For you, anything."

A grin played at his mouth. "Okay."

Daniela and Karla cheered.

Aunt Ginny raised a fist. "Yay. Are you making one of those for me?"

Gia banged the portafilter to release the hot disc and start again. "But I will come help you every afternoon I can when Karla comes to work."

Aunt Ginny sent me some side-eye. "I bet you regret releasing that sparrow now, doncha?"

"We'll be fine." I dusted cinnamon on my latte, and really regretted choosing today to tell Joanne she could go.

CHAPTER 4

An uneasy feeling about this convoluted ghost tour twisted my stomach into a knot during morning yoga. My mind had given up during the first child's pose. Even Figaro had lost interest in winding back and forth through my hair and was curled up in the laundry basket. His ears stood at attention at a faraway sound of what must have been the lid being popped from a can. He shot through his new pet door like a bullet. *Well, Kenny's up.*

For the first week after Itty Bitty Smitty, my handyman, had installed the pet door, Figaro was sure it was a trap. He wouldn't go anywhere near the flap. Smitty put one of Fig's toys on a string and pulled it through to show him how it worked, but Fig's fur stood on end, and he hissed at the plastic sheet like it was an inter-dimensional portal to the dog pound. He'd obviously gotten over his fears once he realized he didn't have to wait for me to get his breakfast anymore. I was just thankful to have a dead bolt to keep the more brazen guests out. If this past summer taught me anything, it's that weirdos had a tendency to cross the velvet rope and wander up to my room in the middle of the night to request pancakes for breakfast.

I showered and dressed and went down to the kitchen to have a leisurely cup of coffee in peace. Because I'm a dreamer. A dreamer of impossible dreams. I must have brain damage from falling off the swing as a kid.

The daily squabble that waited for me had reached new heights of pettiness. Kenny was making sausage rolls and eggs. And Joanne, who had surprised everyone and shown up after walking out in a huff last night, was making one of her specialties—crab Benedicts with a side of *you're doing everything wrong*. Aunt Ginny was sitting at the table calmly reading her magazine. She'd worked up an immunity to their bickering.

I poured myself some Ethiopian Yirgacheffe from the French press. "Joanne. I didn't think you were coming in today." *Or ever again.*

The stocky woman with a permanent scowl adjusted the samurai bandanna over her ash-blond hedgehog hair. "Ginny called me last night and begged me to give you two weeks' notice. And since one of us is a professional, here I am."

Oh, thank God.

I glanced at Aunt Ginny, who gave me a wry look and flipped a page. "You don't need to stick to an exact two weeks' notice if you don't want to, Joanne. I want you to do what's best for you. But I do think two weeks' notice or thereabouts . . ." *Like to the end of the ghost tour and maybe once Momma is back in her kitchen . . .* "Would be appropriate."

Aunt Ginny cleared her throat, flipped her page, and singsonged under her breath, "Taste the crow."

I quickly added, "And very professional of you. Take as much time as you want to find something you like."

Joanne showed her appreciation for my generous offer by slamming the cabinet next to my face. "I'll do what I want. And I can't believe you're going to let him serve that slop to the guests."

Kenny had made fluffy scrambled eggs and the cutest little puff pastry pigs stuffed with sausage links. They had peppercorn eyes and little pastry snouts. I practically swooned. "Oooh, Kenny, these are so heckin' cute! Make sure there are a few without sausage for Owen Rodney. He's a vegetarian. Oh, my word—look at their little curly tails!"

Aunt Ginny cleared her throat loudly, flicked her eyes to mine, and turned another page.

Something had upset Joanne and she was having some kind of angry prayer with God about it when the toaster started to smoke.

Kenny removed one of his perfect pigs from the baking sheet with a spatula and placed it on a waiting rack. "You're burning something, Iron Chef."

Joanne flicked the lever, and two blackened discs sprang from the slots. "That toaster is broken. I should have bought pre-toasted muffins, since anyone can take the easy way out and use store-bought puff pastry. Gordon Ramsay would be so impressed with those grade-school level biscuits."

Kenny lined his pigs up on a rack to cool. "Where do you get your pre-toasted muffins? Feed and tractor supply?"

Joanne ripped another English muffin in half and shoved it in the slots. "Dipwad."

Kenny gave me a *do you see what's happening here?* frown. "Dipwad?"

"Don't look at me. I'm called Buttface."

Kenny sighed. "This two weeks is just gonna fly by."

Please don't poke the bear until the ghost tour is over. I held up my hand. "Shh."

There was a ruckus coming from the other side of the dining room door. "You're the worst kind of con artist. Playing on people's emotions. You're lower than the scum of the earth!"

"You wouldn't know the truth if it marched through the room playing the tuba!"

I swung the kitchen door into the dining room and caught sight of Owen Rodney crouched behind the potted ficus in the corner by the coffee carafe. He was holding a fork like a sword aimed at Gladys Philippot. Gladys was thrusting one of my hundred-year-old dining room chairs out like a lion tamer. Figaro sat on top of the dining room table calmly washing his face in postbreakfast rapture. I wasn't sure where to direct my panic. I chose the naughty feline who knew better than to behave like that. I couldn't say the same for the humans.

"What's going on?" I scooped Figaro into my arms and gave him a look so he would know that we would have words over this later. He licked my hand.

Gladys Philippot stood about five feet two, with a wild mass of silver-blond curls in a ferocious mane. Her bright green eyes flashed anger from deep-set wells. Her cheeks flushed as she jabbed the dining room chair at Owen Rodney like she was a beast master in a pink cardigan and sensible shoes. In a small, raspy voice she commanded me, "Get back! Poppy, do you know who this phony is?"

I looked at the door where all three of my assistants were posed like a wax display of cavemen at Madame Tussauds. I turned my eyes onto the trembling Owen Rodney.

Owen gripped his fork tighter. "No. You can't believe anything she says. She's the worst kind of liar. Lower than a politician."

Aunt Ginny clutched her pearls and gasped. "Good God. A telemarketer?"

Figaro was so stressed out he started to purr in my arms and take a bath.

Owen tried to disappear behind the sideboard, so I turned my gaze back to Gladys. "I take it you two know each other?"

Gladys thrust the chair towards Owen. "Oh yeah. This fraud inna doctah like he wants you ta think."

Owen's head peeked out of the green fronds. "I am so." He disappeared as fast as he'd popped out.

Gladys chuckled bitterly. "He's got a fake PhD from one a them online schools."

The ficus in the corner shook. "I have a real PhD, from a real school, that happens to be online."

Gladys mocked him. "Oh yeah? In what?"

After a pause, Owen answered with less vigor, "Cheese ripening."

"Ha!"

I sent Aunt Ginny a look of silent scolding that she was doing her best to pretend she couldn't see.

Gladys put the chair down to catch her breath. "This cuckoo is Owen Rodney, Pet Psychic!"

Figaro stopped licking his paw and his ears flattened.

Kenny pushed the door all the way through to the dining room. He was still carrying a pastry pig on a spatula. "Wow. A psychic."

Gladys laughed. "Are you kiddin' me? He's a phony with a podcast called *Paws for Concern*."

Owen popped upright and jabbed his fork in Gladys's direction. "Well, she's a sneaky tabloid reporter who's only out to make people like us look like weirdos. She tried to ruin me!"

When did we become an us? Don't lump me in with your weirdness. I had that feeling you get when you think you might have texted something objectionable to the wrong person and you're scared to look. "What do you mean, people like us?"

Owen looked from Gladys to me like he regretted the direction he was headed and was trying to come up with a good alternative.

Gladys filled in the gaps for him. "He means people who fake paranormal activity like saying they been cursed to find murder victims, or they can read animals' minds and stuff like that. You two might be in the same camp of crackpots. Time will tell."

Aunt Ginny took a giant step backwards into the kitchen. Followed very quickly by Joanne. Kenny wasn't sure what to do, so he left the sausage pig and the spatula next to the coffee carafe and followed the other traitors.

Wait a minute. People plural? There's more of us?! I'm googling that later. "I thought you were a retired librarian."

Gladys shrugged. "It's a good cover story. Until some yahoo like this outs me, that is." She shot a look across the room and Owen jabbed his shaky fork out a little further.

"Wait, are you here to investigate me or him? I don't want you harassing anybody." *That's Aunt Ginny's job.*

"I have to follow wherever the weird rumors of a juicy story lead me. And this time they led me to you." Gladys hooked her hands on her hips. "As long as you've not misrepresented yourself for fame or fortune, you don't have to worry about being exposed as a fraud. You haven't, have you?"

Misrepresented like being on a ghost tour when I'm not haunted? "What? No. I wouldn't . . ." *Not on purpose.*

Gladys pulled a square of paper from her pocket and unfolded it. It was a screenshot of the website advertising the Haunted Homes Tour. "See. Since you're on this Haunted Homes Tour, as long there really is paranormal activity here, you're good."

I swallowed so hard my throat let out a loud strangled gurgle. "And if nothing otherworldly manifests?"

Gladys cocked her head and narrowed her eyes. "Then you'd better not be saying that it is. I'm here for a whole week to check it out for myself." She pointed at Owen. "But this whack job needs to stay outta my way. I told you months ago I'm not printing a retraction. I stand on my journalistic integrity."

Owen took a tentative look out from behind the plant. "Journalistic integrity? You work for a supermarket tabloid called *The Chatterbox*. Your last story was about a potato shaped like Leonardo DiCaprio." He looked at me. "Don't you have the right to refuse service to anyone? It said so on my contract. You could just cancel her reservation. Do it for Figaro. He's very nervous about her being here."

Figaro yawned his fish breath in my face.

Gladys took a step around her chair and dropped into it. "Yeah, like that won't look suspicious. Like there's no way I could investigate you from one a your competitors. I'm sure you don't know anyone who would spill the beans for a chance to get their picture in a newspaper that's sold at every checkout stand on the East Coast."

My knees were feeling a little weak. "I don't understand why you would come here."

"One a my readers sent me that viral interview your aunt gave. The rest is research. Somma your neighbors say you got a curse on you. The cops say you been involved in eight homicide investigations in one year. They think maybe you're a weirdo who shows up when they hear the sirens. Maybe we can do an interview later. You can give me your side of the story."

I put Figaro down and he pounced at the quivering ficus in the corner. "What if I never claimed to be haunted?"

She waved the paper in my face. "I don't see you trying ta deny it neither."

"I'll think about it." *There, I thought about it. No.*

I returned to the silent kitchen and shotgunned my cold coffee with three sets of eyes watching me. "Okay, let's review what happened here."

Everyone started talking at once.

Aunt Ginny twisted her hands together. "I may have been a little too trusting when Owen Rodney said he was a doctor."

"Ya think? We have a process for this very reason."

Kenny chewed the inside of his cheek. "Maybe

while he's here he can convince Figaro to stop swatting everything off the counter."

Joanne put a new English muffin in the toaster. "Maybe if you'd kept your nose out of those police investigations you wouldn't have Geraldo Rivera and Dr. Dolittle staying at your B and B."

Aunt Ginny poured me a fresh cup of coffee. "These two slipped through the cracks because they falsified information about who they are. I'll be more careful from now on. I'm sure it won't happen again."

I took her peace offering and added coconut creamer and two packets of stevia. "You have to try harder, Aunt Ginny. You've let in more weirdos who are only here to dig up dirt and make us look bad. I can't have people reporting that the Butterfly Wings is cursed. You need to pay closer attention to the guests you're reserving. I reverse search their email address; I google them, check their social media; I ask where they work, how they heard about us. If they say anything about murder or curses, I tell them we have no vacancy."

Joanne rolled her eyes. "Soon you won't be able to book anyone here."

"I vetted a professional group of four coming in from a California tech company next week. I just want you all to try harder and follow the procedure I've set up."

Aunt Ginny sucked her teeth. "I think you're making too big a big deal out of this. I'm seventy years old. I should be retired."

I sipped my coffee. "You're eighty. And most of this was your idea." *I only give you enough work to keep you out of trouble and that doesn't even help.*

Aunt Ginny narrowed her eyes and was about to deny everything, but Kenny held up a serving tray of sausage pigs ready for the dining room. "I just want to know how we're going to convince the tabloid journalist that there's paranormal activity here."

Aunt Ginny grabbed the bowl of scrambled eggs. "Oh, I have some ideas."

CHAPTER 5

It was time to enter the belly of the beast on the down-low. I walked over to Gia's mother's restaurant, Mia Famiglia, to check in with the chef in charge.

The two-story red building with snappy white shutters and a green awning sat across the brick-paved courtyard a few doors down from La Dolce Vita. Clay pots of oregano, rosemary, and thyme graced either side of the carved white door, tempting passersby to sample the old-world Italian cuisine created within.

I walked through the terra-cotta-tiled dining room to a kitchen of white subway tiles. A row of potted herbs sat on a painted shelf under the lone window. The black floor was covered with rubber anti-fatigue mats at every stainless-steel station.

Chef Oliva Larusso's sous chef, Marco, was standing at the cold prep station chopping tomatoes. What sounded like a horse race was playing in Italian on a little black radio over his head. "*Ciao*, Poppy." He put the knife down and hurried over to kiss me on both cheeks. "Thank you. I hear you gonna help wif da bread and dessert. I show you what we have."

Marco gave me a tour of the walk-in filled with fresh vegetables and enough butter and cream to make Julia Child dance the macarena. There was an entire shelf dedicated to the meal grand finale.

"We have two tiramisu, one lemon ricotta cheesecake, dis da filling for da cannoli, and dis da filling for da *bombolini*. We gotta make da shells every day." He opened the freezer and pointed to three plastic tubs marked gelato. "Dis one da *stracciatella*, dat da *nocciola*, and dat da peestahkio. Dis also good for affogato wif biscotti."

I nodded along. I may have very rudimentary skills in Italian, but it was a good thing I was fluent in menu. *Stracciatella* was vanilla with hardened chocolate drizzled on top and all throughout. *Nocciola* was hazelnut. And peestahkio was pistachio. That last one was usually the test as to whether the gelato was truly artisanal or bought from some factory. Momma's was made right here in the Carpigiani batch freezer. "How long do you think this much dessert will last?"

Marco shrugged. "Weekend? Gelato maybe longer. Chef Oliva make da bread yesterday before she fall, and da cannoli shell is ready to fry when cannoli is order."

"What do you need today?"

Marco led me to the stove top where he had a giant pot simmering. "I already make da sauce for da pasta. I make da pasta for da ravioli now. Giampaolo, say you make da lasagna, *sì*?" He pointed to two industrial casserole dishes the size of sheet pans and raised his eyebrows awaiting my confirmation.

I grabbed an apron from the wall and slung it over my neck. "Yep. I can do that."

Marco clapped his hands. "You gonna make it delicious."

I grinned. "I'll do my best." *God help me to not destroy the reputation Gia's mother has spent twenty years building for herself. Even though she hates me and would cut me for a nickel. Amen.*

Two other line chefs arrived. One was a slim man with caramel skin and straight black hair. The other was a chubby, jovial man with perfect chocolate eyes and a poufy Afro he had to tuck into a pink hairnet. They both grinned at me and waved as they went to work.

I checked the menu to see how the lasagna was described. Did it have meat or just cheese? Was it a red sauce or béchamel? The official description was "baked lasagna." *Well, that tells me nothing.* I asked Marco, "Does Chef Oliva make red or white lasagna?"

He was rolling a pasta wheel across a long sheet of dough on the counter, but he stopped long enough to shrug. "Whatever she feel like."

Okay. Well, today she feels like red sauce. I took the fresh pasta sheets from the walk-in, and gathered large containers of ricotta, mozzarella, and Parmesan. After I added eggs, herbs, and minced garlic to the ricotta, I started building my layers. Sauce, noodles, ricotta, shredded cheese, repeat.

My phone buzzed a text from Aunt Ginny:

This psychic weirdo just told me Figaro is unhappy with the African violets in the sitting room window. They're obstructing his view of the birds. He wants to know if he can move them to the table.

I typed back: **Sure** and shoved my phone in my pocket.

Behind me, the three chefs all yelled, "*Buona sera!*" in unison, and a familiar voice called it back before a man started nuzzling my neck.

I grinned when the stubble hit my cheek. "It's a

good thing I recognize your voice. I might have thought Marco was getting fresh."

Gia growled in my ear. "He would not dare."

I turned and gave Gia a kiss but noticed his eyes were on the lasagna. "Something wrong?"

"Si." He looked around the kitchen. Gia disappeared for a moment and came back to hand me an aluminum bread pan.

"What's this for?"

"That is for my lasagna. Someone needs to be quality control." He wiggled his eyebrows.

All I could do was shake my head and put sauce in his personal lasagna pan. *I can see how he's his mother's favorite.*

Gia washed his hands and dried them with a paper towel. "What can I help with?"

"Grab a pan and follow my lead. Your mother left the restaurant in good shape for the weekend. I've got some dough rising overnight. I'll have to come back early tomorrow to make the bread."

Gia wrapped his arms around me. "Then I will be here. You can teach me many things."

With his lips on my neck, I couldn't even remember how to make the chocolate chip cookies I'd mastered in junior high.

I worked all afternoon to get the casseroles ready for tonight. It was hard to tear myself away from the man I loved, the camaraderie of the kitchen, and the smell of oregano, but after Gia put the lasagnas in the industrial oven for the first bake I had to go. Marco was in charge of taking them out. After they cooled, one of the chefs would cut the casserole into squares for reheating when lasagna was ordered.

Marco gave me a key to the back door so I could come in whenever I needed, whether he was there or not. If Momma ever found out I had a key to her private domain, it would be the final nail in both our coffins.

I kissed Gia goodbye and hit the road. I had a meeting at the Inn of Cape May that I couldn't be late for. Aunt Ginny had signed my life away on that contract like she was applying for an account with Fingerhut. And I had to get a handle on what I was doing before the tour groups started arriving for dinner tomorrow night.

The Inn of Cape May was a stunning five-story mansion built in the late 1800s. The fifty-one-room white hotel sat across from the beach, and they had my favorite porch in all of Cape May. For months I'd been sneaking over there to read in one of their rocking chairs when things were quiet at home. That stopped when I was discovered by Aunt Ginny and the Biddies camped out under the purple awning with iced teas and poker chips. They had told me they were going to the hospital to read to coma patients. Then I got roped into taking them to Urie's for shrimp cocktail. I'm not sure what I did to become their designated driver.

A row of orange lights were strung across the roofline, and a cluster of gourds were piled up with some dried cornstalks on either side of the front door. Linda was waiting for me at the foot of the stairs in the Inn's powder-blue lobby. She was a petite brunette with plum highlights and an obvious fondness for purple judging from her sparkly aubergine eye shadow down to her violet fingernails. "Oh good, you made it."

"I wouldn't miss it." *Because I don't want to get sued.*

Linda linked her arm in mine and led me towards the dining room. "The night manager isn't in yet, so

I'll be giving the ghost tour. The bookings have been incredible. All the inns are thrilled. We may extend through Thanksgiving. You'd like that, wouldn't you? I wish we'd asked you last year. We were in a real slump."

"I didn't even have an oven this time last year."

We walked through the bar, and I did a quick scan for pink hair and familiar faces—force of habit after being ambushed by crafty Biddies in beach robes. We passed into Aleathea's Restaurant—a bright room facing the ocean with two sides of floor-to-ceiling windows. The classic white scroll back chairs and pink tablecloths gave the room an air of relaxed nineteenth-century beach chic.

Linda adjusted a stack of menus. "We're going to start with the house tour, then dinner in the private dining room. Scallops or prime rib. Chef is hoping they go with the prime rib since it's been roasting for hours. And when the dessert and coffee come out, I'll tell them about some of the sightings we've had here. We end with a ride in the haunted elevator."

"The elevator is haunted?"

Linda patted my hand. "That's what they tell me. Oh look." She pointed across the room to a romantic table in the corner. "That couple is with the tour group that goes to your house tomorrow. They're staying with us this week."

We approached a dramatically handsome man with sandy-brown hair in a sharp suit. He had a square jaw and movie star good looks. The woman next to him was about twenty years his junior and could have been a Bollywood celebrity. She had long straight black hair and dark almond eyes.

Linda swept her hand to the couple to make an introduction. "Mr. and Mrs. Beck, this is Poppy McAllister. The owner of the Butterfly Wings Bed and Breakfast. Your Haunted Homes Tour goes to her house tomorrow."

I tried to mask my fears about being a fraud with a smile. "Hi. We're so looking forward to your visit."

The woman's eyes lit up and she flashed a row of perfect teeth. "We are really excited about it, aren't we, Simon?"

The man grinned at his wife, then turned the wattage on me. It was the kind of smile that made you come out of menopause and lower your hair from a tower to be climbed. "Absolutely. Brooklyn here's been buzzing about Cape May and this tour for weeks."

Brooklyn put her hand on her chest to show long, graceful fingers and a French manicure. "I hear so much about what Simon does for a living, I've been dying to come see it for myself." Something must have been funny, because she looked at her husband and they laughed at a joke that went right over my head. Even Linda gave me a glance with an eyebrow shrug.

Simon let out a little laugh. "Sorry. Inside joke."

Brooklyn waved her hand. "He's too modest. This is Dr. Simon Beck. He teaches at Staunton University. He was recently published in a very prestigious scientific journal." She finished her thought with a rush through a laugh. "I can't remember the name of it now. But it was a big deal."

"Oh, that's wonderful. Congratulations."

Linda pulled my elbow. "They'll see you tomorrow night for dinner and the ghost tour."

They both smiled and Brooklyn's eyes sparkled. "I can't wait."

Linda took me through a door into the main dining room. "It's a five-night dinner tour with a paranormal breakfast and a walking scavenger hunt. Those two start the tour with you and end with me. Each group stays together for the whole week. It gives them a chance to get to know each other and helps us make sure they don't repeat houses."

I was trying to focus on her instructions, but meeting Dr. Simon Beck left me feeling a little envious. Why couldn't I get university professors instead of paparazzi and nut jobs like Owen Rodney, Pet Psychic?

Linda gripped my hand. "Listen, Hunny Bunny. I know you're uncomfortable with all this. But it's really important for the tour guests to have a good time. They signed up to hear about ghosts and paranormal activity. We don't want to let them down. You understand?"

"Are you trying to tell me to make some stuff up?"

Linda stopped walking. "No. Of course not. You don't have to lie. No one's lying about anything. But we don't want you to freeze up because you're embarrassed. Just go with the flow and tell them about the murder victims and the curse that's following you around. That's what they signed up to hear."

And Gladys Philippot will get her front-page story next to alien babies and Elvis sightings.

CHAPTER 6

Metallic buzzing like the sound from a radio-controlled mosquito woke me. I bolted upright when whispers in the hall outside my door followed. Figaro rolled down the bed like a potato bug. He let me know he didn't appreciate the interruption with a glare and some irritated tail swishes.

Someone bumped the wall right outside my door.

"Kenny, is that you?" I was still getting acclimated to having someone else living down the hall from me on the third floor. Victory had stayed in a boarding-house, but Kenny's room was just thirty feet away.

I hopped out of bed and grabbed my baseball bat and cell phone just in case. I had the first 9 and 1 typed and ready to go by the time I unbolted and threw the door open.

The hall was dimly lit by a plug-in air freshener that had heaved its last puff of buttercream. I hoisted the bat up to my shoulder and stepped out expecting to see Owen or Gladys—the only two guests currently in the house. Instead, a slim Asian man holding what looked like a Star Trek tricorder stopped in his tracks, looked at the bat, then scrambled backwards in alarm.

Oh, heck no! I took off after him with Figaro thundering backup on my heels. Either I would whack the bejeezus out of the intruder or Fig would flop and trip him down the stairs. We'd worked out the plan after the last guest appeared in our room unannounced. "What are you doing in my house?!"

The man passed the stairs and a short, busty girl with pale skin, long dark hair, and crimson lips came out of the bedroom behind him. She wore designer blue glasses and a Berkeley sweatshirt. She took one look at the bat in my hand and screamed before flying back into the room.

A giant red eye about six feet off the floor moved down the hall towards us and Figaro abandoned the maneuver. He jumped ship and tore off down the stairs with his tail between his legs. *Deserters get shot, Fig!*

I hit the final number 1 on my phone. "I'm calling the police. They can be here in two minutes." *Give or take twenty.*

The man with the tricorder spun around and held his arms up. "Don't do that! We're guests. I'm in the orange room."

The red eye blinked and then drooped three feet towards the floor.

A voice came on the line. "Hey, Poppy. Did you find another body?"

I lifted the phone and cleared my voice. "Hold please." I looked back at the Asian man. "What do you mean, you're guests?"

"We booked weeks ago. We flew in from California?"

I lifted the phone back to my face. "False alarm."

"Okay. We'll talk soon, eh?" The dispatcher, who I was sure was Gloria-who-thinks-she's-a-comedian, disconnected.

I reached up and turned on the hall light. There were four people all dressed in black, shading their eyes and blinking. Two women and two men—one of whom was holding a professional-looking video camera.

The Asian man came forward with his hand out to introduce himself. "We got off to the wrong start. I'm Clark Richards. The host and producer of *Paranormal Pathfinders*—the ghost-hunting show."

Why in Saint Peter's name . . . "What are you doing here?"

The busty girl slipped her headphones down around her neck and blinked a couple of times. "We thought you were expecting us."

The hall light flickered.

Clark put his hand down since I'd made no move to take it. "We were tipped off that you were having paranormal activity by a loyal viewer. I believe she recently stayed with you. Elaine Grabstein? We're here to help."

I stared dumbfounded until the cameraman reached out and gently took the bat from my hands.

Clark continued speaking his gibberish. "If you've seen the show, you might recognize my lead investigator, Harper Reed."

A chocolate-skinned woman with long, straight ebony hair raised her hand. "Hey-ey."

Clark pointed to the man under all the tech equipment holding my bat. "This is my camera operator, Ritchie Grubb."

Ritchie Grubb looked more like a cop or a Boy Scout than a paranormal investigator. Tall and broad, with close-cropped hair and a clean-shaven face. He had a tattoo of an eagle holding a globe running down one muscled arm. "Sorry, I hit your door. It's tight up here with all the equipment."

I snatched my bat back but kept it low. "It wasn't built with television crews in mind."

Clark put his hand on the back of the busty girl's shoulder. "And this is our newest investigator, Paisley Bordeaux."

"Hi. Sorry I screamed. You were really scary looking." The device in Paisley's hand beeped. She looked at it, then held it out in my direction. It beeped again. "Wow. There is a lot of activity around you."

I pushed her hand away. "Stop that. You all can't just come here and start an investigation for your TV show. And why now of all times?"

The four of them looked around at each other. Harper answered for everyone. "The Haunted Homes Tour."

Paisley adjusted her headphones. "We get press releases for haunted tours across the country. There's a dozen of them happening in Southern California this month alone."

I twirled the bat in my fingers. "I can't believe anyone on my staff would book rooms for *Paranormal Investigations* or whatever you called it."

Clark gave me a weak smile. "*Paranormal Pathfinders* is the name of the TV show. We booked under the production company's name. The girls are sharing a big purple suite and Ritchie and I have the orange suite with the twin beds."

The camera operator quietly added, "The Monarch."

Aunt Ginny, you didn't. "Come with me." I marched two flights down the main staircase and around the hall to the kitchen with the rest of them in tow. *I can't believe she did it again. And this time, a TV show. With an assist from that whackadoo Elaine Grabstein.*

I crossed the kitchen and knocked on Aunt Ginny's door. She responded with a sharp, "What!"

"Can I speak with you please?"

Her door flew open. She was wearing a pink kimono robe and had a single curler in her hair. "Do you realize it's half past midnight? Only drunken sailors and casino workers are up this late. Oh, hello."

She had spotted Clark Richards. And judging from the blush in her cheeks, he'd already won her over.

She adjusted her robe and pulled the pink foam roller from her hair and threw it behind her into the bedroom. "Is there a problem, boys? You don't like your room?"

I gave her a stern look. "Aunt Ginny. Do you know who these people are?"

Clark gave Aunt Ginny a charming grin while the other three tried to shrink into the background.

Aunt Ginny came farther into the kitchen. "Of course I do. These are the kids I checked in tonight while you were at that *ghost show* at the Inn."

"They're from a paranormal TV show, and they're investigating us. Did you book their reservation?"

Aunt Ginny raised her eyebrows to her hairline. "Why do you think it was me?"

"Do the words 'pet psychic' mean anything to you?"

The pantry door flew open, and Kenny leapt from the hidden staircase into the kitchen wearing Underdog pajamas and holding a tennis racket like a samurai sword. *"Yaaaaaaa!"*

Aunt Ginny clutched at her chest. "Sweet Pickles! What're you doing?"

Kenny stood to his full height. "I heard voices. I'm here to defend your honor."

I had to remind myself to pick my jaw off the floor. "With a tennis racket?"

He looked at my hand. "The bat was taken."

I put the bat on the counter. "You can hear us down here in the kitchen but not outside your room where I caught them creeping around?"

He ran his fingers through the orange pouf on top of his head. "I was blow-drying my hair. Nothing looks this fabulous without some work."

I can't even process that on two hours of sleep. "Kenny, did you make a reservation for *Paranormal Pathways?*"

"*Pathfinders.*" Ritchie calmly adjusted his camera.

Kenny tsked. "It was probably Joanne."

Clark turned to Harper and whispered something, but I had built up too much steam to hear him. "When I find out . . ." I let the threat hang in the air with the scent of Aunt Ginny's Noxzema and Clark's woodsy aftershave.

I stomped out to the hall. The group shuffled behind me. I picked up Figaro, who was in the process of swatting things off my desk, and put him on the floor. He launched into a frenzy batting the fallen pens down the hall.

I angrily thumbed through the reservations folder, and when I found the agreement for Clark Richards I pulled it from the stack and said, "Look right here . . ." *Oh crap.*

I tried to shove it back into the file. "You know. It doesn't matter who made the reservation . . ."

Aunt Ginny's eyes narrowed. "Oh. I think it does. I can admit when I'm wrong. Let me see it."

"No. That's okay. Really."

Kenny tried to pull the paper back out. "It wasn't me. If it says my name, it was probably Joanne trying to frame me."

Aunt Ginny snapped her fingers. "Poppy Blossom. Now."

I pulled the document from the stack, and there, signed in purple ink on the bottom line, was a glowing horrific *P-o-p-p-y* in my handwriting. *This is my tech company from California. I will never live this down.*

Kenny wiped his hand across his brow. "Phew. Thank God. I wasn't really convinced I hadn't done it."

I cast a glance at the group. "I wasn't expecting you until next week."

Aunt Ginny handed me back the reservation agreement. "It *is* next week."

Clark put one hand behind my arm and the other behind Aunt Ginny's. "We promise to stay out of the way. You won't even know we're here."

"If that were true, I'd still be asleep. You told me you were with Ethernet Studios."

Paisley looked over my shoulder and pointed to the contract. "'Ether Net' is two words."

I shoved the agreement back in the folder. "Well, this is embarrassing. I guess I lost track of days. I'm sorry about the confusion, but we have to be careful with who we allow to stay here. We've had some . . ."

"Crackerjacks," Kenny supplied the sentiment I was trying to avoid.

"Problems," I offered. "I hope you have a wonderful visit, but you can't film your show here. We've had too much publicity of the viral kind already."

Aunt Ginny cleared her throat and patted her chest. "Frog."

Harper returned and handed Clark one of those interoffice envelopes with the string looped in a figure eight around a disc. He unwound it. "We would never push ourselves on anyone who didn't want our help. But we do have a shooting schedule to keep."

Uh-oh, where is this going?

"My research assistant was here weeks ago to do the preliminary site survey." He pulled an ivory paper from the envelope and handed it to me. "We've already spent the budget for this episode, and you did sign the waiver . . ."

I looked at the ivory sheet in my hand. I had to hold it a little further away to make out the letters, but I was holding a contract giving all access permission for *Paranormal Pathfinders* to film in my house. It was dated the week after the Antique Show and signed by Aunt Ginny. Countersigned by Victory. I turned it so Aunt Ginny could see it better.

She blushed. "I thought that girl wanted our autographs. We were famous that week."

I sighed. "It's okay. But new rule—you don't sign things anymore."

"Sure. As long as there's a rule that I can check behind you to see who you're booking."

"Fair enough."

Kenny put his arms around the both of us. "We've all said things that we regret. Mistakes have been made. Contracts have been signed. I may have forgotten to make those lemon squares for tomorrow's check-in. The point is, we forgive each other because we're like a family."

Aunt Ginny muttered under her breath to Kenny, "You need to make those lemon squares in the morning. I promised I'd sneak half of them out to Book Club."

I turned back to Clark. "Well. Obviously, this says I can't forbid you from filming, but you can't go in the guest rooms that are occupied without their permission. I don't care what that paper says. You can sue me."

Paisley and Harper nudged each other in silent victory. I, however, felt about three inches tall. I was zero for three. I needed to stop fooling around with Gia and pay more attention to things around here.

Clark grinned. "We won't go in any guest rooms without a signed agreement, and we promise to keep the interference to a minimum. If we don't find any paranormal activity, we'll say so on the air and maybe that will cut down on the weirdos who keep calling you."

You'll help with the weirdos? This feels like a pot versus kettle situation.

Paisley rubbed her eyes and yawned, "Then we can move on to the Physick Estate. They're reporting all kinds of activity."

Aunt Ginny's fist flew up to her mouth. She sucked in some air. "Oh no."

I could feel the piggyback panic galloping to the surface. "What?"

"The tabloid lady. What do we do?"

Kenny groaned and started to pace. "Why did I become a housekeeper? I should have been an exotic dancer."

Ritchie adjusted the camera back on his shoulder. "Which tabloid?"

"Gladys Philippot with *The Chatterbox.*"

Clark nodded. "We've dealt with them. They can never make up their mind about us. Either paranormal investigation is a hack, or they want to sensationalize everything we find. What are they threatening to print?"

I took a breath. "That I'm a fraud who lied about having ghosts so I could con people out of money with this ghost tour. Plus, if you say on the air we have *no* paranormal activity you'll put me in breach of contract with the Haunted Homes Tour." I slid my eyes to Aunt Ginny, who slid her eyes away from me.

Clark's eyebrows shot up. "So, if we say there aren't any ghosts, you're in trouble with the tabloid and the tour contract, and if we say there *is* activity, you'll have every kook around trying to stay here to spot the ghosts."

Ghosts that I don't have. Because we aren't haunted.

Figaro came skittering through the circle of our feet batting a Pilot pen like David Beckham.

Aunt Ginny watched Figaro flip around and run into the sitting room. "We've got a weird cat. Do you want to film that?"

Clark tucked his envelope under his arm. "I tell you what. We usually sleep all afternoon and do most of our investigating at night anyway. So, while we're here, we're just regular tourists. We'll do our best not to say a word about the show or the investigation around Gladys Philippot. Maybe she won't get wind of the show until after she's written her article. Deal?"

He put his hand out and this time I shook it.

The group of them went back up the stairs and we waited until we were alone to speak. Aunt Ginny faced me. "Why didn't you tell him Gladys is threating to print that you keep finding murder victims?"

"I don't want them to think I'm weird."

Kenny snorted.

Aunt Ginny tapped her fingers on the desk. "Somehow we need to keep the paranormal people away from Gladys, Gladys away from the pet psychic, and you away from murder victims."

Kenny blew out a breath. "We can do this. It'll only last a week."

So did Hurricane Katrina.

CHAPTER 7

I was running on two hours of sleep and forty years of disappointment. I just couldn't relax after that disastrous confab in the kitchen at oh dark thirty. The ghost hunters went right back to where they'd left off when I caught them—outside my bedroom door. *They whisper about as quiet as Aunt Ginny in church.*

Around four a.m. I gave up on sleep and shifted into another gear. One that ran on coffee and gluten-free streusel. I pulled out my phone and googled *Clark Richards.* I was pretty embarrassed about not knowing who the Paranormal Pathfinders were considering they were on cable and their YouTube channel had about two million followers.

I was pulling my fourth batch of muffins from the oven when Figaro jumped off the windowsill, pawed the cabinet open, and dove inside. I cracked the door to peek at him. "What's gotten into you?"

Fig's ears flattened and he turned his back to me. When I raised up, Owen Rodney was standing a wooden spoon's distance behind me. My heart tried to jump out of my chest, and I might have said something Aunt Ginny would not approve of.

"Geez, Owen. You nearly scared me half to death. What are you doing in here? It's five thirty in the morning."

He was wearing rust-colored corduroy pants, a blue short-sleeved button-down shirt with a yellow bow tie, and he had a metal colander resting on his head like a World War Two German helmet. A Peppa Pig Band-Aid was wrapped around one arm of his black glasses. "You have a very talkative squirrel outside my bedroom window."

What do I say to that?

I stared at the colander on his head. Little patches of nut-brown hair poked through the holes like short dry spaghetti.

He pulled at his bow tie like it was poking him in the Adam's apple. "I was looking for some tea when I heard you in the kitchen."

"The tea box is out on the buffet, and I'll bring some water in momentarily. Why don't you go make yourself comfortable?" *In the other room.*

Owen blinked twice. "Also, Figaro would like the beef stew for breakfast this morning."

The cabinet thudded with the unmistakable sound of a fourteen-pound Persian flop.

Owen looked at the cabinet, pulled at his bow tie, then looked back at me.

"Thank you, Owen."

Once he'd cleared the kitchen, I opened the cabinet and gave Figaro a stare down. "Sound travels, my friend."

Figaro gave me his best unblinking stare back. I put the water on, then took out a can of his favorite crab and salmon, and—pushing down my pride—

one of the beef stew supreme. *This is ridiculous.* I opened both cans and sat them on opposite sides of the kitchen floor. Then I took Fig out and showed him the salmon. "Look, your favorite." I knew it was cheating, but I didn't care. I left nothing to chance.

I sat Fig in the middle of the room, and he looked between the two cans. Then the traitor minced his way over to the beef stew and licked it in the universe's biggest coincidence. He gave me the look that meant *put it in my crystal bowl, woman. I'm not feral.*

I picked up the beef stew and dumped it in his pedestal pudding bowl with the last shred of my dignity, then placed it on the floor. His purring was almost loud enough to drown out his lip smacking.

By the time Joanne showed up around six thirty, I had filled the hot-water carafe, set out all the ingredients for breakfast, and baked a coffee cake. Kenny had come down and started his lemon bars. We decided it was too risky to mess with Joanne's breakfast enchiladas because neither of us was willing to face her wrath this early.

Joanne chose to forego her usual greeting of, "Good morning, Buttface." Her eyes roved from the racks of muffins to the stack of flour tortillas to Kenny frozen over his shortbread crust and she opted instead for, "I can't wait to be out of this dump."

It was on the tip of my tongue to bid her a hasty sayonara, but I was already going to pull three shifts today with Momma's restaurant and tonight's ghost tour dinner, so instead I shoved a gluten-free pecan pie muffin in my mouth and thought dark thoughts.

Aunt Ginny entered the kitchen fresh and peppy wearing her "Keep On Truckin'" T-shirt and capris. "Look what I pulled out of the closet. I haven't seen these pedal pushers in years. They still fit." She cast her eyes at Joanne angrily stuffing tortillas and grabbed the coffee carafe. "I'll just take this to the dining room for you."

Kenny sidled up next to me and said in a low voice, "I sense imminent danger to my person over in the hot zone."

I took a sip of coffee and nodded. *You and me both.*

Aunt Ginny flew back into the kitchen in a snit. "Of all the ridiculous. Did you see what that weirdo pet psychic is wearing?"

I've been waiting for this moment all morning. "Really? What is it?"

"The most ridiculous bow tie you've ever seen. Who wears a bow tie with corduroy?"

"That's what you found the most disturbing? Not the metal strainer on his head?"

Joanne dropped the tortilla she was stuffing with scrambled egg and cheese and ran to the door to peek through the crack. With the door open, sounds of Gladys Philippot's arrival in the dining room eclipsed the shock of Owen's headgear.

"I'm surprised you're not out organizing raccoons to take over city council or somethin'."

"Very funny, Ms. Philippot. For your information, the raccoons in this town are already organized."

Joanne let the door swing shut and snickered to herself. "That was worth coming in for." She topped the enchiladas with salsa and cheese and put them in the oven to bake. "You might want to take some of those muffins out to the dining room. The new guests just arrived for breakfast, and these won't be ready for thirty minutes."

"I thought we agreed to keep the guests away from each other." I grabbed a basket of pecan pie muffins and the maple butter and backed into the dining room. The *Paranormal Pathfinders* group were positioned around the table not making eye contact with each other. They sat perfectly still and silent looking straight ahead—except for Harper, who was staring at Owen's metal bowler.

I put the basket in the middle of the table and tried to make small talk. "We also have seating out on the sunporch if anyone is interested." No one would look at me. "No takers?" *Sigh.* "Have you all signed up to go apple picking yet?" I knew they hadn't. "Since you're all here for the fun fall activities. Every group of tourists—like yourselves—should go apple picking. While you're on vacation." *God, even I don't want to go apple picking. I sound like an idiot.*

Owen caught Harper's eye and adjusted his chin strap. "This helps keep my mind clear from unnecessary interference."

She nodded. "Mm-hmm. Sure."

Paisley leaned towards Owen and her tricorder beeped under the table. She shot upright and made a face at Ritchie.

Harper's pocket made a loud whirring noise, and she stuffed a napkin in it to muffle the sound. "Sloppy eater."

Gladys cleared her throat and stared at Clark. "Don't I know you?"

Clark smiled. "I don't believe so, ma'am."

She cocked her head and examined him from a couple different angles. "Are you sure? Did you go to NYU? You look very familiar."

Clark picked up his orange juice glass and used it for cover. "No, ma'am. Virginia. Must be another Japanese American."

The muffled notes of the theme from the eighties

Ghostbusters movie began to play. Ritchie ripped his cell phone from his back pocket just as it sang out, "Who you gonna call?" He jabbed the screen frantically until the phone went silent. "Sorry."

So, I'm gonna be in a tabloid. I wonder if Gladys would like to use my nineties Glamour Shots photo for the front page.

CHAPTER 8

As soon as the guests were served, I slipped out to Mia Famiglia to meet Gia for hot bread class. At least that's how I was thinking about it. Seeing Gia was the bright spot in my day even when I was sleep-deprived.

He was waiting for me in his mother's kitchen, and he'd brought along two surprises. A large pumpkin spice latte and a small scruffy boy in thick glasses. The latter one launched himself at me. "Poppy!"

"Heya, sweets." I wrapped my arms around Henry and gave him a bear hug. "How was preschool last week?"

Henry shrugged. "There's a bossy girl named Mary Jane who says I have to push her on the swing because I'm older."

Gia made a big deal of rolling his eyes. "Women, am I right, Piccolo?"

Henry nodded very seriously. "Women are bossy."

"Oh dear." I wrapped an apron around my waist. "I think it only gets worse as you get older."

Henry sighed very melodramatically. "I'm es-austed from it already."

"I'll get you some almond milk. Then we're going to make an easy bread called focaccia. Sound good?"

Henry thought for a minute. "Maybe something stronger."

"Like what? Chocolate almond milk?"

"Maybe coffee. I'm really tired."

I bit my bottom lip and looked at Gia, whose shoulders were shaking with silent laughter.

I gave Henry a solemn nod. "I'll see what I can do."

I kissed Gia hello in a very non-sexy way and pivoted my mind to family time. I greeted Marco and the other chefs, Frankie and Esteban. Esteban didn't speak a lot of English, but he was able to translate most of Marco's broken Italian-English combo into Spanish so they could all understand each other. The men waved hello and gave me welcoming grins while they worked on Sunday brunch.

I went out to the bar and requested a shot of decaf espresso and a teaspoon of honey in warm almond milk—served in a demitasse cup.

When I returned to the kitchen, Henry had climbed on a stool by the counter and was waiting to begin. "I love gotcha bread."

Gia chuckled. "You love it, huh?"

Henry gave a single nod. "Nonna makes it all the time."

I set the junior cappuccino in front of him and pulled out my recipe. "She does?" Gia and I must have had the same thought at the same time, because our matching looks of horror met over Henry's blond head. *Oh no. Children are notorious blabbermouths and I'm not supposed to be here.*

Gia tousled Henry's hair. "You know what I hear is fun, Piccolo? Secret bread."

I held in a snicker. *This will come back to bite us. You just wait.*

Henry took a sip of his "coffee." "Oooh. Secret gotcha bread."

I wrapped the little apron around his tiny body. "Yes. That would be fun."

After getting Henry two tiny biscotti to go with his coffee. And a napkin. And a little spoon. And washing our hands. I spent the next hour talking about yeast burping gas into the dough, cleaning the dust cloud of flour off of everything that Henry had spread like an explosion, and stealing kisses from Gia. When the dough was complete, I wrapped it in plastic and put it in the refrigerator to rise overnight. Then I took out the ball of dough I'd made yesterday and let Henry flatten it with his hands—just washed for the twentieth time. I walked over to the herb window to cut a couple sprigs of rosemary and all three chefs flew into a panic.

"No no no! Not there. Oliva, she will know."

My hand hovered over the veritable shrub of rosemary. "I just need a couple sprigs for the gotcha—focaccia bread."

Marco gingerly took the scissors from my hands. He turned the potted herb and examined it like a bonsai artist. "Chef Oliva no like when we make da herbs uneven. We has to be very careful."

I glanced at Esteban, who held his hands in front of his chest in prayer position.

Frankie breathed a sigh of relief. The dark-skinned man picked up his chef knife. "That old lady rules this kitchen with an iron fist. You gotta watch yourself around here, girl."

I took the rosemary sprigs Marco offered me and smiled. When I returned to the bread station, Gia raised an eyebrow. "What was that all about?"

"I don't know. But I don't think I'm the only one your mother terrorizes."

After we poked leaves of rosemary into our bread and sprinkled it with sea salt, I drizzled it with olive oil and Gia took the pans over to the proofing oven.

Once he was out of earshot, Henry took my hand. "I have a secret."

I bent down to be closer. "Oh yeah?"

Henry nodded. "I have a plan for Tricks or Treating." He crooked his finger for me to come closer and he whispered in my ear. I looked into those giant blue eyes behind his glasses and nodded. Henry's grin split his face and Gia caught us.

"What are you two being so sneaky about over here?"

I shrugged and Henry copied me.

"That is between me and Henry."

Gia narrowed his eyes in a playful way and grabbed Henry around the waist to tickle him. "What are you up to, Piccolo?"

Henry giggled. "It's a secret."

I watched the two of them playing and my heart warmed. Then Gia put Henry down and advanced on me with a wicked gleam in his eye.

"Hey, I'm just an innocent bystander. The kid's the one you want."

Gia grabbed me and pulled me to him while growling. Henry laughed so hard he doubled over and squealed. "Daddy!"

The door to the dining room opened and the hostess shushed Gia for causing a ruckus. Then she took Henry to the dining room to have some macaroni and cheese—Italian-style.

Suddenly alone. Gia gave me a proper hello kiss in the walk-in refrigerator. He kissed the inside of my wrist. "Bella, if you keep looking at me like that, we will melt the butter. I can only take so much."

I giggled. "Then you'd better let me get busy." I reached for the Parmesan cheese, and he grabbed my hand.

Gia grumbled playfully and nuzzled my neck. "I am trying to get busy."

The walk-in door opened, and Frankie strolled in, grabbed a wedge of fontina, and strolled back out. "I saw nothing."

"Here. Keep your hands busy with this." I filled Gia's arms with different cheeses. I had to get to work on the manicotti so I could get home in time for my tour dinner. Gia followed me to the workbench, grinning. I pointed to the counter and tried to cover a yawn.

"Bella, it is my fault you are working too hard. Let me help you."

We each took a pan and a mixing bowl and Gia followed my instructions. I did the tasting to balance the herbs, then gave him a taste when it was right. Once we had two pans of cheesy saucy goodness layered, Gia put them in the oven, and I checked the focaccia. It was nice and puffy, so I put it in the other oven to bake.

"I was going to make a cheesecake, but there isn't enough time. And there's still half a pan of tiramisu in the walk-in."

Gia wiped off the counter. "So, make something new. Marco can have the front of the house put it on with the specials."

I assessed the ingredients in the walk-in. "Marco, what is this crate of lemons for?"

Marco shrugged. "I don't know. I think, Oliva, maybe she making da lemon sorbetto?"

"Can I use them?"

"Si si si." He waved me on. Or brushed me off. It was hard to tell with these particular Italians in this kitchen. They were both a little sly.

I washed the lemons, then handed them to Gia with a Microplane.

"What do I do with this?"

I checked his expression for a second to see if he was teasing me. *Nope.* I took his hand in mine and dragged the Microplane across the lemon so the peel shaved off into zest. "I need you to do this to about twelve lemons."

Gia grinned but didn't look at me. "Okay, you got it, boss."

Marco said something I didn't understand in Italian and Gia giggled. He glanced at me, then looked away and giggled again.

Are they making fun of me for being bossy? Gia hasn't seen anything yet. Wait till he sees how bossy I get when it's time to decorate for Christmas.

For now, I grabbed a box of tea and put the kettle on. I went through to the dining room to check the bar for a very unusual liqueur. I was going to attempt something completely different that could get me banned from Momma's kitchen once and for all.

CHAPTER 9

Two loaves of rosemary focaccia rested on the rack. The kitchen air swirled with the scent of oregano and garlic. One pan of my avant-garde dessert special was safely tucked into the walk-in, and a smaller pan for tonight's gourmet dinner was ready to go home with me. I'd already worked twenty-seven hours today, and it was only four o'clock.

I tried to pay Marco for the ingredients before I left, but he refused. "No. What is a few ladyfinger and mascarpone compared to six-hour chef prep? Not even Gia's kisses are worth dat much."

That's what you think. I kissed my fellas goodbye and went home with a Sicilian dessert set to stun.

A loud kerfuffle was underway in the front yard. Owen sat on a low branch in my red oak and Gladys stood below, hollering at him, "The only nut in that tree is you!"

Owen gripped the branch over his head. "Will you please stop shouting? You're upsetting Charles."

Gladys stomped the fallen leaves like a Halloween

Godzilla. "Oh, so the squirrel's name is Charles now? You need to be committed."

An acorn dropped from the tree and pelted Gladys on the forehead.

"Ow!"

I'm sure that was just a coincidence. I paused long enough to look up into the branches. Above Owen's head, a squirrel shook its tail and climbed higher.

Owen made clicking noises with his cheeks. "The squirrels in your yard are very stressed. They say Figaro taunts them from the window."

I glanced at the curved window ledge where Figaro was lying on his back in the sun, sound asleep with his tongue hanging out. "Yes, he can be very menacing."

Owen started to fall and grabbed the branch above him with both hands. "I think I'll have a talk with him."

Sure. You do that. "Please be careful getting down."

I left him dangling eighteen inches above the ground, hanging by the strength of his delusion.

Gladys seemed more interested in heckling than helping, and I left her to it.

Inside, I peeked into the library where the *Paranormal Pathfinders* team were spread throughout the room, each holding an open book from the shelves. Four sets of eyes were on me.

"Hello."

Paisley breathed out a chuckle. "It's Poppy." The four visibly relaxed and their books dropped to reveal handheld electronic devices that whirred and flashed.

I stepped into the room. "What are you all doing?"

Clark sprang to his feet. "Taking some preliminary

readings before tonight. Ritchie is setting up the motion sensors. Harper and Paisley are using Tri-Field EMF detectors." He turned a gray box that looked like a video game for me to see the screen. "And I have the data logger. It records electromagnetic fields along with environmental conditions and vibrations."

A row of lights on one side lit up like a pinball machine hitting the bonus round. I nodded towards it. "Well, you certainly did something there."

Clark moved the device away from me and the activity stopped. He gave me a scan from head to toe. "Interesting."

Harper sidled up next to Clark and looked at his device readout. Then she looked at the pan I was holding. "Ooh, what's in there?

I held it out. "Sicilian tiramisu. Earl Grey tea and bergamot liqueur–soaked ladyfingers layered with lemon curd and bergamot mascarpone. Topped with powdered white chocolate."

Ritchie inched closer to peer into the pan. "What's a bergamot?"

"It's a citrus fruit. Like an orange crossed with a lemon and a lime. It's what makes Earl Grey tea taste Earl Greyish."

Paisley's eyes were the same shade of blue as her glasses and about twice as big since she'd heard about the dessert. Her bright red lips were parted, and her mouth hung open a little while she listened. "Is that for us?"

"I'm afraid not. It's for tonight's event. For the dinner tour. It's been booked for weeks."

Clark raised an eyebrow. "What's for dinner?"

"Beef tenderloin, garlic mashed potatoes, and

carrots in a brandy cream sauce. Plus, Joanne and Kenny have a few treats they're making for the other courses."

Harper put her hand on my wrist. "Girl, I will pay any price to come to that. I'll sit in the corner in the dark. You won't even know I'm there except hearing me moan in delight over those potatoes."

Well, that would help sell the haunted theme.

Ritchie tapped his mouth with his finger. "What if we book the tour now?"

Clark quickly nodded in agreement and pulled out his wallet. "We can pay cash."

Paisley snapped her fingers. "We could be like background actors."

They were advancing on me like a wild pack of geese, and I was holding the last loaf of bread.

"Absolutely you can join us if you pay in cash." The voice of a four-foot-nine conniving redhead boomed into the room behind me and cut me off at the knees.

I gave her a warning with my eyes. "But Aunt Ginny, we're only prepared to feed the official tour." Not to mention the lunacy of adding four *ghost hunters* to an ersatz *ghost tour*.

Aunt Ginny took the cash from Clark and stuffed it down her sweater. "Pooh. Joanne bought extra, so we'll be fine. What's this?" She took the Sicilian tiramisu from my hands. "Mmm. I'll just put this away."

Aunt Ginny left me in the middle of the TV crew, empty-handed and red-faced. "Well, I guess we'll see everyone at dinner. The tour starts at six. The um . . . ghost stories are not an admission to being haunted. Please keep that in mind."

They didn't care. They were already celebrating the tenderloin.

Great. I chased the scent of Earl Grey and Giorgio down the hall to shake some sense into Ginny the Conniver. I found her fork deep in my tiramisu with Kenny and Joanne flanking her sides with spoons in their mouths.

Aunt Ginny brushed at the white chocolate powder on the tip of her nose. "What is this?"

Kenny waved his spoon in circles like he was roping a steer. "This is amazing. Is it for tonight?"

I walked to the island and replaced the plastic wrap over the pan. "It's Sicilian tiramisu and yes, it's for tonight."

Joanne narrowed her eyes. "Didn't you trust that my hazelnut torte would be good enough?"

For the love of bacon. I was in no mood for her peevish attitude. "Joanne. Please. Not now. Aunt Ginny just invited four more people to dinner. Let me see the roast."

I walked to the fridge to take out the tenderloin. The room behind me was silent. "Why are there three tenderloins in here?"

When no one answered I turned around. Aunt Ginny was trying to sneak into her room. "Whoa! Where do you think you're goin', Martha Stewart?"

Aunt Ginny attempted a grin. It rivaled the sagging jack-o-lantern out front. "If the B&B guests are paying under the table, we don't have to split it with the Inn. Plus, I already told Gladys and Owen they could join the tour, so what's four more?"

I tried to control my frustration, but some of it spilled over. *Crazy old woman.* "So you planned this. What happens if Linda finds out about your little side hustle? What's that gonna do to our reputation?"

Kenny's chin dropped so far you could fit one of the potatoes he was peeling right into his mouth. He disappeared into the pantry and brought out another ten-pound bag without saying a word.

Joanne blew her breath out real slow. "You invited the tabloid reporter who wants to nail us for being con artists to a ghost tour in a house with no ghosts along with the professionals who can prove it?"

Aunt Ginny looked at each of us in turn. "They overheard me talking to Edith about dinner and they cornered me. What was I supposed to say? 'We're serving a fancy dinner and you can't have any'?"

So, this is how I die. I always thought it would be heart disease, but it will be Aunt Ginny. At least it's hereditary. "You tell them it's an organized tour that the others have paid for in advance."

I pulled out one of the untrimmed tenderloins, sharpened my knives, and searched my cell phone for an appropriate song to match my mood. I typed in "Bon Jovi, 'Blaze of Glory'" and answered Joanne and Kenny's questioning looks when it began to play.

"Theme music for the ride down."

CHAPTER 10

"Under no circumstance are you to tell anyone that we are or are not haunted. The tour people need to believe we are, and the TV people are going to find out on their own that we aren't. Most importantly, we need to keep things ambiguous so the tabloid lady can't quote us."

Royce and Kenny were dressed in tuxedos with brilliant green vests to match Aunt Ginny's emerald evening gown. Figaro sat at their feet in a matching emerald bow tie. That was definitely Aunt Ginny's doing. She said he could get away with a certain amount of begging if he was following the dress code. She was probably right. The best I could do was fancy my hair into a French twist and put on a black velvet dress. Mind you, I looked really good in that black dress.

Spooky classical music for Halloween was quietly playing throughout the house over the speakers, and enough candles were lit to create a fire hazard that I could ill afford after my last warning from the fire chief.

Everyone fancy was lined up in the kitchen next to Joanne, who wore jeans and a "Roar to the Shore" T-shirt. That was her passive-aggressive way to ensure she wouldn't have to help serve tonight.

Aunt Ginny raised a gloved hand. "What if they ask outright? You want me to fake a seizure?"

"Let's save that for the backup plan. For now, just tell them that we've never had any personal ghost sightings, but guests have reported their own."

Joanne snorted. "Like who? Those psychos from last summer?"

Kenny snapped a look to her. "If we sell it, they'll buy it. And I'm gonna sell it."

Royce held out one hand to the imaginary audience and broke into a scene. "'Thou canst not say I did it. Never shake thy gory locks at me.'" Royce made a slight bow. "Macbeth denying everything to Banquo's ghost."

Aunt Ginny patted his arm. "Yes, that's great, dear. But Poppy. What if the reporter asks me outright? I guess I could accidentally poke her in the eye. That would distract her from the questions."

"Please don't poke anyone. And just try to be diplomatic. We'll seat Gladys Philippot in the back corner at the overflow table with Owen and one of the *Paranormal Pathfinders* people. Owen and Gladys don't get along, but he's the safest dinner partner for her to have. She already knows he's nuts. Maybe we'll get lucky and dodge a scandal."

Royce put a hand on my shoulder. "Don't worry . . ." His eyes clouded over as he tried to come up with my name but couldn't quite reach it. ". . . Francine. Everything will be magical."

I smiled and squeezed his hand. "Thank you, Royce. I know you'll be great."

Aunt Ginny raised her hand again.

"Yes?"

"Did you know we have exactly thirteen people coming to dinner tonight?"

I mentally counted. As far as omens went, I'd had better. "No. I did not." *No one on the tour's named Damien, are they?*

Kenny shuddered. "Nuh-uh. How did we let that happen? Oh Lord, I need some salt to throw over my shoulder, quick."

I moved the salt closer to him in hopes that it would quell his panic before he had to call the horoscope network for an update. "It's just a number."

Kenny muttered, "A number so ominous most hotels don't have a thirteenth floor."

"I'm sure it's fine."

The doorbell rang and I checked the clock and sighed. "They're early."

Joanne muttered. "If they have a chain saw, I'm outta here. I'm telling you, 'cause you're the type to open the door anyway."

Kkkhh. "I am not." I popped the bacon-wrapped scallops into the oven and took off my apron. Figaro ran after me to meet the guests at the door. He got as far as the library when he slid into a hundred-and-eighty-degree Tokyo drift and galloped back towards the kitchen with his ears flattened.

Owen Rodney stood in the library doorway, sans colander. "Figaro senses doom on the other side of that door. Cats are very sensitive, you know. You may want to cancel tonight just to be safe."

I thought it was more likely that Figaro was avoiding Owen after the squirrel heart-to-heart they had earlier this afternoon. "Thank you, Owen, but I'm committed now, so I'm afraid we'll just have to take our chances."

Dr. Simon Beck stood on my front porch with his beautiful wife on his arm. They had taken the formal attire suggestion very seriously. Dr. Beck wore a tuxedo and Brooklyn was in a gorgeous gold halter dress that was covered in tiny crystals. She gave me a brilliant smile that glittered as brightly as the beaded purse that hung from her shoulder. "I love all your outdoor decorations. What fun. Especially the skeleton on the porch swing."

My nervous system launched a PTSD panic, but then I remembered. *Oh no, wait. I did put a plastic skeleton in a pirate hat out earlier. We're fine.*

"We're a bit early. I hope that's not too much of an imposition."

"No, of course not. Come on in." I stepped aside to let them enter and looked behind them for the horse-drawn funeral wagon. All I saw was the spider's web that I'd hung, and our flickering jack-o'-lanterns lining the walkway. That one on the porch had an eye patch now. *Who put that there?*

Dr. Beck shrugged out of his overcoat. "We didn't come with the rest of the tour. Brooklyn doesn't agree with the transportation."

Brooklyn gave her husband a biting glance. "I think it's cruel to make those horses do all that work in this weather; don't you, Poppy?"

Uh-uh, don't pull me into this. "Well, I've never been a horse person, so I don't really know what they like or don't like to be honest. I just know that they're well treated by the drivers. They always seem to be eating apples when I see them."

"They don't mind it."

I'd forgotten Owen was still in the library. Apparently, he'd gotten his information straight from the horses' mouths. "They say it gives them a sense of purpose to be useful. As long as no one has sticky hands."

"Well. There you have it." I led Dr. and Mrs. Beck into the wood-paneled library and introduced them to Dr. Owen Rodney—intentionally leaving out the pet psychic part of his title.

Kenny had lit the logs in the stone fireplace earlier and the room was nice and toasty. "Why don't you make yourselves comfortable. Help yourself to the wine and sherry on the sideboard."

Brooklyn gave a sniff and her nose twitched. "Do I smell bacon?"

"Bacon-wrapped scallops are the first course. They just went into the oven when you arrived."

Dr. Beck's expression fell, and he slid a look to his wife.

Brooklyn's eyes went wide. "They did tell you I'm vegan, didn't they?"

They who? No one told me anything. "I'm afraid I did not receive that information. Who did you tell?"

"It was in the notes on the tour reservation online."

"I see. I assume no shellfish. No butter?" *No nothing that I've made tonight.*

"None whatsoever."

"Okay. Don't worry." *A vegetarian and a vegan.*

Thank God for salad. "I'll figure something out. Why don't you help yourselves to the crackers there on the table? You can just avoid the cheese."

I took off for the kitchen—a maelstrom on the inside—running a mental inventory of my cupboards. I threw the dial on the side oven to 425 and grabbed my apron from the hook. "Did you put butter and cream in the potatoes yet?"

Joanne gave me a look like Figaro had come riding sidesaddle on my shoulders. "No. It's too early. What's wrong with you?"

I assessed the four sets of eyes on me. "One of them is a vegan."

Aunt Ginny wasted no time in declaring, "I'm almost positive this one is not my fault."

Kenny drummed his fingers on the microwave. "What are we gonna do?"

I pulled out my cell phone. "Roast a beet and call Sawyer."

Fifteen minutes later, my best friend was at my back door with a box of quinoa and some cashew cheese. I kissed her on the cheek. "You're a lifesaver."

Sawyer peeked in the oven. "Thank me with the vegan lady's tenderloin."

I piped the cashew cheese onto some roasted fig halves and drizzled a little sriracha-infused olive oil over the top. "There. One vegan appetizer. Leave the goat cheese off the salad; the sorbet is good; I'm making her cherry and almond–studded quinoa with roasted beets for her main."

Sawyer picked up the cashew cheese and sniffed it. "What about dessert?"

I groaned. "How about a poached pear in dessert wine?"

"I'd eat that."

"You'll eat anything."

"Just so long as I get some of those potatoes."

I looked around the kitchen, frustrated. "If only I'd known she was coming sooner I could have made her something special."

Aunt Ginny put her hand on my arm. "Would you calm down. She'll be thrilled with this."

Joanne handed me the tray of bruschetta covered in shaved Parmesan to take to the library. "Kenny will follow you with the vegan bruschetta. If it goes in first the wrong people will grab it."

"Good idea."

Sawyer wound her chestnut hair into a bun and double-wrapped an apron around her waist to tie it in the front. "What do you need me to do?"

The doorbell rang and Aunt Ginny patted my arm. "I'll get it this time."

I told Sawyer, "Fill a saucepan with Riesling and peel two pears."

"Why two?"

"Insurance." I backed out of the kitchen into the hall with Kenny on my heels. Paisley and Harper descended the steps whispering to one another excitedly. "Hello, ladies. We're in the library waiting on the rest of the official tour, who I believe Aunt Ginny is greeting right now."

While Aunt Ginny let in the rest of the tour group, I entered the library and smiled. Clark and Ritchie were introducing themselves to Dr. Beck. Just as Clark reached out his hand and said it was an honor to meet the professor, the blood drained from Dr. Beck's face, and he jumped like he'd seen a ghost. Which I realize now is a terrible expression under the circumstances.

"Oh shrimpgrits!"

Only he didn't say "shrimpgrits." But he did stumble over the ottoman and fall backwards onto the sofa.

I turned around to look behind me. Two honey blondes who appeared to be mother and daughter had come through the door in the midst of a loud discussion, and now stared at me in silent shock in the entryway next to the Pathfinders and a very surprised Kenny. A pair of young kids piled into the foyer behind them.

I've seen that look before. Either they're familiar with my unfortunate history from YouTube, or these people know each other and they're not friends. I was stuck standing there holding the silver tray of bruschetta. Simon tried to compose himself while the Paranormal Pathfinders awkwardly tried to blend in, and the two new ladies stared at me.

I held out the tray. "We have some without cheese over on Kenny's tray."

Brooklyn bent down to face her husband. "Simon, what's wrong with you?"

I looked around the room full of strangers not sure what to do when one of the guests was making a scene out of *Night on Bald Mountain.*

Kenny, who had been loitering by the bookshelf unsure of when to bring over the vegan appetizer, now held out his silver tray. His earlier bravado had left him faster than my credibility with the Chamber of Commerce. He cleared his throat and stared into the chandelier. "I have vegan bruschetta here."

Simon chuckled and patted himself down in a personal frisk. "It's silly. I—I think I left my reading glasses at the other B&B. I didn't mean to startle everyone—including myself. Heh."

I put my silver tray down next to the cheese and crackers. "Do you need to read something important? I have a couple of pairs in the lost and found. We can try them out." *You know it's a full moon when you have a reading emergency.*

He held up his hand. "No. I'm sorry for causing alarm. It's fine." He coughed and his eyes flicked around the room. He swallowed hard. "You know, on second thought. Maybe we should call it a night. Go back to the Inn."

Brooklyn's mouth was agape. "Go back? We just got here. We've been waiting for this for weeks."

Simon looked around, then stared at the fire. He muttered something I didn't catch, then cleared his throat. "You're right. We'll stay. Do you have any Scotch?"

Brooklyn examined Kenny's hors d'oeuvres. "Are those vegan?"

"Yes, ma'am."

As if someone pressed resume, the room cranked back to life. The hors d'oeuvres were received and the tour group was greeted and settled into the library. I told them we'd head into the dining room in about ten minutes.

I passed Paisley and Harper as I left the room for the kitchen. Harper gripped Paisley's arm. "Do you know who that is? That's Dr. Simon Beck. He's a legend in paranormal circles. That gorgeous woman must be his wife."

Paisley's bright red lips hung open as she craned her neck to look at Dr. Beck and his wife. "How is that possible?"

Harper gushed, "He's famous for his work with the parapsychology lab at Staunton University. He's the whole reason I got into paranormal investigation."

"He certainly looks like he's just seen a ghost."

CHAPTER 11

"People ought not to say they're doctors if they're hinky professors of pseudoscience at some scammy university!" Aunt Ginny started for the library to give Simon Beck *what for* and I had to grab her by the shoulders.

"Oh no you don't. It's just one night. One dinner. And he's just one nut cluster in a whole box full of pecan turtles out there."

Sawyer turned the heat down on the pears. "I'm pretty sure Staunton U is a real university. Kenny, didn't you say you went there?"

Kenny shot a look at Sawyer. "What are you implying?"

"I'm saying it's a real place, that's all."

Kenny scowled. First at Sawyer, then Joanne, then the rest of us, then at the pears. "It's time to seat them for dinner anyway."

I checked the scallops. "Okay. Why don't you go tell them?"

Kenny swallowed hard. "Can't you do it?"

"What's gotten into you? You've been jazzed about this event since we announced it."

Kenny shrugged and wouldn't look me in the eye. "I didn't know they'd be so agitated."

Royce straightened his bow tie. "I will tell them."

The guests filed into the dining room and found their name cards. We were still waiting for one more, but I told the kitchen we should get started.

Aunt Ginny had set both tables with her Irish linen tablecloths and the sharp cobalt and white Imperial Lomonosov China. While the guests took their seats, I lit the tapered candles.

Kenny and Royce were taking drink orders from the far end of the room, so I started at the head of the table with Simon and Brooklyn Beck.

Brooklyn opened her little crystal purse and put a bottle of liquid stevia next to her water glass, and two little blue pills in front of her husband. "We'll just have iced tea as long as it's unsweetened." She rolled her eyes to Simon. "I'm trying to get this one off the sugar with me."

Simon chuckled. "She has me throwing back a pound of vitamins by lunch."

She put her hand over his. "Well, he was drinking way too much coffee and it was like twenty-four teaspoons of sugar a day. Diabetes was knocking at the door. We all have to stay healthy to live our best lives, right?"

Simon's eyes darted back down the table as he twisted Aunt Ginny's linen napkin to a sharp point. He glanced at me. "She exaggerates." Then his eyes shot around the room again while he worked his lower lip between his teeth.

I was moving around the table to a couple in their

twenties. The boy had an old-fashioned beard like he was from a cough drop ad in the 1800s, and big black spacers in his earlobes like he was from a science fiction movie four hundred years later. He gave me a very timid smile. "Just a Coke, please."

The young brunette he was with had a nose piercing, and full-color sleeve tattoos up both arms from wrists to shoulders. They looked like they'd jumped out of a Portland indie band photoshoot. I didn't have time to dwell on their looks because Simon Beck had started yelling at the older blonde on the far end of the table.

"What are you doing here, Felicity?"

The older woman wore a short and stylish hairstyle and a hip-hugging scarlet wrap dress. She appeared to be a little older than me, but in her case, fifty was the new thirty. In my case, forty was the sad fifty that didn't exercise enough in her thirties. She calmly lobbed her answer down the table. "Probably the same thing you're doing here, Simon. Research."

Simon's lips disappeared into a thin line. "How did you all know I'd be here?"

The woman laughed. "You never change. You're so vain."

The younger woman, who I'd mistakenly thought was her daughter when they first arrived due to their matching shades of L'Oréal Honeybadger, flicked her napkin out and laid it across her lap. "I arranged this trip for Dr. Van Smoot and myself. We had no knowledge of your plans. Despite what you think, the rest of the university doesn't revolve around the great Dr. Simon Beck."

Royce appeared at my side. Having taken all the other drink orders, he put his hand out for my order slip.

I mouthed to the young girl with the tattoos, *Drink?*

She mouthed back, *Root beer?*

I nodded and wrote it down. Then I handed the paper to Aunt Ginny's sweetheart. The waiter–turned Broadway legend–turned unpaid waiter with early dementia disappeared into the kitchen. I hoped he would return.

I smiled down the table. "I take it you three know each other. Perhaps we should make some introductions for the rest of the group."

The older woman at the end of the table made a huge production of a smile. "Why, I'd be delighted. I'm Dr. Felicity Van Smoot with the Staunton University Parapsychology Ethics Department. An *award-winning* department. I'm here with my research assistant, Miss Verna Fox, who set up this trip for purely academic purposes. I'm very interested in talking to you, Poppy, about your bed and breakfast being dubbed 'the murder house.' "

All eyes turned to me. *Five years just fell off my life. And not in the good way.*

The younger blonde to Felicity's left raised her hand and smiled. She had daytime drama good looks, and I got the feeling her cat-eye glasses were less to assist her eyesight and more to raise her IQ. "Hi. Verna Fox. PhD student and research assistant to the brilliant Dr. Van Smoot. I read about the Cape May ghost tours in one of our campus newsletters and set up this research trip for purely academic purposes."

I forced a smile onto my face. "And where are you ladies staying?"

The older woman hunched her shoulders. "Verna and I are at the simply divine Southern Mansion."

Simon gripped the arms of his chair, not facing anyone at the table head-on. "You all know who I am. I'm here for a little time away from the university. For purely *personal* purposes. And I'd like to keep my privacy if you don't mind."

Verna leaned against the table to look down her side past Ritchie and Harper at the beautiful woman of Indian descent. "And I'm sorry, who is this woman you're with?"

Brooklyn shifted in her seat and looked at her husband for rescue. "I—I'm Simon's wife. He's always talking about his work, and I wanted to see him in action. Simon's current research is in ESP. Sensing things through the mind that can't be gained through the physical senses."

I wonder what he's sensing right now.

Aunt Ginny came out of the kitchen to be nosy and started filling everyone's glass with unsweetened iced tea—whether they had ordered it or not. Brooklyn handed her husband the stevia, and he added enough drops to his glass to set my teeth on edge, then downed his two blue pills.

Dr. Felicity Van Smoot purred to Aunt Ginny, "You wouldn't happen to have any real sugar, would you? I like my tea the way I like my men. Honest and hot." Then she reached up and rubbed the back of Kenny's arm. "Well, hey, handsome. Don't I know you?"

Two ripe apples appeared on Kenny's cheeks. He ducked his chin and looked away. "No, ma'am. I don't think so." He practically dove back through the kitchen door with a full pitcher of tea.

The older woman followed him with her eyes, then grabbed her napkin and sneezed. Twice. Three times. And a black smoke feline in an emerald bow tie jumped into her lap. She hollered and shook her hands in front of her face. "Get it off of me. I'm allergic!"

I had to extract my offended fourteen-pound baby and send him with Royce to Aunt Ginny's bedroom with the promise that he would get room service later. *So much for that bow tie being charming.*

A voice from the small table in the corner spoke up. "Figaro thinks you're most likely sneezing from that horrid perfume you're wearing since he just had a bath. He was complaining about it when you were coming up the walkway earlier wrapped in that dead animal you were wearing."

Dr. Felicity's jaw clattered to her heavy gold necklace, and she cranked her head in the direction of the voice.

I sighed and wished I'd hidden the liquor earlier. "Dr. Felicity Van Smoot—Dr. Owen Rodney, Pet Psychic." Owen raised a hand in greeting. "And next to him is Gladys—."

Gladys interrupted me. "Smith. Retired librarian." She gave the Queen's wave of benevolence, but her eyes glittered with a much sneakier intention.

Something under the table banged against the floor and Owen lurched forward. "Ow."

Clark introduced himself to move things along and said he was a tourist here for the cider festival at Cold Spring. Followed by Ritchie, Harper, and Paisley, who each introduced themselves in exactly the same way. Verbatim. Every one of them. Not suspicious at all.

I turned to my shy young couple, who were on my check-in sheet as Sable and Jax, but I had no idea who was who. Before I could ask them, the doorbell rang. Royce answered it, and a very tall man with a head full of dark curls burst in like an explosion. He started tugging off his overcoat, but he stopped mid-tug and pointed at Simon Beck.

"You! Are you here to take credit for more of my research? I won't make that mistake again!"

Brooklyn leaned into her husband. "Who's that?"

Simon groaned behind a hand covering his mouth, "Eli Lush."

Harper shook her head in disbelief. "Good grief! Do you teach at the university too?"

Simon answered, "He's a student in a different department."

Eli let his overcoat drop to the floor. "A PhD student. In the more prestigious Philosophy Department."

Simon made a bitter little chuckle. "He wishes."

Eli threw his arm out to the side and dramatically pointed at the professor again. "You are a hack!"

Harper looked across the table to Paisley. "Thank God we went to school in California."

Paisley nodded. "I guess the rumors about Staunton University are true."

Refueled with indignation, Simon launched another verbal assault down the table. "What are you all doing on my tour? Are you setting me up?"

Dr. Felicity Van Smoot laughed in his face. "It's a coincidence, Simon. Get over yourself."

"How can it be a coincidence when this trip has been posted on my class schedule for weeks?"

Eli took the last remaining seat next to Owen Rodney, which made me wonder who had switched the name cards around to be at the main table. I was supposed to keep the tour group together. Of course, I didn't know then what I knew now, or I would have sat them in different houses.

Eli brushed a short hair from his immaculate black

dress shirt. "No one here is in any of your classes, Simon. How would we be aware of your schedule? It's a big university." He gave the man the flash of an insincere grin that sent a chill up my arms.

Dr. Felicity Van Smoot's research assistant, Verna, stood to her feet and pointed. "I can't believe that's your wife! Are you kidding me!"

Simon shot her a very nervous scowl and took a long drink of his tea.

Paisley tinkled her fingers at Mrs. Beck. "Have you and the professor been married long?"

Mrs. Beck squeaked out an answer that no one heard through the yelling.

Felicity laughed down the table. "You're a narcissist, Simon. You are. You know what? I think you followed me here! So *you* can spy on *me*. Aren't you still suspended?"

Clark, along with the other members of Paranormal Pathfinders, swiveled their heads back and forth in unison. Either paranormal investigations weren't as exciting as I'd thought, or this train wreck of a dinner tour would be talked about for days. For once I was thankful my household wasn't involved.

Verna took her seat and leaned to look down the table at Brooklyn again. "Are you really his wife?"

Brooklyn was too shocked to answer. She sputtered, "Wh—"

Simon grabbed her hand and yelled, "Yes. Now drop it!"

Sawyer and Joanne were watching through the open kitchen door. Twin looks of horror on their faces.

Aunt Ginny bent over Verna's plate to get a better look at her. "Verna's usually a name for an old lady. You look like you're maybe twenty-six. Am I right?"

Verna looked down her nose and over her cat-eye glasses. "Twenty-eight. It was my grandmother's name."

Aunt Ginny straightened up and accidentally dragged Verna's napkin with her. "See. Old lady name."

I shrugged and shook my head. *Maybe the intense Halloween music was a mistake. Everyone's all riled up.* I picked up a water glass and a fork and made a little *ding ding ding* to get everyone's attention. It was either that or raising my hand while covering my mouth like Henry's preschool teacher docs to get the children quiet. "You're a very spirited bunch." *Of psychos.* "But we still haven't met this young couple up here. Sable and Jax. You're staying at The Hotel Macomber I believe? Do you two go to Staunton University as well?"

The kids looked at me with as much pleading in their eyes as I felt myself giving back to them. The girl shook her head and dropped her eyes. "We go to school in New York."

The boy added, "NYU. Sable is a liberal arts major and I'm taking music theory."

The room was blissfully silent, and I tried to draw more out of them to hold it just a little longer. "And what brings you to Cape May?"

The boy glanced at me, then down the table. "We thought it would be fun."

Aunt Ginny was standing behind Felicity holding the iced tea pitcher. "Are you having fun yet?"

I sent her a look of rebuke, and she filled the top quarter inch of Paisley's glass with tea, then tried to disappear into the wallpaper.

The heat was rising from the table like a bonfire and making my cheeks flush. They were all locked in attack mode. *Maybe if we move around, we can reset the tone.* "You know what might be nice?" No one looked at me. "Why don't we do the house tour first? Kenny and Royce can show you where we may or may not . . ."—I glanced at Gladys—"have had ghost sightings."

Thirteen chairs scraped across my parquet floor, and I gave a nod to Kenny and Royce to take their places on the third floor.

Everyone filed out of the dining room and followed Aunt Ginny up the stairs to begin the ghost stories.

Sawyer appeared at my side. "You know those scallops are ready."

"Well, keep them warm. I'm worried they'll try to kill each other if we don't distract them with tales from the other side."

Sawyer chuckled. "They don't call this the murder house for nothin'."

CHAPTER 12

I told Joanne to make a warm sweet-and-sour sauce for the scallops and took the stairs in the pantry up to the third floor. Royce had corralled the group into the storage room next to my bedroom.

Ritchie was trying to act natural with a giant video camera plastered to his face, like no one would notice that. Paisley was a little more subtle about it—watching everything through a smaller handheld camera. She glanced at me and gave a thumbs-up.

"And this is the spot where guests have reported seeing poor little Alice Mosby."

Gladys cut her eyes to me and lowered her voice. "I thought you said you never claimed to be haunted."

I whispered, "I personally have never claimed we are haunted. I can't control what the guests say."

Royce waved his arm in a circle in front of the window. "You'll notice it is very cold here and there's a draft."

Harper reached behind Royce's back with a little teddy bear that had an antenna sticking out of its head. She waved the teddy bear up and down, then shook her head no to Clark.

Aunt Ginny stood in the back of the room behind everyone else and waved a paper fan at arm's length. She caught my eye and turned the fan on herself.

Royce continued his tale of little Alice Mosby, who was entirely a figment of Aunt Ginny's commercialism. He had the guests eating out of his palm with tales about sightings of her appearing in the window, wearing her blue dress and watching the street below.

Gladys took out a red notebook and started scribbling.

Great. I tapped Clark on the shoulder. I craned my neck for him to follow me behind the Christmas tree. "I thought we agreed you would keep a low profile during the tour."

"We're trying. But I don't think you understand who you have here. Dr. Simon Beck is the foremost expert on paranormal activity in the country. He wrote the book on ghost study. If anything is going to happen, it'll happen with him around. He's the leader in paranormal research at Staunton University which studies after-death activity. Anyone who is anyone in the paranormal field was taught by him."

"That's bologna."

Owen was sitting on a storage bin of nutcrackers. He crossed one leg over the other. "Some people were born with gifts from God."

The branches of the Christmas tree jiggled and parted. Simon's face appeared from the other side of the tree behind a snowman ornament that had been missed last January. "That is ridiculous, sir. Everyone was born with the same abilities. They just don't all know how to access them."

A pale hand with scarlet-painted fingernails and a silver ring wound its way over the branch and touched Simon's hand. He turned to his left and jumped back. "Ah! Stop it!"

Royce cleared his throat loudly. "As I was saying, ladies and gentlemen. That if you listen on a quiet night, you may hear little Alice singing 'Frère Jacques.'"

I looked directly at Gladys and whispered, "That has been reported by past guests and no one on staff can disprove it."

She narrowed her eyes in return.

The whisper of a moan floated over the room. Everyone went silent. I turned my eyes to Aunt Ginny. She was running her finger around the rim of a crystal champagne flute behind a dressmaker dummy.

I mouthed, *What are you doing?*

She pursed her lips and made a face at me to shush.

Owen grabbed his head and bent over. "Ooh. What are they doing in here? Their devices are messing with my brain waves."

Sable and Jax pulled out cell phones and pointed them at the little man on the plastic bin.

All eyes turned to Owen. Something Royce did not care for at all.

Owen pointed to a box in the corner. "Figaro doesn't like it either. He says they're running unsanctioned tests."

I sighed inwardly. "Figaro is in Aunt Ginny's room." I took a step to my left and tapped the box with my foot. Figaro shot out of the box and ran through the door trailing tinsel behind him.

Huh. I definitely did not see that coming. I waved my hand at Royce. "What other stories do we have about little Alice?"

Royce cut his eyes to Verna Fox pulling Simon Beck from the room. She ran her other hand down the length of his tuxedo jacket.

I cleared my throat. "Why don't we move on to another spot?"

Most of the tour followed Royce to the next location, where Kenny was waiting. Paisley fished a device out of her boot. She ran it over the cold spot in front of the window and checked the screen. She huffed a sigh and looked at Ritchie. "I need to get a new battery pack. Something in here drained mine."

She left the room. Ritchie and I followed the tour group to the vacant bedroom down the hall. I looked for Verna Fox and Dr. Beck but didn't see either one. A green light started flashing from behind me and several people turned to look.

Ritchie raised a hand. "Sorry. I got too close to the bedroom back here and it set off the EMF reader."

That's my bedroom. They'll be all over this hall again tonight.

Kenny led the group to a spot over by the dresser and did a quick vocal exercise. "Red leather yellow leather. He-he ha-ha ho. Okay, gather round, children."

Someone entered the room and bumped me from behind. When I turned around, Felicity Van Smoot had entered with Simon Beck. Eli pointed a finger in Simon's face. "You need to stop competing with me and keep your nose out of my research. You won't ruin things for me this time."

"Stop blaming me for your shortcomings, Eli." Simon shook himself and waded through the crowd to his wife standing up by Kenny in the dimly lit room.

Kenny had switched into another mode and was channeling the spirit of Alfred Hitchcock. "A séance was held in this room not long ago. Some believe there was an Irish servant girl named Siobhan on staff early in the twentieth century. They say she died of smallpox in this very bed in 1920, and she's been trapped here ever since, trying to cross over."

Gladys started scribbling again.

I leaned in and whispered, "We didn't begin that story and we've never publicized it anywhere."

Gladys rolled her eyes at me. "If you have, I'll find out."

Eli tugged on his tie and groaned. "Some people are so gullible."

I tracked Aunt Ginny skirting along the edge of the room, a high-pitched whistle of a hearing aid with a low battery whining behind her. She caught my gaze and shoved her hand in her pocket.

Kenny raised his hand. "I haven't been fortunate enough to experience Siobhan, but I'm told if you're quiet, you can hear her cries."

I looked back at Eli. "If you're not part of Simon Beck's Paranormal Department at Staunton University, then what are you studying?"

"I'm working on my doctorate for paranormal mind control in the Philosophy Department. I'm here this week to research how people are quick to believe nonsense and trick themselves, and the tricks that charlatans use to lure people into lies."

Gladys looked from Eli to me with her notebook aloft.

A vision of my face blown up on the news with the words "Ghost Fraud" splashed across the frame danced before my eyes and made my breath catch in my throat. "But of course, you don't blame innocent innkeepers for the tales that their misguided guests tell, do you?"

From the corner of my eye, I saw Aunt Ginny nudge the dresser and step aside. The nudge set off a tinkling of the drop pendants on the ancient lamp at the other end.

Kenny called out, "Siobhan, is that you?"

Harper did a sweep over the lamp with the teddy bear. She checked the back, then showed it to Paisley, who was recording on the handheld camera. They both shook their heads.

Simon grabbed me by the elbow. "Excuse me. Where is the restroom?"

"There's one on the first floor between the library and the sunroom. Across from the front desk."

He darted from the room.

Ritchie was just coming back in, holding a medium-sized video camera up to his face. He gave me an apologetic look. "Battery died. I'm just getting B-roll footage. Don't worry, we can't legally put anyone on the air who hasn't signed a consent form."

"Then why are you filming now?"

"You never know what might happen."

Verna sailed past me and left the room, and I gave Kenny a look to speed it up.

He kicked the histrionics into overdrive. "Oooh. How she is suffering, Siobhan. Many have heard her cries up here on the third floor."

Those are my cries. Because of stuff like this.

"Clattering around in pain . . ."

Aunt Ginny stepped on a loose floorboard in the corner knowing it creaked under the bed.

Brooklyn clapped her hands. "I hear her."

I sent Aunt Ginny a dirty look and she softened her face to look like she had no idea what I was upset about.

The lamp on the nightstand started flickering and the room went silent. Felicity lifted both of her palms to the ceiling and her chunky gold bracelets clattered together. "I feel a presence now. It's trying to communicate with us."

Clark, Paisley, and Harper all pulled handheld scanners from God knows where.

"Really, guys?" *On what planet does this pass for discreet?*

The young kids from New York asked the *Paranormal Pathfinders* team what devices they were using and started taking pictures of the equipment.

Kenny waved his hands. "Look up here please. Storyteller time."

I nudged closer to Aunt Ginny. "What are you doing?"

She whispered, "It's not me."

Felicity sneezed and ran from the room with a hand over her nose.

I saw the unmistakable swish of gray fur under the nightstand and snapped my fingers. Fig shot from the room and the light stopped flickering.

Owen chuckled. "He is just trying to help you." Then he grabbed his head and moaned. "That's it. I'm getting my psychic blocker from my suite."

To think, all this time I've been draining spaghetti in a psychic blocker. Who knew?

Owen left the room and Kenny sucked his teeth and gave a deadpanned look to Royce. "Any questions so far?"

Eli launched a catalog of questions asking Kenny if he really believed the nonsense he was talking about or if he just took other people's words for it. Then Clark stepped in to defend paranormal activity and cited different examples from Simon Beck's research to back up his claim.

Gladys Philippot snapped her fingers. "Of course. That's where I know you from. You're on that TV show, *Ghost Hunters.*"

Paisley gave Gladys a sour look. "That's our competitor on another channel. We're *Paranormal Pathfinders.*"

Verna peeked her head into the room. "Is Dr. Van Smoot in here?"

No, Felicity was not. And I'd had enough. "I think it's time for dinner, everyone. Let's head back to the dining room." I heard a couple groans of disappointment, so I let the rest of my dignity fade away and added, "We'll tell you all about the bodies I keep finding and the time I was a prime suspect in a murder investigation."

Sable and Jax were glued to Clark's side and peppered him with questions about the TV show while the tour group thundered down the steps.

Brooklyn got trapped in the back with Verna clutching her arm. "You seem very healthy."

"Oh, thank you. I'm vegan. And I do CrossFit to stay slim."

"Is that it?"

"Other than no sugar, yes. Why?"

"No miracle smoothies?"

Brooklyn laughed nervously. "No."

"Are you sick often?"

"Never."

They disappeared around the landing, and I took the back stairs for a moment to form my defense plan for my fraud trial. *Note to self: Google lawyers specializing in family members signing you up for ill-advised tours.*

I stopped in the kitchen for a quick bite of tenderloin, grabbed the scallops from the warming tray, and recapped the deception for Joanne and Sawyer.

When I made it to the dining room, Eli and Dr. Simon Beck were just coming in red-faced and puffing. And the two kids from New York had moved over to sit with Gladys, the tabloid journalist, and Owen, the pet psychic, who, once again, was wearing the colander on his head. It was a sad day when those two seemed like the sanest options.

Someone had moved Verna's name card down the table past the Paranormal Pathfinders. Now she was sitting on the other side of Simon where his wife should have been.

Simon grabbed her name card. "Oh no. Uh-uh." He moved it back down the table next to Dr. Felicity Van Smoot where it sat before the tour, then took his seat and downed his iced tea.

Brooklyn quickly sat down next to him with some side-eye to Verna, who pouted about being moved, and claimed that she was just following the name card.

Royce refilled the empty glasses while Kenny and I served the appetizers and Aunt Ginny told the guests about the time she was a murder suspect and put on house arrest.

We were able to keep them relatively calm with the wealth of material from our past misfortunes through the appetizer, salad, sorbet, and beef tenderloin. But all the while I couldn't shake the feeling that a weird vibe was running through the room.

There was an undercurrent of something I couldn't put my finger on. Simon was rage-drinking the iced tea. At first, I thought he was tired of the *Paranormal Pathfinders* team's unrelenting questions about his groundbreaking research in communicating with the spirit realm. Clark Richards peppered Simon with questions about what he was working on now and asked him to be on the show. Something Paisley and Harper both jumped on immediately and said he could show their viewers the proper way to make contact.

Or Simon could have been angry over the inappropriate comments Verna kept making about Brooklyn's age and constitution. She was unusually affronted about his wife's level of fitness.

Gladys appeared to be transcribing every moment as it happened in her notebook, which was super weird. But then I overheard Sable and Jax having a discussion in the hall bathroom about turning up the heat and I forgot all about the tabloid reporter.

Dr. Felicity Van Smoot made a general comment about the ethical violation of professors having affairs with their PhD students and the sexual harassment suits they brought before grabbing Kenny's butt as he walked past with the mashed potatoes. Something in the exchange made Eli Lush laugh out loud, and Simon drained another glass of iced tea.

Dr. Simon Beck left the room several times for the restroom, and each time he returned he shot wide-eyed, furtive glances around the room and checked his watch.

Even Kenny was acting strange—and that's saying

something. He wouldn't look at Dr. Simon or Dr. Felicity when he served them the béarnaise sauce, choosing instead to ask Paisley and Clark to pass it to the far end of the table.

The clock struck nine and "O Fortuna" began to play through the speakers. It was time for dessert and coffee and getting the tour group the heck outta here. I called the Victorian hearse and had the horse-drawn wagon on standby for pickup. Then Aunt Ginny and I brought in plates of hazelnut torte and lemon Earl Grey tiramisu while Kenny served the poached pear and Royce took the coffeepot around.

Brooklyn put her hand over her coffee cup. "None for me, thank you. I only drink one cup of coffee in the morning."

Verna leaned into Dr. Felicity and stage-whispered, "I hear coffee robs the skin of collagen. Maybe she's really forty and that's her secret."

The older woman replied, just as cheerfully snide, to her young protégé, "I bet it's the beets. Let's ask these gorgeous young things. Do you ladies eat a lot of beets?"

Harper giggled and patted her face. "Can't you tell?"

Paisley grinned. "Obviously I'll have to start when I get back to California."

Simon glared down the table and swallowed hard. "I think we should go back to the B&B. I'm really not feeling well."

At first, I thought he'd had enough of the indignities that had been coming his way all night from his colleagues. But he did look about one shade of green lighter than Oscar the Grouch.

He put his hand over his stomach. "I think it might be food poisoning."

Eli snickered. "Maybe it's karma. You know, since you've been making everyone sick for years."

I did a quick visual survey of the guests. *Everyone else looks fine.* "Would you like some peppermint tea?" *And to retract your statement about the food poisoning?*

His wife gave him a hopeful look since she clearly wasn't ready to leave, and he nodded. "Sure. I'll try the tea."

I ran to the kitchen and grabbed the herbal tea bags. "Time to bring in the big guns. The words 'food poisoning' have been uttered."

Aunt Ginny sighed and went to her room.

Joanne narrowed her eyes and made an umpire's signal. "No way. Uh-uh. I cooked those scallops perfectly and held them at the right temp."

Sawyer started to breathe faster. "I triple-washed the salad leaves. Joanne watched me."

Joanne nodded. "She did. It can't be the food."

I poured the steaming water over the fragrant peppermint tea. "Then let's hope this does the trick." I carried out the tiny china teapot and placed it before Simon.

Aunt Ginny brought in the horrible troll that we'd bought last summer, in hopes that it would seduce the tour group away from attacking each other.

Royce began telling them about the Antique Auction while I loaded the haunted house soundtrack on my phone for the grand finale. "It was a day like any other . . ."

The sound of wind blowing through the trees and a quiet moaning of tortured souls came through the speakers as Dr. Felicity took a sip of her coffee and interrupted the Broadway legend who'd won a Tony for his portrayal of Hamlet. "So, if all those murders happened outside of here, why is the Butterfly Wings called the murder house?"

Royce threw his hand in the air. "I scorn you, scurvy companion!" He made a show of glaring at the older blonde.

Gladys wrote some notes in her little red book and giggled about uncovering a scandal for the tabloid.

I answered nervously, "No one has ever been murdered here."

Simon gulped his tea. "But there is an energy here. In this house. Something that doesn't belong."

Dr. Felicity Van Smoot sneezed.

Not again.

Figaro trampolined onto Felicity's lap, then sprang to the table. He ran down the length of it in a showing of mischief that was beyond anything I'd ever seen him do. The breeze from his tail blew out all the tapers that had melted down to nubs.

I jumped forward and grabbed the naughty boy midair as he leapt for the floor. "I'm so sorry, everyone. I don't know how he keeps getting out." I cast my eyes to Aunt Ginny, who pursed her lips and looked at the carved troll talisman in her hand as if she could shift the blame to it somehow.

Sable and Jax steadied their phones on Dr. Beck while he continued voicing his observations. The entire *Paranormal Pathfinders* team leaned forward in their seats, listening to Dr. Beck as if to glean some new professional insight for their show.

"Or it could be you, Poppy. It could be that your own negative thoughts bring it on to you somehow."

Say what now?

The curly-haired Eli Lush jumped to his feet and threw his arm out dramatically. "I knew it! You are here to steal my research on the power of suggestion."

Simon hurled his napkin to the table. "I've had enough of you. All of you! Some of you shouldn't even be in the same room as me legally! And my paranormal lab is doing research in ESP—seeing the future. I have less than zero interest in your little paper on coercion, Eli."

Royce soldiered on, reading from his note cards as if we weren't in a nuclear meltdown. "'Poppy was on her way to the Antique Auction with the gorgeous Virginia.'"

On cue, Aunt Ginny hit the sound effect on my iPhone and a boom of thunder came through the Bluetooth speakers, followed by the peal of Toccata and Fugue in D minor—Dracula's pipe organ. The theme song of every haunted house. A power surge from the speaker overloaded the weak electrical system. The lights flickered and everything went black.

Owen Rodney whimpered. "Oh no. Figaro was trying to warn us."

Joanne hollered from the kitchen, "I got it!"

She must have flipped the breaker in the mudroom, because the lights came back on to reveal Dr. Simon Beck lying facedown in his tiramisu.

Gladys Philippot tapped her cell phone and snapped off a couple pictures. "Whoa. That'll go on the front page."

His wife reached out to nudge him. "Very funny, Simon. Joke's over."

His head flopped over to the side, and she pulled back her hand shaking it like it was covered in fire ants.

I said a prayer and put my finger on Simon's neck to check for a pulse. I looked to Aunt Ginny and shook my head. "He's dead."

Dracula's pipe organ gave out a repeat of its earlier cry and Aunt Ginny gasped. "I wonder if he saw that coming."

CHAPTER 13

Sawyer and I dragged Simon out of the chair and laid him on the floor. I wiped the whipped cream from his face and began chest compressions. Aunt Ginny cut the spooky Halloween music and muttered to herself about people having the nerve to die in the middle of a performance. Royce turned up the lights and blew out the rest of the candles while Joanne called 911.

The tour group suddenly had nothing but praise for the late Dr. Simon Beck. Now he was "a great man." And they'd "lost a pioneer in the field of paranormal science."

Sawyer knelt on the floor beside me, ready to take over if needed. "Soon he'll have been able to walk on water."

"That's the guilt talking. Please don't let it be murder. Not another one."

Owen was on his hands and knees looking under the sitting room couch. "Of course, it wasn't your fault. You tried to warn everyone."

Royce put his arm around Aunt Ginny. "Heya, Ginger. Isn't it almost time for our brunch reservation?"

Aunt Ginny patted him on the hand. "You need to go drink some water, dear."

Royce obediently headed to the kitchen. When the door closed behind him, Aunt Ginny knelt beside me. "I think he's sundowning. This was a lot of activity with his dementia, but he does love being onstage."

An ambulance arrived, and the paramedics took over. They tried for several minutes to resuscitate Simon, but it was no use. When they reluctantly started to pack up, Verna threw herself over the body and wailed, "No, Simon, no!"

Brooklyn curled into a tighter ball. "Oh God, oh God."

Aunt Ginny and I went to the sitting room to wait for the police. Within minutes, the black-and-white squad started pulling up in front of the house like it was free cone day at Ben & Jerry's.

Officers Birkwell and Consuelos arrived first. They had been here more times than I cared to admit. Always in an official capacity. They were followed by the very pink Officer Simmons with a female rookie I had not met. Then the new big cheese, Chief Kieran Dunne, pulled up in a blue sedan and started giving orders to two more officers who arrived right behind him.

Aunt Ginny tugged the curtain back from the sitting room window and watched them assemble on the front lawn. "Good God. If there was ever a time to rob the liquor store it would be now. Every cop in Cape May County is here."

Kieran looked around the yard and spotted us watching him from the bay window. He turned his piercing blue eyes in my direction, and they were definitely not happy to see me.

Heading onto the porch, he took his time brushing the mud off his shiny black shoes onto the welcome mat before he entered the foyer. Then he feathered his windblown black hair into place. Looking up to read my expression, he adjusted the starched white cuff on his midnight-blue dress shirt, turning the square gold cuff link until it was perfectly lined up with his watchband. "Ms. McAllister. We meet again."

"Chief Dunne. Is it customary for the chief of police to personally investigate a death?"

His hands rested on his hips while he assessed me. "Interim Chief. And it is when you're involved. What transpired tonight? Just the overview."

I offered him the basic bullet points, knowing I'd have to give a full drawn-out statement before we were done. I kept watching the door waiting for a little blond cop in a top bun to arrive.

Kieran kept his eyes fixed on mine, giving a slight nod every now and then.

How can one man be so calm and yet unnerving at the same time? "I can't help but notice that Sergeant Fenton isn't here. She usually shows up right away."

"Mm. You're right. Show me the body."

Well, that was disappointing. I would have to wheedle Amber's whereabouts out of Birkwell or Consuelos.

Chief Kieran followed me into the dining room and studied Simon Beck's lifeless body lying across the floor. Aunt Ginny, Royce, Sawyer, and Joanne stood on one side by the kitchen door, while the B&B guests had clumped together on the other side of the room. Right in the middle was the tour group. One person was missing.

Where is Kenny?

I looked at Aunt Ginny, then Joanne, and gave them a questioning shake of my head while mouthing his name. They both shrugged. Joanne looked in the kitchen, then back at me, and shook her head.

Felicity and Eli had their heads together, whispering quietly, looking around like they were waiting for something to happen.

The two kids, Sable and Jax, were plastered to their cell phones. Sable was feasting on her nails, and they both looked like they wanted to crawl under a rock.

Paisley and Harper were holding hands and quietly crying while Clark and Ritchie looked on shaking their heads in dismay.

Brooklyn had moved as far away from her husband as possible and sat on the floor with her knees pulled up to her chest. She was hugging herself and gently rocking back and forth.

Verna, on the other hand, was right up near the body. She was sobbing and dabbing her mascara with Aunt Ginny's white linen napkin. "He was such a great man." She reached out to stroke his hair.

Kieran took a little notebook from his inside pocket. "Ma'am. Please don't do that. I'm going to have to ask you to take a seat away from the deceased."

Kieran was a small man with a big presence.

People usually did whatever he said without question. Verna pulled herself to her feet and stepped away from Simon and the interim chief of police did a lap around the room. Not looking at the body but examining the living.

I stepped towards Brooklyn. "Chief, this is the widow, Brooklyn Beck."

Brooklyn's mouth hung open and her eyes were pleading and vacant. Her lips moved like she was speaking, but only a squeak came out.

Kieran beckoned me out to the foyer. "And you said the group from the university were fighting with the deceased all night?"

I nodded.

"Please don't clean up or touch anything until we've finished." He opened the front door and motioned in the other officers who were waiting on the lawn. "Simmons, call Kat Hinkle at the Coroner's Office and tell her we have a possible homicide. Tell her it's McAllister again. We'll wait for her to pronounce TOD."

I tried to keep the alarm out of my voice. "Homicide? No one touched him. Isn't it more likely to be a heart attack?"

Kieran raised an eyebrow. "Did the victim grab his arm or his chest, complain about pain or trouble breathing, or cry out for help at any time?"

My confidence was evaporating as fast as Aunt Ginny's bottle of crème de menthe she'd won at poker. "Well, no. But—"

"And do you seem to have a penchant for being in the way when someone has been murdered?"

"I wouldn't say it's a penchant, exactly. Bad luck maybe."

Kieran's eyelashes gave a flutter. "Then what would make you suspect a heart attack?"

Other than wishful thinking? "God owes me one?"

"Uh-huh. I think you're going to have to keep waiting for that."

"There are other things that happen without warning. Aneurism. Stroke. It doesn't have to mean murder."

"In any other house I would agree with you."

While Kieran gave the squad of officers instructions on the porch, I poked my head back into the dining room. The *Paranormal Pathfinders* team had a black box on the floor in front of the body. Harper was holding out a meter and Ritchie had the small handheld camera up to his face. Paisley stood in the corner nervously watching the door. She took her glasses off and rubbed the tears from her eyes.

Clark asked, "Dr. Beck. Can you hear me?"

I swatted my hand in the direction of the lot of them. "Zzzst! What is wrong with you?"

Aunt Ginny pointed at Clark. "I told them not to."

Harper gave her some side-eye. "You said to see if we could get him to say it wasn't food poisoning on camera."

Aunt Ginny looked to me. "Yeah, but that's it."

I grabbed Joanne and Sawyer "Don't clean up or touch anything until the police are done."

Sawyer tsked. "Can't I just finish the tiramisu I already started before the guy died?"

I eyed the Fourth of July parade of cops coming in. "Don't get caught. Actually, go hide me a piece too."

The ladies slipped into the kitchen *to take care of*

some business, while Officer Shane Birkwell walked into the dining room and looked around. He spotted his four-foot-nine adversary and his hand instinctively reached for his sidearm. "Mrs. Frankowski."

Aunt Ginny squared her shoulders at the tall sandy-blond cop. "Oh, it's you. Just remember, I can come and go whenever I want now."

"Yes, ma'am. And it's nice to see you not trying to sneak out of a window for a change."

They stared each other down, then went their separate ways.

I opened the dining room door and Sawyer craned her neck to see who was coming in. Her face split into a grin when she laid eyes on Officer Ben Consuelos. And not just because he was gorgeous. They had been living together for a few months, and she was still on cloud nine.

He pointed at her. "Ma'am. Come with me to give your statement."

She whispered to me on the way by, "I got your back."

Most of the guests were placed in the sitting room under guard to wait their turn while the rest of the cops took statements and collected possible evidence. Clark mic'd up and went out to the front porch followed by Ritchie carrying the big camera. They were setting up what they called the confessional next to where the rookie was guarding the front door.

I was left alone, sitting on the bottom step in the foyer feeling sorry for myself and wondering if an actual murder violated the terms of my tour contract or just made my house more desirable on the circuit.

The front door creaked open. "What'd you do now, McAllister?"

It was a very unusual sensation for me to hear my high school nemesis's voice and feel a flood of relief. I started to tear up, but I made myself choke it back. "I hope it was just a heart attack or people will never stop calling this the murder house now."

Amber breathed a little chuckle. "I think that ship sailed long ago. I would have been here sooner, but I was dealing with a break-in. An hour later and I'd have been off duty."

An hour later and I may have been on my way to Canada. "Well, everyone else is here. I'm surprised Gloria from dispatch hasn't arrived."

"She couldn't get anyone to cover the switchboard." Amber gave me a tiny smile. "You know there are two men on the front porch filming an interview about the murder."

"I figured."

"Kieran'll have to deal with that." She looked towards the library. "Where is everyone?"

"Spread out. Giving statements. Most of them are in there."

Amber took a step back towards the sitting room where the majority of tonight's unfortunate guests were in limbo, awaiting their turn to give their statements while an officer stood by silently taking mental notes. Amber put a finger to her lips and opened the door a crack.

Jax was speaking. "We had nothing to do with this."

Followed by Sable: "I just want to go home. This is all a horrible coincidence."

Amber lifted her eyes to mine.

I nodded. "That's probably true. They did take a

lot of pictures and some video, though. You may want to look at it."

After an awkward silence, Felicity started speaking. "Simon was very charming back in his day. We were both in the same department before he got tenure and became full of himself."

Paisley spoke with a soft voice. "Were you a student of his?"

"No, not exactly. But then I am several years younger. He would have loved you. You're just his type."

Paisley was silent for a moment. "I think he was the same age as my dad. Is Staunton University a big campus? Did you see Professor Beck or his students often?"

"No. Why would I? Our departments don't really have that much crossover. He was in the Psychology Department and ethics falls under Philosophy. We were aware of each other, but I teach a very specialized area of paranormal science. Look, there are several different fields of paranormal study. We don't all sit around and eat lunch together."

I whispered to Amber, "Defensive much?"

Felicity's voice developed a sharp edge. "Eli is the one who really hated him. They can't even be at the same cocktail party on campus."

Eli was cold and brusque. "I didn't hate Simon."

Gladys snorted. "Keep tellin' yourself that, honey. We all saw you."

Harper's voice was low. "You did threaten him as soon as you came in the house. I'm just hoping Ritchie got that on camera. Clark loves when stuff like that happens on *Paranormal Pathfinders.*"

"I would never let you put me on your show. I just have low blood sugar. And I missed the Victorian hearse and had to walk here from the Southern Mansion, so I was a little cranky. Simon and I were friendly competitors. We had a mutual respect for one another."

Amber raised her eyebrows in question, and I shook my head no.

Felicity snorted. "Since when?"

Amber beckoned me to follow her down the hall. "Who are those people?"

"Two of them are students from New York, two of them worked with the victim at the same university, one is a tabloid reporter, and two of them are from a ghost-hunting TV show on cable. The last three are staying with me."

Amber laughed. "That figures. Where's everyone else?"

We passed my desk and walked farther down the hall to the kitchen. Aunt Ginny was sitting at the banquette with Royce and Sawyer. Joanne was over by the mudroom giving her statement to Officer Simmons while another cop was confiscating the rest of the expensive tenderloin and half a pan of tiramisu to be tested. *I really wanted to eat that.*

Amber motioned for me to stay in the hall while she opened the door to the sunroom across from the kitchen. Kieran was interviewing Brooklyn Beck.

Brooklyn had her arms wrapped tightly around her. "He was fine this afternoon. I have no idea what happened. I know he just got some bad news at a recent physical." She threw her hands out in frustrated karate chops. "Maybe his heart gave out. Call his university. They'll handle everything."

Kieran watched her, his eyes sharp, thumbs poised to tap notes into his smart phone.

Brooklyn hugged herself again. "When can I return home? You don't need me in your way."

Kieran replied, "I would implore you not to leave yet, ma'am. We haven't even determined the cause of death. And we'll need more information from you."

Amber shut the door. "He sounds irritated. It's not going well."

If you say so. He sounded business as usual to me. Confident on the edge of cocky.

She nodded towards the room. "So, who's that?"

"That's the wife, Brooklyn Beck."

A shadow moving outside the back door caught my attention. "Someone's on the patio."

Amber walked over and put her face to the window. "Birkwell's with a pretty young woman in cat-eye glasses who's sobbing. Are you sure she isn't the widow?"

"I'm sure."

Amber watched for a moment. "Hm. Now she's yelling and pointing to the house."

Verna's voice rose loud and clear. "You need to be questioning that woman. That's who killed him. It's always the wife, isn't it? I bet she stabbed him under the table. Did you check for a knife?"

Amber looked my way. "Any wounds?"

"Not that I saw. It looked like he just fell over dead in dessert. He was extremely agitated and paranoid all night. And he kept excusing himself for the bathroom. Of course, he drank iced tea like a camel. He could have been given something before he came over."

"Interesting." Amber turned and went back down the hall towards the front foyer where we started. She looked through the library door and gave a chin-up greeting to someone before turning to me. "Consuelos is interviewing a guy with a colander on his head."

"That would be Owen Rodney, Pet Psychic."

She glanced at me, and the corner of her mouth twitched.

"Yep. He's one of mine."

"Do you advertise in a special newspaper for these guests?" She cracked the door open. Owen's voice came wobbling through, full of emotion. "You need to check the water bowl. It was moved."

Officer Consuelos sighed loudly. "I don't know what that means, sir."

Owen sounded frustrated. "Figaro saw something."

Amber shut the door. "Well, does that account for everyone?"

I hadn't seen Kenny since we found Dr. Beck in the tiramisu. I swallowed hard and looked at my hands.

After a moment, Amber's voice took on a familiar edge. "Spill it, McAllister."

"My housekeeper is missing. I'm sure it's nothing."

"Then why are you trying to hide it?"

"There's a dead body in the dining room. It looks suspicious even to me."

Amber quirked an eyebrow. "You know you can't cover for her. You have to disclose that information in your statement."

"Him."

"What?"

"My housekeeper's a him."

There was a knock on the front door; then it

opened. Kat Hinkle, the Cape May County Coroner, entered the foyer followed by two men dressed in white crime scene suits.

Amber fell back into cop mode and caught them up.

I knew Amber was right. I couldn't protect Kenny. I just hoped Aunt Ginny knew where he was, and that he had a darn good reason for being there.

CHAPTER 14

"Expect a lawsuit." That was the last thing Interim Chief Kieran Dunne told me. Okay, not really. But he may as well have. What he really said was, "Your kitchen is shut down until we can clear everyone on your staff, and rule out poison," and that meant the same thing. The stroganoff was about to hit the fan with the Haunted Homes Tour leaders.

"Can I at least bring in food from outside restaurants?"

Kieran took out his smart phone. "Is there a place where you can do that?"

"Either La Dolce Vita or Mia Famiglia. Both are on the mall." *I mean I'm still the one making everything, but maybe this could be a see no evil–say no evil kinda sitch.*

Kieran made a note in his phone. "I'll allow it for your B&B guests because I don't want them leaving until we're finished investigating, but you'll have to cancel your dinner tours for new people. We aren't taking any chances considering your peculiar history. I'll try to get the toxicology results quickly so you can open again."

"If you closed every establishment where someone dies at dinner there wouldn't be an open casino in Atlantic City."

"You know I could shut you down entirely until we've ruled out homicide. This could be an active crime scene. It's only out of deference to Sergeant Fenton that I'm letting you stay open at all."

"Well, not to mention that I've helped the department catch murderers like a half a dozen times in less than a year, so no way I'm a suspect."

Kieran widened his stance and placed his hands on his hips. "From where I'm standing you've gotten in the way of actual police work, contaminated crime scenes, and compromised open investigations. It's only because of Sergeant Fenton that those arrests were made, and the cases were closed."

What kind of revisionist history is this? A few months ago, you thought she was on the take.

"I can see by your expression that you don't agree. Nevertheless, do I have your word that you'll stay out of my way with this one?"

It was like negotiating with a twelve-year-old in a designer suit. "Look, I don't want anything to do with your investigation. If I could still pay my bills without this week's reservations, I'd beg you to send everyone home and shut me down." *I'm already working at a loss because of Aunt Ginny's freewheeling tenderloins. So much for taking January off.*

Kieran gave me a long look, followed by a nod.

Once the crime scene professionals had left, and everyone had given statements and was released to their own lodgings, I locked the front door and picked up Figaro. He gave me a head bonk with a sympathetic purr.

"You would not believe what I've been through tonight, Fig. It happened again. Who did I cheese off to bring this curse down on me?"

Figaro licked my chin.

I took out my cell phone and checked the notifications. I had twenty-four missed calls and six messages. Most of them from Linda at the Inn of Cape May. News had reached her that my house was living up to its name. Wait till I filled her in that I couldn't use my kitchen by order of the police.

"I don't even think that's a real thing, Fig. It sounds like an unreasonable show of force by that control freak Kieran Dunne. Like I couldn't poison food brought in from the coffee shop just as easily."

Clark Richards called to me from the top of the stairs, "Is the coast clear?"

"Everyone's gone."

"Come on, guys." He trundled down the steps carrying a black box made of rugged-looking plastic. I had one just like it in the garage for my drill set.

I didn't get a chance to ask what he was doing before the other three members of his team followed him down in rapid succession. Ritchie had his cameras and a pole with a furry duster on the end of it. Paisley had a black-and-silver box, and the headphones from the other night. And Harper had two of the handheld devices that lit up and beeped whenever she came near me.

"What's going on? And what are you dusting?"

Ritchie held out the pole with the furry tail on it. "It's a dead cat."

Figaro's tail started flicking in an *I will scratch your eyes out* kind of way.

"What?"

Paisley tsked and looked to the ceiling. "Don't listen to him. I mean it really is called a dead cat, but it's just a synthetic wind muff for a microphone."

Ritchie brought it over and showed it to me, then Figaro. "It cuts down on wind noise when we shoot outside."

Figaro was more titillated by the muff than I'd given him credit for. He gave it a sniff, then grabbed it and subjected it to rabbit kicks until Ritchie could work it out of his clutches.

Harper held a small gray device towards me and checked the readout.

"What are you doing?"

"This is a Mel Meter. It measures electromagnetic fields and ambient temperature. If we get an electromagnetic spike coupled with a hot or cold spot that could mean paranormal activity nearby."

If it detects levels of irritation I expect bells and whistles any minute. "I really meant what are you doing down here. With all that?" I circled my finger around the room. "I thought you were keeping your investigation to the third floor where the ghosts are." *Nothing lit up, so they obviously don't have a device that detects sarcasm.*

Clark opened his case and took out a gray box the size of a two-pound Whitman's Sampler—so I've heard—and set it in the middle of the dining room table. "That was before Simon Beck died during the tour. We have an unprecedented opportunity here to communicate with his spirit entity."

Paisley opened her black-and-silver case and took out two smaller devices. Her voice was full of emotion. "Whether Professor Beck died of very unfortunate natural causes, or someone killed him, he may still be around to tell us what happened." She waved her hand in front of her face. "I'm sorry. My father died a few months ago. They were about the same age. It's all coming back."

Harper reached out and squeezed Paisley's shoulder. "I know you miss him." She looked at me and mouthed, *Cancer.*

Figaro jumped out of my arms and trotted to the dining room table to get all up in that equipment.

The four of them were setting up what looked like an Ocean's Eleven sting, and Figaro jumped immediately into the empty case that Clark had on the table. Clark picked Figaro up and placed him gently on the floor.

That's going to last maybe sixty seconds. "What makes you think Dr. Beck would even talk to you if he were still around?"

Harper set a couple devices around the room at various angles. "We may never get another chance like this. Clark is setting up the SLS Camera. It'll pick up any ghost that passes the projector and show it on-screen as a human figure. I'm setting up motion sensors. We're usually dealing with entities who died long before any of this technology existed, and they don't understand what it is. If anyone will know how these devices work, it will be Dr. Beck."

Figaro jumped back on the table and into the case.

Clark gently removed him again and put him back on the floor. "Simon Beck once had the leading program in paranormal detection back in the day before he lost his funding and his department turned on him. If his spirit is still here, we can communicate with him, and ask him what happened tonight."

Paisley lined up four flashlights and started replacing their batteries. "Like did his wife kill him somehow?"

"Wait a minute. Why did he lose his funding?"

Ritchie was testing the lighting levels with a laptop. "Some big scandal involving a student who had to be sent away."

Figaro circled the table to the other end and jumped onto it, determined to get into that black box. He spotted the line of flashlights Paisley had set up and his whiskers twitched.

Harper took three different handheld devices and set them up on the buffet. "If I was Dr. Beck's wife, I would have launched my fist neck-deep into that crazy cat-eye-glasses-wearing Verna Fox. I bet she's one of his students."

"She was so inappropriate," Paisley said.

Clark strapped a microphone pack to the back of his black jeans. "Simon Beck had that reputation. There have been rumors circling him for years that he's had numerous affairs. He had a brilliant mind and a wandering eye."

Figaro got low and his butt started to wiggle. He was going to pounce on the row of flashlights like a toddler with a tower of blocks. Paisley snatched him up midpounce and held him aloft over her face. "You are a beautiful kitty, but so naughty like my Mittens." She hugged Fig to her chest and put him gently on the floor. "We had a professor in California who was caught with a grad student."

Ritchie opened one of the cameras and replaced a little plastic disc. "What happened to him?"

Figaro hurtled onto the table and slid into the row of flashlights knocking them all down in a lucky strike. His ears flattened in newfound regret, and he ran in place on the polished mahogany table trying to find the traction to escape.

I grabbed him around the middle and looked into his wild eyes, tucked him under my arm, and turned my attention to Paisley. "Did he get fired?"

Paisley picked up the flashlights and lined them up again. "Nope. He married her."

I was too tired to watch the ghost busting first-hand. And the only advice I knew to give was "Don't cross the streams." I left them to it and climbed the stairs to the third floor. I stopped down the hall and knocked on Kenny's door. "Are you in there?"

There was no reply.

I didn't feel comfortable barging in. The door was locked anyway. "We need to talk, Kenny."

No answer.

He better hope to God that Simon Beck wasn't murdered. Because if he was trying to get a spot on the suspect list, he found the quickest way to the top.

CHAPTER 15

Aunt Ginny sat on the end of my bed holding Figaro. She'd shown up at seven fifteen to check if I was still alive when I hadn't surfaced in the kitchen to make coffee. "At least you won't have to worry about the tabloid reporter saying you're a fraud."

"Yeah. Now she'll say I'm a murderer."

Aunt Ginny scratched Figaro between the ears. "Oh. She won't . . . I'm almost nearly sure. Are you getting dressed, or are you staying in those ratty pajamas?"

I pulled the covers up to my chin. "I'm never coming out. You can tell everyone to go home and report me to the Better Business Bureau."

Aunt Ginny smacked her lips and stroked Figaro's fur. "Are you sure about that?"

I turned my face into the pillow until I couldn't see her anymore and I had barely enough air to survive. "Yes. I'm done."

"Well, you might want to brush your hair."

What is she up to now? Television interview for the

Crime Scene Network in the kitchen? Photographer for *I'm Haunted* monthly magazine on the porch? "Why?"

A different voice, warm as honey and sexy as McSteamy, answered me instead. "Because your latte is getting cold, Bella."

My eyes popped open, and my heart sank through the mattress. *Oh crap! That's it. Aunt Ginny, you're dead to me. Also, I'm buying new pajamas today.*

Aunt Ginny put Figaro down next to me and stood up. "Oh, I forgot to tell you. Gia's here. I called him about the kitchen being closed and he brought coffee and pastries for the guests."

Aunt Ginny giggled all the way down the hall. Then Figaro abandoned me in my time of need and galloped after her in the name of filling his belly. I peeked at my boyfriend's gorgeous blue eyes, knowing I had not taken my makeup off last night before I cried myself to sleep.

Gia had that quizzical look on his face that a man gets the first time he sees what a train wreck his woman really is. Then he chuckled to himself and put the cup of coffee on my nightstand. "Don't I get a 'good morning'?"

"I had different expectations for your first time in my bedroom."

He sat on the bed next to me and put his hand on my back. "Wow. You are a mess."

"Thank you. You were bound to find out one of these days."

He reached out and smoothed a lock of my hair away from my eyes. "I heard what happened."

"Was I on the front page today?"

"No, but the dead professor was. You . . . may have been mentioned a little bit."

Every cell in my body heaved a sigh. "Maybe God's trying to tell me something. Maybe being an innkeeper just isn't for me. Or living in America."

Gia touched my temple and ran his finger down my cheek. "Then where should we go?"

"I'm a death magnet. Maybe you should get it over with and break up with me now."

I could feel his eyes on me without looking up. The heat coming off of him sitting on my bed was making me start to sweat.

"No, Bella. That is not the direction I want us to go in."

My breath got caught in my throat. That was a lot of emotional heat that I wasn't prepared to face before brushing my hair. I had to deflect, so I gathered my courage to ask Gia the one thing that had been haunting me since Simon Beck died during Dracula's pipe organ. "Do you think someone learned that we're called the murder house, and decided to come here to murder Simon on the tour because it would make a good cover story to hide their crime?"

Gia was quiet for moment. "If they did, that is not your fault. You had nothing to do with what happened to that man."

I lay there hoping I would wake up and find this was not real. Maybe this was a diet dream. I tried to think back. *Was there any point last night where I dreamed I ate a can of frosting?*

"Are you going to get up?"

So, I am awake. Rats.

"Or are you going to let this beat you?"

"I don't know yet."

"I promise we will get through this together."

"Okay." I flipped the corner of my blanket away from my face.

"Okay." Gia stood.

"I've got to get dressed first."

"Don't let me stop you."

I turned my mascara-smudged face and looked at him in all my Gene Simmons glory. "I'm not letting you see me in threadbare shorty pajamas."

"Then take them off."

I reached for the pillow behind my head and threw it at him, but I could not keep the crooked smile off my blotchy face.

"Okay, okay. I will wait in the kitchen."

Twenty minutes later, I was scrubbed, fluffed, spritzed, and repainted. And I had put on a burgundy sweaterdress and tall suede boots to try to erase the last image of me that might still be lingering in Gia's mind. When I entered the kitchen with my latte, the look on his face was almost enough to make last night bearable.

Gia groaned. "I should have stood my ground."

The back door banged open and Joanne stormed in. "What are you doing here? We're not allowed to bake anything until we're cleared by the police."

"I just came to get some of my things before you threw them out." She grabbed my Alice in Wonderland mug and poured herself a cup of coffee.

"I would never just throw your things out, Joanne. Why would you think that?" *It does, however, sound like something Joanne would do to me without blinking an eye.*

Joanne dropped down to the bench seat and blew on her coffee.

Gia glanced my way and raised his eyebrows.

The bedroom door opened, and Aunt Ginny swished into the kitchen wearing a yellow nylon jumpsuit. "Kenny won't be down today. He called in sick."

"He called in? From upstairs?"

Joanne's lips flattened into a line. "Good. I don't want him here."

I crossed the kitchen to Aunt Ginny. "When did you talk to him?"

She adjusted a cord dangling from her waist. "This morning."

"What happened to him last night? He just disappeared."

"I gave him a pill and sent him to bed. He wasn't feeling well."

"He needs to give his statement so the police will let us prepare meals again."

Joanne smirked. "Pretty convenient timing."

Gia sipped his espresso. "Why is that?

Joanne crossed her arms over her chest. "I think he may have tampered with the guests' drinks."

I blew on my latte. "What? Don't be absurd. Why would he do that?"

She smirked again. "Because I saw him put something in one of them."

"Why didn't you say that last night?!"

Joanne leaned back and shrugged. "You said you don't need me. And I don't work here anymore. It sounds like you should ask your golden boy what he was doing."

Of all the ridiculous, petty . . . I would not give Joanne the satisfaction of seeing me nervous. I picked up my cell phone and texted Kenny:

We need to talk. ASAP.

Aunt Ginny slid a pair of rose-gold sunglasses up to the top of her head. "Well, I'm off."

That's the word on the street. "Off where?"

She opened her mouth, then looked me in the eye. "Never you mind."

We stared at one another, each daring the other to flinch first. Then she grabbed one of the pumpkin cheesecake muffins from the basket on the island and swished from the room.

After the front door closed, I joined Joanne and Gia at the table. "What was that all about?"

Joanne shrugged. "I wouldn't know." She sipped her coffee. "But that's the kind of jumpsuit you wear when you jump out of a plane."

"What?" *Oh, heck no!* I leapt from the table and ran through the door into the dining room. "Aunt Ginny, wait!"

Owen Rodney was squatting down in front of the wing chair, eye to eye with Figaro. "It's okay now. It's all over."

Skydiving panic paused, I stopped to examine my feline for injury. "What's okay now? What happened?"

Owen adjusted his square glasses. "Figaro has seen a lot of death in his lifetime."

Please. Figaro has caused a lot of death in his lifetime. But we haven't had a mouse or moth problem in months.

Figaro turned his body like a corkscrew and stretched his paws out past his head.

Owen grinned at me. "He sure does love you."

"Well, yeah. I know how to work the can opener."

Gladys Philippot strode through the dining room, up to the sideboard, and grabbed a coffee cup and a muffin. "You're in luck. You won't have to worry about an exposé. You might be a serial killer, but you're not a fraud."

That's not exactly a win.

"And the rumors are certainly true about you attracting death." She poured herself some coffee. "I was wondering if I could get an exclusive?"

"No, I told you I'm not doing an interview. And I'm definitely not a serial killer."

Owen straightened his bow tie. "Figaro thinks you should do the interview."

I looked at Figaro, who had curled into a ball with his eyes closed. "I didn't know Fig was so concerned with my reputation."

Figaro cracked an eye open for a brief second to glance at me before going back to dozing.

Owen laughed. "Good one, Figaro."

"What'd he say about me?" *Why, in God's name, did I just ask that? Commit me now.*

Owen chuckled. "He thinks you don't know how to mark your territory."

I stared at the gray ball of fluff, then at Owen. I had too many questions forming at once to pick through and ask the right ones. It seemed I didn't have time to anyway; the *Paranormal Pathfinders* crew were dragging themselves down the stairs at impulse speed.

Harper was the first to come around the corner. She yawned and turned bleary eyes towards the pastry buffet courtesy of La Dolce Vita. "Oh, I hope the coffee is ready."

Clark came right after her. "The equipment is packed up for the day so it will be out of your way. We worked all night, so after I have breakfast I'm going to turn in."

"How did it go last night?"

Ritchie dragged himself to the table and shrugged. "It was okay. You have a lot of doors that open and close on their own. And I'm missing a lens cover to the small handheld."

Harper stirred cream into her coffee. "It's not unusual for items to disappear when you have a ghost in residence."

Paisley reached for the juice. "I'm missing a pink pom-pom off my pen cap. The ghosts may be letting us know they don't like our interference."

Owen took his mug over to the tea chest. "I heard last night was a dud."

Clark narrowed his eyes and looked at his team sitting around the table. "From who?"

Gladys cackled. "From the cat. Who else do you think he's been talking to?"

Owen poured steaming water over his tea bag. "Figaro supervised the operation until very early this morning. That's why he's so tired today. He says you didn't see anything."

I looked at my sleeping feline. *Figaro does seem very tired today. Snap out of it, Poppy.* "I'm so sorry there isn't a hot breakfast. The police won't let us prepare any food in the kitchen until they determine Simon's cause of death. And again, I can't apologize enough for last night. I know that was a terrible experience for everyone."

Ritchie poured himself a cup of juice. "No one blames you for what happened. It was probably just a heart attack."

Paisley gave me a tremulous smile. "I'm just sorry it happened at your house."

Harper helped herself to a pumpkin cheesecake muffin and a piece of cherry coffee cake. "I've been thinking about it, and I think that guy from the university murdered him. The cute one with the curly hair who almost strangled him at dinner."

Ritchie snorted. "How can you think he's cute and he murdered someone at the same time?"

Harper pulled out a chair and sat down. "I don't think those things are mutually exclusive. Killers can be good-looking."

Gladys pulled out a chair and joined the group. "Since the cat is out of the bag so to speak with you-alls being on TV and everything, what made you go into ghost huntin' as a career?" Gladys took out a little recorder from her pocket, pressed the button, and set it on the table.

Clark sipped his coffee. "As far back as I can remember, I've been interested in the paranormal. That's why I got a degree in paranormal studies. I wanted to help people feel safe when strange things were happening around them."

I can't say it's been helping.

My phone buzzed in my hand, and I was so startled I almost threw it into the ficus. It was a reply text from Kenny:

There may have been a problem with Simon Beck's food.

CHAPTER 16

"What are you talking about, Kenny?" I stood outside of his door on the third floor and pleaded with him to open it.

"I don't want you to see me like this. My cheeks are pink and splotchy, and I have dark circles under my eyes. You've only ever seen Marilyn Kenny. Right now, I look like Norma Jean Kenny."

"Yeah, well. You wouldn't believe the sight Gia got this morning either. Why do you think someone tampered with the food?"

"He was obviously poisoned, wasn't he?"

"Did you see anyone put anything in his food?"

"No."

"He could have had a heart attack."

"Nice people have heart attacks. Self-important connivers are poisoned."

"How do you know Simon was a conniver?"

Kenny was silent for a beat. "He had that vibe."

I wanted to argue with that, but seeing as how I'd had more than my fair share of experience in the area, Norma Jean was on to something. "But are you feeling sick? What did you eat last night?"

"Nothing. I never eat anything other than a Lunchables before a performance."

"Then how are you sick?"

Kenny's voice lowered. "I don't want to talk about it."

"Someone said you put something in Simon's drink."

Kenny was silent for a moment. "Stupid Joanne is going to get me sent to jail. It was sugar, okay. He said the stevia wasn't sweet enough. He didn't want his wife to know."

The alarm went off on my phone. It was time to go to Mia Famiglia to make desserts and dinner rolls. "I've got to go, but I want to talk more about this tonight, so spruce yourself up, kitten."

Unspecified grumbling came from the other side of the door, and I took it as disgruntled acquiescence.

I took the hidden staircase down to the pantry. Gia was deep in conversation with Joanne. I popped out just as he said, "Why don't you tell her?"

I looked between the two of them. "Tell me what?"

Joanne made a face at Gia. "It's nothing, Stupid. Go away."

Gia gave me a lopsided grin. "How did that go?"

"He's being a diva. So . . . same old same old. Are you ready to go to your mother's to make cannoli?"

Gia threw his paper cup in the trash. "I will follow you anywhere, *cara mia.*"

I pulled the fry basket from the hot oil. Even with tongs as long as my arm, I still managed to burn myself for the third time as I attempted the extraction of the shell from the metal cannoli form. "Son of a biscuit!" I dropped the shell onto the counter, and it shattered. Every jagged edge mocked me.

I grabbed another ice cube to rub on my wrist. "These metal tubes hold on to the grease like my hips on Jenny Craig."

Marco gave me some side-eye. "Maybe dis just not your ting."

Six cannoli shells in varying degrees of "doneness" lay in shards on the workbench.

Gia took the bottle of lavender from the counter and let a couple drops fall to the angry red blotches on my arm. He gave me a pitiful look and gently patted the soothing oil around the burns.

"There has to be a better way to do this."

Marco shrugged. "Momma, she no let anybody make da cannoli but her."

I looked the little sous chef in the face. "How about this. What if I make a Sicilian cassata instead? I can add some orange peel and chopped cherries to the cannoli filling and spread it between layers of rum cake with an almond glaze? Will that work?"

Marco's eyes lit with interest. "Yeah. Dat sound delicious. Plus dis." He waved his hand at my fractured dignity before us. "Dis you no good at."

Yes. Thank you, Marco. I got that. The bell dinged for the oven and Gia removed the pans of chicken and artichoke manicotti that we had made for tonight's special. We spent the first two hours here stuffing pasta shells with a mixture of chicken, spinach, artichoke, and cheeses.

His cell phone rang, and he fished it out of his pocket. "Yeah? . . . *Si*. On my way." He hung up and told me it was Sierra, his daytime barista. "I have to go unload a delivery for the coffee shop. I will see you a little later." He kissed me and then he kissed my wrist. "Maybe stay away from frying things."

"Understood."

The garlicky Parmesan sauce bubbled around rows of pasta soldiers making me wish I'd made some gluten-free ones for myself. I sprinkled Romano cheese over the top with my good hand and set the pans on the workbench to cool.

I was just about to throw together a batch of pumpkin pie Danishes when the hostess stuck her head in the kitchen.

"Psst!"

"Hey. What's up?"

"The cops are here."

I chucked the box of puff pastry and sprinted for the back door. I had my hand on the doorknob when I froze. *Wait a minute. I'm not doing anything wrong. Why am I running?* "Here for what?"

The hostess shrugged.

The wrong side of the kitchen door swung open, and Amber entered through the exit. "Aunt Ginny said you'd be here. Are you leaving already?"

I cut my eyes to the box of puff pastry wedged a few feet off the floor, between the Hobart mixer and the bin of flour. "What? No. I'm just . . . doin' stuff . . ."

The line of chefs were watching me with more than a little amusement on their faces.

Amber's eyes narrowed and she looked around.

I took a step towards the workbench and made an attempt at a casual smile. "So . . . What do you need?"

"Why are you acting suspicious?"

I wiped my hands on my apron. "What? No." I looked at the hostess who was still watching from the doorway. "Why don't you get Sergeant Fenton a pop. On me."

Amber held up her hand. "That's okay. I'm good. I've got a Mega Slurpee in the squad car."

I pulled the box of puff pastry from its nook and took it to the workbench with a glance at the tiny blond cop. "That's where we keep it."

Amber shook my comment off like it was more ramblings of a crazy person. Which it was. "Whatever you need to tell yourself."

"So, to what do I owe the pleasure of this visit?"

"I want you to do something."

"No."

"You don't even know what it is."

"Yes, I do."

"What?"

I pulled on a vinyl glove over my burns and opened the box of pastry. I unfolded it on the floured bench into a rectangle. "You want me to stick my neck out for you again with this newest murder case and your boss has already made me promise not to get involved."

Amber shrugged. "Okay. If you don't want the B&B kitchen opened again that's entirely up to you."

I pointed a floured finger at her face. "No! You will not lure me into this with your undercover promises."

"McAllister. Will you relax? Chief knows I'm here."

I opened a can of pumpkin and dumped it into a mixing bowl. "Yeah. I don't think so, lady."

Amber took a couple steps towards my workbench. "Would I lie to you?"

"Yes." I took a step backwards. "And you're not handcuffing me to anything until I agree with you. Fool me once."

Amber stopped moving. "Kat doesn't think Simon

had a heart attack. She doesn't think it was natural causes at all."

"So, he *was* murdered."

She nodded. "It's most likely poison, but she's still waiting on the full tox screen to know which one."

"Did you check the NYU kids' photos?"

Amber shook her head. "They'd deleted them by the time we questioned them. IT ghosted their devices to look for hidden files."

"Ha-ha. Ghosted. Very funny."

Amber leaned against the counter. "No, really. That's what they told me."

"Great. Well, how does that help me?"

"Because I convinced Kieran to let you resume dinners for the ghost tours." Amber picked up the tin of cinnamon I kept eyeing from a distance. "I promise not to cuff you."

I took a tentative step towards my mixing bowl and accepted the offered spice. "He's going to let me open my kitchen again?"

"No. But I told him you could probably find a professional kitchen to cook in while yours is awaiting clearance. Which I can see you already thought of and neglected to mention when you asked him if you could bring food in from your boyfriend's mother's restaurant."

I cracked an egg and dropped it into the pumpkin mixture, realized what Amber had just said, and looked her in the eye. "He didn't ask for specifics."

"He doesn't know you well enough yet to realize he needs to. Which reminds me, I still need to get your housekeeper's statement."

My cheeks flamed and I looked deeply into my mixing bowl to avoid Amber's gaze.

"There are a couple of caveats to this little arrangement."

Oh, here it comes. "And they are?"

"One, you have to join the ghost tour."

"I'm already on the ghost tour." *At least I will be once I tell Linda I'm back in.*

"No. I want *you* on the ghost tour. While your staff hosts dinners to a new group at the Butterfly Wings every night, you'll be traveling with the group who came to your house with Dr. Simon Beck."

"What! To do what?"

"Just keep your ears open. See how they interact. You'll know better than the other innkeepers if anyone is acting suspicious. Then report to me anything unusual you hear."

"You want me to spy for you again."

"In exchange for letting you resume dinner tours, I want you to be nosy like you usually are. It's surprisingly effective."

I am losing a lot of money by canceling those tour dinners. "And Chief Kieran okayed this? After he made a big deal about me getting involved?"

It was Amber's turn to look away. "He approved enough. This one is problematic because most of the main suspects are from out of town. We have a very slim window before we have to charge them or lose them."

"Don't you have an undercover cop who could do this better?"

Amber blinked twice. "*Every* undercover cop could do it better. But you were there when Simon Beck was murdered. You'll pick up on changes in their behavior. Plus, they already know you. They're less likely to open up to a stranger who starts asking questions about their motives out of the blue."

"And what happens if I get caught by your boss nosing around these people and asking questions?"

Amber looked deep into my eyes. "I've got your back. I won't let you get into any trouble."

I knew she would keep that promise if it was the last thing she did. Amber was a good cop. And she just wanted to put the bad guys behind bars. She was willing to bend a couple rules to do it. Apparently, I was one of those rules. "What's the other caveat?"

"I've got Joanne cleared to help you."

"Joanne gave me two weeks' notice. She's been mad about something lately, so she definitely won't be doing me any favors."

"She's the only one on your staff without a record that I trust to help you make dinner. So, if I were you, I'd do whatever it takes to get her back."

CHAPTER 17

I thought Kieran was overstepping his authority, but I still sped home from Momma's kitchen with interrogation on my mind. I was going to be both good cop and bad cop. Forget Simon Beck's murder. How is Joanne the only one in my kitchen who has a clean record? Maybe I should get a bare lightbulb for intimidation. *No. There's no point. Aunt Ginny isn't intimidated by anything. I'll hide the peanut butter until she breaks.*

I found Aunt Ginny and Kenny sitting at the kitchen table drinking amaretto that was weakly masquerading as hot cocoa.

"Just tell me what you have a record for, Aunt Ginny. I know it wasn't that murder business from a few months back because those charges were dropped."

She shrugged. "Who can remember? It was so long ago."

"Obviously Amber remembers." I turned my eyes to Kenny, who'd had a miraculous recovery that was brought on by thinking I'd be gone from home longer. "And how is it you were *not* cleared to work in this kitchen during the investigation?"

Kenny tipped his chin from Aunt Ginny to me. "I think it's racial profiling."

"You're a white guy."

"It's not that popular right now."

I pointed in his face. "Kenny, I did a background check before I hired you. Did I miss something I need to be worried about?"

Kenny sipped his ethanol cocoa. "No. Wait . . . Did I put the Melon Patch club down as a reference?"

"You didn't list any clubs. Why?"

He waved his hand. "Psh. Never mind. That was someone else."

These two were locked down tighter than a *Gilmore Girls* reunion script. My cell phone buzzed, and I fished it out of my pocket. "I'm just gonna ask Amber. She owes me one." *Again.*

Aunt Ginny muttered into her cocoa, "Good luck with that."

I pushed the button to answer the call I'd been anxiously awaiting and dreading at the same time. "Joanne. Hi."

"What."

Lovely. I need a vacation. And some chocolate. "Thanks for calling me back." I pulled open the drawer where I'd stashed the bag of Halloween candy. "I was hoping we could talk for a minute." I pulled out the empty bag of Reese's Peanut Butter Cups and shook it at Aunt Ginny.

She shrugged. "I think we have a possum problem."

Joanne huffed into the phone. "Make it quick. I'm busy."

I narrowed my eyes at Bonnie and Clyde seated at

the banquette. "So am I. And it looks like I need to stop at the drugstore and buy more Halloween candy on my way out tonight."

"What does that have to do with me, Buttface?"

I see our little heart-to-heart about being nicer has done wonders. "I'm calling to ask you for a favor."

Joanne's voice perked up. "Oh, are you now?"

I filled her in on my conversation with Amber and the stipulations placed upon me. "Do you think you can help me make dinner at Mia Famiglia for the next group of ghost tour guests at the B&B, then serve them by yourself starting tomorrow night?"

"And why exactly can't Ginny and Dipwad help serve?"

I looked across the kitchen to the two gingers who were watching my every move like cats tracking a fly. "Only you were approved by law enforcement to handle the food in my absence."

"Uh-huh. And where you gonna be?"

I checked the schedule Linda had sent over in an email. "Tomorrow, I'll be with the group at The Chalfonte." *Eavesdropping on Brooklyn to see if she's planning to flee the country.*

"Well, I don't see why I should do this for you. My two weeks' notice only commits me to the morning shift."

"That's why it's a favor, Joanne. You have the prerogative to say no."

"Still . . ."

She wants me to beg, doesn't she?

"I mean it is a big inconvenience, and I do have other offers from more reputable establishments . . ."

Figaro trotted in and headed straight for me. He rubbed against my ankles and purred. I picked him up and kissed his forehead.

"Are you still there, Buttface?"

"I'm here. I'm just wondering if my life insurance would cover what I owe for the tour contract if I tell Amber no and we cancel the remaining nights." *Aunt Ginny can always bury me in the backyard.*

"This investigation could go on for weeks. Not days. So, how badly do you want me there?"

"What's your price, Joanne?"

"I want you to admit that I'm a better cook than Kenny."

I rolled my eyes, thankful that this wasn't a video call. "Of course you're a better cook, Joanne. No one can touch your sugar art. And everyone says your croissants are amazing."

"Just amazing?"

"Made from angels' wings! Okay. I mean they always look perfect. I've never eaten one because I can't have gluten, which you seem to insist on telling me is in my imagination."

Aunt Ginny loudly cleared her throat and I realized I may have gotten off course.

I took a breath and softened my approach. "Joanne. You know you are very talented, and I am asking you to please come back and help me make the tour dinners off-site until my kitchen is cleared for food prep again so we don't lose a fortune."

Aunt Ginny gave me a nod.

I breathed out the last of my dignity and put Figaro down. He immediately began a full-court press for dinner.

"Are you begging me?"

Is she serious? "Joanne!"

"Fine! I'll do it for the sake of the guests, but I'll need some help. Kenny'll just poison someone else. Tell me when and where to meet you."

I gave Joanne the details and hung up. Kenny and Aunt Ginny were watching me closely, waiting to be filled in on the other side of the conversation.

"She'll do it, but she'll abuse me the entire time."

Kenny tsked. "I bet her mother beat her with wire hangers." His eyes grew wide. "Did she make you say she was a better cook than me?"

"Look at the time. I need to get dressed for the tour."

Aunt Ginny laughed. "Oh, that Joanne's a sneaky one."

Kenny looked at Aunt Ginny, then back at me, his mouth hanging open. "No, really. Is that what I heard you say?"

Figaro moved on to plead with Aunt Ginny while I filled a plate of lemon squares for happy hour in the library. "Well, to be fair, Kenny, she's a better pastry chef than both of us."

He sputtered and fanned himself. "If you like those hard, tasteless icing flowers maybe. But can she perform the Katniss Everdeen monologue from *Hunger Games* flawlessly—I think not."

"Okay. Calm down. You both have your talents. The more important factor to remember here is that only one of you has an arrest record. And I'm still angry with you for disappearing last night. What exactly was that all about?"

Kenny cleared his throat and his eyes shifted to the left. "Is that how you're going to wear your hair tonight?"

"Don't try to change the subject. What's wrong with my hair?"

He shook his head. "I don't know where to begin. Go with a chignon. It's classy and you don't have the time or a magic wand for anything else."

"It's just the Southern Mansion, not Buckingham Palace."

Figaro squalled the world's longest meow and we all stared at him until it was finished.

Aunt Ginny broke under his demands and walked over to the cabinet where the prince's top-shelf mush was stored. "It is formal attire, though. And you are representing the Butterfly Wings."

I picked up the plate of lemon squares and a packet of napkins for the library. "You can both rest easy. I will call my plus-one, and we will fancy ourselves up appropriately. You just need to be prepared to perform the ghost stories at tomorrow's dinner tour without me."

Aunt Ginny gave me a thumbs-up. "I've got the coroner on speed dial."

CHAPTER 18

I yanked on a pair of Spunks and poured myself into a red swing dress and leopard high-heeled booties. While I fussed over my hair, I recounted all the ways I was blessed to keep myself from sliding into depression over having someone else die in front of me. I'd worked too hard to break through the darkness after my husband passed, and it was a slippery slope back down.

Joanne had pitched such a fit about serving alone that I'd gotten approval for Kim to come help her. Even though we'd been friends since high school, she felt she still owed me from that Wine Tour fiasco. I did not disagree.

I had just fastened the last hairpin to hold my chignon into place when a car horn wailed from the front of the house.

Aunt Ginny waited for me at the bottom of the steps. "Is that Sawyer I hear?"

"She's going to help me blend in."

Aunt Ginny cocked a hip. "Blend in, or break in?"

"That depends on what Amber is sending me into." I pulled the door open, and we stepped out into the crisp night.

Aunt Ginny grabbed my arm. "Flippin' chestnuts!!"

I put my hand out to steady her and looked around to see if she was freaking out over something real or imaginary this time. "What in the world?" Someone had added about forty creepy jack-o'-lanterns to our front lawn, and every one of them was glowing and glaring in the direction of my front door.

Aunt Ginny's voice was a little shaky. "It's like the valley of the dammed."

I steadied myself. "That may be an exaggeration. It's just a bunch of pumpkins."

That have come out of nowhere.

All looking at us with malice in their triangle eyes.

Okay, calm down, Poppy. "I'm sure it's just the neighborhood kids pulling a prank."

A couple of teenagers walked down the sidewalk and ignored us completely.

Aunt Ginny shook her fist and shouted at them, "If I see so much as one egg splattered on my porch for Mischief Night, I'm giving out raisins this year!"

Sawyer was hunched over the steering wheel watching us through the passenger window. She lifted her hands and gave me a shrug.

I hugged Aunt Ginny goodbye. "Don't worry. I think it's just harmless fun. Why don't you go watch *Wheel* until you have to do the ghost stories? Kim is coming to help Joanne serve and I'll be home soon. I'll bring you some of those peanut butter pretzels you like."

She patted the back of my shoulder. "If someone dies on the tour tonight you call me right away."

"I always do."

I opened the door to Sawyer's little car and climbed in. She had dressed in a short black taffeta cocktail dress that showed her long legs down to silver sparkle high heels.

"Your yard looks great. You spent a small fortune on pumpkins."

I eyed the field of demonic orange spheres, and a little shiver ran up my spine. "It's definitely an eerie effect."

Sawyer pulled away from the curb. "I was thinking about this curse you're under."

"I see our days of adding 'alleged' are long gone. Go on."

"What if it's not you? What if it's the house?"

"Like we're built over an ancient Indian burial ground?"

"Don't laugh; you probably are. The Kechemeche tribe lived in Cape May long before rich people came in and put up summer homes and minigolf."

"Yeah, but I grew up in that house. No one was getting murdered when I was in Mr. Wilson's fifth-grade class at Consolidated."

Sawyer eyed me briefly before turning onto Washington Street. "Maybe the curse needed time to warm up to you."

"Then why hasn't Aunt Ginny had a lifetime of finding murder victims?"

"Chaos theory."

"If ever there was a theory surrounding Aunt Ginny, that would be the one."

Sawyer slowed the car. "Think about it. You can either cause chaos, or chaos will be caused around you. We both know which one is Aunt Ginny. You're like a chaos lightning rod."

"I don't think that's what chaos theory means."

We pulled in front of the looming beige-and-green palace. "Well, it should be."

Sawyer drove around to the red rock parking lot on the side of the building and parked just as the Victorian hearse was trotting away to pick up their next group. We stepped out of the car and followed the paper bag lanterns that lit up the redbrick pathway to the double doors at the front.

If you could pick up an antebellum plantation and move it to the beach, you'd have the Southern Mansion. Its low-pitched roof and square cupola were almost out of place amongst the witches' hat towers and spindles of the Queen Anne dollhouses. I expected Scarlett O'Hara to be sipping mint juleps on the huge covered porch with a *Fiddle-dee-dee*. But the mansion's sprawling manicured lawn and relaxed gardens brought you right back to the Victorian seaside ambiance. Right now, that ambiance had orange and purple lights strung across the roofline of the porch.

We stepped inside the entryway and were greeted by a lovely dark-haired woman in a bright red scarf and a pointy black hat. "Hi. You must be Poppy. I'm Denise, the manager here. I'm so sorry about what happened at your house last night. Sergeant Fenton said you'd be joining us tonight."

I took her offered hand and gave it a squeeze. "Thank you for having us on such short notice. I'm Poppy, and this is Sawyer."

Denise patted my hand. "So nice to meet you both. Why don't you follow me, and I'll get you set up?"

Sawyer and I followed Denise through a wild-looking foyer. The walls were emerald green, the carpet leopard print, and two fire engine–red chairs sat under heavy gold gilt mirrors, one on either side of the expansive hallway.

We paused at a beautiful aqua-blue room with a yellow tray ceiling. Eli was drinking a martini in front of a large marble fireplace with a glowing fire. Across from him, Felicity sat on an ivory barrel back chair while Sable and Jax were huddled together on a matching damask sofa. *Where's Verna and Brooklyn?*

Sawyer whispered in my ear, "You didn't say we were getting free drinks. I would have shown up a half an hour earlier."

"I must have forgotten about that while I was distracted by tonight's eavesdropping assignment."

Denise was already down at the other end of the long hallway. "That's the double parlor. Come along. We're just past here."

Where is she going? The tour group is by the fire.

We quickstepped to catch up to her, passing through an enclosed solarium with gold linen–covered tables and down the stairs to the kitchen. Two chefs were buzzing around sizzling grills and steamy pots. Denise took two aprons off a row of hooks and held them out.

I stared at the black canvas in her hands. "What's this?"

"These are your aprons for tonight. You don't want to mess up your pretty dresses. And we want the guests to know who the servers are."

If I had a hamster running my brain, she had fallen off her wheel and was lying in the water bowl. "Servers for what?"

A flash of uncertainty passed Denise's brow. "For dinner. For the Haunted Homes Tour. Sergeant

Fenton said you were looking to work tonight to observe how we conduct the tour because yours was such a disaster."

Amber . . . you little . . . I didn't reach for the apron due to shock. My heart was willing, but my brain was still rebooting.

Denise gave it a little shake. "When Sergeant Fenton requested my assistance, she suggested waitstaff. I already sent my other guys home. I thought she cleared it with you."

Sawyer took the black canvas and tied it around her waist. "Did she now? Poppy, remind me to thank Officer Amber for taking care of these specific details."

I gave Denise a wan smile and took the offered apron. "Thank you, Denise. I really do appreciate you letting us join you tonight."

Denise breathed out a relieved sigh and filled us in on the flow of the event.

When another server came in to get her help with a table, Sawyer pulled a grimace for my eyes only. "These are not walking shoes. They're sitting and looking sexy shoes."

"My feet hurt already, and I've only walked from the car to the kitchen."

"We're getting pedicures on my next day off."

"I'm buying."

Sawyer gave me a wry look. "Oh, you'd better believe it."

CHAPTER 19

"**A**mber. Why the heck are we waitresses?" I held my cell phone under my chin while I wrapped the apron around my dress.

"Calm down, McAllister. It's a cover story. Don't you think they'd start asking questions if you were just going to all the ghost tours for the heck of it?"

Denise walked past us to talk to the chef, and I turned in to my phone. "You couldn't give us a little warning?"

Amber laughed. "Let's just say we're even for that time you threw the frog at me."

"It hopped."

"Mm-hmm. You keep saying that and maybe one day I'll believe you."

Sawyer jabbed me in the side. "We're on."

"I gotta go." I clicked off and turned to Sawyer. "She's getting even for the ecology field trip."

"Oh, my word, Amber. It hopped!"

"I mean . . . that's what frogs do for Kermit's sake."

The first course was pumpkin soup with bacon. I

thought I saw Sawyer brush a tear away when the chef loaded her tray. Neither of us had eaten anything all afternoon in preparation for dinner tonight.

Denise rushed over and replaced one of the bowls on my tray for one without bacon. "Don't ask why they aren't sitting together. It's a whole thing. Apparently, the woman in the orange silk is vegan. This one is for her."

I wasn't the only one ambushed by the dietary news flash. I carried the tray up the steps to the solarium—praying there would be soup left in the bowl when I arrived—and spotted my tour guests spread out amongst three different mostly empty tables. Sawyer went in the direction of Dr. Van Smoot sitting with Eli, and I took the New York kids.

"Hey, guys."

Jax's eyebrows shot up. "Do you work here too?"

I put his soup in front of him. "Just for tonight. Innkeepers help each other out for special events." *Starting now.* "How are you doing today?"

Sable gave me a one-arm shrug and adjusted her spaghetti strap. "I want to go home, but the police said it's better if we stay in case they need to ask us more questions."

Jax made a face and his beard quivered. "They already cloned our cell phones. Can they make us stay? We'd never even met the guy."

"Technically, no. They can't *make* you stay. But they can hold you for questioning if they feel they have reasonable cause."

Sable chewed her lip. "What kind of reasonable cause?"

I shrugged. "Like if there was a suspicious connection between you and the deceased. And with you being from out of state, they might play that card if you push them. So you might as well enjoy the rest of your tour while you're here. Do you have a good lawyer?"

Sable pushed her soup away in a deep sigh. "My stepmother is working on it."

"That's good." I felt sorry for the kids. New York was a long way from home just to get stranded in a police investigation. "I'm surprised you didn't have a haunted homes tour closer to where you live."

The kids looked at each other with tight mouths and wide eyes. Finally, Sable looked my way again. "We've been to all the local ones. We want to visit all the ghost tours on the East Coast before we graduate in the spring."

Jax cleared his throat, loudly. He gave me a grin that didn't reach his eyes. "Cape May has a lot of them."

Denise was making faces at me from across the room and shifting her eyes in Brooklyn's direction. Apparently, I was not serving fast enough.

"That is definitely true. Well, I hope you find some way to enjoy the rest of your stay." I gave the kids a smile and headed over to the widow who was sitting alone at a table for four.

I placed her bowl of pumpkin soup on the decorative black charger plate meant to keep the table festive. "Good evening."

She looked into my face and blinked a few times. "I thought you owned the bed and breakfast we were at last night."

"I do. I'm just helping out. How are you holding up?"

Brooklyn touched her forehead. "Not well. I had a migraine all morning. I've only come out now because I have to eat something and this dinner is already paid for."

"I'm sure you're exhausted. My husband died a year and a half ago. I know how stressful it can be to plan and pay for a funeral. I hope Simon had life insurance to help you with the expenses."

She took a spoonful of soup and shrugged. "I don't know if he had any or not. He kept all that to himself."

"Well, do you at least have some support? Are Simon's family coming up to be with you?" I felt eyes on me and followed the creepy vibe two tables down. Felicity Van Smoot was staring at me like she was memorizing my anatomy for a sculpture class.

Brooklyn put her spoon down. "I don't know. Do you think I should call them?"

"You haven't told them yet?" *Is she in shock or insane?*

"I don't even know their number. How do I say 'your son had a heart attack on vacation'? I knew his blood pressure was too high. That's why I put him on a diet and reduced his sugars. But I guess I was too late, and I don't know what he told them."

Sawyer brought out a tray with little tarts and served Brooklyn first. "These are apple and pear crostini. They are supposed to have Roquefort on them, but they've left it off of yours." She made eyes at me and nudged in the way of Denise, who was hovering over the tables nearby.

I caught Felicity's eye and mouthed to her, *What?*

She just looked away and bent her head to say something to Eli.

Sawyer moved to the table with Sable and Jax, and I squatted down to be face-to-face with the widow. "Brooklyn, please forgive me for asking, but I overheard a couple things the other night, and I was wondering if maybe in his past, before you of course, Simon was known as a ladies' man? Could there be a jilted lover who maybe is holding a grudge against him?" *And could she be at that table over there?*

"I dunno. He was very private." She picked up her fork and stabbed at the pastry. She took a bite and chewed thoughtfully. "We agreed not to talk about our pasts when we got together. He did tell me that he had a relationship years ago with a student who became obsessed with him. He tried to break it off and she began stalking him. He was really afraid."

"What happened?"

She took another bite of the pastry. "I think he had her transferred to another department just to get her away from him."

I flicked my eyes up to the honey-blond professor two tables down. She was talking to someone at her table, but her eyes were on Brooklyn. "Did he ever mention a name?" *Does it rhyme with* Felicity?

"Not that I remember. Do you think I could get some hot tea?"

My calves screamed in protest as I straightened up and one of my knees popped. "Of course. Let me go tell the kitchen." *Down the stairs. Who puts a kitchen in the basement?*

She doesn't seem jealous over her husband's past lovers. Of course, if the rumors are true, they may not all be in the past. I ran into Sawyer hobbling out of the kitchen with a basket of bread on her tray. "If I take my shoes off, do you think anyone will notice?"

"Maybe. But I won't judge you. Go for it. What can they do? Dock your pay?"

"By the way. That guy who looks like he's been constipated for twenty years . . ."

"Eli Lush."

Sawyer nodded. "He said the people who believe this stuff are idiots. He claims he only came on this tour to prove there are no real hauntings. Doesn't that go against everything the dead guy believed?"

"Definitely." I ordered the tea, and the chef placed a cup and saucer with a tea bag and a small metal teapot on the counter in front of me. I put it on Sawyer's tray and took the basket of bread instead. "Here, trade with me."

I took the bread out to the table with Eli and Felicity. They were deep in a conversation that stopped the moment I arrived. "Hey. How are you both holding up?"

Eli narrowed his eyes to slits. "What are you doing here?"

I tried to color my words with a shade of perky. "I'm here to serve. You're my tour group, so you might just see me every night."

He cocked his head and examined me with a long appraisal.

"So . . . Doing okay?"

Felicity wiped at her dry eyes. "As well as can be expected. We lost a great man. And a good friend."

Are we still talking about Simon Beck? "I'm so sorry. It was quite a coincidence that you all ended up on the same tour. How did you hear about it?"

Felicity played with the ghost-shaped tea light in the middle of the table. "Verna set it up for me and her. She's my research assistant. She's always on the lookout for good opportunities."

Eli gave me an insincere smile in return. "I follow a Google alert for *haunted homes tours.*"

Google alert? Note to self: Set up a Google alert for Cape

May murder houses *and* weird cursed lady. "Speaking of Verna, where is she tonight?"

Felicity stole a quick glance at Eli before answering me. "She's upstairs in her room. She's still very emotional. Simon's death was quite a shock, you know. He's revered by all at the university."

Eli added in a snide tone, "She's not ready to be in public yet."

I accidentally let my guard down and glanced over at Brooklyn. She was smiling and chatting with Denise.

Felicity caught my gaze. "Disconcerting, isn't it?"

I crouched down next to the professor. "When you and Verna arrived at my house. You both seemed startled by something. At first, I thought it was me, but now I'm wondering if it was someone else in the room."

Sawyer came over with two plates of seafood pasta and placed them in front of Eli and Felicity. She gave me a look and rolled her eyes to the front of the room where Denise was holding a microphone. "Better hurry up."

Felicity picked up her fork and started tossing through her pasta. "To be honest, I was totally dumbstruck to see Simon standing there. I think he'd been following me."

Eli pierced a juicy shrimp. "He must have been. Once is a coincidence. But four times?"

"He's always been obsessed with me. I just can't figure out how he discovered I'd be here."

Denise tapped on a portable microphone to check the sound and I stepped away from the tables.

"Welcome to the Southern Mansion Haunted Dinner Tour. We were built in 1863 by a man named

George Allen. His niece, Ester, loved the mansion so much that she's never left. In fact, if you stay in room number nine, she may visit you, and tickle your face with a feather while you're trying to sleep."

I tiptoed my way to the kitchen. Partly not to disturb anyone listening to the presentation, and partly because I felt like there were cactuses inside my boots. Sawyer was sitting on a case of Kentucky bourbon, eating a bowl of pasta. An empty wineglass next to her. "Poppy, this is Chef Frank. Chef, Poppy."

A man in striped gray chef pants and a starched white coat gave me a grin. "Has Denise mentioned the ghost activity in the kitchen yet?"

I shook my head. "She's just getting started."

He nodded and shook a sauté pan on the burner. "Civil War soldiers are through the kitchen all the time."

I glanced at Sawyer.

She put her fork down and rolled her eyes to mine.

Chef flipped the shrimp in his pan. "It's like a supernatural party out there at the bar. The other night, the maintenance guy saw a dark shadow walk through the basement over by the time clock and go into the office. When he went to open the door to ask the man what he was doing—no one there." He nodded to us. "Denise should bring the tour down here. There's more activity in the basement than anywhere else in the building."

I think he had more to say, but one of the waitresses for the main dining room brought him an order and his attention shifted back to cooking.

Sawyer whispered to me, "Do you believe all that?"

"I don't know. I've never seen anything. If you ask

Eli, it's a scam. But if you ask the Paranormal Path-finders, they'll tell you they have proof."

Sawyer's eyes lit up. "Can I come watch them?"

"Sure, if you want. I owe you big after tonight."

Denise popped her head into the kitchen. "We're going on the house tour now; then we'll return for dessert. Want to join us?"

My mouth said yes, but my feet cried, *You are out of your flippity flippin' mind, lady.* My feet needed to speak up faster next time.

Denise had already stepped aside and was curling her hand for me to join her. She led us past the solar-ium and the aqua double parlor, up leopard-car-peted stairs to the second floor. Leading us down the long hall, she pointed out rooms with reported para-normal activity. "Room fourteen has a middle-aged couple who've been having the same argument for about two hundred years. The woman is always sit-ting on the bed while the man is getting undressed. She warns him that she doesn't think they should take the steamboat the next day to leave Cape May."

Brooklyn gushed, "That is fascinating. Do you think they died in a steamboat accident leaving Cape May?"

Denise shrugged. "I've always wondered about that, but I can't find any report of one. We had a wedding here and the people staying in the room next door asked to be moved because the couple in here were arguing all night. We didn't have the heart to tell them that the room was empty. Another time twin sisters were staying. One could see supernatural activity, but the other could only hear it. The twin who could see it saw the woman sitting on the bed ar-guing with her husband. The next day she asked her sister, 'Did you hear them?' Her sister said, 'Yes, but I didn't want to get up, so I pretended not to.'"

Felicity ran her hand along the chair rail. "I can feel psychic energy outside their room."

Uh-huh.

Denise smiled and nodded. "A prominent psychic named Wendell Dennis stayed here a few years ago. He could feel it too. He said the couple is still here because they have unfinished business." She continued down the hall telling of another incident, but Felicity hung back.

She looked at me. "I have always had the ability to communicate with the departed."

If you see Simon, tell him I said hello.

"Simon and I were in opposite areas of theory in paranormal studies. I believe psychic ability is a rare occurrence like a gene mutation and we should protect people from con artists. Simon felt everyone was born with psychic capability. He ran a development group to help 'normal people' develop latent psychic abilities. He took so much money from people, giving them false hope."

"Is that why you came on the ghost tour? To communicate with the dead?" I guess that would be a new motive for murder. To prove you're psychic.

Felicity shook her head. "No. I'm doing further research on ethics in ghost hunting. Some people don't agree with disruption of the entities. Trying to capture them on camera, getting them to perform and interact with devices. There are always protests going on about the methods used to communicate with them. Or extract them."

"Extract them? Like in the movie?" *I'll have to ask Clark if he uses proton packs.*

Eli shushed me over his shoulder, and we picked up the pace towards the rest of the tour group.

"Do you know anything about professor-student relationships?"

Felicity narrowed her eyes, and her voice was guarded. "Like what exactly?"

"I heard Simon was in a relationship with a student and it got out of hand. He had to have her transferred."

Felicity pursed her lips and swiveled her pucker to the side. Her eyes remained dead ahead at the back of the tour group. "That's just a rumor. Besides, relationships between a professor and a student are forbidden at our university due to sexual harassment lawsuits. Why ruin your whole career for one night of sex that will never go anywhere?" She sighed. "It would be career suicide."

CHAPTER 20

"It's amazing how quickly you can get out of a ghost tour when you don't have to wait around to give a witness statement." Sawyer and I pulled up to my house at a half past ten. The tour group was gone, and Joanne had texted that she was going home for the night with a middle finger emoji. Kim had sent me a text that just had a GIF of a woman giving a hateful look and rolling her eyes. I showed it to Sawyer. "I think I may owe Kim a dozen of those Fruity PEBBLES cookies she likes so much."

"You better double it. The price of being bossed around by Joanne all night." She looked towards my house and gasped. "What happened here?"

Almost every single jack-o'-lantern in the yard had been smashed and pumpkin shells were strewn about from the massacre.

Sawyer, who was now barefoot, hobbled up the walkway. "Aw. Someone destroyed all your pumpkins. And Mischief Night isn't until Friday."

I stepped over a splotch of seeds. "At least they left the one on the front step."

Kenny came through the front door carrying two commercial-sized black trash bags. "That's only because I caught her in time."

I stopped short of stepping on half a head. "Oh no. Is the *her* in question who I think it is?"

Kenny picked up a broken gourd and dropped it into the bag. "Don't ask me. Go ask Babe Ruth in the kitchen."

I took my booties off at the door and left them by the coatrack. I couldn't feel the bones in my feet. They were entirely numb, and yet somehow on fire.

Sawyer and I both minced our way to the kitchen. Aunt Ginny was sitting at the banquette splattered in pumpkin gore. My baseball bat, now stained orange, lay on the floor at her feet. She was calmly drinking a mug of cider that I was certain would catch on fire if you lit a match near it.

Sawyer murmured, "Oh dear."

I scanned Aunt Ginny head to toe. Her hair was a wild tangle, and she had a chunk of orange over her eye. "Do you want to talk about it?"

Aunt Ginny sipped her cider. "Nope."

I took out a plastic tub and dumped in a bag of rose-scented Epsom salt. While it filled with hot water, I flicked my eyes to Sawyer. "You know what I'm in the mood for?"

She raised her eyebrows.

"Pumpkin pie."

Sawyer snorted and turned her face to the side with strangled laughter.

Aunt Ginny drained her mug, picked up the bat, and went into her room with a slam.

We eventually stopped laughing. I set the tub on the floor and Sawyer and I put our feet in the basin of water.

Kenny came in the back door, dragging two full trash bags to the mudroom. "It was like a live-action *Attack of the 50 Foot Woman.* Why couldn't anyone get *that* on video? We'd be rich."

Sawyer and I started laughing again and didn't stop until the front door chimed.

The three other Biddies rumbled in like an earthquake, leaving menthol aftershocks in their wake. They pulled out Dr Pepper and whipped cream and a Pepperidge Farm Pound Cake. "Hey, girls."

They were wearing matching pink satin jackets that said *Biddies* in white embroidery across the back. "Where'd you get those?"

Mrs. Davis, who had done a new rinse on her hair to deepen the shade to eye-popping pink to match her jacket, took out a carton of strawberries from her bag. "Lila ordered them from her bowling catalog."

Mother Gibson flashed me a grin. "I ordered them weeks ago. They just came in today, child."

I felt my stomach drop a little lower inside me. "You ladies know that I love you dearly, right?"

The three octogenarians stopped setting up their dessert station to stare at me.

"It's just, I hope I've never offended you by referring to you as 'the Biddies.' I mean it with love and the deepest admiration. You're like grandmothers to me."

Mrs. Dodson tilted her cane against the island and folded her hands. "What else?"

Sawyer nodded. "Each one of you is an inspiration and a role model for your strength, your love, your friendship, your loyalty, and the way you embrace life."

The women stared with blank expressions that could go either way. Then they burst out laughing.

Mrs. Dodson waved a hand. "We were calling ourselves the Biddies long before you came back to town. We've never been offended. Life's too short."

Mother Gibson shook a can of whipped cream. "Good Lord. Some people make it their full-time ministry to be offended at everything."

Kenny came back into the kitchen just as Mrs. Davis took a package of paper plates from her grocery bag. "We love that you have a pet name for us. We have one for you too."

"What is it?"

She smiled a mile wide. "Murder Magnet."

Oof.

Kenny laughed so hard he sucked in air until he was wheezing.

Mother Gibson reached into her tote bag. "And we couldn't get jackets without getting one for both of you too."

Uh-oh.

She pulled out two Barbie pink satin jackets and handed them to us. They had our names over the heart and *Biddy in Training* across the back.

I put mine on and wrapped it around me. "I love it!"

Sawyer held it up to read it, then dropped her hands to her lap. "I always wanted to be in a clique. Now I have one that gets twenty percent off before five p.m. Thank you."

Aunt Ginny re-emerged in the kitchen wearing white footie pajamas and her satin Biddy jacket. Her hair was piled up in a towel that made her almost tall enough to ride Space Mountain. "Did you remember my pretzels?"

You know what it feels like when you get punched in the heart? I do. It feels like somebody wants you to walk your canned-ham feet out to the car to get the bag of peanut butter pretzels you forgot. "I remembered to buy them."

"But?"

"I forgot to bring them in."

Kenny took pity on me. Plus, he was still trying to make up for being a sneaky diva and not telling me what was going on with that calling in sick business. "I'll get them."

He put his hand out to Sawyer and made gimme motions.

She moved like a sloth in molasses to get her purse, then dug through it for a full minute. Finally finding her keys, she held them out to Kenny.

He snatched them from her. "For the love of Bela Lugosi, woman. If you move any slower, we'll be eating those pretzels for Christmas."

We heard the muted murmurings of Kenny talking to someone on his way out.

Aunt Ginny clapped her hands. "That must be them."

I strained my ears but didn't hear anything. "Who?"

She ignored me and poked her head through to the dining room. "Oh, it's just you. He did, did he? Well, you tell him for me that he can mind his own business, or I'll tell Poppy she needs to put him on a diet."

Aunt Ginny closed the door and went over to the island for a piece of cake.

I took the strawberry Mrs. Davis held out to me. "What was that all about?"

"Owen Rodney, Pet Psychic." Aunt Ginny topped her cake with a mountain of whipped cream.

The Biddies snickered and looked at me.

"Aunt Ginny booked him."

Aunt Ginny wasted no time dragging me under the bus with her. "Yes, but I didn't know he'd be staying here with the cast of *Casper*."

Sawyer was eyeing the cake, but she made no move to get any for herself. "What did he say to irritate you so much?"

Aunt Ginny rolled her eyes. "He said Figaro wanted me to know that I missed a pumpkin over by the bird feeder."

The front door closed, and Kenny came in with the bag of peanut butter–filled pretzel nuggets. He handed them to Aunt Ginny. "Milady."

"Thank you." Aunt Ginny ripped the bag open with her teeth and grabbed a fistful. "Are the TV people setting up yet?"

Kenny nodded. "They were just coming down the stairs. And the pet psychic guy is in the sitting room reading a book to Figaro. Although Figaro has his back to him, and he doesn't look as into it as the guy thinks."

I snickered. "What's the book?"

Kenny took the piece of cake Mrs. Davis offered him. "*Of Mice and Men*."

Mrs. Dodson nodded. "Figaro will be too wound up to sleep later."

I can't tell if Figaro's being spoiled or taking one for the team this week.

Mrs. Davis held a slice of cake with some strawberries in our direction. "Would you like some?"

Sawyer put her hand out. "Yes, please."

As Mrs. Davis walked the plate over, she looked at me and rolled her lips in. "Um, Poppy? Do you think you could ask the ghost team if we can stay and watch them work?"

Mrs. Dodson took some napkins out of the basket.

"If they need any help, like maybe an eyewitness interview or something . . ."

Aunt Ginny threw her some sass. "What exactly have you witnessed?"

Mrs. Dodson came back with a sharp retort. "Well, I've witnessed you eating a plate of chicken wings in your bathrobe and that was as frightening as any specter."

Aunt Ginny narrowed her eyes and took another shot of whipped cream straight to her mouth.

Mother Gibson shook her head. "Well, I'm not stayin'. I want nothing to do with any of it. When you all are ready for that nonsense, I'm going home to pray for your safety."

Aunt Ginny frowned. "I thought the whole reason you came over was to watch the TV show people in action."

Mrs. Davis tilted her head my way and said through clenched teeth, "Ginny, you said, 'Make it look unplanned.'"

Aunt Ginny suddenly found something on the counter that needed to be scrubbed.

Mother Gibson held up her plate. "Nope. I'm here for cake and companionship. I want nothin' to do with that demon stuff. Like I told my Sunday School class back when I was superintendent, it's either totally fake, and them people are charlatans conning you outta your hard-earned money. Or it's totally real, and comes from the Devil masquerading as an angel of light. Some people have an unhealthy fascination with the wrong kind of spirits. No sir. Not for me."

Sawyer reached for the whipped cream and added a dollop to her cake. "So, you don't believe in ghosts at all, Mother Gibson?"

"No, ma'am. Least not like you all do. The Bible has a spirit in it, but it's the Holy Spirit."

"Then what's going on with all these places that say they're haunted?"

Mother Gibson shook her head. "All those so-called ghosts and trapped souls—that's a lie of the Devil. When you die, you don't hang around wandering the earth till Judgment Day. The Devil's greatest trick is to convince you he don't exist, or that he exists and he's harmless. If you got a real demonic spirit here, you're gonna need a higher help than those TV peoples can give you."

CHAPTER 21

"What does this button do?" Mrs. Davis's hand hovered over a black device covered in red buttons.

Paisley snapped her fingers by the woman's hand. "Hey! Ma'am. Please stop touching things. I've calibrated that box three times already."

The TV crew was setting up their base for detecting in the dining room again. Clark Richards had originally told Aunt Ginny and the Biddies that they could not stay and watch. Then Aunt Ginny pulled out the contract that she had erroneously signed and pointed out that there was no clause banning the occupants of the home from being present if they desired. Only from being on camera without consent. So he had to change his stance so that the three older women could stay and observe as long as they stayed out of the way and kept quiet. It was not going well.

We couldn't light a fire in the sitting room fireplace because of the flickering glare for the TV cameras. So, instead, Sawyer and I were curled up on the couch with warm apple cider and fuzzy blankets. Figaro was coiled into a tight ball in my lap, a front-row seat to the sure disaster that tonight would be.

"But what's it do?" Mrs. Davis touched the red button, and the device blared a deafening peal like a smoke detector on steroids.

Ritchie ripped off the sound-amplifying headphones he was wearing. "Aah! What did I say about that?!"

Sawyer tried her best to silence a snicker, but it squeaked out like a snort.

Mrs. Dodson had Clark trapped in the back of the room by the kitchen where the team had set up their monitors. "What does that do?"

"That measures temperature fluctuations."

"What's this for?"

"It's a digital voice recorder."

"In case the ghost speaks?"

"Yes."

"Then what's this one?"

"That's an EMF recorder."

"What's an EMF?"

Clark sighed.

"Don't get upset if you don't know. I can ask one of the girls. They seem to know what they're doing."

Sawyer snickered again.

Aunt Ginny was following Harper around "supervising." She didn't have questions so much as a better way to do everything. "There's a draft there. I think it would work better by the piano. Maybe you should put those flashy cat toys at the bottom of the steps."

Harper stopped so fast Aunt Ginny ran into the back of her. "Mrs. Frankowski. There's a reason the homeowner usually vacates the premises when we investigate."

Aunt Ginny shrugged. "Why? 'Cause they're scared? I'm not scared. I've lived in this house my whole life. If there's a cold spot, I'll know how to find it."

Sawyer whispered to me, "You should have had the Biddies over the first night they filmed. The TV crew would have checked out by now."

"You are not wrong. Who knew Aunt Ginny and her friends were like paranormal pest control?"

Clark Richards stood in the center of the room and gave a whistle. "Ladies. Can you please take your seats and remember to be silent? We're about to begin filming. Remember, if something happens over in this area of the home and we have to pan over here you've agreed to sign waivers to let us show you on the air."

Mrs. Davis sat a little taller. "Where are the waivers? I'll sign mine right now."

Mrs. Dodson grabbed a pen from Paisley's hand. "Let's do it."

Clark held up a hand. "Alright. I misspoke. That one's on me. Let's just wait and see what happens. Okay, ladies?"

The three women hustled to the cluster of sitting room chairs that they had pulled under the arch and spun around to face the dining room.

Paisley and Harper turned out the lights. Ritchie put his headphones back on and started the camera.

Clark stood in front of the dining room table with Simon's chair from our haunted homes dinner directly behind him. The red light glowed softly against his face. He counted down from three with his fingers. "Simon Beck died under mysterious circumstances in this spot right behind me."

Aunt Ginny raised her hand. "Oh, Clark."

Clark sliced his hand across his throat. "Cut!" He softened his voice. "Mrs. Frankowski. What did we say when the camera light is red?"

"You said that meant you were recording and it cost you ten dollars a minute to film an episode."

"Yes, ma'am. And every time you interrupt us, we lose money."

"Yes, I remember."

"So, what was it that you absolutely had to tell me?"

Aunt Ginny folded her hands in her lap and smiled primly. "I just wanted to tell you, that Simon Beck was definitely murdered. The coroner called it this afternoon."

Ritchie's mouth dropped open, and he gasped. "You're kidding."

Paisley dropped into one of the dining room chairs and teared up. "Oh no. That's terrible. I'm so sorry."

Harper held out a device towards the dining room chair where Eli had been sitting. "Simon, was it the man in this seat? Did he kill you?"

Paisley added, "Do they think it was the wife?"

Lights started flashing in the foyer by the front door and a tinkling little bell sounded.

Clark shook his hand at Ritchie. "Camera!"

Ritchie hoisted the camera on his shoulder and the red light came on.

Clark took a step towards the foyer. "Simon? Are you with us?"

The flashing ball rolled across the floor, and everyone held their breath. Including me—but perhaps for a different reason than the rest of them. I knew something they didn't know.

Right behind the flashing ball, a gray pouf pounced and trapped the sphere between his fluffy paws.

Sawyer snickered again. "Figaro!"

Okay, well, now they all knew. Figaro had left my lap the moment the lights went out.

Clark sliced across his throat again. "Cut!" He cast a look of frustration in my direction.

"In Fig's defense, they *are* cat toys."

Paisley picked Figaro up and held him over her face. "You are so smooshy. Those are for the ghost to play with. Not naughty kitties."

Figaro put his paw over her red lips and shushed her.

She spoke through his paws. "Maybe you need some Pounce treats."

Clark asked me to lock Figaro in another room while Ritchie and Harper reset the devices. So, I took Mr. Troublemaker to Aunt Ginny's room while chastising him for ruining the take. He purred the whole way.

When I got back to my seat, Clark counted down again. As soon as he hit zero, Mrs. Dodson turned to Aunt Ginny. "You know who they should try to contact?"

"Mmm, who?"

"That old lady who was so mean to us when we were kids. She died in the room right above here, didn't she?"

Aunt Ginny's eyes brightened. "Oh, that's right. I think she had a stroke. Serves her right, the old bat. She wanted Papa to beat me with her cane because I ran through the front parlor with a sand crab."

Harper stepped towards the three older women and eyed them conspiratorially. "Which room was this?"

Aunt Ginny looked at the ceiling, her eyes squished in deep thought. "Poppy, what suite is above us?"

"The Monarch is above the sitting room. The Adonis is above the dining room."

Paisley turned to Clark. "Maybe we should move up there and try to contact that lady. We haven't had any luck with Professor Beck."

Ritchie looked at the dining room chair where Simon Beck had been sitting. "But he was murdered by someone on that tour. That's Haunting One-Oh-One."

Clark looked at the Biddies' grinning faces. "What else do you ladies know about the history of this house?"

Aunt Ginny and the other Biddies looked at each other blankly. Then Mrs. Davis said, "Ginny made out with Arthur Boyd behind the garage at her sweet sixteen birthday party."

Aunt Ginny punched Mrs. Davis in the arm. "That's supposed to be a secret, Thelma."

Mrs. Davis laughed. "From who? He's been dead twenty years."

Clark threw his hands up. "Okay, ladies . . . Could you . . ." He sighed. "Take five."

Ritchie approached Clark, who was getting himself a drink from his private thermos. "You know, it wouldn't be a bad idea to do some research on the history of the home. It could give us some new angles."

Clark sighed. "You're probably right. But that will have to wait until tomorrow. Tonight, I'd like to get back to Simon Beck, and whoever else may present themselves."

The team tried for an hour to get one of their devices to light or blink or beep, but nothing happened. Then Harper held up a hand. "Shh. Do you hear that?"

Everyone was silent. Except for Mrs. Davis, who was snoring. Mrs. Dodson gave her a jab with the end of her cane, and she jerked upright. "Hide the bacon. What?"

The team listened intently. Clark looked at one of the devices on the table. "It's picking up something. There! There it is again."

He turned the dial on the device to amplify the sound. *Shhk shhk shhk.* I covered my eyes so no one would see me roll them. They were picking up Figaro scratching on Aunt Ginny's door to get out of prison. Aunt Ginny caught my eye and put a finger to her lips.

Mrs. Davis wrapped her sweater around her shoulders and whispered, "Oh, it's very exciting, isn't it?"

Yes. And it will be even more exciting when he begins to moan for me to come break him free.

It was nearly two a.m., and I could barely keep my eyes open. I stood to silently excuse myself and go to bed. Ritchie panned the camera away from me, so I had a clear shot for the steps. As soon as I got near the big box they called a spirit scanner it lit up like New Year's Eve in Times Square.

Paisley stepped closer to me with something that looked like an old TV remote control. It was humming like the Jetsons' spaceship taking off. "Whoa! Look at that field light up."

Harper came to join Paisley with another device that looked like a Game Boy. "And look at the heat signature around her."

Clark looked over Harper's shoulder. "Sometimes paranormal activity manifests as a cold spot, and sometimes it's a heat signature. You appear to be in the latter."

"You know what else manifests as a heat signature?"

They shook their heads.

"A hot flash. I'm going to bed." I turned and headed up the stairs, but behind me, on the couch, Sawyer snickered again like she'd shot milk out of her nose.

It would have been a small victory if I hadn't heard Clark tell the girls before I'd hit the landing, "That's where all the paranormal activity in this house is coming from."

CHAPTER 22

"You're sure you can come to work today? You're over the scaredy-cat flu?"

Kenny slid his eyes to mine and smacked his lips while he measured coffee for the French press. "Very funny. As long as those university people aren't coming back, I'll be okay. What a bunch of freaks."

I took out the pastry box from La Dolce Vita and put the gluten-free apple cinnamon coffee cake on a plate shaped like a pumpkin. "Did something happen the other night with Felicity Van Smoot?"

Kenny answered way too fast. "What? No! Why would you even suggest that?"

"Well, I saw that she was really flirty on the dinner tour, and I thought maybe that was what wigged you out so bad."

He smirked. "She wishes. I am a tasty snack, but no way was I letting her get her claws into me. Especially when she clearly had one claw deeply pierced into that other guy."

"Simon Beck?"

"No. The broody one who came in yelling, then sat in the corner and pouted all night."

"Eli Lush."

Kenny shrugged. "If you say so."

I picked up the plate of tender yellow cake with cinnamon apples and brown sugar streusel. "Okay. Well, as long as it wasn't that one of them made you uncomfortable or anything."

Kenny picked up the carafe and headed for the dining room. "Please. I'm your very own Mr. Cool. The picture of calm in the face of danger." The door swung open, and he hopped backwards. "Jiminy Christmas, what are you doing!"

Kenny had slammed into me, and the plate of coffee cake smashed against my chest. I brushed the crumbs from my plum sweater back onto the crumbled mess and craned my neck to see what had spooked Mr. Calm.

Figaro was sitting awkwardly in one of the Biddies' chairs from last night, still facing the dining room. His back was against the chair and his tail, and all four legs were straight out in front of him. He looked like a zombie cat.

Sitting in the next chair over where Aunt Ginny had been, Owen Rodney, in full colander regalia, had one leg crossed over the other and he was taking notes on a steno pad. He held up a finger for us to wait quietly while he listened. I can only assume he was listening to Fig.

Finally, Owen nodded. "And how does that make you feel?"

Figaro's tail flicked like a *West Side Story* gang member starting a dance fight.

Owen replied to Kenny, "If we could have just a minute, please." Then he turned back to Figaro and said, "You could ask him to respect that this is your sanctuary, your rules. After all, you don't poop in his nest."

Figaro yawned and gave me a slow blink. He was on his own. As far as I was concerned, he deserved extra treats just for keeping Owen occupied.

I took the ruined coffee cake back into the kitchen and set it on the counter. Kenny flew in right after me. "I am so sorry."

"It's okay. But we need to move to plan B. Get out the vanilla yogurt and the nutmeg."

Someone banged the back door. Joanne's face plastered against the glass and Kenny threw his hands up in mock horror. "Is today Halloween? Where's the bowl of candy? A witch is at the door."

Joanne's eyes narrowed to a glare. Kenny opened the door and she "accidentally" stepped on his foot when she came through holding a casserole dish. "I made my egg, cheese, and potato casserole for this morning." She placed it on the island in front of me so I would be sure to get a good look at it.

"Oh, Joanne! It's adorable!" She had placed cut black olives to make Halloween Spiders randomly across the cheese.

She opened a cotton bag that was hanging from her wrist. "There are sausage links wrapped in croissant dough that look like mummies in here."

I opened the foil and squealed at the sight. She'd even attached little eyes on the mummies.

Joanne looked away and busied herself at the sink, but not before I saw the hint of a smirk appear.

Kenny frowned. "Eww. No one wants to eat spiders in their eggs. Even if they aren't real."

She gave him a look so frightening I thought he'd melt on the spot.

I took a serving spoon out of the drawer. "I think they'll love it. And you really saved us this morning too. There was an incident with the coffee cake that we're now turning into apple pie parfaits."

Joanne plated the sausages. "Well, I figured you'd be in trouble because as usual you've gotten in over your head."

I looked at Kenny for a moment to catch him roll his head and scoff. Joanne could make an entire bitter meal from the smallest of compliments. "Let's take this out to the buffet. I want to see if Owen Rodney is finished psychoanalyzing Figaro before we go to Mia Famiglia."

I picked up the tray of parfaits and Joanne grabbed the casserole. "He's doing what to the cat?"

"I'll explain later." We pushed through the door to the dining room. Owen and Gladys were on opposite sides of the table. Only Harper had joined them from the TV crew. No one was in Simon Beck's seat. No one had sat in that seat since he died there.

Joanne placed the eggs in the center of the table between Owen and Gladys, then returned to the kitchen for the sausages. I had no sooner put the tray of parfaits on the table than Gladys began her interrogation.

"So, including the last guy, what's your body count to?"

"I don't think this is appropriate breakfast talk in front of guests." I gave Harper an apologetic smile.

Gladys waved her hand. "She don't care. She looks for dead people for a livin'. Do the police think you're psychic or psycho?"

Probably both.

Owen gasped. "Don't you ever stop? Why are you so duplicitous?"

Gladys ignored him. "Okay, I can see by that vein throbbing in your neck that you don't like that one. How 'bout this? Can you tell when there's a dead body nearby? Or is it always a surprise to you?"

A spark of irritation ran through me like static. "If I could tell there was a dead body up ahead, don't you think I'd run the other way?!" I cleared my throat and looked for Owen of all people to throw me a lifeline. "How did the session go with Figaro?"

Owen shrugged. "It was okay. He's very shy."

Figaro galloped through the sitting room and jumped for the coffee table, slamming into the African violets that were no longer in the window. He failed to stop in time and knocked a pink violet to the floor with a crash. After a reflective moment of staring at the violet and presumably contemplating the laws of gravity, he sat back on the table and began to tidy his undercarriage.

I passed Owen a parfait. "Yes, he has always been very reserved."

Kenny looked through the kitchen door, sighed, then disappeared. A moment later he walked through to the sitting room carrying a broom and dustpan to clean up the Persian-induced carnage-of-the-day.

Harper added some eggs to her plate. "There was a lot of activity last night with the doors. They kept opening on their own."

"Is that right?"

She nodded. "I don't think it was Dr. Beck, though. I'm sure he would have set off at least one of our spectrometers."

"Naturally."

Paisley entered the room and accepted a parfait. "Could you please keep an eye out for my bracelet? I had to take it off last night because it was clicking against the EMF meter and the audio was picking it up. I left it on the end table in the other room, but it disappeared."

"I will tell my staff to be on the lookout, but what if a ghost took it?"

Paisley grabbed a mug and poured herself some coffee. "That's what I expect happened. They can only move things, so it should be around here somewhere. Oh, and you'll never believe what we found last night after you went to bed."

"What?"

"Clark picked up an electromagnetic surge on the EMF reader. We were so excited. The guys are checking the readings on the computer now. They'll be down for breakfast soon."

Gladys took a spoonful of the egg casserole. "Have you been able to reach the guy who bit the dust yet?"

Harper frowned. "No. Not yet. But we're confident he'll reach out soon. He might not know he's dead."

Well then, he's having the worst vacation ever. I picked up the empty tray and turned to go back into the kitchen.

Gladys poured herself a cup of coffee. "You know I saw him leave with that woman the night of the tour."

On second thought, I'll just rearrange these tea bags out here.

Harper's eyes went very wide. "When?"

"During the tour. When we were all upstairs, right after that older fella talked."

Owen stirred honey into his tea without taking his eyes off Gladys. "Where'd they go?"

"I saw them sneak back into the storage room with the Christmas tree and the coats. The one where little Abner was supposed to be."

"Alice." I said it before I remembered I wasn't supposed to admit or deny anything. "So past guests have told me."

Gladys blew me off. "Sure. Whatever. I thought they were sneaking away for a little bam bam since they'd been going at each other all night. Opposites attract and all."

I finished playing with the tea bags and stepped closer to the table. "Which woman was it?"

Harper grinned and tossed her hair. "It had to be the one with the cat-eye glasses. Verna. She's half his age. Did you see his wife? He liked 'em young."

Gladys leaned in. "Did you see that Verna switched her name card with one a the kids' so she could sit next to him? That takes some big cojones."

Owen sat back against the chair with his tea. "Figaro says she didn't switch the cards."

"Who switched them?" Heat rushed to my face. *Dude! I did it again. Stop encouraging him.*

Owen shrugged. "He says it was the one who has a cat at home."

We all stared at Owen for a beat, contemplating his sources.

Gladys shook her head. "Anyway, it was the older one in the red dress sneaking off with him. I saw them leave the room together right in front of his wife when she was listening to the tour guide. I don't know where they went, but you know he was up to no good with that hoity-toity Dr. Felicity Van Smoot."

CHAPTER 23

"I can't believe they let you in here to cook for them." Joanne spoke in hushed tones like she was in a cathedral as she surveyed the professional kitchen of Mia Famiglia. "How are they not afraid you'll drive away all their customers?"

I grabbed an apron off the hook and counted to ten, although I'd need to count to a million for Joanne not to rub me the wrong way. "I know it's hard to believe, but not everyone thinks I'm a worthless screwup in the kitchen."

Joanne stared at the stainless-steel grill station and shrugged. "I'll have to take your word for it."

I checked the supplies to make a punch list for today. "Joanne, do you think you could make pumpkin pancakes and candied bacon for breakfast for the B&B tomorrow?"

Joanne grabbed an apron. "I thought you said this was going to be hard."

"No, I said it was going to be busy. Amber's got me informing on the university people in exchange for not going bankrupt and I have another night of spying ahead of me."

"How does she keep getting you to help her with these homicides?"

I've been asking myself that same thing for six months now. "There always seems to be something she can use as leverage over me."

Joanne took out a mixing bowl and started opening drawers. "If you weren't always the first one to find the body maybe she'd stop. Have you asked yourself who's got the most to gain by the guy being dead?"

"Of course. And it depends on whether or not he has life insurance and who the beneficiary is."

"So, the wife then?"

I shrugged and checked my dough in the walk-in. "Probably. She's not acting like a grieving widow—so that's the first thing that's suspicious."

"Even an idiot would know to fake some grief to avoid suspicion if they killed somebody close to them."

"Yep. And that's the second thing that's suspicious. She's not even trying to cover it up."

Joanne took out a dozen eggs. "What do you want to make with these pancakes?"

"Let's do a compote of baked plums. We can serve them with cinnamon whipped cream. Then for the tour dinner tonight . . ."

"Aren't we doing the tenderloin?"

"Not at that price. We lost too much money on the tour of the damned and it went into the trash. A whole tenderloin was confiscated by the police. I was thinking we could go with butternut squash ravioli in a sage brown butter sauce. And for the entrée—

stuffed pork roast in a ruby port wine sauce, whipped potatoes, and green beans. Sound good?"

Joanne nodded. "Any vegan options?"

"I have been assured that no vegans are attending your dinner tonight. The only vegan will be with me at The Chalfonte."

"Good. How about crab and cheese puffs for the hors d'oeuvres?"

"You'll have to go pick up some crab at the fish market."

"You may not be much of a chef, but you sure know how to eat."

"Thank you. Wait. Are you calling me fat?"

Joanne snickered. "Dessert?"

I checked the shelves. "I think I'm going to make two pumpkin cheesecakes. One for us and one for the restaurant."

"That's not Italian, ya moron. The old woman will have a cow if she finds out."

"Maybe so, but it's perfect for this time of year. And keep a tab of ingredients you use so we can pay them back." *We don't need Vinny-the-hook showing up to whack us in the middle of the night for stealing eggs. And by* Vinny-the-hook *I mean Momma.*

Joanne got a mixing bowl and started measuring ingredients for pancakes. "Are they going to let us heat these up in the kitchen tomorrow or are you serving them cold and hoping no one notices?"

"We can heat them up before serving; we just can't make them in my kitchen fresh."

"That logic's even dumber than you are."

"I wasn't about to point out the flaw in the chief of police's plan in case he changed his mind."

I started with the dinner rolls, so they'd have plenty of time to rise before I made the cheesecakes.

Then I'd make gelato and some muffins for La Dolce Vita. The lasagna I could do in my sleep. And as tired as I was after staying up to watch the *Paranormal Pathfinders* team in action, I just might have to.

Joanne hummed a little tune while she flipped pancakes and fried bacon on the grill. I had never seen her so happy. Come to think of it, I'd never seen her happy, period.

I bloomed my yeast for tomorrow's bread and Joanne hollered from across the room, "Are you sure you don't want me to do that? Bread seems way above your skill level!"

I muttered to myself, "At least common decency isn't above my skill level."

"What!"

"I said *no!* Just make the pancakes."

Marco came in all bouncy and smiles. "*Buongiourno. Buongiourno.* Hello, ladies."

I stopped measuring flour long enough to make the introductions. "Marco, this is Joanne, my kind-of sous chef."

Joanne scowled. "Actually, I'm the senior chef and I'm a free agent at the moment. So, if you're hiring let me know."

Marco looked from Joanne to me, nodding. "Never discuss business before espresso." He held up three fingers. "*Tre, si?*"

Joanne replied like she'd spent her summer in Tuscany instead of bullying me in Cape May. "*Si, Marco. Grazie.*"

Marco disappeared through the door to the dining room to make espressos while I was elbow deep in flour. I smiled to myself as I remembered making gotcha bread and Halloween plans the other day with Henry. I couldn't wait to go trick or treating with that little boy. I put today's dough in the refrigerator for its overnight rise and took the dough I'd made yesterday out of the walk-in to form into rolls.

Joanne held up the basket of broken burnt cannoli shells I should have thrown away last night. "What's this?"

"It's nothing. How are those pancakes coming along?"

She sneered at me like I told her to lick a doorknob. "I finished the pancakes and the plums while you were squashing the life out of that dough. So, what is this? Something you burned?"

Marco came in with three espressos and grinned. "Ah, you find Poppy's masterpiece." He placed an espresso on the workbench in front of me and winked. "Everybody love the cassata. We sell half last night."

Marco handed Joanne an espresso and she gave him a Julia Roberts grin.

Who is that? Has Joanne been snatched by aliens? And can this version come work at my house instead?

Esteban and Frankie arrived for the day and the kitchen cranked up full throttle. Joanne worked on dinner for tonight's tour group of ten, while I made the cheesecakes. My cell phone alert said "*ciao!*" and I knew Gia was texting me.

Are you across the courtyard, mi amore?

Yes. For a little longer.

I will be right over. You want that pumpkin spice latte you ladies all seem to love?

Heck yeah! "Joanne, do you want Gia to bring you a latte?"

Joanne pursed her lips. "Are you buying? I mean it's the least you can do since I'm helping you out."

Bring 2 plz xoxo

I put my phone in my pocket and moved the

Amarena chocolate gelato mix to the blast chiller to get cold enough to run through the batch freezer. The back door opened, and my heart gave a little flutter. "That might be your fastest latte ever."

"Just what do you think you're doing!"

Marco started to mutter in Italian what sounded like a desperate prayer.

I had expected to see my sexy boyfriend holding two paper coffee cups, but I was sorely disappointed. It was his sister Teresa. The sour one.

Gia had six sisters and two brothers. Karla was the baby and the one who worked at the coffee shop. Stefania was the one making a career out of going to college. Daniela was number three and currently the black sheep with their religious mother having had baby Violetta out of wedlock. And then there was Teresa. Baptized in lemon juice, born in a bitter mood, the stick up Momma's butt—Teresa. Every family has a tattletale. Teresa held that position for the Larussos.

"Why are you in my mother's kitchen!"

Um . . . Why am I here? Maybe I'm sleepwalking? No. Maybe I'm lost? That doesn't explain the pan of lasagna I'm making. Think, Poppy.

Joanne stepped to Teresa and put her hand out. "Hi. I'm Jo. I'm betting you're related to that gorgeous Italian across the courtyard. You have his eyes."

Teresa blushed and her hand flew up to her chest. "Oh, thank you. People don't usually notice."

Probably because you're always squinting in fury.

Joanne shook Teresa's hand. "I just started working here and this pitiful baker from a local B&B asked if she could use the kitchen to make dinner for her tour group tonight."

Teresa leveled her squint on me.

See. There it is.

Joanne leaned in towards Gia's sister and lowered her voice. "She's the one with the dead body problem."

Teresa pursed her lips. "Mm-hmm."

"Well, apparently her kitchen was closed by the police, and your brother said she could make her dinner here."

Teresa's face flamed pink. "How dare he give you that permission without asking our mother—who is home laid up with a broken hip." She crossed herself. "Godblesshersoul."

Gia came in from the dining room with two lattes. "Bella . . . Teresa."

Teresa made a fist and pointed at Gia's face. "You!"

I started stacking the lasagna layers twice as fast in case things went south. I hate to leave anything half done before I get thrown out of a place.

"Momma would be so ashamed of you if she knew you let this . . ."

"You need to mind your own business, Teresa!"

Marco crossed himself and muttered some more. Esteban and Frankie worked the line without taking their eyes off the two screaming Italians.

Gia's eyes narrowed and he took a step towards his sister. Teresa balled her fists at her sides and the situation went the full Fukushima. Gia was yelling in Italian and Teresa was screaming over him in Italian. She appeared to be winning, until Marco stepped over to Gia and took the two lattes from him. Once he could flail hands around his argument picked up steam.

Marco handed me my latte and whispered, "What is left?"

"Tiramisu."

He nodded. "Okay. If she kill you, we make do."

My timer dinged and I put the raised rolls in the second oven. I went back to the lasagna and Joanne crossed the room to check the gelato mixture. She turned on the batch freezer and poured in the mix.

While Gia and Teresa yelled over each other in Italian, one of the waitresses came through the door, picked up a lunch order, and left again.

Finally, somebody won, or they both ran out of words, and Teresa folded her arms in a pout.

Joanne stepped towards the sourpuss like nothing had happened. "So, I figured it would be good press for your family if you were kind enough to lend your kitchen to a local in need. I'm so sorry if I overstepped. Should I call off the interview?"

Teresa's eyebrows shot up and her natural pinched pucker relaxed. "Interview? Hmm. Okay. She can do this week only. Then she go. The interview will go forward, but I talk to the press on behalf of the family. Capisce?"

Joanne nodded. "Absolutely."

Teresa glared at Gia, then bit her thumb and threw it at me. She turned back to Joanne. "You be in charge of her, though."

Joanne shook Teresa's hand again. "Don't worry. I will make sure she toes the line."

Teresa stormed out the back door and Joanne gave me a wicked grin.

Marco strode across the kitchen and pulled Joanne into a hug. "Dat was incredible. Maybe you should work here for the good."

Okay, hold on now. "Let's not get carried away."

Joanne giggled like a five-year-old princess who just got her first pony and blushed to the roots of her hedgehog hair.

I was bothered by the whole situation. Marco and Joanne. It was very upsetting, but I wasn't sure exactly why. All I knew for sure was, I didn't like it when Joanne gloated over me. And if Joanne's head swelled any bigger, Macy's would enlist her for next month's parade.

CHAPTER 24

Crunching through fallen leaves on the broken concrete, I tried to shake off my icky feeling on the walk back home. Joanne was having *so much fun* in Mia Famiglia's *true professional* kitchen that she decided to stay and whip up a couple frittatas and a Dutch pancake for the B&B breakfasts later this week. *La-di-da. Whatever. Maybe they'll keep her on and she can punish someone else for breathing too loud for a change.*

I was approaching home when I noticed several of the neighbors sitting in lawn chairs along the street. It was a delightfully warm October evening, but there was a chill following me that might have added to my unreasonable nervousness. The faint smell of wood-smoke urged me to relax. The passing kids pointing at my house and laughing urged me that I was right the first time and dread was the more appropriate course of action.

I passed Mr. and Mrs. Sheinberg and gave a wave.

"Heya, Bubbala."

"Hi."

A little further down I passed Nell. "Hey, darling."

"Hello, Ms. Belanger."

Mr. and Mrs. Collazo were sitting in the front of their yard with a cooler between their chairs. Mrs. Collazo waved a wineglass. "Good evening, Poppy."

"Good evening."

Mr. Murillo had pulled a camp chair across the street to sit with Mr. Winston and Mrs. Pritchard. They each gave me a smile and a wave. Mrs. Pritchard reached her hand for mine. "Hello, dear. Lovely weather, isn't it?"

"Beautiful. I hear a storm is coming in. Why is everyone staring at my house? And what's that all over my lawn?"

Mrs. Pritchard cocked her head to look at me. "Marshmallow Peeps."

"Why are they green?"

"Because they're zombies, dear."

Mr. Winston grinned, and his eyebrows wiggled like fuzzy black caterpillars belly dancing. "Watch the leaves."

A few seconds later, a giant pile of leaves under the tree in my yard started to quiver. The center section raised up about six inches, and a large pair of black binoculars did a sweep left to right, then disappeared into the leaves again. Mr. Murillo started to giggle and bit his fist.

Owen Rodney came out the front door wearing his brain wave–dampening colander. He had made a breastplate out of tinfoil and was carrying a paper bag. A team of purple grackles descended to the grass and started pecking at the green globs stuck into the ground.

Owen shook his paper bag and chased them. "You'll get bird diabetes if you eat that! Go find some corn in one of the fields. I don't know where. There are farms all around here. Then check the sunflowers. Anything is better than processed sugar. You can't take that home to your nests."

Nell tittered from over in her yard. I asked the three neighbors at my side, "Who put all the zombie Peeps in my yard?"

Mr. Murillo shook his head. "No one knows."

Mrs. Pritchard giggled. "That's what Ginny's trying to find out."

Owen shook his finger up at the red oak. "Don't do something you're going to regret, Charles. You said your stomach was already hurting from that spoiled acorn."

The bad news is, Aunt Ginny looks crazy. The good news is, she only looks half as crazy as Owen.

I looked down the street into the neighbors' yards. There was not a Peep to be found. *Why is our yard the only one being pranked?* The kids aren't usually this selective for Mischief Night. I smiled at the neighbors to my side. "If you happen to spot whoever's been doing this, could you please give me a call?"

Mr. Murillo snickered. "Eventually."

Mrs. Pritchard smacked his arm. "Right away, dear."

Mr. Winston thought I asked to watch his VHS copy of *Hoosiers* and I had to wait for him to get it from the house.

I crossed the picket line of green zombie Peeps impaled in squadrons across my lawn on kabob skewers. Owen was sitting on the front step adjusting his tinfoil. "The chatter is deafening right now. All the squirrels can talk about is what's covering your yard. They want to move in before the raccoons arrive."

The front door opened, and Gladys marched

across the porch and pulled out a camera. She took a couple pictures of me standing in the field of green marshmallows backed by the cast of *The Best Exotic Marigold Hotel* in their lawn chairs. "I'm on fire." She gave herself a fist pump and disappeared back into the house.

"I'll get Kenny out here to clean it up." I pulled out my phone and texted him that the zombie apocalypse had happened as predicted and please bring a trash bag to the front yard.

Owen let out a pent-up sigh and his shoulders relaxed down away from his ears. "That's good. Figaro bet me a piece of cheese that the giant raccoon would show up before the yard was cleared."

"So, if you win, Figaro has to get *you* a piece of cheese?"

Owen shrugged. "A deal's a deal." He went back in the house, and I turned my attention to the pile of leaves.

"Do you want to go with me to The Chalfonte for the tour tonight? Kim had an emergency with her iguana, so Sawyer's coming here to help Joanne serve the guests."

The pile of leaves quivered. "What's for dinner?"

"Probably fried chicken since it's their specialty."

Aunt Ginny rose from the pile. She was wearing a safari outfit and a pith helmet covered in leaves. Webby strings of hot glue hung off the rim. The giant binoculars swung from her neck and she licked her lips. "I could do with some fried chicken. But who's gonna watch the yard for hooligans?"

I pointed across the street and the neighbors waved. Aunt Ginny gave a salute in return. "I guess I'll go get myself gussied up."

Aunt Ginny passed Kenny, who now stood on the

porch holding a trash bag, surveying the yard. "I thought we agreed that when the zombie apocalypse came, we'd move underground and hoard Hershey bars and Diet Dr Pepper."

"Think of this as a dry run."

Kenny started yanking the sticks from the ground. "Okay, but I think this at least earns me a KitKat."

"Yeah. Knock yourself out."

A fat raccoon waddled out from the hedge by Mrs. Pritchard's yard, pulled a stick from the ground, and disappeared back into the hedge. I looked to the front bay window and saw Figaro's bright orange eyes looking back at me. In the background, Owen said, "Dang it, Figaro."

Kenny ripped another zombie from the ground. "What was that all about?"

"Apparently, Owen Rodney will be needing a piece of cheese."

A blue sedan pulled up to the curb. Kenny appraised it and sidestepped towards the backyard. The car door opened, and Chief Kieran Dunne got out. Kenny started meandering a little faster. Chief Dunne let out his breath in a huff. "Kenny Love? I'm just here to get your statement. Don't make this worse by trying to run."

Kenny dropped the bag of Peeps and took off at a sprint. Kieran hopped the wrought-iron fence and tore through the yard after him. I gave a little wave to the neighbors who were all on their feet and making a very slow mad dash to get a better view of the side of my house.

Moments later, Kieran came out front leading Kenny with his hands behind his back. "If you have nothing to hide, then why are you running?"

Kenny gave Chief Dunne his most innocent expression. "Those were interval sprints. I've got to get buff before my next audition and Mrs. Frankowski doesn't like eating Halloween candy by herself."

Kieran led Kenny to the front porch and sat him on the step. He tried to look down his nose at me, but he'd have to walk up a flight of steps to do so. Instead, he clucked his tongue and chuckled condescendingly. "Ms. McAllister. I was coming to check on you to make sure you're adhering to our agreement about the use of your kitchen. I didn't realize your housekeeper was so skittish."

"Maybe your fancy shoulder holster intimidated him."

Kenny nodded. "I thought you were Doc Holliday come back from the dead to kill me."

A flicker of irritation passed Kieran's eyes and he turned away to look at the front of the yard. While he was shooing the neighbors back to their homes, I shrugged my shoulders and mouthed to Kenny, *What was that?*

He looked at the ground and blushed to his roots.

Kieran turned his gaze back on me. "I'll give you a choice. You can either give us some privacy while I question Mr. Kenny Love, or I can take him down to the station to do it in a cell."

"Take all the time you need. I have to go get the cheese anyway." I pointed to his legs. "You've got mud on your slacks."

Kieran's look moved like a slingshot towards his trousers, and he swatted at the dirt in disgust. "Now, let's start again, Mr. Love. How well did you know Dr. Simon Beck?"

I listened to the whole thing through my bedroom window while I dressed for dinner at The Chalfonte. Kenny gave his statement and denied having ever met Simon Beck or the rest of the university guests before the tour dinner. Then Chief Dunne threatened to charge him with obstruction of an investigation if he tried to run again. Kenny sounded sincere, but he was as nervous as a long-tailed cat in a room full of rocking chairs and that made my stomach very quivery. I hadn't known him long, but I liked him and I considered him a friend. A friend who has a criminal record he won't tell me about, who just ran from the police.

CHAPTER 25

One hour and three outfit changes later, Aunt Ginny emerged in a salmon silk cocktail dress. I hung up with Amber and waved goodbye to Sawyer, who was pouting from the front window—imploring me to take her with me—and we walked over to Cape May's oldest original hotel.

The green sign out front proudly announced that The Chalfonte was established in 1876. Built like a square wedding cake, the three-story white hotel had layer upon layer of ornate scrollwork trim up to the center cupola topper.

The bottom layer of the two-tiered wraparound porch was sometimes dressed in striped awnings like a billowy skirt. And there was always a battalion of rocking chairs lined up for duty. Considering this was Cape May, where no one bats an eye if you have a pink house, The Chalfonte was rather sedate, all things considered.

Today a black cat sculpture with an arched back sat on the porch by the door and the front steps were covered with pumpkins and hay bales. I reached for

Aunt Ginny's hand. "You okay? Not having flash-backs from the other night, are you?"

Her lips flattened and she smacked at me. "Very funny."

Amber had promised me I didn't have to waitress this time, but I had flats in my tote bag just in case I was bamboozled into mopping the floor or some-thing. Aunt Ginny had made it clear that she'd walk home before she waited tables. "If they try to hand me an apron, I'm outta there, right after I get my fried chicken and biscuit."

The general manager met us at the door dressed in a tuxedo. "I'm so sorry about your tour. Do the po-lice know what happened yet?"

As usual, Aunt Ginny applied her sass like her makeup—with a heavy hand. "Dillon, if the cops knew what happened we'd be home eating cheesy puffs right now instead of standing on your front porch starving half to death."

I put my hand on Aunt Ginny's arm. "What she means is, they're following every lead, but they haven't made an arrest yet."

Dillon was about my age, with chestnut-brown hair and kind eyes. He smiled indulgently at Aunt Ginny. "I hope you can make do with one of Miss Lucille's crab cakes."

Aunt Ginny puckered her lips. "That might just hit the spot." She gave me a nudge. "I'll be waiting for you in the King Ed. I want to see if I'm still hanging on the wall over the bar."

I had no idea what she was talking about, as usual. But at least I would know where to find her.

Dillon leaned towards me like a coconspirator and lowered his voice. "There is only one guest from the tour here right now. She didn't want to come with the carriage. Something about unethical treatment of horses."

"That's probably the widow. How does she seem?"

Dillon clenched his teeth and his eyebrows shot up. "Well . . . Fine? She asked if we were going to see the haunted cupola on the tour, and if she could sit in it by herself to see if the ghost would talk to her. I guess everyone handles grief differently."

"That is certainly true." I didn't get out of bed or shower for two weeks after I buried John, but I wouldn't want anyone else to know that. "Her late husband worked in paranormal science, so maybe she expects him to reach out from the other side? I'm going to go say hello to her."

I took a step towards the door. "Sergeant Fenton didn't volunteer me for anything in particular, did she?"

Dillon shook his head. "She just said you were here to observe how we run the tour at The Chalfonte."

"Oh, okay."

"Since yours was the biggest disaster to Cape May tourism in the past twenty years."

Oh . . . oh-kaaay. "Well, thank you, Dillon. I'm looking forward to getting some pointers."

"Of course. Anything I can do to help. We just want you to relax and enjoy yourself. I'll send the bill over to the Butterfly Wings for you tomorrow."

And I'll just send it to Sergeant Fenton for you. I grinned at Dillon to cover my irritation with the former cheerleader who always seemed to have a way of sticking it to me. At least I would get to sit and eat tonight.

I found Aunt Ginny in a little nook just off the library, sitting at a massive old-fashioned wooden bar.

The bartender was busy playing the bossa nova on a copper martini shaker. "So, where is this picture of you on the wall?"

She took a sip of something pink and fizzy from a champagne coupe. "Right over the bar."

"The topless mermaid?"

She nodded and gave me a demure smile. "You know my second husband was a painter."

"That's supposed to be you? She's a brunette."

Aunt Ginny shrugged. "Artistic license."

"I'm going to look for the tour group and try out Owen's cockamamie intel about the one who had a cat at home moving the name card at dinner. You can come with me unless you have to give an interview to *Nudist Monthly*."

"Psh." Aunt Ginny slid off the stool and took my arm with her free hand. "I can look at that in the mirror whenever I want."

I want that magic mirror in my room.

The genteel apricot dining room was set aglow with shaded chandeliers gracefully dangling from intricate plaster medallions. The dark polished wood floor was a striking backdrop to the white linen—covered tables, each one with a vase of sunflowers and cattails.

Brooklyn was sitting at a table by the window, a half-eaten Luna bar next to her water glass.

"Hello again. Mind if we join you?"

She looked up and didn't smile. "Hey."

Aunt Ginny pulled out a chair and sat even though we had not been invited. "You look like a woman who could use some company."

Brooklyn gave her half a smile. "I want to leave. There's no reason for me to still be here. I don't know anything about Simon's murder. The vacation is ruined. I just want to go back home and get on with my life, but the police are pressuring me to stay. They think I'd be more useful here until they release the body."

"Who's taking care of your cat?"

Brooklyn's eyebrows dipped. "What? I don't have a cat."

"Sorry. My mistake." *Why am I even taking Owen's word on anything Figaro says? What an idiot.* I pulled out the chair next to Aunt Ginny. "I actually wanted to ask you about Simon. When you were at my house, was your husband with you the whole time?"

She shrugged and pushed the Luna bar further away. "Not every second. He disappeared a couple of times, but I thought he was going to the bathroom. He kept saying his stomach was upset."

"Was he sick before you came over?"

"No. He was fine. If he was sick, I would have left him at the Inn and come alone."

Aunt Ginny's eyelashes fluttered. She'd had five husbands. I wondered if she would have left any of them at the hotel to go on a tour if they were sick. *Probably.* "Did Simon ever leave the room with Dr. Felicity Van Smoot?"

She looked out the window. "I dunno. I wasn't watching him." She turned and looked towards the kitchen. "Do you think they could at least make me a fruit cup?"

Aunt Ginny's eyes narrowed just for a second. "I'm sure they could. Oh look, here's the rest of the tour group. Won't you excuse me?" She picked up her drink and left the table to catch Sable and Jax.

I had used Aunt Ginny as my excuse many a time, and tonight was to be no different. I pushed my chair back. "I have to go with her. She's off her meds."

Verna had joined the rest of the university people tonight. Although her presence appeared to have been under protest. She wore no makeup, her hair was a wispy mess, and she had chosen to go with the formal combo of sweatpants and SU T-shirt. She was being half dragged to the table by Felicity with Eli shuffling behind them, his hands stuffed in his pockets.

"It's good to see you all again. How is everyone?"

Eli gave me a look like he thought he was talking to one of those contestants on a reality TV show who you really hope is pretending to be that dumb; otherwise, DNA owes them an apology. "How do you think? We can't get a refund, so we're stuck on this amateur hour dinner tour with food that I can only assume passes as gourmet to people who've never left this backwater island."

I felt a flash of anger so hot the corners of my eyebrows singed. "Well, this backwater island is about to serve you fried chicken that has been featured on several nationwide cooking shows and gourmet travel magazines, so hopefully you can rally."

Eli's face paled and he swallowed hard.

Felicity left her young assistant at a table, took my arm, and led me through the dining room to the lobby, back towards the King Eddie bar. "Don't mind him. He's grumpy because the university newsletter pushed the announcement of his upcoming publication to next month so they could print the staff condolences about Simon. Even in death, Simon is still stealing Eli's thunder. Come with me to get Verna a drink."

"Is she okay?"

Felicity waved her free hand. "She's fine. I wanted to ask you something."

"Oh?"

"Whose idea was the Haunted Homes Tour and who set the prices for the event?"

"I think Linda at the Inn of Cape May set it up. I'm not sure whose idea it was, just that they've done events like this in the past and this is the first time they've asked me to join them."

She eyed me and nodded. "How was the price of the tour determined?"

"I have no idea. I wasn't consulted. I think it's only fair if I get to ask you a question now."

"Shoot."

"An eyewitness has come forward who says they saw you and Simon leaving the tour group to go back in the storage room together. Is that true?"

Felicity made a slow nod of her head. "Well, yes. Technically."

"Were you in a secret relationship?"

Felicity threw her head back and laughed. "Simon wishes. He's been after me for ages, but I have far too much self-esteem."

"Then what were you doing?"

"Running interference. I saw him corner Verna when we first got up to the third floor. Simon was a lech. It would be just like him to go after an impressionable young girl, and my Verna is a very promising PhD student. I don't want her lured into his clutches under false pretenses just so he can seduce her and wheedle all my department's secrets out of her."

"You think *he* was coming on to *her*? I really had the impression that it was the other way around. We all thought Verna was trying to seduce Simon on the tour."

"No, that's ridiculous. Don't get me wrong. Verna

worshiped the ground Simon walked on, but in a purely academic way."

There was nothing academic about it when I saw her grab his butt in the hall.

I waited a minute for Felicity to order a pumpkin spice White Russian and a maple toddy from the bartender. When she was done, I asked, "How did Eli feel about Simon?"

"Nope, my turn. Do you get a lot of tourists who want to stay at your B&B just because you're listed as haunted?"

The heat rose to my face. "Where are we listed as haunted? Surely that one lady's blog isn't undeniable proof. It's true that some people want to stay with us because they've heard certain stories." *Stories that my tour contract forbids me from telling you are not true.* "So, Eli?"

"Simon Beck was a pioneer in modern parapsychology. Eli had the utmost respect for him, as we all did."

"Are you sure about that? I sensed something more akin to rage. He rolled up to my house and launched into a brawl."

Felicity shrugged. "That little tiff was nothing to be concerned about."

"He ripped into the man the moment he laid eyes on him in my dining room. He left his coat on the floor."

Felicity picked up the drinks and took a long sip of both of them. "Simon liked to test the knowledge of our doctorate students. What you saw was just normal academic rivalry."

"I guess." *Don't ask it. You're being an idiot.* "Felicity?"

"Yeah?"

"You don't have some kind of hypoallergenic cat at home, do you?" *Does that even exist?*

Felicity snorted into one of the drinks. "Are you kidding? I'm wearing a velvet cocktail dress. Does it look like I have a cat? I don't have time for anything so needy."

I'm oh for two. That'll teach me to take clues from pet psychics.

We took the drinks back to the table where the crab cakes were being served. Felicity put one of the drinks next to Verna and whispered something in her ear before taking the seat across from her. Verna looked at me, then quickly looked away. I was left with the empty seat across from Eli. "We were just talking about you at the bar."

He checked the silverware for spots. "I'm sure you were."

The waiter placed a gorgeous brown crab cake in front of me. I picked up my fork, but Aunt Ginny swooped in from two tables down and snatched my plate. "Hey!"

"These have gluten in them. I'm just saving you from yourself."

"Don't you have your own?"

She grinned. "Yep. I'll make room."

I put my fork back on the cloth napkin and allowed myself a moment of self-pity. "Felicity was telling me there was some work-place jealousy between you and Simon."

Eli scoffed. "Felicity needs to have her head examined."

"So, what happened at my house then? Just routine hatred?"

Eli scowled coldly without blinking. "Simon Beck

was the last person I wanted to see. I thought he was there to steal my ideas again."

"Again?"

Eli took a fat bite of crab cake before he answered me. "I was a visiting lecturer from another university when I met Simon. I made the mistake of confiding in him that I was working on a breakthrough thesis about psychic development and mind control. He stole my entire premise, and published a very similar paper a week before I could get mine out."

"What's wrong with that? I'm sure your paper was still good."

Eli's fork hovered over his plate. "No one remembers who publishes second. It's publish or perish in academia, and Simon wasn't content with being top dog. He wanted to be the only dog. He didn't see any room for two stars in parapsychology. So he did what he always does and unfairly wielded his position to sabotage others. In this case, me. I lost all credibility with my university after that and had to transfer my credits to SU to finish my doctorate."

"So, when you saw him on my tour, you figured he was here to scoop you again?"

"Simon Beck may have looked the suave, debonair college professor, but he was a basic, garden variety bully. One of his favorite moves was to humiliate a student early on in the semester until they dropped his class in disgrace. He said it was healthy to put fear in the rest of the students to weed out the weak ones who didn't have 'it.'"

"What was 'it'?"

"It was whatever Simon thought would set you apart from the pack and show excellence. Although I think it was really whoever he could steal credit from or manipulate into sleeping with him."

A plate of fried chicken and mashed potatoes landed in front of me like it had been delivered by angels. It was glorious. Then a devil in a salmon cocktail dress attacked my parade with a flamethrower. She grabbed the plate with one hand and the waiter with the other.

"'Scuse me, hon. Can we get hers wrapped up in a doggy bag for me to take home?"

The waiter took the plate and absconded with my hopes and dreams for crispy chicken. *This was probably payback for the mashed rutabaga on the shepherd's pie.*

Aunt Ginny rolled her lips to a pout. "Don't hangdog. You know you can't have anything on that plate. I'm only looking out for you."

"What am I supposed to eat? I'm starving."

"You want me to go shake down Brooklyn for the rest of that Luna bar?"

"No." *I'll shake you down.*

The hunger was causing me to lose all self-respect and I heard these words come out of my mouth before I could snap it shut. "So, Eli, do you have any pets at home? A cat maybe?"

He looked me up and down like he was trying to decide if I was mental. Then he looked away. "Not anymore."

Verna shot up from her table and fled the dining room in tears. Since I obviously wasn't going to be allowed to eat with my personal diet coach shadowing me, I excused myself and went after her.

She was standing in the lobby by the fireplace, crying softly.

I handed her a box of Kleenexes from the side table. "What's wrong?"

Verna's eyes were red and swollen. Her scarlet fingernails were bitten down to jagged edges. "Who are you, again?"

"I'm Poppy. I own the Butterfly Wings. You were just there two nights ago."

She still looked blank.

"Simon Beck died at my dining room table." *Geez. Maybe you need a new prescription.*

Her eyes filled with tears. "Oh, that was your house."

"Yes. You and Simon must have been very close."

She stared into the flames. "Simon Beck was a genius. Despite what *Newsweek* said about him, he was a brilliant scientist and the leading expert of parapsychology in the fields of telepathy, precognition, paranormal investigative techniques, and ESP. His loss will be the greatest tragedy of our generation."

Sure. Right up there with the cancellation of All My Children. "You were definitely a fan of Dr. Beck. Is that why you signed up for the same tour he was on? To be near him?"

She threw her head back to face me so quickly that my eyes popped in surprise. "Certainly not! It's part of my job as Dr. Van Smoot's research assistant to find credible investigative opportunities. I'm only here to assist her in said research. We had no idea Dr. Beck would be here with his *wife.*"

There is no way a bunch of university people just happened to sign up for my tour at the same time. How big is this field? I took out my phone while she ranted at me and looked up universities offering parapsychology degrees. The list was small, but SU was the closest one to Cape May.

Verna wound down her tirade with a sniffle. "And I would never have come had I known he'd be here at the same time."

"Okay, okay. So, Felicity is only here to research—what?"

Verna sighed like she could scarcely believe I didn't know the answer myself. "The ethics of psychic investigation, or profiting from the paranormal. You know, like charging people a lot of money to see the ghosts in your house."

"I served dinner too."

She rolled her eyes and huffed. "I'm not the one you need to convince. I've only been in Dr. Van Smoot's department for a few months, but one thing I've learned is that when she has her mind set on a goal, nothing will keep her from it. And she's on to your shady dealings. I hope the money was worth the exploitation of trapped souls."

"I swear to you, not one ghost has complained about being exploited. Were you in love with Simon?"

Verna started to sputter, "Wha . . . Of all the . . . Absolutely not! He was married!"

"An eyewitness says you left the tour with Simon Beck for a few minutes. And when I say 'an eyewitness' . . . I mean me. What were you doing?"

"You must be remembering wrong. Because I never left the tour group. But I did lose track of Felicity for a few minutes. If you want to question someone who's been sneaking around go find her."

The tour group emerged from the dining room with Dillon leading them. "The gifted psychic Wendell Dennis has visited us on several occasions, and he himself has not only seen a woman rocking a baby in the cupola, but he's felt the presence of a woman sitting on the end of his bed in room eighty-four. Let's head up there now and you can see for yourself."

Dillon cupped his hand and motioned for me to join him.

I nodded and took a step towards the tour group. "Do you think Simon was having an affair with Felicity?"

The blood drained from Verna's face, and she picked a short white hair from her sweatshirt. "What have you heard?"

"Just that Felicity and Simon keep showing up on the same research trips."

The corners of Verna's eyes pinched tight as she watched the tour group move away. "I have wondered if maybe Felicity's been spying on Simon, professionally. She does a lot of sneaking around and doesn't always tell me where she's going. But I don't know what she would gain. They're in totally different fields of study."

"Maybe it was romantic?"

Verna snorted. "Please. He would never be into her. She's much too old for him."

CHAPTER 26

Aunt Ginny and I walked around the block to home while I searched for articles in *Newsweek* about Simon Beck. "Hey. Guess who wrote an article titled 'Paranormal Investigation—the Great Hoax'?"

"Please tell me it was that whackadoo, Gladys Philippot."

"You got it. It was a long time ago. I wonder how she ended up working for a tabloid."

Aunt Ginny swung her takeout bags at her sides. "Maybe it's more money."

"More than *Newsweek*?"

"Unflattering celebrity sightings might be big money. You think she killed him?"

I shoved my phone back in my purse. "It certainly can't be a coincidence. But that seems more like a motive for him to kill her."

"I suspect you have to get in line to kill Gladys Philippot."

"You're probably right." I wished I'd worn a coat; the wind cut me right through to my bones. I rubbed my arms and picked up the pace. My stomach rumbled and Aunt Ginny gave me some side-eye. "You should have taken something with you so you could eat."

"Maybe I should have left you home so I could eat."

She swapped hands with her double takeout bags to shift the weight. "Oh, you don't mean that. Besides, you'd be up all night scratching and complaining your stomach hurts. Isn't this better?"

"That bread pudding looked like it would be worth it."

Aunt Ginny lifted the bag. "It was."

I started planning a gluten-free bread pudding with whiskey sauce for breakfast to quell my regret. "Did you get anything out of Sable and Jax?"

"Just that the girl's boyfriend is coming up this weekend if she isn't home by then."

"Her boyfriend? I thought Jax was her boyfriend."

Aunt Ginny shrugged. "I dunno. That's what she said. I can't understand these kids today. She also called her father to ask him to Venmo more money. Apparently, they had not planned on attending the tour past yesterday, but they're afraid if they leave it will make them look guilty."

"Sure."

"What's Venmo?"

"It's an electronic payment app." I pulled out my phone to show Aunt Ginny, but my attention was diverted by a polite argument on my porch. The house was dark, but Owen and Gladys were sitting side by side in rocking chairs, bickering like an old married couple. Their voices sang like a lullaby but cut like a razor blade.

Owen pulled his sweater tighter around him. "People can be different without being crooks."

"In my line a work, you learn real fast that everyone is out to make a buck. And they'll steal from their own grandma to make that happen."

"Well, that must be a very sad life you live."

"At least I'm not the neighborhood whack job."

"How would you know? You probably don't have any friends to tell you whether you are or not. Oh, hello, Poppy. Beautiful night."

I smiled at them both. "Is the dinner tour over?"

Owen nodded. "Your friend ran out of here a few minutes ago muttering about hazard pay."

Gladys nodded. "Yeah. But you'll be glad to hear this group had no casualties."

Aunt Ginny kicked a lone piece of pumpkin shell that Kenny missed towards the garage. "At least no one's blaming Poppy this time."

Gladys stopped her rocker in midswing. "You know things are not looking good for you?"

"Why not?"

"This crew inside ain't found any evidence of a ghost, specter, or poltergeist. I talked to my editor about you not being haunted and he thinks the fraud angle is ovahdone."

"That's good news."

"Nah. He wants me to shift angles to the murder victims."

My mouth went dry, and my throat closed like invisible hands tightened around my neck. "Oh?"

Owen adjusted the colander on his head. "Leave her alone. Can't you see she's just an innocent victim in all this?"

"Owen's right." *That felt weird.*

Gladys shot him a dirty look. "Like you would know innocent if it marched up here and gave you a noogie. Anyway. I been talking to some people around town. They say every few weeks someone dies and you're the first person to find the body."

Aunt Ginny shrugged. "So. That isn't a crime."

Gladys leaned her head to the side and back. "It is if you're the one killing them."

"I thought we were through with this. What reason would I possibly have to kill all those people?" *Except for maybe the first one. Barbie was really mean.*

Gladys shrugged. "Maybe you're trying to get your own ghost to compete with the other haunted houses in Cape May—since you obviously aren't one a them."

My jaw clenched, and I lost the ability to speak. Aunt Ginny cracked her knuckles and I put my hand out to stop her from doing something rash.

Gladys put her hands up in surrender. "Hey, I'm not the enemy here. I'm just following up on a story. If it wasn't me, it'd be someone else who isn't as sympathetic to your predicament."

Aunt Ginny's hand shot to her hip. "So, this quiet threat is what passes as sympathy these days?"

Gladys shrugged. "I gotta make a livin'."

The front door opened, and Clark stuck his head outside. "Oh, hi. I thought everyone had gone up to bed already." He called into the room behind him, "False alarm. Just people on the front porch!"

"I'm going inside to make a sandwich." I went through the front door with Aunt Ginny on my heels. Ghost-hunting equipment was spread out all over every room of my first floor.

Clark and Ritchie were in the dining room sitting in the dark. The recording light on the camera was lit, and they were watching a black box. I quietly walked past the piano and Clark put his hand out. "Did you see that?"

I stood perfectly still, waiting while they received some questionably authentic paranormal readings.

Ritchie just said, "Wow."

"That was one heck of a surge." Then he spoke to the darkness. "Hello. We just want to talk to you. Can you do that again, please?" A moment later. "Whoa! Awesome, man."

Paisley called from the sunroom, "Where is my SD card? I left it right here!"

Harper answered from the hallway, "I didn't touch it."

Paisley called, "Clark, I need a confessional. The ghost took my SD card!"

Clark waved his hand across his throat. "Cut. Girls! We had something."

Harper came rushing into the dining room followed by Paisley. "Was it Professor Beck?"

I watched the playback in Ritchie's camera. "Is that the only thing that's happened all week?"

Clark shook his head. "No. We have footage that shows where doors keep opening and items have moved. You seem to have a playful ghost who likes pranking you."

Is her name Ginny Frankowski? 'Cause I think she just doesn't remember where she puts things. "Is that right?"

Harper sidled up next to me and craned her neck to see the screen. The device in her hand beeped. She held it closer to me and it beeped again; this time the beep got quieter. She looked at the readout, then at Ritchie, then at me, then to Clark. "*Something* just drained the battery on my EDI meter. I'll be right back."

Clark and Ritchie both looked right at me. Then Clark said, "How do you feel?"

"Fine." *Other than hungry.*

"Do you have trouble wearing a watch? Like does it stop working after a few hours?"

"Yes."

Paisley grunted.

Clark rolled the footage of their power surge back and played it again.

I tiptoed into the kitchen and opened the drawer to the Halloween candy. An empty bag of peanut butter cups mocked me with its perfect flatness. *Doggonit, Aunt Ginny!*

I opened the freezer and took out a loaf of gluten-free bread, then got the peanut butter and jelly.

Kenny bounded down the back stairs and through the pantry door. His hair was a pouf of orange. "I need a new hair dryer. Every time I put that one on high the lights flicker." I paused with my knife over the peanut butter and considered my options. Tell the truth and have Gladys report me as a fraud and a serial killer. Or let them believe they've just made contact with a spirit and not Kenny's hair dryer creating power surges on my ancient electrical system.

Clark came to the door. "Hey. You wanna see one of the things we got?"

I looked longingly at the peanut butter. "Sure." I followed him down the hall to the library where they had set up a laptop and headphones. "What'd you find?"

"I was looking through the B-roll footage from the night Simon Beck died, and I found this."

We sat side by side on the couch and he clicked the mouse to play a video. It was a camera sweep of my empty dining room before dinner. Everyone's drinks were already on the table, so I knew we must be on the third floor.

"We get background shots of each room so if something happens later we can show the before and after."

I nodded.

"Look at the little bottle on the table." He pointed to the bottle of stevia in between Simon's and Brooklyn's iced teas.

"Okay."

"Now look." He advanced the video to an hour later when everyone was coming downstairs from the tour. "It's moved over there."

The bottle had moved down the table to the other side of Brooklyn's plate. The group started filing back in to take their seats and Verna went to sit next to Simon. He had to snatch her name card from the place setting where Brooklyn had been and moved it back to the end of the table. "So, someone moved the bottle and the name cards while we were on the tour? Do you have any footage of that happening?"

"No. I was on the third floor when it was switched. Some ghosts love to move things on you."

"But why would a ghost . . . *if I had a ghost* . . . want to change place settings between Verna Fox and Brooklyn Beck? Isn't it more likely that someone on the tour came down here and swapped the cards while we were all upstairs?"

Clark minimized the screen. "That's why we usually do these investigations with an empty house. We want to re-create the scenario tonight and see if we can get it to happen again. Do you think we could borrow that bottle?"

"That wasn't mine. Simon's wife brought it with

her. I would assume the police have it now. You want to use my eyedropper bottle of vitamin D? It looks just like that."

Clark stood. "We can try. But usually, when an entity moves something, it holds a significance that we don't understand."

CHAPTER 27

I pulled the door open at La Dolce Vita, having left the kitchen at Momma's restaurant in good shape. As it was the middle of the week, there was nothing Mia Famiglia needed other than some fresh bread. I could make that here in the coffee shop without Gia's sour sister, Teresa, harassing me. Then I could take advantage of a little snuggle time with a certain Italian boyfriend.

Joanne had taken Gia's sister's words about being in charge of me like a directive from the NSA. She bossed me through breakfast at the B&B. She bossed me through making tomorrow's bread dough at Momma's. And she was determined to boss my every step through the coffee shop, past the espresso machine, into the back kitchen.

"You don't have to stay with me, Joanne. I can handle baking a few muffins on my own."

Joanne looked around the tiny commercial space. "I agreed to this favor, and I'm not having you say I didn't hold up my end of the bargain."

"I'm not gonna say that. Amber said you could help me. Not that I was a flight risk."

Gia swiveled his gaze from me to Joanne, fascinated with the verbal tennis match.

Joanne, for her part in the conversation, huffed and puffed and yanked down an apron. "If I leave you, there's no telling what disaster you'll create. And you still need to tell Amber about that moving bottle."

"Geez, Joanne. Unclench. I texted her a while ago."

Gia swiveled his gaze to me with a gleam in his eye. "Looks like you brought your own sous chef today. You need me to do anything?"

"Kiss and a latte?"

He pulled me close. "How about this one, *mia cara*?" He gave me a long, sweet kiss

Joanne wove her hand in between us and took the wrapped lump of dough I was still cradling for today's ciabatta rolls out of my arms.

I pulled back to look at her. "What in God's name are you doing?"

"Don't let me stop you from sucking face. But one of us has to get these rolls started or they won't be ready in time for dinner."

Gia snickered and made a face for my eyes only that said, *That was awkward.* "What are you making, Bella?"

"I'm thinking apple butter sheet cake and some apple cider donuts."

He gave me a lopsided grin. "And which of those are you making because you've been craving them?"

"Both. And while we're on the subject, I'm making

that bread pudding with whiskey sauce even if you and I are the only ones who will eat it."

"I am there for you, my love." The bell jingled out front that a customer had come in. Gia pointed to Joanne. "Latte?"

"You know it."

He swiveled his hand back and forth. "What kind you want?"

Joanne clapped her hands together releasing a puff of all-purpose flour that I would now have to sanitize from every surface in my gluten-free kitchen. "Surprise me."

Gia returned to the dining room with a promise to make us both fancy lattes while I gathered my ingredients for the donuts and moved to the far corner away from the Pillsbury Doughboy's cross contamination.

My apple cider was simmering and just starting to reduce when Gia brought back two new creations. "Bella, for you, snickerdoodle with extra whip cream. And Joanne, you have lumberjack latte. Sweetened with maple syrup and a tiny pat of butter."

Joanne covered her ciabatta rolls with a clean cheesecloth and sipped her latte. "Nice job, GQ. You should add this to the menu."

Geez Louise. How is she the Ambassador of Pleasantville to everyone but me? I slurped my latte and shot Gia a grin.

He chest puffed a little at the praise. He chuckled and wiped the whipped cream off the tip of my nose. "Two winners, eh?"

I gave him a lazy grin. "Definitely. Hey, you want to go with me tonight to the Macomber's ghost tour?

Sawyer has to work, and Joanne said last night's tour at my house was too much work and she needs Aunt Ginny to help."

Behind me Joanne grumbled. "I didn't say it was too much work. I said I need Ginny to stay and help wrangle Royce. He got lost on the tour and started quoting someone named Oberon."

I turned the heat off under my cider to let it cool. "Aunt Ginny does help ground him. So, what d'you say, GQ?"

Gia grinned and his eyes narrowed playfully at my teasing. "Sure. Aunt Ginny has been asking to baby-sit. What could go wrong?" The bell jingled over the door in the dining room again and he disappeared to answer it.

Joanne hooked her hands to her hips and scowled. "What's next, Buttface? I finished forming the rolls while you were making out. They need to rise for about an hour. You want me to start on the apple butter cake?"

"I want you to stop calling me Buttface. What is your problem with me anyway?"

"If you can't figure it out, I'm not gonna tell you."

"Figure it out? I don't have the slightest idea." I turned on my peacock stand mixer and whipped together softened butter and two kinds of sugar.

Joanne shrugged. "What can I say, you can't like everyone."

Well, that was true enough. God knew I was having occasional fantasies about slapping that scowl off her face.

I took another sip of my latte. "Do you think you could make some of those maple pecan bars for the pastry case? And I want to try a new muffin."

"What are you thinking?"

"You know that apple spice muffin everyone likes?"

"Yeah?"

"What if we put some chopped dates and figs in with the apples."

Joanne's eyebrows shot up.

"And maybe some toasted pecans?"

She shook her head. "Uh-uh. We got pecans in a lot of things. How about roasted hazelnuts?"

My heart leapt with a mixture of excitement and irritation that I hadn't thought of that on my own. "That sounds fabulous. I don't know if we have hazelnuts, though."

"My pal Marco has some. I'll run over and get them." She took off her apron and walked through to the dining room.

My pal Marco, her voice mimicked in my head. I turned off the mixer, and Joanne flew back into the kitchen. "You'll never guess who's in the dining room."

"Who?"

"Eli Lush."

"Get outta here!"

Joanne pointed towards the other room. "He's at the bar drinking coffee and looking at his phone."

I peeked around the corner and spotted the surly PhD student just as he swiped left on his screen. "I'm gonna go talk to him."

"Aw, you're gonna blow it."

"How? I just want to talk."

"Well, don't spook him."

I waved my hand at her to back away and grabbed my snickerdoodle latte.

"Hey, Eli. Fancy running into you here."

Gia was cleaning the espresso machine. He looked from me to Eli and raised an eyebrow.

Eli looked behind him. "How are you everywhere I go? You aren't actually triplets, are you?"

I sat on the barstool next to him and sucked in some whipped cream. "It's a small town and this is the best coffee."

He went back to his cell phone. "What do you want?"

"I wanted to say I was sorry for bolting on you at dinner last night. Verna seemed really upset and I just wanted to check on her, you know?"

Eli sent his eyes in an arc across his face. "Verna needs to get a grip on reality."

"About Simon?"

He clamped his lips down.

I waited him out.

"Felicity has done all she can to help Verna. She needs to start helping herself and let Felicity get on with her life."

"Because Verna's in love with Simon?"

"I don't see how that's any of your business."

"She did have a meltdown at my house. I want to be able to comfort Verna without encouraging her in the wrong direction, you know?"

"Trust me, you aren't smart enough to help someone like that."

"How would you know how smart I am?" *I don't have a degree in psychology, but those Dr. Phil reruns have to count for something.*

"Verna Fox has a brilliant mind. She'll make a phenomenal PhD one day. She just needs to keep

her focus on things that are important. Not a waste
of time like Simon Beck."

"I heard Dr. Beck used to have quite the reputation with the ladies. Do you think Felicity was ever
drawn away by his charms?"

A flash of anger passed through Eli's eyes, and I
had to take a medicinal swallow of my snickerdoodle
latte.

"Many a silly girl falls in love with her professor."
He tsked and sighed of boredom. "It's such a cliché.
And Simon was a playboy. But the dirty little secret in
academia is that relationships between professors
and students are more common than they want you
to know. You're both adults. You spend eighty hours
a week on campus. Where else are you going to meet
someone? Most universities have the archaic rules of
making professor-student relationships forbidden,
and punishable."

"Punishable for which one?"

"If any favoritism or cheating is suspected, the student can be expelled, but the professor gets suspended
and eventually fired if they don't break off the relationship. It's against the code of conduct. If Verna,
or Felicity, were involved in a forbidden relationship,
they knew enough to keep it quiet and not to expect
it to go anywhere lasting. If it became public, it would
be career suicide for both parties."

While he was talking, Joanne texted me like a machine gun:

How's it goin?
Did u ruin it yet?
U want me 2 make the donuts?
U know what, I'll just make the donuts.
I can do them better than u anyway.

Where's the GF flour?

NM.

Found it.

I turned my phone on silent and flipped it face-down with a sharp look towards the kitchen. "Everyone said that Simon was well respected with paranormal people." *That's not right.* "People who are paranormal." *That doesn't sound right either.* "Paranormal ghost students? Students studying ghosts?"

Eli stared at me with his coffee cup hovering in front of his lips.

"Are any of those right?"

Gia was facing the opposite wall, but I heard his snicker from here.

Eli sighed and his empty cup dropped to the counter in a clatter. "I didn't respect Simon because he was a liar and a thief. And he was closed-minded to the truth when it didn't agree with his theories and thinking. He obviously recognized that I had the superior intellect. And there is nothing a professor despises more than someone smarter than him."

"You think he resented you?"

"Heaven forbid someone else be in the spotlight."

"But you were never in his department?"

Eli studied the writing on the espresso machine. "No. When I came to SU, I knew well enough to stay clear of Simon Beck. He couldn't be trusted."

"Because he'd already stolen your work."

Eli played with the rim of his paper cup and avoided my eyes. "He didn't just steal my ideas. He claimed that years of my research was his own. Once he published my work in *ParaPsychology Today* I lost my funding and the respect of my university."

"Did you want to kill him?"

He crushed the empty paper cup in his fist. "Yes, I resent him. But I didn't kill him. Simon was threatened that I was rising too close to the sun, so he clipped my wings. He may have stolen my research, but he ruined Felicity's career. If you want to look at someone with a motive, start barking up that crazy tree."

CHAPTER 28

"I wish I'd thought ahead to drive instead of walk this morning." I stood in the doorway of La Dolce Vita and balanced two pastry boxes of muffins and donuts with a gingersnap pumpkin cheesecake and a bag of ciabatta rolls.

Joanne held one aluminum tray of chicken and artichoke manicotti, and another of Caesar salad. "I'm not walking this all back to your house just because you weren't smart enough to plan ahead. Go home and get the car and come back, dummy."

It killed me to not be able to argue with that logic. It also killed me for Joanne to have the upper hand. A devious plot began to form in the back of my mind. "Good idea. You wait here."

I left Joanne with no small amount of suspicion in her eyes, and Gia with a fully stocked pastry case that should last him about three days and walked the two and a half blocks home. When I arrived, a blue sedan passed and parked at the curb in front of the house.

I leaned down to see Chief Kieran Dunne driving

with Sergeant Amber in the passenger seat. "Hey. What are you doing here again so soon?"

They got out of the car at the same time like it was part of a practiced scene for *Hill Street Blues*. Amber pushed her mirrored sunglasses to the top of her head. "We've got a couple follow-up questions about the crime scene."

"Okay. Can you give me a minute?" *I've got to figure out how to bring up the stevia like Amber doesn't know about it.*

Kieran removed his sunglasses, wiped them with a cloth, and folded them into a hard container. "Quickly, please, Ms. McAllister."

I ran inside to send Aunt Ginny to pick up Joanne in the Corvette. "Get your new license."

"I've got it."

"The registration is in the glove box."

"Quit pushing me! I'm goin'."

Aunt Ginny stepped onto the porch and eyed the police. "Do you have a warrant?"

Amber looked the saucy little redhead in the eye. "We're not searching anything."

Aunt Ginny cocked her head and narrowed her eyes. "Okay. I'll be right back. Don't frisk anyone while I'm gone."

Amber gave her a serious nod. "Okay." Then she chuckled behind her back as she went to the garage.

I turned my attention to Chief Dunne. "Do you want to come in this time?"

He put out his arm for Amber to step into the foyer ahead of him; then he followed.

Aunt Ginny flew Bessie down the driveway in reverse and ran over the recycling bin and a patch of orange mums. Then she spun in an arc and headed for the Washington Street Mall.

I shut the door before the interim chief of police could see anything further.

Kieran eyed me quizzically. "What are you so tickled about?"

"Nothing." I looked at Amber. "I sent Aunt Ginny to pick up Joanne."

Amber's eyes widened for a moment, and she immediately looked away. She cleared her throat. "Kat isolated the poison that killed Simon Beck. It wasn't in any of the food we collected the night of the homicide. It was only found in the victim's iced tea."

I led them into the library to sit. "He did drink a lot of it while he was here."

Kieran pulled a smart phone from his inside jacket pocket and tapped it on. "Take a look at the crime scene photos and tell me if anything is missing."

I glanced at Amber and swept through the photos. "Everything looks right to me. Simon took some pills before dinner, so they're missing. Oh wait. A bottle of liquid stevia should be on the table down by the victim. I don't see it in the pictures."

Amber's face remained emotionless, but her eyes belied something else. Amusement? No, gloating. *What's that about?*

The muscles in Kieran's jaw flexed like he was grinding his teeth. "Did you move it?"

"No, I didn't move it! It didn't belong to us. Brooklyn Beck brought it with her. It was sitting right on the dining room table all night. I'm surprised your team missed it."

He swept through some crime scene photos. "Where would it be, exactly?"

"The *Paranormal Pathfinders* crew can show you a video from the tour. You want me to see if they're here?"

Amber grinned. "Would you please, ma'am?"

I said I'd be right back and ran up to the second floor to the Monarch Suite. I knocked on the door hoping Ritchie was in and could show the officers what he'd recorded when he was getting B-roll footage.

There was no answer, but the door to the Purple Emperor opened and Paisley peeked out. "Hey. The rest of the team isn't here. They're at the historical society doing research on the house."

"Oh, darn. I was looking for Ritchie to show the police the taping from before the . . . incident the other night."

She stepped into the hall. "I can help you. I'm just rendering the footage from last night. Hold on; I'll get my laptop."

It was silent when Paisley and I reached the library, but the air was charged with friction. Kieran's face was a subtle shade of pink, and Amber's impassivity now held an air of smugness.

Paisley glanced my way, and I gave her a tiny shrug. She sat on the couch and opened her laptop.

The screech of tires let me know Aunt Ginny was home. Figaro flew to the front door to greet her. She calmly walked in and took off her leather driving gloves. "Anyone harassed yet?"

I shook my head. "So far so good."

She gave a prim little nod and headed down the hall with the Persian trotting at her feet.

A few moments later, the screen door banged open and Joanne stumbled into the hall carrying the manicotti. She was pale and out of breath. The color of her face now matched the hair on her head. She stopped to glare at me weakly.

I gave her a grin and tried unsuccessfully to keep just a little of the delight out of my eyes.

Kenny came down the hall to help bring in the food. He took one look into the library and hid his face like a movie star trying to duck the paparazzi.

Figaro slid around the corner and trotted over to the couch. He jumped on the seat in between Paisley and me.

She reached out and slid her hand over Fig's cottony fur. He settled in and started to purr. "What do you want to see?"

I told her about the video Ritchie had shown me and she found the folder from Sunday night in the files.

She tapped the mouse and a video opened. "This is the footage he took during the tour."

I leaned towards the screen. "Fast-forward to when we were all upstairs. Now keep going until you see the empty dining room."

Paisley slowed the playback when she got to where I'd asked. Both Amber and Kieran leaned in to examine the video.

I pointed to the telltale bottle just as Kenny came in with the pastry boxes. "That's the stevia Brooklyn brought with her."

Kieran gave me an icy stare. "Why do you suppose this one item was missing from the crime scene?"

Kenny stopped and threw me an alarmed look. Then hurried down the hall to the kitchen.

"Either his wife took it home with her, or the killer got rid of it. Or they still have it. I dunno. It definitely wasn't because a member of my traumatized staff chose the one item that didn't belong to us to clean up in the middle of the investigation. And you searched every inch of my house when the crime scene techs were here."

Paisley drummed her fingers on her keyboard and looked around the room to keep from making eye contact with anyone. Figaro reached his paw out and swatted her hand. She reached over and gave him another stroke.

Kieran held my stare for a few seconds longer, then shifted his attention to Paisley. "I want all the footage from the night of the party. Whether you think it's relevant or not."

Paisley paused with her hand on Fig's back. She cut her eyes to me and bit her lip. She sighed. "Okay. Hold on. I'll go get a thumb drive."

She ran up the stairs and I sat in awkward silence with two people who were both staring stiffly into space. Kieran pulled out his cell phone and called the station. "I need a CSI team to do a second sweep of the McAllister house." He looked my way. "Do I need a warrant?"

"You do if you want to search the occupied guest rooms."

"Apply for the warrant and we'll see what we find in the common areas first. Thanks, Gloria."

The front door opened, and Gladys came through. She paused in the doorway to the library. "What's happening here? Someone else die?"

Kieran gave her a charming smile. "Collecting for the Fraternal Order of Police. How much can I put you down for?"

Gladys stepped back. "I'm a little short right now. Let me get back to you." She disappeared down the hall.

I tried to nonchalantly insert her story about Simon into the conversation. "So, have you seen the article Gladys wrote for *Newsweek* on paranormal investigation?"

Amber's eyes narrowed. "When was this?"

"Several years ago. I think she called Simon 'a con artist of condolence.' Apparently, he was approaching people who had recently lost loved ones and offering to contact them in his lab at the university."

Amber made a note in her little black book. "Send me a link to that."

Kieran looked back and forth between the two of us but said nothing.

Paisley returned with a little rubber Daffy Duck and yanked his head off. Then she shoved his neck into the side of her laptop. After some clicking around, she pulled the thumb drive back out and reattached Daffy's head, handed it to Kieran, and shut her laptop.

I gave Amber a tight smile that she did not return.

The two officers stood to go. Figaro raced past them out to the foyer and flopped in front of Kieran just as Aunt Ginny was coming down the hall. "Don't mind that crazy cat. He's got a screw loose."

Kieran reached into his pocket and pulled out a vibrating cell phone. "Dunne.... What's that? ... You're kidding?"

I grabbed Amber's arm and lowered my voice. "What's going on with you two?"

Amber cut her eyes to Kieran for a second. "He's suddenly coming with me on every call. I don't like being micromanaged."

"Listen. Simon Beck was having an affair with a student that got too intense. He had her transferred to a different department. There may be a restraining order on file."

Amber nodded. "I'll look into it. I'm pretty sure we're heading over to talk to Brooklyn Beck right now."

"On our way." Kieran hung up his cell and nudged his head to Amber for the door. "We need to go to the station. A new witness has come forward."

CHAPTER 29

Figaro was in a right state. He galloped back and forth through the dining room, with his tail low and his ears pinned while I set the table for the tour dinner. He lost traction coming around the hutch and slid into my leg in a furry pileup.

"What has gotten into you?"

I picked him up to look at him, forehead to fluffy forehead. Blue eyes to bugged-out orange ones. "What's that in your mouth?"

Fig fought me as I tried to force his mouth open. I pulled out a soggy ball of pink yarn. "Figaro! Is this Paisley's pom-pom? I swear the ghost busters think the paranormal activity in the house is coming from me, but ninety percent of it is just you being naughty. Here comes the other ten percent now."

Aunt Ginny pushed through the dining room door carrying the silver tray of maple bars. "Fig's wound up from that Owen Rodney. The man tried to convince him that he was sleeping too much and needed a calisthenics routine."

"I simply told Figaro that he needed more exercise

to deal with that middle-aged pooch he was develop-ing." Owen Rodney was calmly sitting in the wing chair next to the fireplace reading a book. How long he had been there I had no idea.

I gave Aunt Ginny a sharp look and her cheeks flamed up to her sketched-on eyebrows.

She forced a chuckle and tried to backpedal. "Your little pep talk has him running around like he's Rocky Balboa."

Owen adjusted his colander. "He needs to work off some of his nervous energy. He's been very stressed."

"The squirrels?" I asked, despite knowing it would be almost too much for Aunt Ginny not to say some-thing snarky. Her eyes went wild, and she clamped her mouth down so tightly her teeth rattled.

"He still feels responsible for the murder that took place here three nights ago."

Well, if he does, he's punishing himself with a good purr right now.

The doorbell rang and Figaro wiggled to get down so he could run to the foyer and flop for whoever was on the other side of the door.

I opened it to three familiar little old ladies in bright pink jackets. Mother Gibson was carrying a glass bowl with something orange inside.

Mrs. Davis flashed me a grin. "What's shakin'?"

"My cat's stressed."

Figaro thudded to the floor next to me.

Mrs. Dodson stared down at him. "Maybe he's hit his head too many times."

I stepped aside for them to enter. "That's a strong possibility. What's in the bowl?"

Mother Gibson held it out to me. "My mandarin orange Jell-O salad."

"For what?"

Aunt Ginny appeared in the foyer like a magician and grabbed the bowl. "I'll just take this to the kitchen. Come along, ladies."

What are they up to?

The Biddies followed the sneaky hobbit down the hall, and I felt a sense of unrest begin to crawl through me. I looked at Fig, who was staring at me from his position splayed out on the floor. "You can get up now. It's over."

The screen door opened again, and Clark, Ritchie, and Harper stepped in buzzing with news. Ritchie was carrying a long roll of tightly wound paper.

Clark hung his suede jacket on the coatrack. "We found something fabulous about the history of the house. Where's your aunt?"

"In the kitchen plotting something with her pack of elder hooligans."

Harper's eyes glowed with excitement. "You're not gonna believe it." She called upstairs, "Paisley, bring the handheld!"

Figaro flew down the hall ahead of us to warn Aunt Ginny we were coming because he was a stool pigeon. We walked into the kitchen and caught the four Biddies hunched over an iPad. Aunt Ginny turned the screen off and flipped the device over.

Clark approached the table and greeted the ladies. "Wait till you hear what we discovered through the historical records."

Aunt Ginny's eyes twinkled. "Did you discover that I'm the last remaining heir to royalty in some far-off land and they need me to take the throne?"

I crossed my fingers.

Harper snorted. "It's exciting, but I wouldn't start dressing for a coronation yet."

Aunt Ginny's mouth twisted to the side. "Darn it."

Paisley came through the kitchen door with the little camera. "What's going on?"

Clark called her closer and pointed to the table. "Get all this recorded."

She put the camera up to her face and pushed the button.

Ritchie rolled out the translucent paper he was carrying. It was a blueprint of our house. "We found some building records. Did you know there is a hidden chamber off the kitchen? In here."

He tapped on the pantry closet on the document, and I snorted.

Aunt Ginny blushed and looked at the other Biddies.

Mrs. Davis giggled. "Everybody knows about Ginny's grandfather's whiskey hatch."

Harper bounced on the balls of her feet. "Can we see it?"

Aunt Ginny shrugged. "I mean, there's nothing there."

The other Biddies and I said in unison, "We hope."

Aunt Ginny's lips flattened. She got up from the table and toddled over to the pantry closet that hid the back staircase. When she threw the door open, Kenny was backing away. She startled and swatted at him.

Now it was Kenny's turn to blush. "I was just coming down for some juice."

Paisley was still watching through the screen of the digital camera. "I can edit that part out."

Aunt Ginny pushed by the sneaky housekeeper. "Uh-huh." She kicked aside the crate of potatoes and revealed a trapdoor. We all held our breath as she pulled the little ring—although, some of us for very different reasons.

There was a collective sigh when it was empty.

Aunt Ginny pointed to the cubby in triumph. "See."

Ritchie tapped the blueprint. "But see here."

The ten of us were packed tightly in the little pantry. Paisley and Harper moved up a couple of the spiral stairs while the rest of us smooshed together a little more to see the paper.

"These lines show the original root cellar is under this room. And it's a lot deeper than that box."

Clark squatted to examine the wooden hole. He took a penknife from his back pocket and gently dug around the top rim. He found a notch and started to wiggle the knife until the wooden box wiggled ever so slightly. When he had it moving freely, he was able to get ahold of the side and pulled the wooden crate up from the notches it had been built into.

"What in the world!" Aunt Ginny took a step closer and peered into the hole.

Ritchie rolled up the blueprint. "We need a flashlight."

Kenny called from the kitchen, "I'm on it!"

I touched Aunt Ginny on the shoulder. "Did you know about this?"

She shook her head. "Pee Paw hid his hooch in here when I was little. No one ever mentioned a root cellar."

Kenny returned with a flashlight and shone it down the hole. There were filthy wooden steps leading into an earthen vault.

Clark looked to Paisley. "Get ready."

Before the camera was in place, Aunt Ginny grabbed the flashlight and dove for the steps. "I can't wait to see what's down here."

Clark sputtered, "Mrs. Frankowski! The cameras." He hurried into the hole and tested the first step.

Aunt Ginny's voice called up to me, "Poppy. You've got to come see this!"

Clark blanched and snapped his fingers. "Harper, quick. Get me an EMF reader. Mrs. Frankowski, please wait."

Harper disappeared for a moment and was back to hand him the device.

He turned it on and gingerly followed Aunt Ginny. Paisley followed to record every moment.

I took a deep breath and squatted to find the first rung. I shimmied towards the fragile wood, praying that it wouldn't splinter under my foot. "Kenny, get the stepladder from the garage. Just in case."

My sinuses immediately closed up from the mold. I couldn't see anything other than the dim light from Aunt Ginny's flashlight bouncing around like a wasted firefly. I turned the light on my phone and shone it in front of me. Big mistake. If you've ever wondered where all the spiderwebs go after Halloween, I found the mother lode.

Aunt Ginny squealed in delight. "I found a box. Oh wait. Never mind. It's just a brick."

Clark tried pleading with her. "Mrs. Frankowski. Ginny. Don't you want this on camera?"

"Oh, I don't care. So long as I get to see the treasure first. There could be gold coins down here."

My eyes were adjusting and the only treasure I saw looked a lot like a rat skeleton. There were a couple of empty barrels and some old sacks that might have held potatoes or apples at one time. I caught up with Aunt Ginny, who was pushing against the brick wall.

"What are you doing?"

"Maybe there's a secret door somewhere."

"Please be careful. I don't want them trying to contact your ghost tonight."

Aunt Ginny hmphed. "If I come back as a ghost, I'm setting off all those devices right outside of your bedroom."

I shone my light on the ground next to a wooden wheel and saw a square clod of dirt. Aunt Ginny dove on it. "A treasure. I got it. I got something, Clark!" She lifted a filthy wooden box that could fit a pair of boots and hugged it to her chest.

Clark and Paisley were at her side immediately. Which wasn't very hard seeing as how the root cellar was about the size of the kitchen.

Harper called down the hole, "Bring it up, Mrs. Frankowski, so we can all see it!"

Followed by a chorus of Biddies: "Ginny. Quit being selfish. Bring that treasure up here for everyone to look at it."

I was able to corral Aunt Ginny back to the steps. She would only climb up them after I promised I'd hold the box and not open it but give it right back to her when she was out of the cellar. "I promise."

She climbed the ladder, then reached down for me.

I reached my hand to hers and she smacked it away. "I don't want that." She took the box from my other hand and disappeared. I could hear everyone in the pantry clomp out to the dining room.

Clark and Paisley were silent. All I could do was hurry up the ladder to let them get what they could on camera.

Aunt Ginny was sitting at the table with a grin that could cut glass. She had one hand on the box. "Whenever you're ready, Clark."

Good Lord.

Clark pulled up a chair next to her, while the rest of us crowded on one side of the table behind Paisley and the camera. The other Paranormal Pathfinders explained on camera everything that had happened that afternoon. Aunt Ginny spun her fingers in a spiral to tell Clark to hurry it the heck up. "I want to see what my ancestors left in the house."

Clark gave her a nod and she opened the box.

She gasped and reached inside. "Hey. A gun!" She pulled out an antique pistol and waved it around to see it better and we all dropped to the floor.

Clark put his hand on hers and coaxed the weapon from her grip. "Maybe we can look at that later." He handed the firearm to Ritchie, who immediately pointed it away from everyone and checked to see if it was loaded. Mercifully, it wasn't.

I tried to peer over the edge. "What else is in there?"

Aunt Ginny pulled the items out one by one. "A newspaper from 1898. A small chest of spoons, probably silver. An empty silver hip flask. A dead beetle, eww. And a leather book."

The Biddies oohed and aahed over the silver. Mrs. Dodson rubbed a spoon against her blouse, then held it up and squinted. "I wonder how old it is."

Harper reached her hand for the book. "May I?"

Aunt Ginny handed it to her, and she delicately opened the cover. "It's a diary. Callum McAllister."

Aunt Ginny practically swooned. "Callum was my great-great-grandfather who bought the house after it was built."

The diary looked dirty as an old potato and about as beaten up as a grocery list that had gone through the wash. But you could still make out most of the words. "What do you think was so special in here that they hid it in the cellar?"

Aunt Ginny squinted at the gloppy ink on thin

pages. "I might need to get one of those pairs of reading glasses from the lost and found."

Harper gently turned a page. "If you like, I can read it tonight and tell you what it says. I have a degree in history from Berkeley."

Aunt Ginny handed Harper the diary. "Okay, but be careful with it. No one has touched it for ages."

Harper gave a huge smile to the other Pathfinders. "Maybe there will be something in here that can help us understand the paranormal activity in your house."

Ritchie handed me the blueprint. "Especially since Dr. Beck is being very difficult to communicate with."

Clark vogued for the camera. "I can't believe that Dr. Simon Beck has moved on that quickly. Murder victims almost always have unfinished business until they're given justice."

Paisley turned the camera off and placed it on the table. "We need access to other rooms. We aren't getting much from the third floor. Except when Poppy's up there."

"Don't look at me. There are reasonable explanations for everything." Since my life was averse to making sense, that's when the sitting room door slammed shut of its own accord.

CHAPTER 30

I pulled on my red flats and smoothed down the black satin of my skirt. Amber wasn't satisfied with what I'd overheard so far. Everyone from that university had a motive. It was the means and opportunity I was still not sure of.

So, tonight I was following the tour to The Hotel Macomber and Gia was my plus-one. If I had to put on Spunks I was counting it as a date. So, I zhuzhed myself up with an extra layer of mascara, sprayed an invisible net over my auburn hair, and applied my bombshell scarlet lipstick.

I crept down the back stairs to the kitchen and put my ear to the door. Aunt Ginny and the other Biddies were up to something, but I had yet to catch them in the act. I could hear whispered giggles and Mrs. Dodson said, "But what do I do with my cane?"

That was never a good sign.

The door to the pantry flew open and I stumbled into the kitchen practically landing in Aunt Ginny's arms.

She licked her lips and gave me a look up and

down. "You should know by now to turn off the pantry light when you're hiding in there so your shadow doesn't move under the door. You should ask Kenny for some tips."

The Biddies broke into a series of cackles that left me more nervous than I already was—and at least a little embarrassed for getting caught. It was a rookie move leaving that light on. "Why won't you tell me what the Jell-O salad is for?"

Mrs. Davis cocked her hand on her hip. "We're going to eat it."

Aunt Ginny tsked. "What are you, some kinda nut? What do you think we're going to do with it?"

I gave her what I hoped was a cautionary look at her bright green eyes. "With you, the possibilities are endless."

The front door chimed and a bouncy five-year-old ran into the kitchen and launched himself against my legs. "Poppy!"

I hugged Henry tight against me. "Hey, sweet boy. I missed you."

Gia came in right behind and I forgot to breathe. I felt the smile slide off my face. Six feet two of Italian sexy was turned up to eleven in blackest blue formal wear.

Mrs. Davis snapped her fingers in front of my face. "It's no use. We've lost her."

Gia leaned against the counter, a sly grin working across his face, and he unbuttoned his crisp jacket. He didn't move his eyes from mine. "Do I look okay, Bella?"

Aunt Ginny snapped a dish towel on his butt. "If you looked any better, she'd be pregnant. Now quit crowing and give me a hug hello."

My face flamed. *Geez Louise, Aunt Ginny! I couldn't be pregnant without divine intervention.*

Mother Gibson picked up the magazine they'd been poring over and fanned me with it while Gia took the dish towel from the little troublemaker and gave her a hug.

Henry crooked his finger to me. I bent my head down, and he whispered in my ear, "Did you get them?"

I nodded. "They're on the way. Don't worry. Everything will be here on time."

He glanced at his father, who was watching us suspiciously, and pointed. "Don't tell you-know-who."

Gia made a face, and his hand flew up to his chest. "Am I supposed to be you-know-who?"

Henry giggled and nodded.

"Your papa? You keeping secrets from me now, Piccolo? After all I do for you?"

Henry giggled again. "Yes."

Gia went on a tirade in Italian, which made Henry giggle harder.

I wrapped my arms tighter around the little boy. "All part of Operation Trick or Treat."

Gia wiggled his eyebrows at his son. "I will deal with you later." He looked at his cell phone. "We need to go if we're going to be on time."

Henry reluctantly let go of me. "Why can't I come too?"

Gia ruffled his blond hair. "You don't want to go, Piccolo. Is going to be very boring."

Henry scrunched his nose and his glasses bobbed up and down. "Boring like Zio Luca watching football boring?"

Gia grinned. "Worse. Zia Teresa shopping boring."

Henry stuck his tongue out. "Yuck."

Aunt Ginny pulled the sweet boy into a hug. "You can help me and the gals tonight."

I gave Aunt Ginny a narrow look over Henry's head. "And that's help you do what, exactly?"

All four Biddies shrugged in unison. "Nothing."

"Sit around."

"Shoot the breeze."

I don't buy that for a minute. I whispered to Henry, "You keep a close eye on them."

He wisely side-eyed the Biddies and gave me a nod.

CHAPTER 31

"Am I allowed to make fun of the ghost stories?" Gia parked his Maserati along Beach Drive.

"No. You have to behave yourself. I'm already on thin ice with the tour council."

His grin slid into a disappointed frown. "Fine. But I will be mocking on the inside."

I gave him one of Henry's serious nods. "Understood."

The Hotel Macomber was a beautiful five-story mansion turned family-run boutique hotel. Over a hundred years old, it was famous for being the largest cedar shake structure this side of the Mississippi.

The clouds were coming in, so we hurried down the sidewalk. I looked across the street to Convention Hall and a skeleton chill danced across my shoulders. Another place in Cape May I couldn't walk past without my blood pressure rising—even though future Beauty Expos would likely be canceled for years to come after that last one.

Gia gently put his hand on the small of my back.

"Are you ready to face the suspects?" I nodded and we ascended a flight of steps up to the wraparound porch. The second-story entrance was flanked with a cluster of cornstalks and a smattering of pumpkins. We muscled through the heavy door and into warmth.

The cream-and-green lobby was dominated by a massive antique sideboard that had built-in bookcases on either end. Forest-green carpet with a swirly pattern of cream-colored tulips made a vibrant contrast to the white punched-tin ceiling dripping with glass chandeliers.

The tour group was spread around the living room like Kleenex boxes in a funeral parlor. Verna stood next to a silver granite fireplace, running her fingers through a giant fern like she was playing a harp. Eli and Felicity had their heads together whispering from a burgundy Jacobean antique carved sofa. Sable and Jax were huddled tightly between one of the heavily fringed Tiffany lamps and a reclining mermaid statue on the mantel. Brooklyn sat forlorn at the back of the room, tracing a lamp of three frolicking bronze dolphins with her finger.

Gia ran his hand down my arm. "I think Queen Victoria designed this room herself."

I snickered and entwined my fingers in his. "I didn't expect to see Brooklyn here tonight. I thought the police were detaining her."

"She must have given them some good answers for them to let her go."

I wanted to go question her, but Felicity was waving us over. I tugged on Gia's hand gently to lead him into the fray.

Felicity gave herself whiplash watching Gia cross the room. She unfurled from the sofa, her back arched, one hand resting seductively on her shoulder. "Well, hel-lo, gorgeous. Where have you been all my life?"

Gia gripped my hand tightly. *"Signora."*

Eli wrapped his suit jacket tightly over his reedy rib cage like he was afraid to catch cold from the tailwind of Felicity's pounce towards the attractive new man in the room. He gave me a sour nod.

I raised my hand and gave a wave. "Hello, Dr. Van Smoot, Eli Lush. This is my *boyfriend*, Giampaolo." I shifted my gaze to Gia, who nudged closer to my side.

Felicity couldn't rip her eyes from Gia's chest. She replied with a growl-purr combo that made everyone uncomfortable. Even the fern.

A woman in a silver-sequined floor-length gown approached me with caution. "Is that you, Poppy?"

"Hello, Crystal." I held out my hand. "You look gorgeous."

"Thank you. So do you." She grasped my hand in hers. "I've been waiting for you. It's in here."

I cut my eyes to Gia, and we passed a spark of concern between us. "What's in where?"

Crystal led us back through the lobby and into the dining room. Six tables covered with black tablecloths had been set up in the center of the room. "We've partnered with the Union Park restaurant to host the tour dinner in here. We've also offered it to guests staying with us as part of a midweek special so there are forty-one in all. Your offer to help couldn't have come at a better time. Our bartender went into labor this morning."

The back of the room had a high counter draped in black satin and wispy cotton cobwebs with a wall of liquor behind.

I looked at Crystal. She nudged her head towards the wall of booze.

I looked at Gia and he answered me with a raised eyebrow.

Crystal put her hand towards the high table. "We're offering a cash bar just for the event. Sergeant Fenton said you've done this before."

Seriously, Amber? I made virgin piña coladas for my sweet sixteen birthday party and you count that as bartending experience?

Gia took in my expression and his lip twitched. "You want us to make the drinks for tonight?"

"For forty-one guests?" *This isn't worth it. Amber can come here and investigate by herself. I'm taking Gia and going home.* I fished out my cell phone and typed a quick text to Amber:

Bartending! Are you insane!!!

As soon as I hit send it dinged and I checked the screen. It was from Sawyer. She sent three fire emojis. Then it dinged again with a text from Joanne:

Apparently, your aunt and her rowdy friends are attending the tour dinner tonight. They brought a Jell-O salad as payment. They've got the kid dressed like a butler and they're calling him Ahnree. He says it's the most fun he's had in his whole life. Come back here!

I shoved my phone in my purse. "The corkscrew is where?"

Crystal nodded. "It's behind the counter with everything you'll need. Menu, price list, cashbox. You get it."

"I can help you, but my boyfriend didn't sign on for this. Maybe he could sit at a table with the rest of the tour?"

The tour group from the university came in led by an older woman in a black pantsuit. She took them to the center table and lit the candle. Felicity winked at Gia and ran her hand over her body.

Gia put his arm around my shoulders and pulled me into his side. "No no no, lady. We are a team. If you serve the drinks, I serve the drinks."

Crystal clapped her hands. "Oh good. I really don't think just one person can handle it to tell you the truth. And I'm not exactly dressed for bartending."

I took a look at my white silk blouse and black skirt and wondered if I'd brought this situation on myself.

My phone dinged a text from Amber:

After that Hawaiian-themed birthday party you kept bragging about in high school, this should be right up your alley.

Another group of eight were led in and waited to be seated. Crystal nodded to the back of the room. "I've got to go help Mom. I'll be back to check on you in a bit."

She scampered away to seat the guests. "We will never see her again."

"Not until time to go home." Gia chuckled and took off his jacket, draping it over a nearby chair.

I went behind the bar to look at the setup. "I'm so sorry about this. After The Chalfonte didn't put me to work, I thought Amber had only set me up at the Southern Mansion as a joke."

Gia picked up a bottle of red from the Cape May Winery and reached for a corkscrew. "This is not a big deal. No one is dead." He looked my way. "At least not yet."

"Ha-ha. If these tourists had any idea about who was pouring their drinks they'd leave immediately."

Felicity prowled up to the bar in front of Gia. "Hey. How can a girl get some Sex on the Beach?"

"Er . . . sorry, *signora*. My English eis no so good."

I stepped closer to Gia and gave Felicity a smile. "I can make you something if you like. How about a Crazy Cow or a Menopause Mama?"

Felicity's eyes shot to mine. "I don't think I've ever heard of those."

Gia grinned. "Eis local favorite."

Felicity pressed her lips together and looked very unsure of herself. "I'll just have a glass of white wine please. And a rum and Coke." She put one hand over Gia's. He pulled it away to get the bottle of chardonnay.

I took down the Bacardi and a shot glass and sat it in front of Felicity. "I heard you had quite the grudge against Simon Beck."

Felicity ripped her hand back to her neck. "I beg your pardon. I had no such thing."

Gia handed me a glass of ice and a Coke.

"Even though Simon Beck ruined your career?"

Her eyes narrowed and she looked over her shoulder. "Did Verna tell you that? The little . . . Simon may have derailed my career temporarily, but he didn't destroy it. He wasn't that powerful." She made an unconvincing throaty laugh.

"Then what?"

"At one time he was my mentor, and I thought my friend, but he turned out to be just another small-minded man with a big ego who couldn't bear to see a woman in power."

Gia poured the glass of white wine and remembered how to speak English. "What did he do to you?"

Felicity leaned down towards the counter to better display her cleavage. "I had made an exciting breakthrough in a discipline of parapsychology that Simon wasn't working on. The university Chancellor was *very* interested in the potential acclaim that would accompany my research. Naturally, I wanted to apply for the tenure track."

A line was forming behind Professor Cougar, and I knew people would start to get irritable if their drinks were delayed. I put a straw in the rum and Coke and nudged it towards her. "So, what happened?"

"Simon was on the tenure review board. He denied my application. We could have been an unstoppable force together, but there was only room for one in the spotlight. His jealousy drove me to another department."

Gia poured three red and three white wines and lined them up.

One of the men in line made a rude comment about how long it was taking. I slid one of the whites to Felicity. "You were transferred?"

Felicity took a long gulp of her wine. "The university thought it was best that I move to a branch campus and continue my career as a fixed-term professor. So, I had to start over. Reinvent myself. After a few years and a few publications, I applied for tenure in the Philosophy Department and was approved. And it was Simon's loss, because my department has made more advances in parapsychology ethics than his little Paranormal Basics program ever could."

Gia called to the ladies in line behind Felicity, "Red or white, step up here. Anything else, see the lovely lady!"

Eli strode to the counter and mugged Felicity with a slow eye roll. "Really?" He grabbed the rum and Coke and went back to his seat.

"Eli, wait." Felicity pulled some cash from her cleavage and dropped it on the counter before chasing him back to the table with her chardonnay.

I kept eyeing Brooklyn and trying to will her to

come to the bar. "I need to talk to Mrs. Beck. The TV people have evidence that the stevia bottle may have been tampered with before Simon died. Unless you want to believe a ghost moved it."

"I do not."

"Yeah. Then she should be their prime suspect right now, and yet she's here." I was about to leave the bar when Crystal gave me a thumbs-up from the front of the room.

Gia passed me a glass of red wine for a stout woman at the counter. "You look for an opportunity when we are not being watched and I will cover for you."

We slipped into a rhythm where Gia poured the wine and I poured the shots while I waited for the right moment. I tried to keep an eye on my tour group's table when I could. Their sour faces told me the conversation was anything but friendly. Dinner was served, so that slowed down the press for drinks. Then three giggling twentysomethings came up to the bar and wanted obscure cocktails. A Salty Dog, a Horcrux, and Death on the Riverbank.

They had Gia googling recipes and me combing the shelves for elderflower liqueur and "something pretty."

I whispered to Gia, "These can't be real drinks. I think they're making them up."

Gia whispered back, "Do we even have a muddler?"

I turned to the girls. "You know what I hear is good? A screwdriver."

The middle girl, who reminded me of Marcia Brady with a post-football-in-the-face nose, dropped her lips to a pout. "That's not fancy."

Exasperated, and with a growing line who were

not in the red or white lane, I offered to make a super special signature cocktail for them. They agreed and I shook together a bunch of different fruit juices with some rum, ice, and vanilla syrup. Then I poured it into champagne coupes that Gia had rimmed with pink sugar. I layered on this shocking violet gin I found on the back of the bar and added thin wedges of pink grapefruit. "Here you go."

The girls oohed while Marcia Brady took the glass and held it up to the light. It looked like Sorority Punch. At least from what I could remember of that one time I went to a sorority party. From the bottom up they were yellow, then pink, then shocking violet up to the sparkly rim.

"What's it called?"

Gia and I looked at each other.

Gia shrugged. "Ghost Tour?"

I turned to the girl and grinned. "That is absolutely what it's called."

They paid and skipped back to their tables.

It very quickly became clear that I had made a horrible mistake. The line doubled in minutes. Everyone was requesting a Ghost Tour. Even Sable waved to me from the back of the line and pointed to the purple drink as it passed her.

The bottle of violet gin was almost gone, and I was starting to panic. "I hope Crystal starts the tour soon."

Sable made it to the front of the line and showed me her ID by the time I made it to the bottom of the violet gin. "You're getting my last one, girl." She grinned and threw a twenty on the counter.

"Yes!"

Marcia Brady crept up to the bar at Sable's side. "Oh my gosh. I know you!"

Sable turned her face away from the girl. "I don't think so."

"Yes, I do! We follow you. Bobbi, come here. It's Sable. Is Jax with you?" She craned her neck and looked around the room.

"I don't know what you're talking about." Sable grabbed her drink and took off down the aisle to her table.

The girl followed her. "Are you here to do one for Halloween?"

I wiped down the counter and asked Gia, "What do you think that was about?"

"I am afraid to ask."

"Sometimes I feel like the older I get, the more I'm out of the loop."

Gia's lip twitched. "Baby, I've never been in the loop."

I pulled out my cell phone to google *Sable* and *followers*, but the room dimmed and a tiny light shone on Crystal over by the double doors to the library.

"Welcome to the haunted Macomber. We're so glad you're here with us during the spookiest season. The Macomber has a unique past on the island. Soldiers were in and out of here daily during World War Two because our basement served as the Naval brig. Reflections of men in uniform will often appear in the mirror at the top of the stairs. Sometimes you can still catch them out of the corner of your eye. When you're not looking, that's when they're there. I see them when I'm working at the front desk, and it always startles me."

Crystal waved everyone out of their chairs. "We have a very grumpy spirit in the basement who doesn't like to be disturbed, so let's head up to the second floor and hear about some of our friendlier visitors who've never checked out."

I shoved my phone back in my purse, and Gia and I followed the large group out of the double doors, through the lobby. I looked around for Sable and Jax to see if Marcia Brady was still harassing them, but the kids had disappeared.

Eli spotted Gia and his lips twisted into a sour Mick Jagger frown.

Gia muttered, "What did I do?"

I took his hand in mine. "You're too handsome for your own good."

We ascended the stairs and Crystal started walking slowly backwards down the hall with Brooklyn right next to her. "Our saddest story is one of our former owner, Sarah Davis. Her daughter became ill with encephalitis and died when she was very young. Sara could not live with the grief of losing her child and she took her own life in the hotel."

Verna started to cry, so Felicity reached over and patted her shoulder.

Crystal paused in front of a white door. "This room is famous. Some of you may have already heard about Irene Wright, the Trunk Lady. Irene was a single woman who visited the Macomber every summer in the forties. She loved room ten and returned to stay every year. Guests have reported seeing a woman dragging her large steamer trunk down the stairs to the lobby. Miss Wright can be quite playful and flirtatious. We had one gentleman staying in room ten who woke up to find his clothes were missing and he could smell a lady's perfume around his bed."

Eli rolled his eyes and spoke under his breath. "Please. That happens to me all the time. And it's never been a ghost."

Felicity sent him some stink eye. She reached out to Gia and felt his biceps.

Gia jumped away like he'd been tased.

Brooklyn raised a hand. "Does room ten get booked a lot? How far in advance does someone have to call to reserve it?"

Crystal smiled. "The hotel stays busy all summer, so book early. But we usually know when someone requests room ten that they're interested in meeting the Trunk Lady. In fact, psychic medium Wendell Dennis stayed in room ten and was able to record an EVP of her speaking."

Wendell Dennis really gets around.

Gia made a face and rolled his eyes. "That is nothing. My momma once put the evil eye on my cousin Fabrizio and his hair turned white overnight."

I willed myself not to giggle out loud. "I think you're confusing ghosts with witchcraft."

Crystal moved further down the hall with Brooklyn on her heels. "Guests staying in room nine often report that they hear children playing and doors slamming above them even when there are no other guests in the hotel."

Verna wrapped her arms around herself and leaned against the wall. "I'm never going to have children now."

I put my hand on her back. "Don't be ridiculous. You're so young. You have plenty of time."

She looked startled like she was unaware that she'd spoken out loud. "What? Goodness. Of course I do."

"Verna, do you need to talk to someone about Simon? Maybe a compassion counselor?"

Verna shrugged and searched through the crowd for someone. "No. Why?"

"It's obvious that you had deep feelings for him. I know professor-student relationships aren't allowed and all, but I don't think you were the only one. Someone will understand."

"What do you mean?"

"Well, didn't you say Felicity has been sneaking around, not telling you where she was going, and you'd lose track of her? Did you ever think that maybe she's having an affair of her own?"

Verna stood ramrod straight. "Absolutely not! Dr. Van Smoot would never . . . With Simon? No. She knows how I feel—felt . . . She may have had feelings for Dr. Beck when she was younger, but that's been over for a long time."

I never said Felicity's affair was with Simon Beck.

"Felicity would never be involved with Simon. She wouldn't hurt me like that. She's like a mother to me."

Eli cocked an eyebrow and looked directly at Verna. "I think you're forgetting that some mothers eat their young."

Hmm. Okay, maybe it was.

CHAPTER 32

"That was weird, right?"

Gia nodded. "Every one of them . . . What is that that Aunt Ginny calls Miss America contestants and members of Congress?"

"Unstable whackadoos?"

"That. Unstable whackadoos."

We drove to the Point and parked overlooking the ocean. The tide was going out, but the sound of the waves was still hypnotic. "I could not get a moment alone to question Brooklyn. She was stuck on Crystal like a freckle."

"There must be a reason the police let her go. And you did get to witness that breakdown with the one in the weird glasses."

I put my hand in Gia's. "That one's Verna. And she's clearly in denial. She was so obviously in love with Simon. It's like she thought she had a future with him that included having a family."

Gia nodded. "But was she having a real affair with him, or just imagining one?"

"Either way I don't think she would kill him, do you?"

Gia breathed out a chuckle. "No. But I would not put anything past the sour one. He looked like he wanted to kill me just because the handsy woman would not leave me alone."

"I have a feeling Eli's interest in Felicity goes deeper than just student-teacher admiration."

"Who?"

"The handsy one."

Gia put his arm around me and pulled me closer. "A man needs a suit of armor around her."

I snuggled into his side as much as possible with the center console in the way. "You did a good job deflecting her."

Gia kissed the top of my head. "There are a lot of miles on that model. I could believe she would have an affair with her professor."

"I could too. Plus, she was transferred to another department when things went south just like Simon's wife said."

"The wife . . . She is *sospetto*."

"*Sospetto?*"

"Not right. She does not act like the widow. Where are her tears?"

"Oh, suspicious."

"I would never love again if you died."

"Aw." I kissed the back of his hand.

"The wife could have poisoned him at breakfast. Maybe he took a long time to die."

"You're right. I'll have to share that theory with Amber. And you know, we never did see where Sable and Jax disappeared to."

"Maybe the ghosts got them."

"Where would a ghost take you if it got you?"

"Maybe there is ghost pyramid scheme. Knock ten years off your afterlife for every new ghost you sign up."

I looked into Gia's face. The muscle in his jaw was working overtime so he would not laugh. "You're ridiculous."

He snickered and kissed me. When he started to kiss me deeper my cell phone buzzed. "Give it to me. I'll throw it in the ocean for you."

I pulled the phone out of my purse and checked it. Gia was kissing my neck while I was giggling, and I was having a hard time focusing on the screen. "We gotta go."

Gia didn't stop kissing my neck as he asked, "What has Aunt Ginny done now?"

"I don't know. But that text was from Kenny. It just says 911."

A few minutes later we pulled up to the house and saw Kenny's emergency with our own eyes. An undead army of plastic skeletons were hanging from the trees, the porch, and the bird feeder. There, in the middle, was Aunt Ginny in her flannel nightgown and polka-dot rain boots, whacking the skeletons with a broomstick like Jason and the Argonauts.

Gia shook his head. "What is she doing?"

I sighed. "Nothing sane."

We got out of the car and Gia reached for Aunt Ginny. "What is happening here, *zietta*?"

Aunt Ginny tried to whack him with the bristles, but he dodged. Her eyes were wild, but when she looked into his face her expression softened. She let Gia take the broom from her hands and pull her to his chest. He put his hand on the back of her head. "How about we go inside?"

Aunt Ginny nodded, buried in his arms.

Kenny stood in the doorway wringing his hands. "I

tried to stop her, but she wouldn't listen. She was in some kind of furious trance."

I looked around the yard. "I bet this looked great before she attacked everything. Who did all this?"

Kenny shrugged. "I have no idea. I was doing laundry on the third floor when Figaro came flying upstairs and wouldn't stop howling at me. I only came downstairs because I thought he was hungry."

Figaro is always hungry.

Gia led Aunt Ginny inside and sat her down in the kitchen away from the guest areas. I fetched her the chenille throw from her bed while Kenny put the water on for tea.

Once we had Aunt Ginny toasty and comfortable, she turned a little embarrassed. "I don't want anyone making a fuss over me."

I put the sugar bowl down next to her teacup. "Since when?"

She sent me a glare. "Since now, Lippy."

Gia sat across from the little redhead who was swallowed up in a pink fuzzy blanket. "What has gotten into you with the smashing things outside, eh?"

"I think someone is trying to scare me to death." Aunt Ginny sipped her tea and screwed her face to a frown. She held the cup up to Kenny. "What did I tell you about that?"

Kenny sighed and opened the cabinet over the sink. He took down a bottle of bourbon and added a splash to Aunt Ginny's tea. "Happy?"

She sipped the tea again and nodded. "Better."

"What do you mean, scare you to death, Aunt Ginny? These are just routine pranks."

Kenny muttered, "Really good ones, though."

Our eyes met and I nodded. Then I caught Aunt Ginny giving me the scowl of death and I stopped.

Aunt Ginny placed her cup in the saucer. "I've lived here my whole life, and nothing like this has ever happened before. I'm usually on top of things. Nothing gets by my constant vigilance."

"Constant vigilance? Just the other morning I found one of your pot pies in the microwave. It had been there for two days."

Aunt Ginny gave me a quick glare and continued her speech. "But these kids seem to be able to swoop in and prank my yard without me even hearing them. I don't like it at all."

"Maybe you need to get your hearing checked."

"Girl. I will knock you flatter than a flitter."

Just trying to help. I'm not the one going Karate Kid in the yard.

Kenny grabbed a glass of water and joined us at the table. "Okay. Well, what would make you feel better about this?"

"I need to catch them in the act."

Gia rubbed his stubble on his chin. "You want me to set up surveillance?"

She sat up as tall as four feet nine would go and the throw fell from her shoulders. "You can do that?"

"With motion sensors we can record anything that moves in the yard bigger than a squirrel."

Her eyes began to twinkle, and a warm glow rose to her cheeks. "When can we set it up?"

Gia grinned at me. "I will go pick up what we need tomorrow."

"Hot diggity." Aunt Ginny slurped her tea with a renewed evil gleam playing about her eyes. "They're gonna pay alright."

Uh-oh. "I don't want you to launch into some kind of war with the neighborhood kids, Aunt Ginny."

"What war? I'm just gonna do a little strategic retribution."

Kenny blew out his cheeks and took the whiskey back down for himself.

I braced myself for a fight. "Settle down. We don't even know who it is yet. And I hate to tell you, but revenge is generally frowned upon these days."

"I don't want to hurt anyone." Aunt Ginny grinned like the Grinch when he came up with his own devious plan. "I just want to scare them a little bit."

Oh, good heavens. My phone dinged in my purse, and I pulled it out to check my texts. "Tsk. Amber. I don't have time to do that."

Gia stretched back in his seat. "What does she want now? We just served cocktails to forty tourists. She want us to throw a barbecue at the prison or something?"

I looked the world's best boyfriend in the face. "She wants me to go to the Physick Estate in the morning for their Haunted Breakfast Tour. She says she has a huge surprise for the university people and she wants me there to catch their reactions."

CHAPTER 33

I ran through some morning yoga poses while Figaro cheered me on by swatting the dust in the sunlight. I'd been to three ghost tour dinners and hadn't gotten a single bite to eat. Everyone's house was way more exciting than mine if you didn't count an actual murder. *I really hope no one is counting that.*

I didn't have a lot of free time this morning because Amber had set me up to go on this cockamamie paranormal tour of the Physick Estate. *I'd better get to eat something this time.*

Aunt Ginny was listening to the radio in the kitchen while she drank her coffee.

Murder is up eight hundred percent in Cape May from just one year ago, leaving law enforcement officials scratching their heads, trying to figure out just what has changed in their sleepy little town.

Aunt Ginny glanced my way and shut the radio off.

Joanne poured this morning's coffee delivery from La Dolce Vita into a waiting carafe. She did not look at me. "Why don't you take the pastries out to the buffet, Murder Magnet?"

Sigh. I grabbed the silver tray and went through to the dining room. I paused when I saw Owen was letting Figaro sit on the table next to his plate and the door swung back and banged me on the hip.

Owen adjusted his colander. "He knows he's not allowed up here, but he likes to feel included."

I put the tray on the sideboard. "Can't he feel included from the floor?"

Owen looked at Figaro, then up at me. "He says no. The floor smells like a hundred dirty feet."

I looked at Figaro. "It does not."

Owen took a sip of his tea. "Figaro says, agree to disagree."

Why am I even entertaining this? At least no one else had come down yet.

Gladys breezed through the room and reached for the coffee carafe. "Hey, can I get a rebuttal from you for my piece?"

"A rebuttal? What did you write?"

She blew on the steaming brew. "Ya know what, no hurry. I'll get a comment from you before I send it off."

"What did you write?"

She waved me off. "It's a work in progress."

I returned to the kitchen to count the peanut butter cups. If one or six should happen to fall into my mouth, so be it. I pulled an empty plastic bag from the drawer and shook it at Aunt Ginny. "Why?"

She looked at me through her eyelashes. "Don't give me your sass this morning. I'm in no mood. Gia better hurry over here to set up those cameras or I may just go off half-cocked."

Kenny snickered. "No one wants that." He was sitting at the table in his Underdog pajamas. Not being cleared to touch the food for guests didn't keep him from eating his Froot Loops with the rest of us. He looked my way. "We have Almond Joys. Why don't you have one of those?"

Aunt Ginny took her coffee cup to the sink. "Those are for the trick or treaters."

I shook the bag again. "So were the peanut butter cups."

"Yeah, but I like those." She sailed from the kitchen to her bedroom. "Gotta work out my battle plan."

"I'll think of something to do with the Almond Joys. For now, I have to go pick up Sawyer for this breakfast. Cross your fingers for me that someone will say something incriminating and we can be done playing Nancy Drew and get back to work."

Kenny gave me a Vulcan salute. "Go forth and be nosy."

I drove to the Washington Street Mall and waited on the corner by the bookstore.

Sawyer opened the passenger door of Aunt Ginny's convertible and dropped onto the white leather seat. "Do you ever think you'll get married again?"

"That depends. Is this a proposal? 'Cause I'm gonna need coffee before I commit to anything."

"Just so you know, there'd better be coffee at this Physick Estate breakfast or I'm withdrawing the offer."

"Fair enough." I pulled away from the curb. "So, why are you asking? Are things that serious with Ben?"

"I think so. We've been living together for months, and it's been amazing. Mind you, he won't tell me anything about the investigation or who the cops suspect—which is super annoying. But last night I overheard him talking to his mother and I swear he said the Spanish word for marriage. I couldn't sleep all night. What about you and Gia? Have you talked about marriage?"

"Definitely not. We've only been dating since Easter. And we're moving at a much slower speed than you are. Between having a five-year-old, Aunt Ginny forever skirting the edge of fiasco, and the shadier members of Gia's family finding new intrusive ways to hijack our lives—it's a wonder we have time to hold hands."

"But you want to eventually get married, don't you?"

"I dunno. I'm really happy with the way things are between us right now. We're still in the best part of the relationship before you start getting on each other's nerves and fighting about laundry soap and whose turn it is to take the trash out. Besides, can you imagine being Oliva Larusso's daughter-in-law? You think I'm cursed now? She's been trying to put the evil eye on me since the first day I walked into the coffee shop."

The Physick Estate loomed ahead of us. It was a green stick-style mansion with a steeply gabled orange-tiled mansard roof and upside-down chimneys, built by Dr. Emlen Physick around the time my house was built, and he and his family members are rumored to still haunt the mansion today. I couldn't imagine sticking around to haunt Aunt Ginny's house after I died. There's got to be something better in the afterlife than that.

I pulled into a parking spot over by the tennis courts and cut the engine. It was a warm day with a rustling breeze, and I took a deep inhale of sunshine. The air was fresh with the scent of fall leaves.

Sawyer took off her fleece and threw it back on the car seat before shutting the door. "What are we here for?"

"The tour group will be attending a special ghost tour breakfast. We're spying on them. What's going on over there?"

Sawyer shielded her eyes with her hand. "It looks like a craft show. Oh, I bet this is the scarecrow weekend."

"What?"

"Scarecrow Alley." She started walking towards a grouping of canopies between the main estate and the gift shop. "Once a year, local businesses and community groups compete by entering scarecrows for judging."

We passed an Elvis scarecrow in a rhinestone-studded white suit with a red scarf tied around his neck. A little further down was a scarecrow pair that loosely looked like Snoop Dogg and our eleventh-grade English teacher. "Is that Mrs. Sandridge?"

Sawyer laughed and pointed to a sign on the ground with the number 6 on it. "It's Martha Stewart."

"I wish someone would have told me about this. I could have entered."

"What would you have made? It's supposed to reflect who you are in the community."

I shrugged. "You think they'd frown on a chalk outline around a bunch of loose hay surrounded by police tape?"

Sawyer laughed. "Your crime scene scarecrow can't be any more gruesome than that zombie over there."

I followed the direction of her hand. "Hey. Look behind the dentist scarecrow. That's Sable and Jax from the tour. What are they doing?" Jax was holding a cell phone on a long selfie stick, and they appeared to be talking to the camera.

Sawyer craned her neck. "It looks like they're making a video."

"Let's go say hello."

We took a couple of steps towards the kids and heard Jax say, ". . . laying low for obvious reasons."

Sable looked over and caught my eye. I waved. She looked as though she might faint dead away. She jabbed Jax in the side and he pulled the cell phone off the stick.

His eyes shifted from me to Sawyer. "Oh, hey. What are you doing here?"

I tried to disarm them with a smile. "We're checking out the competition. Are you here for the breakfast tour too?"

He shoved the cell phone in his cargo pocket. "Um. Yeah. Aren't we, Sable?"

She nodded with her mouth set in a flat line. "Mm-hmm."

Sawyer looked behind the kids. "Is this one your favorite?"

They both looked at her like she'd sprouted a second head. "What?"

She pointed to the scarecrow in a tattered wedding dress just behind them. "The ghost bride scarecrow. Is this one your favorite? I saw you making a video of it just before we came over to say hello."

"No, we weren't." Sable looked past us and waved madly. "Look, it's starting. We don't want to be late."

I turned to see who she was waving to. A woman dressed in a Mid-Atlantic Center for the Arts sweatshirt was consulting a clipboard. Sable ran up to her frantically waving her hands. Then the kids headed past a parked trolley into the Carriage House. The woman turned and hollered after them.

"It's not just me; that was odd, right?"

Sawyer nodded and looked again at the ghost bride scarecrow. "Definitely. Maybe that was a marriage proposal and we interrupted it?"

"I don't think so. They aren't supposed to be a couple. Besides, he wasn't talking to her. They were both talking at the phone."

"I bet they were live streaming."

"Someone at the Macomber claimed to have recognized them last night. She said she followed them. You think they're on Facebook or something?"

Sawyer pulled out her phone and started moving in the direction of coffee and breakfast. "Do you have their last names?"

"In my email." I checked messages from a few days earlier and read off the list of names.

We entered the Carriage House gift shop and checked in for the breakfast tour. We were seated in the empty tearoom, ordered coffee, and left to await the rest of the group. Sable and Jax were nowhere to be seen.

Sawyer tried searching a few things on her phone. She shook her head. "Do you have an email address for them?"

"Not with me. Can't you find them?"

"Not on Facebook."

Aunt Ginny texted me.

The cops are here. They have a warrant to search the premises.

For what?

Donut

What?

I donut

I donttttt know

I closed the text screen. "The cops are searching my house again."

"For what?"

"They're probably looking for the stevia. Sable and Jax must go by different names online." I pulled out my cell phone and started googling all the tour guests. "Here is Dr. Felicity Van Smoot on Instagram."

Sawyer leaned over to look at my screen. "That's a lot of selfies."

"That's her whole account. Selfies and food. Apparently, she's big into brunch. Everything has a poached egg on it."

Sawyer turned her phone for me to see the screen. "Eli Lush is on Twitter. I think he's using hashtags ironically. #GeniusLife. #KnowledgeisPower. #SexyMind."

I snickered. "Is there a hashtag sourpuss?"

"He has a lot to say about mind control."

"Anything about coming on this tour?"

Sawyer scanned his tweets for a moment. "He tweeted about it a week ago. Cape May Ghost Tour #ExposeTheFraud."

An ice pick of irritation stuck me right in the temple "Am I supposed to be the fraud?"

Sawyer shrugged. "I think it could be any or all of you."

The waitress brought our coffees and I cradled mine like a tiny reward for not slapping the smug off of Eli's face the next time I saw him. "Here's Verna Fox on Instagram. The past six months have been all the same pictures of food that Felicity posted, but from a different angle. It looks like before that she posted a few random pictures of everyday things. Babies, coffee, books, a cat. Wait. Look at this."

Sawyer took a sip of her coffee and leaned in.

"It's from a year ago. Verna took a picture of what I'm pretty sure is her hand entwined in a man's hand. The lighting isn't great, and it's a little out of focus, but that's the same silver ring she had on at my house."

Sawyer nudged me.

A very tall mocha-skinned diva wearing an enormous pink beehive wig and a scarlet Victorian gown was leading Felicity and Eli to our table. Verna was dragging behind them, draining all the sunshine from the room. The diva waved her hand across our table in a graceful arc displaying long golden bejeweled fingernails. "Here you go, kids. Here is the rest of your group. Now have a seat and your server will come around and take your drink orders. Oh, good heavens. Poppy? Girrrl, is that you?"

I looked into the longest fake eyelashes I've ever seen in my life. "Bebe?" I sprang to my feet and gave the statuesque drag queen a hug. "What are you doing here?"

"Honey, I'm a guide. You know how I love wearing a corset. Now I'm getting paid for it. I'm doing the eleven a.m. paranormal tour." Bebe winked at me.

"You're not gonna believe this, but I'm on your tour."

"Why are you paying for a tour on a kitsch weekend?" Bebe's eyes grew to the size of saucers. She looked around the table. "Ooooh. Somebody died."

I grabbed her hand trying to avoid her gold-painted talons and pulled her a little closer to me. "Shh. Yes. At my house this time."

She blinked and her spider lashes fluttered a breeze across my cheeks. "And you're undercover . . ."

"Yep. Again."

"Girrrl. You gotta stop findin' dead people."

"When you figure out how, you let me know."

Her lips dropped to a pout, and she hugged me again. "At least you get a free breakfast. I'll be sure to charge it to the police fund for you." She waved to the tour group. "I hope you're all hungry. After you eat, we're going to start the tour in the room where Dr. Physick made a life-size Ouija board so he could talk to ghosts. Enjoy."

I returned to my seat, and the university people's faces fell like they'd decided as one that they hated me. Sawyer passed the sugar to Verna across the table.

The young woman reached for the bowl. "Why are you giving me this?"

I glanced at Verna's hands and the silver ring she was wearing, then at my cell phone to review the picture she'd posted. "Yep."

Sawyer did the same and mumbled, "Mm-hmm." She smiled at Verna. "I thought you might need that."

The woman with the clipboard found Sable and Jax behind a lattice wall on the other side of the tearoom and migrated them to our table. Sable dropped to the seat next to mine with a long sigh.

"Hey, guys, I was going to watch your channel, but I can't find it. What's it called?"

Sable's nose scrunched like I'd asked her to eat a bug. "I don't know what you're talking about."

Sawyer waved her phone. "We just saw you making a video or something. We're going to follow you."

Sable and Jax looked at each other blankly. Jax

shrugged. "I'm sorry, ma'am. I have no idea what you're talking about."

I sighed. Sure they were being difficult on purpose. "We've been trying to look the tour members up on Facebook to send them friend requests so we can stay connected after this week."

Jax ran his hand through his beard. "Not on Facebook. Facebook's for old people."

I beg your pardon.

Sable tossed her hair in a bored way. "Yeah. If I wanted to be friends with my mom, I'd like—be friends with her in the real world."

Jax laughed. "Weird. Right?"

Sable laughed with him, and I sat back in my seat and counted the days until I could collect Social Security.

My phone buzzed and I checked the screen. It was Amber.

Where R U?

At the PE bk like you requested

omw

Brooklyn Beck breezed into the tearoom in a lovely white pantsuit. Her hair fell in a bouncy cascade down her shoulders. She spoke to Bebe and looked our way. The smile momentarily dropped from her face, and she closed her eyes. When she recovered, Bebe led her to the table, her face shining from superior health and a good night's sleep. "Good morning, everyone. Did I miss anything?"

Verna's face pinched until white lines formed around her lips and eyes. "How dare you act like everything's okay. You killed him. You couldn't be happy, so no one could be happy."

Bebe's eyes were two golf balls with golden centers. She glanced at me and took a step back.

I closed Instagram and opened my camera. I hit record on the video.

Brooklyn steeled herself. "I don't know what you're talking about. I didn't kill anyone."

Verna's eyes welled up and the dam was about to break. "He said you were dying. But you aren't sick at all, you fraud. I bet you were slowly poisoning him all along."

Bebe squealed. "Oooh, girl. No."

Brooklyn's mouth dropped open. She slapped Verna across the face. "Stop saying that!"

Verna arced her hand into a claw to retaliate, but before she could swat at Mrs. Beck, Felicity grabbed her wrist and shushed her. "Have you lost your mind? Get yourself under control!"

It would have been a fantastic explosion, but the lady with the clipboard saw the pending catastrophe and shoved Bebe towards the table to intervene.

"Oh, okay. It's like that, is it? Sure. I guess we can begin in the dining room." Bebe adjusted her gown and silver stiletto boots peeked out from under the hem. "The great Wendell Dennis, psychic medium extraordinaire, has visited the Physick Estate on numerous occasions to speak with its ghostly residents."

Sawyer rolled her eyes. "Oh, good Lord. Wendell Dennis again? How is it everywhere he goes, they end up having a ghost?"

I turned my camera off and lowered my voice to a hush. "You know what I think? I think Wendell Dennis is haunted."

Sawyer snorted.

Bebe shot a look at me, then closed her eyes with her lips puckered and bowed her head to keep from laughing.

The lady with the clipboard glanced my way and cleared her throat to a loud ahem.

Hey, we aren't the ones who were just about to slap it out over the pumpkin print tablecloth. Focus, lady.

There was the crackle of police radio at the front door, and Bebe looked over her shoulder at the arriving cops. "I'll just go check on your food."

She disappeared in a haze of hairspray and pancake syrup, and Amber entered the tearoom with Officers Simmons and Birkwell. The room went silent, and all eyes followed the nervous gaze of the woman with the clipboard.

Amber turned down her radio as she approached our table.

Verna lifted to hover over her seat and frantically scanned the room for another exit, but Felicity gripped her arm. "Stay."

Amber approached the lady with the clipboard. "Excuse the interruption. I need to speak to your paranormal tour group."

The woman examined her notes as if checking to see if police interrogation was on the schedule. "But their breakfast is just about to arrive, and they have to be up at the main house in thirty to get started."

Amber smiled politely like the woman had a choice. "It will just take a moment." She turned to the table occupants. "I thought you all would like to know, I have an update on the late Dr. Beck. The complete toxicology results are in. Dr. Beck died from a lethal amount of tetrahydrozoline hydrochloride in his bloodstream."

Sable shook her head. "What exactly is that?"

Amber ran her finger over her handcuffs. "I'm glad you asked. It's an ingredient commonly found in popular brands of eye drops. Judging from the levels found in the bloodstream, and the absorption rate, the coroner has determined that the drug could only have been administered over a three-hour time period before Simon Beck died."

The table gasped.

So much for Gia's theory that he was poisoned before he arrived.

"A team of officers have been busy this morning searching your belongings. You'll find souvenir copies of the warrant at each of your lodgings." She pulled a crime scene plastic bag out of her pocket. It held a small blue bottle of Visine.

Nobody moved.

"Eli Lush, this was found in your luggage at the Southern Mansion. I need you to come down to the station with me."

"For what? Having dry eyes?"

Officer Birkwell approached Eli while reaching for his handcuffs.

Eli tossed his head, his curls quivering in every direction. "This is preposterous. I didn't even know Simon Beck would be on the tour until after I arrived. And if I poisoned him with that Visine, why is the bottle still full?"

Officer Birkwell cuffed Eli and led him back out to Scarecrow Alley. Amber clicked on her radio. "Okay, bring her in."

Officer Consuelos entered the tearoom with a beautiful, older brunette at his side. She was stylishly dressed and impeccably made up. Her face winked that she was thirty, but her hands whispered that she was closer to fifty. She looked like a retired supermodel who had been demoted to commercials sell-ing probiotic yogurt and fiber-based snack bars. The only features to mar her otherwise flawless skin were the dark circles under her eyes.

She gave a polite nod to our table. "Hello. I'm Jennifer Beck. Simon's wife."

CHAPTER 34

All eyes turned to Brooklyn, who was locked in an apoplectic showdown with Verna. They sat as frozen sentries on either side of Jennifer Beck like beautiful, stunned gargoyles.

Amber took out a little notebook and a pen and turned to face the impostor Mrs. Beck, who had lost her earlier jaunty attitude in a recent avalanche of mortification. "Now ma'am, you told officers the other evening that you were the wife of the deceased. Do you want to change your statement, or was Simon Beck in fact a bigamist?"

Sawyer jabbed me in the side and I grabbed my cell phone to hit record.

Brooklyn tried to melt into her chair. "It was Simon's idea. He said bed and breakfast owners were uptight little old ladies and we needed to pretend to be married or we couldn't reserve the room. He said it was just a little role-play. I should have told the police right away, but I was so shaken up by what happened, and Poppy had already told that scary little policeman that I was Mrs. Beck."

Hey! Don't blame me.

"Then I was too afraid to correct my statement because I didn't want you to think I was lying about killing him too."

Jennifer Beck picked up a menu and gave it a quick browse. "I wonder how many women have pretended to be Mrs. Beck at this point."

Verna's voice was dangerously serene as she looked from Jennifer Beck to Brooklyn. "You self-righteous home-wrecker. Now you'll get what you deserve."

Felicity threw her head back and laughed. "Oh, that is rich. Simon, you've done it again."

Sable and Jax silently pushed their chairs away from the table in an attempt to excuse themselves, but Amber snapped her fingers and pointed for them to sit back down—which they obeyed immediately.

Bebe was hovering by the table and holding a coffeepot. Sawyer made eye contact and held up two fingers. Bebe sidled over and we lifted our empty cups without breaking focus from the nuclear meltdown across the table. Bebe took a step back and hovered in case we needed emergency refills.

Amber had years of playing a dumb blonde in high school. She reprised her role for an encore performance this morning in the Carriage House Tearoom. "So, wait, you lied to us about being his wife even though it's a crime to lie to the police?"

"I didn't know it was a crime."

"You told the officer who took your ID that you hadn't updated your license since the wedding. Why didn't you just come clean then?"

Brooklyn bit her bottom lip and her eyes turned glassy. "I panicked, okay."

"You're a suspect in a murder investigation, but figured you should maintain your identity cover story so you wouldn't be judged for adultery?"

"It was a stupid mistake." Brooklyn's eyes shifted to Jennifer Beck, who stood a few feet away gripping a Chanel bag like body armor. "But I didn't know he was married. Really. He told me his wife died recently from some blood disease."

Bebe muttered, "Mm-hmm."

Felicity shook her head at Jennifer. She chuckled to herself and stared at the ceiling. "Well, you finally died, I see. That took a lot longer than anyone expected."

Jennifer puffed out a bitter breath of air and looked longingly at my coffee cup. She asked Bebe, "Can I get some of that?"

"Here you go, honey." Bebe turned over a coffee cup in front of Eli's abandoned place setting, filled the cup with the last drops of coffee, and took a silent step back. Still holding on to the empty coffeepot in case anyone wanted to inspect it.

Verna skyrocketed through a dozen different emotions, paused for a moment on crazed laughter, then finally settled on loud tears.

Amber made some notes in her flip-book. "Brooklyn, where did you meet Prince Charming?"

Brooklyn reached for a glass of water and Verna spitefully pushed it further out of her reach.

"We met at the gym. I'm a personal trainer. Everything else I told you was the truth. Simon said his blood pressure was high and he was borderline diabetic. So, I suggested some diet modifications and an exercise routine. We only recently started dating." She turned pleading eyes to Jennifer and covered her heart with her hand. "I'm so sorry. I really believed that he was a widower. I swear to you, I would never, ever, in a million years have ever gone out with a married man."

Bebe bobbed her head at Brooklyn and tsked. "Dial it back, girl. You don't wanna stink of desperation."

Verna's face flushed. She glared at the erstwhile Mrs. Beck. "Don't try to act like Miss Innocent. This poor woman has been through enough without your excuses and lies."

Jennifer picked up her coffee and took the empty seat next to Verna. She grabbed two Splendas and shook the packets back and forth before ripping them open. She stirred the sweetener into her coffee, then blew on it and calmly looked around the table. "Simon was a serial cheater. You weren't the first." She looked from Brooklyn to Verna. "Or the second. Usually a student. Sometimes a colleague." She glanced at Felicity.

Amber flipped her notebook closed. "I'll leave you ladies to your coffee and discussion. Oh look, your Benedicts are here."

A waitress placed a tray of eggs Benedict and fruit salad on a nearby stand. She tried to serve, but no one at the table moved to accept the offered plate except Sawyer, who reached for the first one.

"Mmm-mm. Nothing tastes better with hollandaise than a clean conscience."

Bebe snapped her fingers. "I know that's right."

The women sniped at each other while Jennifer Beck drank her coffee. Then after a few minutes my phone buzzed. It was Amber:

Meet me out back.

I excused myself and took a detour out the back through the garden. Amber was waiting next to a cluster of cornstalks and red mums tied up at the corner of the tent. "That was quite an explosive announcement you made in there. Brooklyn looks like she'd rather be arrested than sit in there next to the real Mrs. Beck."

Amber grinned slightly. "I'm more interested in Verna Fox. How did she react to the wife?"

"Stunned. Defeated. She seemed angrier at Brooklyn for being with him in Cape May than at the wife for being home alone."

Amber nodded. "So, what do you think?"

"I would bet my Barbie Dream House that Verna was in love with Simon Beck and thought he was going to leave his wife for her. She had some lofty expectations about their life together until something happened about six months ago. That seems to be when things went south with Simon, and she started working with Felicity."

Amber checked her notes. "That matches what I have. Do you think she killed Simon?"

"I thought you just arrested Eli Lush for killing Simon."

"We're only holding him for questioning. It's still an active investigation and we need to follow every lead while the clock is ticking. So . . . Verna?"

"I just don't think so. She's truly shattered about his death. And it came as a complete shock."

Amber wrote that down in her notebook. "What about Jackson Thomas and Sable Brackenhoff?"

"Sawyer and I are still trying to figure them out. I think they're some kind of Internet celebrities, but they're not on any social media that we can find. I know they're not as innocent and clueless as they seem."

Amber reached into a cargo pocket on her thigh and pulled out another evidence bag. "Speaking of innocent and clueless. How well do you trust your housekeeper?" She let the bag unfurl from her grip. It was the missing bottle of stevia.

I felt my stomach lurch. "Why are you asking about Kenny? That belongs to Brooklyn . . . whatever her last name is."

"We found this buried in that tree in your dining room during yesterday's search. Not one person we interviewed mentioned seeing someone put anything in that pot."

My voice was rising. "That doesn't mean it was Kenny. Don't you have any concrete evidence like DNA or fingerprints?"

"Okay, calm down, CSI. The bottle's been wiped clean of prints. I'm on my way to the lab to have it tested for residue of tetrahydrozoline. If we find out this was the murder weapon, it won't look good for him. He fled the scene of the crime. He tried to run from the chief when he came to question him. He had hours of opportunity to dispose of the evidence after the tour group was gone. And he attended Staunton University when Simon Beck was teaching there. That's not a coincidence."

"He wasn't in Simon's class."

"He didn't graduate from Simon's class. That's not the same thing."

CHAPTER 35

"That was the best brunch I've ever had." Sawyer checked her makeup in a little mirror on the passenger side visor. "Even if the house was super creepy. Who paints a Ouija board on their floor?"

"That was just asking for trouble."

"And what was up with that demonic teacup for reading tea leaves?"

"I bet that bogus psychic you made me see didn't have one of those."

"I bet Wendell Dennis brought it as a hostess gift."

"I wish I'd had my video on when Verna threw her mimosa in Brooklyn's face."

Sawyer showed me her cell phone. "I got a picture when Bebe told her it was a waste of champagne."

"Send Aunt Ginny a copy of that. She'll never forgive me if one of the Biddies shows it to her first."

I turned down Jackson to go around the block and park behind Mia Famiglia. The most important things I'd learned from this morning's ghost tour brunch was that Sable and Jax were up to something and no one could hold a candle to Joanne's crab Benedict. "You know I only have a few days left with Joanne working for me."

"What are you gonna do when she's gone?"

"We're definitely not going to have more of those beautiful little cupcakes she makes. I don't have hours to spend decorating them. I'd planned on Kenny doing more of the cooking. But something's going on with him and I'm not sure he'll still be with us next month either."

"You don't really think he killed Simon Beck, do you?"

"No. Maybe. I hope not. I like Kenny, but he's keeping something from me, and that makes me very nervous. Plus, now he's on Amber's radar. I'm starting to wonder if everyone close to me will be a suspect in a murder at one time or another."

"He did go to the university that Simon taught at."

"Yeah, but that was years ago. And a different area of study. Kenny majored in drama."

"He still does."

I parked behind Sawyer's bookstore. The Italian restaurant was just next door. "You've been awesome this past week. How can I say thank you for working the dinner tours with Joanne?"

"You know I'd do anything for you."

"Same."

"And I want some of those vanilla extreme macarons."

"You got it."

"And for you to convince Joanne to make my wedding cake if the day ever comes."

We got out of the car, and I headed towards the back door of Momma's restaurant. "Do I look like

Hermione Granger to you? I can't even make Joanne stop calling me names. If she suspects I want her to do something she'll pitch a fit and double down. She's been complaining about working for me all summer."

Sawyer had her hand on the back door to Through the Looking Glass. She gave me a funny look. "You don't see it?"

"See what?"

"She admires you."

I started to laugh.

"No, I'm serious. There's something there."

"Oh no there isn't."

Sawyer made a face. "I think she wants to impress you, so you'll accept her."

"Accept her how?"

Sawyer shrugged. "I dunno. She always was drawn to confident people."

"Then I'm the last person she'd be interested in."

"Just think about it."

I stuck my tongue out at Sawyer and went into Mia Famiglia. Marco, Esteban, and Frankie had their hands full of pasta, prepping for an event tonight. They all shouted, "*Buona sera!*" as I entered the steamy kitchen. I returned the greeting and went straight for my apron and punch list of today's baking needs.

The paranormal tour of the Physick Estate sucked away a lot of my time, so I'd have to work quickly to be caught up for the ghost tour at the Inn tonight.

The back door opened, and Joanne breezed into the kitchen in red sunglasses and a white silk scarf. She hailed a hearty, "*Buona sera!*" like she was Audrey Hepburn in freakin' *Roman Holiday*. Then she saw me and sighed. "Hey, Moron."

Sawyer is on crack if she thinks Joanne wants us to be friends.

Joanne took off her sunglasses and scarf and wrapped an apron around her Eat Fresh T-shirt. "What do you need first?"

"Can you form the ciabatta rolls while I make the manicotti? We have a double order for an event tonight."

Joanne nodded and took out the tray of risen dough. "What about dessert?"

I looked at the line of chefs. "Marco?"

"*Si?*"

"*Dolce?*"

He frowned. "Oh. We is outta every-ting. Our regulars, dey like to try da new specials. It been very busy."

My heart sank and passed my blood pressure on the way down. I looked at Joanne forming little square pillows as fast as she could.

She quirked an eyebrow. "There's no time to bake something elaborate. I have ten people coming for dinner and I still have to make the chocolate orange mousse. It's going to have to be tiramisu."

I stuffed my pasta tubes like a factory worker on an assembly line. "I just wish there was time to make a cassata or at least gelato."

"You should have started those hours ago."

I bet they would taste good mixed together. I've never had a cassata gelato. An idea shot through my head that excited me and now I wanted to do it more than anything else. "What about a *semifreddo?*"

Joanne paused midpat over her ciabatta. "It is very Italian."

"I haven't made one in years."

"It's like riding a bike. What kind are you thinking? Not something stupid like pumpkin?"

"Eww. No. What about honey almond with roasted cherries?"

Joanne's eyes dilated and she tried to look disinterested. "I could see that. Maybe with some chopped almond toffee sprinkled over the top."

We both started moving at our tasks a little faster so we could get to the *semifreddo*. Once Joanne finished forming the ciabattas and setting them in the proofing oven, she took over layering one of the lasagnas. Unlike with Gia and virtually everyone else, I didn't have to tell her what to do. She knew exactly what amounts to use.

By the time Joanne had the lasagnas in the oven, I had all the ingredients for a large batch of *semifreddo* set out.

Joanne examined the workbench, then disappeared to the storage room. She came back with a bread pan and set it before me. "We might as well make one for our house while we're at it. It will be a good backup for when you inevitably ruin something."

Our house. I glanced at Joanne. "Good idea." I thought I saw the barest hint of a smile arrive and disappear in the beat of a bat's wings.

We worked side by side—whipping cream and chopping fruit while the kitchen filled with the aroma of tomato sauce, basil, and melted cheese. I passed Joanne half the chopped almonds and she handed me my half of the roasted cherries. The hostess came in at one point and left us both cappuccinos. Saying thank you was the only time Joanne and I spoke. We filled the pans with the creamy Italian ice cream and set them in the blast chiller to freeze.

I cracked the oven to check the lasagna when a breeze filled the room as the back door flew open and banged against the wall. A string of Italian curses peppered off of my back, and I knew before turning around that the gates of Hell were missing a sentry.

Gia's mother was in a wheelchair being pushed by her sour lieutenant, Teresa. Teresa's husband, Angelo, shuffled meekly behind them. He wiggled a finger in greeting.

Marco's eyes grew as big as walnuts. He whipped out his cell phone and tapped furiously.

Oliva Larusso sent another venomous sounding tirade in my direction, and I reached over and turned off the oven. "Hello, ma'am. How are you feeling?"

Joanne came out of the walk-in holding a stick of butter, and Momma started yelling and shaking her fist at her. Marco came over and waved his hands in front of Chef Oliva in a panic. "No no no no no. Poppy, she is helping. She is very good chef."

Teresa grinned, and the deeper her grin stretched, the more malevolent her eyes became. "You are so busted. I checked with the paper. There is no story."

Gia burst through the door from the dining room and jumped between his mother and me.

Momma spewed another onslaught and Teresa was ever so helpful to translate for her.

"Momma wants to know why this tramp is in her kitchen."

Gia faced his mother. "Don't you dare call the woman I love a tramp." He continued from there speaking in Italian until I put my hand on his arm.

The time had come for me to fight this battle head-on. I stepped forward so I was even with Gia and addressed his mother one-on-one. "I've been helping in your kitchen while you recover from your accident, Mrs. Larusso."

Teresa translated what Oliva didn't understand. The old woman pounded her fist against the workbench and yelled at Marco.

"Momma says she never gave you permission to hire this woman, and you don't have permission to change the menu based on years of her family recipes."

Marco tried to appease his boss by taking tiny steps and bowing. "Everyone love da new *dolce*. People even ordering dessert after lunch and dey never do dat before. We very busy."

Momma grabbed the wooden spoon from the counter and threw it at Marco. Marco ducked and the spoon ricocheted off the herbs in the windowsill.

I tried to remain calm. Partly because Joanne was white as a sheet and looked like she might need a defibrillator, and partly because I just didn't want her taking her fury out on the chefs. "Mrs. Larusso, I did the best I could. We've been working very hard to keep business steady so you could pay your staff through to the new year."

Angelo quietly reached over to the counter for a roasted cherry on the cutting board.

Teresa slapped his hand.

Momma glared at me and pointed in my face. She spoke slowly like she was casting a spell instead of firing off an insult.

Gia started to laugh.

"What is it?"

"She's mad because a food blogger came in and said the new artichoke chicken manicotti was the best thing to be added to the menu in a decade."

I glowed with pride. "Oh wow. That's exciting, isn't it?"

Momma understood me enough, and her rage turned up to 11.

Teresa yelled, "Get out! Get out now! She says you are never allowed in her kitchen again."

Joanne looked from me to Oliva back to me. She edged towards the blast freezer and retrieved our *semifreddo* and wrapped it in her scarf. Then she crept towards the back door and waited.

I'd had enough. My relationship with Gia wasn't going to be threatened by this angry little woman, so why did I care what she thought of me? I took my apron off and draped it over the counter. "I'll gladly leave. Because you are a miserable, bitter old woman who doesn't deserve one ounce of the generosity that I've shown you this past week. I was only here because of my love for Gia and Henry. But as far as I'm concerned, you're on your own. I hope Teresa knows how to make chicken manicotti, because I don't give my recipes to anyone who isn't family."

Gia was interpreting for me, and Momma's face was as red as the cherry tomatoes on the caprese. Broken hip or not, I'd been holding my tongue for a year. "I'm going to make a wonderful life with your son. We're going to be very happy together and you have absolutely no say in that. You don't have to love me. You don't have to like me. But you're not gonna bully me. Because I don't give a flying fig about what you think, lady. I'm here to stay. Also, I tweaked the recipe for your tiramisu. Yours was a little bland."

Joanne flung the door open, and I marched through it with her on my heels. Behind us we heard Oliva and Teresa screaming. I didn't know who they were screaming at, but they were someone else's problem now. I reached for the handle on the Corvette, and someone grabbed me from behind.

Gia spun me around and kissed me until my knees started to buckle. "You were amazing back there, my love." Then he whispered something in my ear that I swear I will never tell another living soul, but if Joanne hadn't been standing on the other side of the car I would definitely not have been going home with her.

CHAPTER 36

I floated up the front steps a mixture of fury and passion and furious that my passion had nowhere to go. Aunt Ginny raced to the foyer, dressed in black slacks and a black sweater. She had her hair tucked into a black beret. "What's going on? Gia got a text and ran out of here like the coffee shop was on fire. He was just about to show me how to work the security cameras. I'm all dressed to do cyber recon."

Joanne let the screen door smack against the frame behind her. "The mother showed up."

Aunt Ginny paled. She glanced at me. "Oh no. Do you need chocolate or ice cream?"

I shrugged. "I'm fine."

Aunt Ginny slid her eyes from me to Joanne.

"Buttface here told the old witch where she could go."

Is that my imagination or does Joanne sound slightly complimentary? Minus the Buttface.

Aunt Ginny scanned me from head to toe. She looked back at Joanne and jabbed her thumb in my direction. "This one here?"

"It's not a big deal. I'm just tired of her being rude to me. She's not my mother. Mean old bag."

Joanne snickered, then tried to cover it by clearing her throat. "We made *semifreddo* for dessert tonight. Now we need to figure out everything else. Too bad the old lady and Sad Sack couldn't have been a couple hours later. I would have had a stuffed pork roast and potatoes ready."

"Why don't we get the *semifreddo* in the freezer and we can regroup at the coffee shop to make dinner?"

Aunt Ginny took the *semifreddo* and offered some of her usual customary advice. "Hey, you're only banned from making food here to serve to guests. You can go right in there and make that pork roast for my dinner. There's no law against that."

We started down the hall, but a metallic little *wheek wheek* coughed in front of the house. Aunt Ginny plastered herself against the screen. "What is that? It looks like a bear and a meercat riding a tiny motorcycle."

She was almost right. It was two men riding a white scooter. The driver's Afro was poking out from under a white helmet with a red stripe running down the middle of it. The rider sitting behind was wearing a chef coat and goggles. He held up two silver aluminum pans.

"It's Marco and Frankie."

Joanne and I crossed the yard to greet them.

Frankie unstrapped the helmet from under his chin and more Afro pouffed free. "There she is. The Red Devil with a wicked left hook. How you doin', champ? We wanted to applaud, but Chef Oliva would can every last one of us without thinking twice, and there aren't many jobs for cooks this time of year."

Marco handed us each a warm pan. "*Si.* And Esteban, he send da money home to da family. Dey counting on him, you know?"

I was overwhelmed by their support. "Oh, guys. It means so much that you would come here to encourage me."

Marco clapped. "You a chef. We gotta stick together, no?"

Frankie grinned. "Besides, you'll probably own Mia Famiglia one day. Gia gets everything when the old lady kicks it."

My heart caught in my throat. *What? Is that what everyone thinks? That I'm after Gia to get the restaurant and the coffee shop?* My voice sounded a little weak as I said, "I'm sure that's not true. He has a lot of brothers and sisters." *Not to mention the old lady will cut him out of the will the moment he says,* I do.

Marco laughed. "Sure sure sure. But dey got da houses. Gia, he live in apartment because he get the restaurants. He da smart one."

I didn't know what to say to that. I only wanted Gia for Gia. And Henry, my sweet Baboo.

Joanne pressed ahead, giving me time to regroup. She held up her aluminum pan. "So, what is this?"

"We bring you da Chicken Marsala for twelve peoples." He tapped the pan in my hands. "And dis da whipped potato. We let the party tonight fill up on da bread. Dey never notice. You jus' need da salad and you good to go."

Frankie reached into a saddlebag on the side and pulled out a paper bag of rolls. "Oh yeah. And don't forget your ciabatta. You gonna want to take them outta that bag quick like 'cause they're hot."

I reached out and took the rolls, tears threatening to spill and my voice hovering in my throat.

Frankie snapped on his helmet. "We gotta hit it, ladies. Esteban's by himself."

Joanne took one look at me and raised her hand to the guys. "She would say thank you if she could speak. Let us know if you ever need anything."

They did a U-turn in the street and puttered away with a *wheek wheek.*

"Come on, Moron. If you're done being a pathetic crybaby, I need to get this in the kitchen."

We'd no sooner crossed the threshold when a police cruiser pulled into the driveway. Aunt Ginny took the pan from me and said she'd put it away.

"Okay, thank you." *Wait a minute.* "Do not eat it! It's for tonight's ghost tour."

Aunt Ginny gave me a muffled sounding, "Mm-hmm."

Amber got out of the cruiser and opened the back door. Jennifer Beck climbed out clutching her Coach bag and a pink suitcase.

Oh no.

Amber caught my eye and her expression said, *Buckle up, because this is happening.*

I returned a look that said, *No way! Absolutely not. Just turn right back around and take her to The Queen Victoria.*

Amber's eyebrows locked down, and she sent me a piercing look. *I need you to get on board with this.*

You can bite me!

Jennifer Beck took a step towards the house, oblivious to our silent argument. "Wow. It's so quiet here."

I took a breath and stepped onto the porch. "Hello again. Have you recovered from brunch?"

She smiled. "Not the worst brunch I've ever attended. I could have done without the histrionics, but the fried potatoes were good."

Amber gave me a wide smile for Jennifer's benefit. "Mrs. Beck will be staying in town until Kat can release her husband's body. I told her you had rooms available."

I tried to keep my voice light. "Of course. I have just one room available. I'm surprised Sergeant Fenton was aware of that."

Amber matched my tone. "I remember you telling me the other night when I was here that you had four sets of guests. And I know that you have five rooms."

Mrs. Beck looked back and forth between us. "Your bed and breakfast is lovely. I can't wait to see our room." On cue, a giant rat popped its head out of the Coach bag and looked around.

My eyes slid in Amber's direction. She grinned wider until I was afraid her tightly wound bun would pop off the top of her head and roll down the sidewalk.

Jennifer petted the rat. "You take dogs, right?"

I'm gonna need to see proof that this is a dog. "Of course. Let's go get you settled."

I took the pink suitcase from Jennifer and led her into the house while tossing a glare over my shoulder to Amber. She gave me a tinkling wave of her fingers as she climbed back into the squad car.

"The only room I have available right now is the Scarlet Peacock. It's one of the tower rooms with a beautiful sitting area. The private bathroom is in the hall, but the room has a gorgeous antique Louis the Sixteenth armoire that I picked up over the summer."

"It sounds perfect." Jennifer snapped a pink leash

on a little rhinestone collar and placed the animal on the floor in the library. "This is my baby, Princess. I take her everywhere."

Princess was a bug-eyed Chihuahua with a one-tooth underbite. She immediately started to shake, vibrating herself in an arc.

Figaro stuck his head out from under the couch. He climbed free and took a long look at Princess. Then he hissed, fell over, sprang back up, and hissed again. Owen Rodney came flying down the stairs. "What's the matter?"

How badly could this possibly go? "Dr. Rodney, we have a new guest."

Owen pulled at his bow tie. "Oh dear. Figaro is most disturbed. That rhinestone collar is triggering him. And this little dog is desperate to take a tinkle."

I cast a nervous glance to Jennifer and a tittering laugh escaped my throat. "Owen is a pet psychic."

If Jennifer was offended, she didn't let on. "A pet psychic. How fascinating."

Princess squatted and took her tinkle on Aunt Ginny's antique parquet floor.

Figaro jumped to the top of the desk and glowered at the little Chihuahua in a death threat.

Jennifer dug through her Coach bag and pulled out a pack of baby wipes. "Princess, no! I am so sorry. I should have listened to Dr. Rodney."

Dr. Rodney reached out a hand. "Call me Owen." He shot a look at Figaro. "I am not."

Jennifer shook his hand, then cleaned up the little puddle.

Owen cleared his throat. "I'll just go read my book in the sitting room. The light's better in there." He looked at Jennifer again. "And Princess is very embarrassed."

I don't know how you'd ever tell that. Princess looked to me like she'd been hit in the head with a badminton racket. One of her ears looked like someone had taken a bite of it, her tongue stuck out the side of her mouth, and her bigger eye was twitching.

Jennifer stood upright and looked around.

Owen called from the other room, "Figaro says the trash is outside by the squirrel bait!"

I tsked at Figaro. Realized what I had done, and tsked at myself. "There's a wastebasket by the desk there."

She threw the wipe away, then asked for the powder room. I told her it was just down the hall, and she handed me the end of the pink leash. "I'll be just a moment."

I looked down at the shivering dog. One of its eyes looked in my general direction.

Owen poked his head back into the room. "I feel I should warn you that Figaro is planning an attack."

He'd better not be. "I don't think Fig would hurt Princess."

Owen shook his head. "It's not Princess he's planning against."

I sent another tsk Figaro's way. He swatted a little bell on the desk, and it fell to the floor.

Jennifer came back in the room and took the leash from me. "Thank you."

"Would you like to go up to your room now?"

"Actually, would you mind showing me . . ." The weight of her unspoken request hung in the air between us.

"You want to see where . . ."

She nodded. "It's why I requested to stay with you. Simon and I were separated, but I still loved him."

I took her through the sitting room to the dining

room. "We were in here having dinner. He was sitting at the head of the table just there."

She pulled out the chair where Sable had been sitting that night and sat down. Princess sprang up to her lap and shook herself into a ball. "You're probably wondering why I didn't leave him sooner."

I took the chair across from her where Brooklyn had been sitting. "It's none of my business."

Owen called out from the sitting room, "Figaro wants me to mention that that has never stopped you before!"

"Figaro needs to mind his business. It's almost time for him to eat and I'd hate for him to have to settle for the dry kibble."

The piano hit a sour chord like a fourteen-pound feline just flopped on the keys.

Princess stuck her head up and yipped, then curled back down again.

Jennifer ran her hand over the dog's bony head. "Simon cheated on me constantly. He's what they call a sex addict. I think that's a load of—"

Another sour chord struck on the piano and Owen laughed.

"Anyway," Jennifer continued. "He had one affair after another. I was always getting calls at home with no one on the other end of the phone. But then he'd come home to me, and he'd be so sweet and so contrite—we'd try to make it work. A few months ago, someone sent me a bouquet of dead roses with a card that said, 'Die already and let him move on.' That was it. That was all I could take. The next day I filed for divorce."

"I can't believe you put up with it as long as you did."

"Have you ever been married?"

"Up until a year and a half ago."

"Did he ever cheat on you?"

"No. Never."

"Then you don't know how soul crushing it is. No matter how many times he tells you it isn't you, you still believe that somehow, it's your fault. If you had been a better wife, prettier, younger, thinner. Maybe he wouldn't have gone looking for something else."

"My best friend would know exactly how you feel. Her ex-husband is a so-called sex addict too. She was the best thing that ever happened to him, but he was never content. He always had to see what was under the next skirt."

Jennifer chuckled. "I should have known better. Simon wasn't married when we met, but he was my professor. He pursued me with a lot of passion."

"You were a student in his class when you met?"

She grinned ruefully. "Paranormal Studies One-Oh-One. He wasn't that much older than me. He was a new professor on the tenure track."

"It sounds pretty easy to make enemies in academia. Is there anyone you can think of who would have wanted Simon dead?"

"Sure. The women behind the affairs he ended. Some of them had jilted boyfriends. Some had angry fathers. The faculty at the university had to forbid student-teacher relationships because he was involved in two sexual harassment claims with a third on the horizon. But to be honest, I always thought those women were just being spiteful. Harassment wasn't Simon's way. He was more the catch and release type."

Harper came around the corner into the dining room. "Hey, Poppy. I think we're going to move over to work at the Macomber tonight. Oh, sorry. Hello."

"Harper Reed, this is Jennifer Beck. Simon's real wife."

Harper's face remained perfectly passive. "His what?"

"Brooklyn wasn't really Simon's wife. They were having an affair. Jennifer is his wife."

Jennifer gave Harper a rueful grin. "If I had a dime for every time I was introduced as Simon's *real* wife these stones on Princess's collar wouldn't be made of cubic zirconia."

Harper nodded slowly. "Alright. I see you. Will you excuse me for a moment?"

She tore off around the corner and thudded up the steps. Less than a minute later, a herd of buffalo ran back down the steps, and all four Paranormal Pathfinders members rounded the dining room to get a look at Jennifer.

Paisley stared openmouthed. She pushed her glasses back. "Another one?"

Jennifer smiled. "The only one, actually."

Ritchie was the first to put his hand out. "Ritchie Grubb. Nice to meet you, Mrs. Beck."

Clark reached out and grabbed my elbow. "Forget what Harper said. We'll be investigating here tonight. I think the chances of Simon making an appearance just increased exponentially."

Figaro tore through the room and slid down the table, his orange eyes glowing with mischief. He rose up tall on his back feet and swatted at me twice with powder puff paws. Then he ran in place with his ears pinned flat for a couple seconds trying to get traction before flying off the table and pushing his way into the kitchen.

Owen called out from the sitting room, "I tried to warn you!"

CHAPTER 37

"I don't know what the heck that was all about, mister. But you'd better behave yourself while I'm on Linda's ghost tour."

Figaro swished his tail and knocked my row of perfume bottles over.

I finished fastening my earring and set the bottles upright. "I know you did that on purpose. If you're frustrated about something, why don't you go talk to Owen. Just don't tell him it's my fault. I don't need a pet psychic judging me." *What I do need is a psychiatrist, because I've clearly lost my mind. Owen is obviously just a lonely cat person.*

A tiny yip sounded downstairs and Figaro's ears flattened.

"You know I can't help that. We have to take in pets to justify having your cat hair flying about."

He jumped down from the dresser and disappeared under the bed. He came back out with a charm bracelet.

"What do you have there?" I looked under the bed and found a stash of items the ghost had moved.

"Fig, if you have a stevia bottle full of poison under here you're in big trouble."

Fig turned his back to me.

Silent treatment, huh. Let's see how committed you are to that. "You want a treat?"

He gave me that wide-eyed look that said, *Don't toy with my emotions, woman. There'd better be a snack in your hand.*

"Come on. I've gotta talk to Kenny a sec; then I'll fill your catnip toy before I go."

Figaro jumped off the dresser and followed me down the hall where I tapped on Kenny's door.

"Entrez vous."

I opened the door to Kenny's apartment. It was a lot like mine in that it had walls and a bed. That was where the comparison ended. I was over the Monarch Suite and part of the Adonis with a mahogany sleigh bed and a circular tower sitting room with a white leather Chesterfield sofa and an antique French writing desk.

Kenny was over the Purple Emperor and had a giant black-and-white poster of Jayne Mansfield in a bikini, and a vintage Barbie collection set up in a diorama of *Valley of the Dolls* complete with a tiny bowl of Tic Tacs.

Kenny was raking product through his hair with his fingers to make it stick up like he'd just gotten out of bed. "You look nice. Is that a new dress? Blue is your color."

"Thank you. I'm going to the Inn tonight with Gia. Linda will probably have us working the front desk as punishment for ruining that first tour."

He wiped his hands on a white towel and grabbed his tuxedo jacket off the black satin comforter on his bed. "We're the ones who should be mad. She sent over a homicidal maniac who killed someone at our house."

I brushed the cat hair off his lapel and tied his bow tie into a sharp knot. "You have a good point there. I'll remember that if she gives me any grief. Are you all set for tonight's performance of the anguished Siobhan?"

"Yeah. I'm thinking about adding that Siobhan made contact last spring. Elaine Grabstein's blog says she talked to her when she was here."

I wonder if Elaine Grabstein is related to Wendell Dennis.

Kenny brushed his hands down his sleeves. "I just wish I could serve dinner. Not like Joanne deserves the help, but I hate seeing her boss Sawyer around. Kim will never be back after the way she made her run back and forth hawking those crab puffs. And Aunt Ginny was . . ." He tipped his chin and lowered his voice to match. "Well . . . You know."

"Her usual queen-of-the-castle self?"

Kenny snickered and gave me a tiny nod.

"I just wanted to let you know before I leave that Simon Beck's wife has arrived. His real wife."

Kenny's eyes bugged out. "The other one's not his real wife? Oh, do tell."

I adjusted my hair in the reflection of his backstage light-up vanity mirror. "They were just having an affair. It was a cover story to avoid gossip and judgment from old ladies on the tour."

Kenny gave me a pointed look and fluttered his orange eyelashes. "Well, that worked beautifully."

"Anyway, Jennifer Beck is staying in the Swallowtail. I'm letting you know so it doesn't come as a shock if you run into her in the hall. I'd hate for you to sprain your tennis elbow defending me again."

"Is she another twenty-year-old?"

"No. This one looks more like Cindy Crawford in retirement. She may have some questions for you."

"Why me?"

"Because you went to Staunton University, where Simon Beck taught."

"That was years ago. Besides, I was a theater major. I had nothing to do with paranormal studies." He sat on the edge of his bed and grabbed a silver throw pillow. "I'd never met Simon Beck before the other night. Why would I kill him?"

"Calm down. I just think she might want to ask you how the dinner tour went last Sunday."

He hugged the pillow to his chest and muttered under his breath, "You know how it went. Someone murdered him."

"What are you so nervous about? Is there something you need to tell me? Preferably before I'm under oath."

"No. Everything's fine."

I considered telling him about Amber finding the stevia bottle to see if he'd confide in me, but he clamped his lips down like Beaker waiting for an explosion and wouldn't give me so much as a *meep*. "Alright. I haven't forgotten that you owe me an explanation. I'll be home later to talk."

I went down the spiral stairs to the kitchen. Figaro tried to trip me three times. I filled his ratty little chicken toy and told him to chill out. Joanne and Sawyer were busy warming the hors d'oeuvres from last night, and Aunt Ginny was sitting at the table with her face glued to the laptop. "What are you looking at?"

Her eyes gleamed in a way that made me very nervous. "I'ma catch me a prankster."

"Alright, well. Have fun with that." The doorbell rang and I checked the time. "I hope that's Gia. Otherwise, tonight's tour is very early."

Aunt Ginny's voice trilled, "It's not Gi-a."

I opened the heavy front door to find the wrong gorgeous Italian staring back at me.

Oh no. Maybe I did ruin things between us when I told off his mother. "Karla? Where's Gia? Did something happen?"

"You caused a firestorm this afternoon that he's still bragging about. But he also has to deal with the restaurant and decide what to do now that Momma's being a pill. So, he sent me to go with you."

"Oh, okay."

"Just so you know, if you're supposed to do any manual labor, you're on your own. I don't owe the cops anything and I just had my nails done." She fanned her fingers and all of her long nails were painted to look like black cats with different expressions on their faces. Her ring fingers had acrylic whiskers sticking out both sides.

"Got it." I started to walk down the sidewalk.

"What are you doing?"

"We're going to the Inn."

"I'm not walking. In these shoes?"

"But it's like a half a block."

Karla turned her foot to the side to show off four-inch platform stilettos.

I went back inside and grabbed the keys to Bessie. We drove over to the Inn, which seemed ridiculous, and I parked in the lot across the street. "If I had a stretch limo, the back end would still be parked at my house right now."

Karla tossed her long dark hair. "If you had a

stretch limo I would have insisted you pick me up at my house instead of having Daniela drop me off like a prom date who's your cousin."

A few battery-operated jack-o'-lanterns had been added to the front steps of the Inn since I was here last Saturday. The wind rolled off the ocean and whipped my dress up around my neck. I was yanking it back down when Karla grabbed onto me to keep from blowing into the house next door. We made it inside the lobby and Karla ran to the bathroom to fix her hair before she was seen by any single attractive men.

Moving pretty good in those spiked heels now.

"Hunny, you made it." Linda came out from behind the front desk and grabbed my hand. She was wearing purple slacks and a purple silk blouse tied in a bow at the neck. "We have had so many calls about the dinner at your house since it hit the eleven o'clock news. Everyone wants a ticket. We may make the ghost tour dinner a permanent event."

"Not at my house we won't."

Her eyelashes fluttered and tiny flecks of purple glitter fell to her cheeks. "Why not? You're making a very nice profit."

"For one thing, I've been to every location on this tour, and they all have restaurants. They serve dinner whether there is a tour or not."

Linda rolled her eyes to the side. "That's true. Did I not mention that before?"

"You did not."

She waved her hand. "Well, we can talk about that later. Why don't you come in and relax? Have a drink. On me."

Karla reappeared by my side having touched up everything that could be reapplied. "Where's the bar?"

Linda pulled me closer. "Who's this?"

"This is my plus-one for tonight. Gia's sister Karla."

Linda gave Karla a scan and lowered her voice again. "Don't let her be a bridesmaid."

"I'm not engaged."

Linda took Karla by the elbow. "Right this way. We have a delicious new cocktail everyone is raving about called a Ghost Tour. It's purple."

You can't keep anything a secret in Cape May.

The first thing I spotted when we approached the bar was a very tipsy Felicity. She waved me over, giggling. "I cannot believe she wasn't his wife."

Verna and Eli were on either side of the professor. A few regulars were spaced around the bar, enjoying the happy hour specials. Eli took one look at Karla and a maraschino cherry dropped from his mouth into his glass with a *clink.*

I sat on an empty barstool down by their end of the bar and looked at the man I thought was in police custody. "Hey. What are you doing here?"

He stabbed the cherry with the plastic sword from his drink and held it over his glass. "The police had to let me go due to a lack of evidence. I think they were making a show of force by publicly arresting someone so the community doesn't find out they're really idiots who don't know what they're doing."

"I see."

Verna looked as though she'd been matching Felicity drink for drink, but with a less giddy outcome. "Simon Beck is an *asinus asinorum.*"

Karla sat on the stool next to mine and shifted her size 0 royal-blue dress to make sure the side cutouts were still where they were supposed to be. She waved the bartender over. "I think that means jack—"

I cut her off. "Yeah, I got the general idea."

Verna slurred through her tears, "How dare he. There is nothing worse than a cheater. And a liar. I trusted him . . ." She glanced at me. "As a respected member of the faculty . . . He should be held to a higher standard. Not running around with twenty-year-old personal trainers."

Karla had not even been introduced to Verna, but she didn't let that stop her from giving an opinion. "You sound like you think he was cheating on *you* instead of his wife."

Oh, this will be interesting.

Eli and Felicity shared a look of exasperation.

Verna shrugged off Karla's comment. "I was not in a relationship with Simon Beck. Apparently, I'm *too needy.*" Felicity jabbed her in the side. "Or I would have been . . . if we'd been in a relationship . . . which we were not."

Karla plucked an orange slice from the bartender's garnishes. "Did you kill him?"

Verna's mouth dropped open, and she stared in horror. "Who are you?"

A voice at the other end of the bar joined in commiseration with the young PhD student. "I'm the innocent victim here. I was lured here on a romantic week with him. Why do I keep falling for the same thing? I should just assume every confident attractive man is cheating on a wife somewhere."

I hadn't even noticed Brooklyn sitting at the far end of the bar. For the first time on the tour, she was not dressed for the runway. She was in my daily uniform of yoga pants and a T-shirt that said, *Life is short—Eat the cake.*

Karla ordered her drink. "So, this is what you do? Hang out with murder suspects and listen to them talk?"

"Pretty much, yeah."

"Wow." She called over to Brooklyn, "Did you kill him?"

Brooklyn drained her glass and held it up to the bartender. "No! I thought we were just playing around. He's not allowed to date students and I've been taking a poetry class. Simon was afraid that sanctimonious jerk would report him."

Eli looked affronted. "I can hear you."

Verna laughed so hard she snorted. "You were afraid Eli would report you for sleeping with a professor. That's hilarious."

Brooklyn pointed a finger at Eli. "Simon said you've had it in for him since he denied your application for transfer into his department." She twirled a paper straw in her square glass. "He even showed up after Simon's lecture once to accuse Simon of bugging another classroom."

Karla sipped her Cosmo. She called down to Eli, "Is that why you killed him?"

I leaned my head towards Karla and whispered, "I usually try to be a bit more subtle than this."

"Your way is taking too long. And I have to do my laundry tonight."

Eli froze with his glass up to his lips. "I didn't kill him. Being denied entry to the Parapsychology Department was the best thing that ever happened to me. I couldn't stand working with that scumbag every day. I'm much more suited to the ethics department under Dr. Van Smoot."

Felicity snorted.

Eli ignored her and soldiered on. "Do you have any idea how many people believe they've felt a ghostly presence when it's just everyday electromagnetic waves?"

Linda tapped a spoon against a champagne flute. "Hi there. I'd ask how everyone in here is doing, but the people out on the porch could answer that for me. We're going to head into the event dining room now. Dawn is going to tell you about some of the supernatural activity that is reported to go on here at the Inn."

A young woman with long light brown hair smiled at the group and little crinkles appeared in the corner of her eyes. "Hi. I'm Dawn, the night manager. I see a lot of the ghost activity when the Inn is quiet. Let's go get yooze settled."

We followed her into the private room and were seated around a large round table covered by a white tablecloth. A tall black tapered candle stood in the center. Dawn leaned over the table and clicked a long stick lighter.

Karla stood in the doorway holding her pink drink. "What is this? This isn't gonna be a séance, is it? 'Cause I didn't agree to that."

Dawn waved her in. "No séance. I promise. I don't need a séance to speak to the ghosts. They're right over there."

Everyone turned to look towards the kitchen. Dawn waved.

Felicity craned her neck to look around Eli. "I don't see anything."

Dawn smiled. "It's the kids. They're curious about you."

Karla gave me a look like she was a thin thread snap away from running out of there. "Some prices are too high to pay for your brother."

I jerked my head for her to come closer. She downed the rest of her Cosmo and placed the empty glass on a serving tray by the door before she joined me.

Dawn was relaxed. She held on to the back of a chair as she looked at each of us in turn. "Our spirits are friendly here. They're all good entities. Yooze don't haf to be afraid. We have kids who like to run around and knock on the doors when you're trying to sleep. And they love to play with the TVs."

Verna's voice caught as she tried to speak. "How many kids are there?"

One waitress started filling glasses with iced tea while another brought out a tray with plates of prime rib and whipped potatoes.

Dawn looked to the empty back corner of the room and grinned. "There's a young boy who drowned in the ocean, and a girl about the same age who died from a lung disease. They weren't related or nothing. They met here. They like to play together. Sometimes guests on the third floor complain that there's kids playing with a ball outside their room." She smiled to the back of the room in another area. "Yeah, you. That's them. Go ahead."

No one was touching their food. We were all transfixed on Dawn, who was having a conversation with people that none of us could see.

"It's alright. They came to hear about you."

Eli looked over his shoulder and back at Dawn.

Brooklyn stabbed at her prime rib. "Can your ghosts talk to other ghosts? 'Cause I'd like them to tell us who killed Simon Beck so I can go back home."

Felicity smirked. "I see the veganism has passed."

Dawn cocked her head like she hadn't heard the news about another murder in Cape May. "They don't know anything. They pretty much just stay here at the Inn. They're just like us, doing their thing. Just on a different plane."

No one who had been to my house was touching

their iced tea, but Karla took a long drink of hers. "Are all the ghosts friendly?"

Dawn smiled and nodded. "Yeah. We have a young woman in blue who's very flirtatious." She grinned at Eli. "She mostly shows herself to the men visitors. I'll take you up to her room later and maybe you'll see her."

She turned her head like somebody called her from the kitchen, but no one was there. "I'll tell them." She looked back at us. "Well, I'm gonna let yooze eat. When you're done, I'll take you up two by two in the elevator." She looked at the back of the room again and laughed. "The kids like to play with the buttons, so they're looking forward to that."

Karla pushed her plate away and hung her head. "Our Father, who art in Heaven . . ."

Dawn started to leave, then turned back before she crossed the threshold to the bar. "Just stay out of the kitchen. The spirits in the kitchen don't like anyone in their space at night."

The room was silent when she left, except for Brooklyn, who was devouring her prime rib like a sabertooth tiger.

Eli laughed to himself. "Well, if Simon were here, he'd be in the kitchen."

"Why?" I took a bite of my prime rib and nearly melted. *I'm so making this for Christmas.*

Eli picked up his knife and fork. "Because he was a bully. He loved to intimidate his students. Especially the men."

Verna looked up from her mashed potatoes and nodded. "True."

Eli delicately cut his meat. "I heard that one boy was so traumatized after taking Simon's class that he dropped out and started therapy."

Felicity gasped. "Oh!"

Verna shook her head. "What?"

Felicity bit down on her lip. She sprang to her feet. "I've got to go make a call!" She ran past Linda, who was just coming in to check on things.

Karla chuckled into her iced tea. "Hey. Aren't you the one who's supposed to have some big discovery right about now? You're letting the background actor have the epiphany."

I gave her some side-eye. "The poison that killed Simon Beck was in the iced tea."

She spit a mouthful across the table.

I regret nothing.

CHAPTER 38

I returned home to find the Blair Witch Project had taken over my front yard. Weird little wooden stick people and tattered ribbons hung from the branches and the gingerbread around the porch. The departing tour group was standing around taking pictures of the ominous decorations.

One woman asked me to take a photo of her and her friend with them. "This is the coolest thing I've ever seen. How'd you do all this while we were inside on the ghost tour?"

I took the picture and handed her phone back. "Silent partners."

I entered the house waiting to find a nervous little redhead. Aunt Ginny was sitting in the dark in the sunroom facing the tower window. Figaro was on her lap, and she was petting him like an evil supervillain. "Did you catch your kids?"

"Oh yes."

"You didn't yell at them, did you?"

"I didn't do anything."

Why is the hair standing up on the back of my neck?
"What are you doing sitting here in the dark?"

"Planning."

I swallowed hard. *This won't end well.* "Okay. Good night. I hope you have peaceful dreams about the blessings of children and forgiveness."

Gladys Philippot ambushed me in the hall. "Hey. I heard the cops got you goin' around town asking questions of all the people who were on that tour. It sounds like you're some kinda narc or something. Is that what you do? Murder victims in cold blood, then call the cops and help them question the suspects to throw the suspicion off of you? It's a very clever angle, I'll give ya that."

"You've got to be kidding me, Gladys."

"I'm just wanting to give you a chance to tell your side of the story."

"Good night, Gladys." I went up to bed exhausted and lay there with my fears about news helicopters circling my house and Aunt Ginny being on *Wake Up! South Jersey* to answer why the neighbors' kids are in therapy.

I woke up some time later to banging and whispering outside my door. "Not again. What are they doing, Fig?" Figaro seemed to have abandoned me. His spot on the bed was cold.

I pulled on a bathrobe and opened my door.

Jennifer Beck was standing in the hall with one of the Paranormal Pathfinders' devices. It started to flash. "I've got something."

Ritchie crept closer with the camera up on his shoulder and swung it my way. The red light made my eyes water.

"What are you all doing?"

Clark shushed me. He ran a device up one side of my body and down the other like a wand at airport security.

Paisley was in the middle of the hallway, under headphones and on a laptop. "I've got it too."

Clark called back to her, "Is it Poppy?"

"No. It's next to her."

I beg your pardon.

A yip sounded at my feet, and I looked to see Princess shaking herself into the wall. "Is it this dog?"

Clark looked at the laptop, then down at me. "Can you stand still for a second please?"

"Me or the Chihuahua?"

Harper placed a box on the table next to me. "I've set it up. Go."

Jennifer clapped. "This is so exciting. It reminds me of the early days with Simon, before he started having affairs."

A voice sounded from the storage room doorway, and I discovered Owen Rodney sitting on a box just inside the room drinking a cup of tea. Earl Grey from the scent of it. Figaro sat at his feet. "Figaro says to ask the entity to make that box flash."

Figaro is ghost hunting now?

Harper spoke in my general direction. "We know you're here with us. Could you please push that button on the box there?"

A green light flashed on the box sitting on the table in the hall.

The team made tiny fist pumps and jumped around silently.

Jennifer asked, "Is that you, Simon?"

The hall was silent. Even the air didn't move. The box didn't respond.

Clark spoke into the dark hallway. "If you're here

because of Poppy, could you hit that button again please?"

There was a slight delay; then the green light flashed again. My insides felt like someone had replaced my bones with that Jell-O salad.

Owen gave more helpful advice. "Princess thinks she sees the outline of a man standing there."

Well, Princess is a dog who seems like she has one brain cell left. So, why are we listening to her?

Clark asked the entity, "Are you here to hurt Poppy?"

Oh God! What? I stared at the box planning to hire the first moving company that had a twenty-four-hour hotline. Nothing.

Ritchie spoke from behind his camera. "Are you here to help Poppy?"

The green light started to flash. Something I only found slightly more reassuring than the first option.

Jennifer reached out and grabbed my wrist. "Isn't this fun?"

"That's not what I would call it, no."

Clark moved next to me but faced the camera. "Do you know why Poppy keeps finding murder victims?"

The box started to flash and the emergency lights on the ceiling flickered. Clark's EMF reader whirred, and the needle spun to the maximum reading. Then everything went dark.

A moment later, Kenny opened his door. "Oh. I didn't realize you all were up here. I think we blew a fuse."

Everyone stared at him in anticipation.

"I'll just go check the electrical box." He disappeared down the back stairs.

Clark pulled out a flashlight and checked the box

on the table. "We're fried here too. Let's reset and try again in twenty."

I yawned. "I'm going back to bed. You all have fun and tell me all about it tomorrow."

Their disappointment would have been flattering if it hadn't been so terrifying.

I closed my door and put my ear against the wood. I overheard Clark: "We won't get anything else up here tonight. The entity only responds when Poppy is around. Let's check the purple suite where the girls are staying."

I stood on the other side of the door trying to slow my heart. *Kenny must have been blow-drying his hair again. Or maybe Aunt Ginny is downstairs making waffles. I'm sure there is a reasonable explanation for everything.*

CHAPTER 39

Breakfast was a lively affair. The TV crew peppered Jennifer Beck with questions about her late husband, while she returned questions about their education and how they'd each known Simon. Paisley and Harper eventually excused themselves to bed, followed by Ritchie and a very reluctant Clark, leaving Jennifer alone with Owen and Gladys. I entered the dining room with the coffee carafe in the middle of their conversation.

Gladys was sitting in between Owen and Jennifer with her notebook open on the table before her. "Did you always know your husband was a fraud or did it come as a complete shock to you when he died?"

I nearly dropped the carafe. "Oh my—Ms. Philippot! Please don't harass the guests."

Gladys's lips pursed and she cast her eyes nervously to Jennifer.

Owen stepped in to defend Mrs. Beck, and uncharacteristically raised his voice. "How dare you! Have you no scruples at all, woman!"

Jennifer leaned forward in her seat. "I thought

you said you were a retired librarian. What was your name again?"

Owen gently answered, "This is Gladys Philippot of *The Chatterbox.*"

Jennifer's mouth dropped open. "The same Gladys Philippot from *Newsweek* who my husband sued for defamation?"

I stared at the tabloid journalist, wondering how she would respond. I had not expected her to get up and run from the room, but that's exactly what she did. I wish I could say I felt sorry for her.

The morning dragged, and I was on my fourth cup of coffee just trying to stay awake. I'd already had two calls with Amber to give her updates. Then Joanne and I searched the Internet for mention of Gladys Philippot linked to *Newsweek* and a lawsuit. We came up empty. People just weren't destroying each other on social media that far back. I went up to her room to talk to her, but either she'd gone out or she was ignoring me.

While I waited for her to return, I thought I'd keep busy doing one of the things that I loved—baking. Then I pulled out the empty plastic from the kitchen drawer. "This is the fourth bag of candy I've bought, and Halloween isn't until tomorrow. How am I supposed to make candy bar brownies for this afternoon with no candy bars? And what about the trick or treaters?"

Joanne brought in the plate of leftover maple cardamom breakfast cake and three fall fruit hazelnut muffins. "They're finished eating and the dining room is clean."

Aunt Ginny sat at the table eating a small mixing

bowl full of Kenny's Froot Loops, a laptop open in front of her. "It's not my fault you can't control your bag of candy."

"It is your fault. It is one hundred percent your fault because you've single-handedly eaten all the candy."

Aunt Ginny blinked innocently. "That's not true. I haven't touched the Almond Joys."

I held up two fistfuls of blue-wrapped candy bars. "That's exhibit B that you're behind this because it's the only candy you don't like. We can't give out only these for Halloween. Do you really want our house pelted with egg grenades? We still have to get through Mischief Night tonight."

Aunt Ginny's grin was so disquieting my blood ran cold. "Bring it on."

Joanne wrapped the leftover cake in cling film with one eye on the terrifying old lady at the table who was checking for the plastic Toucan Sam toy in the bottom of the box. "God help us."

"Aunt Ginny, I'm all for retribution as much as the next girl, but I don't want to have to testify to a judge as to why you attacked the neighborhood children because they terrorized you with marshmallow Peeps and toilet paper."

Aunt Ginny ignored me and went back to her cereal. "Don't worry. They'll be too afraid to call the cops."

I started ripping the wrappers off from the coconut candy while Joanne and I shared a look edging towards terror.

Kenny popped out of the pantry dressed head to toe in white looking like the love child of Mr. Clean and Carrot Top. "The rooms are finished, and I thought you should know that Owen Rodney has a roll of aluminum foil on his dresser in case the colander doesn't block enough psychic energy."

I plunged the Almond Joys into the pan of brownie batter just enough so they weren't quite on the bottom of the pan and the batter covered the tops. "Did he tell you that?"

Kenny took a carton of orange juice from the fridge. "He did indeed. I just nodded along and got the heck outta there before Figaro made fun of my outfit again."

Aunt Ginny leaned in closer to the laptop screen. "Someone's coming."

A few seconds later, the doorbell rang and everyone standing around looked at me. "Sure. I'll go get it since I'm clearly not doing anything."

I put the brownies in the oven and walked down the hall with Figaro at a canter by my side. When I opened the door, an ivory envelope fell into the room. Figaro pounced and swatted it a couple of times making sure it wasn't hiding a predator or a cupcake.

I pried it out from under his fluffy paws. It was blank. I looked around outside, but no one was there. After closing the door, I ripped the envelope open and pulled out an official-looking sheet of paper from Staunton University. It was a page from a college transcript from several years ago. One of the classes listed was Paranormal Studies 101 taught by Professor Simon Beck. The student listed was Kenny Love.

I felt the room sway and grabbed something to steady myself. Owen Rodney appeared at my side. "Are you okay? Figaro said you were looking like you ate some bad fish."

I suspected it was more that Figaro had just

flopped at my feet and I was hanging from the coat-rack like the last officer on the *Titanic,* but I tried to be gracious anyway. "I just need to sit down for a second."

Owen led me to the library where Jennifer Beck was curled up with a copy of Jane Austen's *Northanger Abbey* in front of the fire.

She turned the book over and placed it on the table. "What happened?"

I settled myself into the wing chair. "Nothing. I think I just need to drink some water."

Aunt Ginny entered the room and shrugged. "Well? What was that all about? They disappeared before I could get a good look at them. What's that in your hand?"

She took the paper from me. "Sunday biscuits!"

I turned the envelope over to be sure I hadn't missed a return address.

Aunt Ginny looked towards the foyer. "I saw who came to the door. It was just some kid on a bike."

Jennifer craned her neck to see the paper better. "It's from the university. I recognize the logo at the top there."

Owen put his hand on my shoulder. "Figaro wants you to know he's here for you if you need him in your lap."

Figaro was stalking something under the blanket next to Jennifer. He pounced and it yipped. Princess stuck her head out and shivered in Fig's direction.

Owen took his hand away. "Nope. I'm sorry. It's too late. He's forgotten all about it now."

Figaro flew to the desk and stuffed himself behind the monitor to glare at Princess from under the gap at the bottom. "That's the first thing you've said that I know is true."

Jennifer reached for the paper. "May I?"

Aunt Ginny snatched it from my grasp and handed it to her before I could say *plausible deniability.* "I think it's part of a college transcript."

Jennifer looked it over. "This student took one of Simon's classes."

"Can you tell what grade they got?"

Jennifer shook her head and pointed to a line on the page. "It's incomplete. Kenny Love didn't finish the semester for some reason. It happens all the time."

Aunt Ginny leaned in. "And why would a random student that we've never met and doesn't work here get an incomplete?"

Jennifer pulled the blanket up tighter around her and the ball in her lap growled and spun in a circle and settled back down. "There are always reasons why students drop out. Illness, changes to their major, schedule conflicts, poor grades."

Owen cocked his head slightly to the side. "What about a conflict with the professor?" He caught my gaze and rolled his eyes towards Figaro, who was watching me intently. Fig slow blinked and looked away.

Jennifer bobbed her head back and forth. "It happens. Simon had a lot of dropouts in his entry level classes. At least one every single semester. He said kids would sign up who had no business being there and they'd always drop out when it got tough. Occasionally Simon would recommend a student drop the class if they showed absolutely no natural ability with the material. That could be what happened to this Kenny Love."

Joanne came around the corner carrying the carafe. She lifted it towards Jennifer. "Ready for more?"

Jennifer held her cup and nodded. "Yes please."

Joanne filled her cup and glanced at me. "So, you're okay with it?"

"Okay with what?"

She stopped pouring. "What Kenny just asked you."

"What are you talking about?"

"Didn't Kenny just come in here and ask if you wanted to head to La Dolce Vita early to get started for me?"

"No. We haven't seen him, have we, Aunt Ginny?"

Aunt Ginny put her hand over her chest. "Oh no. I bet he was eavesdropping from the hall. He's almost as good at it as I am."

Joanne cocked her hand on her hip. "You know, I thought it was weird that he just ran out the back door and across the yard. I wonder what caused that?"

CHAPTER 40

I called Kenny from my cell phone, and it went straight to voice mail. "He lied to me." I paced back and forth in the sunroom wearing a figure eight in the black-and-white fleur-de-lis rug. Figaro mirrored my movements from the back of the gray sofa.

Aunt Ginny perched on the white leather wingback chair and waited for me to slow down. Her expression was tired and sad. Unlike Joanne, who was tickled pink, sitting across from her in an identical wingback chair.

I could choke them both right now. "I knew something was wrong the night Simon died. Kenny started acting weird the moment he saw Dr. Beck in the library. Then he pulled that disappearing act when the cops arrived. What made you give him that pill and send him to bed?"

Aunt Ginny tilted her palms up. "He told me he recognized someone on the tour who could ruin his life and he had to get out of sight before he was falsely accused of murder. I told him to go to his room and don't answer the door for the rest of the night. The cops would need a warrant to go up there."

I stopped pacing in front of Aunt Ginny. "After all we've been through, and all the murderers who we've been around, didn't that seem suspicious to you?"

"Well, yes. But it's Kenny. He's not a killer."

I smacked the transcript and shook it at her angrily.

Joanne added, "He did put something in Simon's iced tea. He said it was sugar, but we only have his word for it."

The doorbell rang, and Aunt Ginny stood to answer it. She reached out and put her hand on my wrist. "I know this looks bad, but you know as well as I do that Kenny didn't send that here by himself. Who's trying to sway suspicion from themselves? That's the question."

"That may be a valid point, but why would Kenny take off again if he was innocent?"

Aunt Ginny shrugged and disappeared down the hall.

Joanne nodded. "I'm with you. There is something very fishy about that man. I think he's been lying to you from day one."

Aunt Ginny's voice carried down the hall. "Come on in, Amber. Poppy is just down here."

I was immensely flustered from my handful of incriminating evidence. Looking frantically for a place to stash it, I was caught in a feedback loop turning back and forth from the chair to the couch.

Joanne reached out and grabbed the document from my hands. She folded it and stuffed it under her butt. "You're hopeless."

I flopped onto the couch, causing Figaro to bounce

a little. He sent me a reproachful look with just a small amount of judgment about my weight, but I ignored him and sat on my hands.

Amber followed Aunt Ginny into the room. She was carrying a leather attaché. "What are you up to that she's giving you a warning, McAllister?"

"Nothing. Don't you think I have enough to do running this place than to be trying to subvert your every move?"

Amber stared at me with the slightest of quirks to her lips. Her eyes narrowed. She looked at Joanne.

Joanne crossed her arms over her chest. "I don't think she knows what she's doing half the time."

Amber looked back at me. "You know you're the worst liar I've ever seen. I always find out what's going on."

"You could ask Figaro. That's where Owen Rodney gets his intel."

Amber snorted and looked to Aunt Ginny, who for her part remained the picture of calm. She took her seat back and Figaro stretched and yawned his way over to her lap. "So, what can we help you with, Officer?"

"The tetrahydrozoline hydrochloride was definitely in the stevia bottle. According to several of the statements, Simon Beck was unwittingly poisoning himself all night long."

I nodded and tried to look mildly bemused. "Why aren't you pressing charges against Eli? I saw him at the Inn last night."

"We had to let him go. His bottle of Visine was tetrahydrozoline-free. He's not the guy. At least that's not the Visine."

I swallowed hard and Amber's words went down like glass. *Kenny, wherever you are, you'd better get back here and explain yourself, you ginger idiot.* "What'd you find out about Sable and Jax? Did you find their social media accounts?"

"Not yet. We have the IT forensics team looking for recently deleted accounts."

"What about the restraining order?"

"Still waiting. That should come in any day."

Joanne nodded to the case in Amber's hand. "What's that?"

Amber held up the leather bag. "This is Simon Beck's laptop. I was hoping Mrs. Beck might know the password and could get us in. I passed her in the library, but Aunt Ginny seemed so suspicious marching me back here that I thought I'd see what you were up to first."

Fabulous. "Let's go ask her before she heads to her room." I threw my arm out in a move to usher Amber ahead of me. I gave one last panicked look to Joanne before I cleared the room.

Joanne returned my look with the same glare that Grandma Emmy used to give me when I acted up in public. It was not comforting.

We reached the library, where Jennifer was still in front of the fire, head back in her Jane Austen. Princess had moved to Owen's lap in the chair next to the couch. I was about to tell Jennifer that Amber wanted to speak with her privately when the front door opened and Gladys Philippot breezed in stinking of seagulls and suspicion.

"Any breaks in the case, Shaggy? Or has Scooby stopped talkin'?"

Princess raised her head and started barking a tirade worthy of a Great Dane.

Owen chuckled. "You're right. She does look like a cartoon witch."

Gladys balled her fists. "Watch it, cuckoo. I'm just in the mood to run a follow-up story about how you're leading on a local bed and breakfast owner that you can talk to animals."

Owen kept his eyes on his copy of *Black Beauty*. "You have bird poop in your hair."

Gladys put her hand out to feel her hair and spun in a haphazard circle. "What? Where?"

Owen turned a page. "On the back."

One side of her lip curled to a snarl. "And how would you know that if you can't see it from there?"

The little Chihuahua yipped.

"Princess can smell it. Besides, it's all the chatter in the yard."

Gladys took a step towards Owen and knocked his book from his hand. "You're an idiot."

Amber's police radio sounded a high-pitched tone and Princess growled. Amber turned it down and gave a long once-over to the tabloid reporter. "Ma'am. I'd like to go over your statement again when I'm finished here. Please stay nearby."

Gladys took a backwards step into the hall. "Of course, Officer. Excuse me." Gladys calmly walked from the library. There was a splotch of white on the shoulder of her orange sweater.

Amber stepped further into the room and held out the leather case. "Mrs. Beck, do you recognize this?"

Jennifer pushed herself upright. "That's Simon's briefcase."

"Ma'am, do you think you can open his laptop for us?"

She nodded. "As long as he didn't change his password, I can."

I stepped closer to Mrs. Beck. "Would you prefer

to go to the dining room where you can have the table? Or to open it right here in the library?"

"The dining room would probably be easier." She shifted her eyes to Amber, then back to me. "Can you stay with me?"

"Of course." I was considerably taller and heavier than Amber, who could still be a flyer for the Cape May High Cheerleaders, so people often felt safer with me. Maybe it was because Amber had a badge and a gun. More likely it was because she had resting cop face.

Princess jumped down and shook herself into the coffee table. Then she snapped at the coffee table for attacking her and licked her leg to console herself.

Owen didn't look up from his book but spoke to the little dog. "Remember your inner peace. You are descended from the royal Techichis."

Princess wagged her tail and pranced across the hall following Jennifer. I pulled up the rear, casting another quick glance at my so-called pet psychic. He pushed his glasses back on his nose and gave me a thumbs-up.

We took seats around the dining room table and Jennifer powered on the laptop. Princess made a couple of unsuccessful attempts to jump into her lap until Jennifer finally reached down and scooped up the tiny dog.

Aunt Ginny toddled through the room and pointed from her eyes to Amber's. Amber nodded sagely.

"Jenny8675309. I'm in. He didn't change it."

Amber spun the laptop to face her and started typing with one finger. Peck. Peck. Peck. She narrowed her eyes and scanned across the keyboard.

"Are you serious!"

She frowned at me. "I didn't take typing. I didn't think I'd ever need it."

"Here." I spun the laptop to face me. "What are you looking for?"

She tipped her head and gave me a look that said, *Really. You need me to spell it out in front of the wife?*

Jennifer smiled. "It's okay. I assume she's looking for anything incriminating from one of Simon's ex-lovers."

So, all I need is a file marked "this one will kill me" and we'll be all set. I typed in a search and started reading through the subject headings in Simon's email. It was all boring university stuff. I clicked on a web browser with my fingers crossed that his home page was for webmail. For once the paranormal energy was Team Poppy. "He has a Gmail account with the screen name BigGhostDoc. Nothing obvious from women by the subject headings."

I clicked through a few just to be sure they weren't in code.

Amber tapped the table. "Check the trash or archives."

I clicked the trash can icon. "I'm not finding anything other than ads for . . . enlargement pills."

Jennifer rubbed her hand over Princess's good ear and craned her neck to look at the screen. "He probably emptied the trash to hide the evidence from me."

I angled the laptop so she could see it with me. I saw one subject heading that read *Time to face the music.* "This might be something."

"What is it, McAllister?"

"'We're going to destroy you for exploiting the delicate balance of the underworld.'" I looked at Jennifer. "Their words."

She nodded. "Those groups have been sending Simon threats for years. Always accusing him of disturbing the spirit world. I think they have a YouTube channel where they post videos of their protests."

"There's a link." I clicked the link, and it opened a window titled *Underworld Warriors.* The video started on an effigy of a mannequin wearing long black robes. Two college kids in hoods were piling up sticks around the bottom of the dummy while naming the victim's sins. Then one of them doused it with lighter fluid, and the other lit a match and set the whole thing ablaze while a larger crowd of students cheered.

As disturbing as setting a mannequin on fire was, the most unsettling revelation was that I recognized the protesters. *Whoa!* "You've got to see this."

Amber made spinny motions with her finger. "Show me."

I turned the laptop around to face her. "We found Sable and Jax. They knew exactly who Simon Beck was, and they came here specifically for him."

CHAPTER 41

I followed a link to the Underworld Warriors' channel on YouTube.

Amber pointed to the top video. "They posted an update this morning."

I clicked on it, and it started a video Sable and Jax had been making at the Physick Estate in the Scarecrow Alley. "Quick update. We promised to make Simon Beck pay for his crimes and we still intend to follow through with the effigy when we return. We got some good footage of the criminal but had to delete it when the police arrived. Sable and I will be offline for a few days laying low for obvious reasons."

The video ended. There were several other videos of different protests around the New England states, but nothing from my house the other night.

Aunt Ginny's voice came through the closed dining room door. "I think you should go pick up those kids and take them to the station for questioning."

Amber shut the lid on the laptop and called over her shoulder, "How long have you been eavesdropping from the kitchen?"

Aunt Ginny replied, "Jenny8675309."

Amber rolled her eyes.

We hadn't found anything else incriminating on Simon's laptop, so if there were emails from former mistresses it seemed he had deleted them. Amber clicked on the radio attached to her shoulder and called the station to request an arrest warrant for Sable and Jax.

Aunt Ginny poked her head into the dining room. "Your brownies are burning."

"Ugh. I forgot about them." I rushed into the kitchen expecting a pan of charred soot and coconut and came face-to-face with Kenny. Actually, I came face-to-face with Joanne, who was next to Aunt Ginny, who was standing over Kenny tied and gagged at the banquette. The perfectly gooey brownies were cooling on a cake rack.

I shot a look of alarm to the hatchet man and her muscle, Joanne. I hissed at them, "What are you doing? There's a cop on the other side of that door."

Aunt Ginny shrugged. "You needed Kenny. Joanne got you Kenny."

Joanne shrugged. "I caught him trying to steal one of the bikes from the garage."

I picked up a tea towel and swatted Joanne while I hissed, "If Amber comes through that door, how do I explain that he's tied up?"

Kenny muffled a defense and tried to get up.

Joanne pushed him back down with one meaty hand. "We'll tell her he was like this when we found him."

"Do you seriously think Amber's going to buy that Kenny gagged himself and tied his wrists together with a jump rope?"

Kenny struggled and murmured through the Strawberry Shortcake dish towel that had been shoved in his mouth.

Amber hollered from the dining room, and we all froze. "I gotta run to The Chalfonte. I'll be back to talk to Gladys Philippot in a bit!"

"Okay. I'll talk to you later."

Aunt Ginny shooed me towards the dining room. "Go in there and walk her to the porch."

I poked my head through the swinging door. "Can you see yourself out?"

Amber lifted the attaché. "I'm good. I'll let you know if we make an arrest."

"Yeah, yeah. Good good good good. Let me know how it turns out."

Amber narrowed her eyes and gave me a long look. "You alright?"

"Yep. Gotta cut these candy bar brownies for tea-time."

Her eyes lit up. "Brownies?"

"You won't like them."

"How do you know?"

"The only candy bars Aunt Ginny left me were Almond Joy."

Amber made a face and headed through the sitting room towards the front door. "Eww. Okay."

I heard the front door close behind her and turned to face the mounting fiasco that had all the earmarks of an episode of *Dateline.* "Kenny, we need to talk."

Aunt Ginny and I sat side by side on one side of the kitchen table like *Shark Tank* investors hoping to be impressed. I'd made them untie and ungag Kenny because we already had enough bad juju in our lives to add kidnapping to the list.

Joanne was humming a little tune and wiping down every surface in the kitchen for the umpteenth time and I was afraid she would polish the copper right off the stove.

Kenny stuffed his hands in his pockets and considered Joanne's mood. A dark cloud shadowed his expression. "Am I fired?"

"Um . . ."

Aunt Ginny bit her lip. "Well . . ."

Joanne's humming shot up an octave.

"Joanne, you don't have to be here. Breakfast is over and we don't have to be at La Dolce Vita yet to start dinner. You want to take off and have some time for yourself?"

Joanne grinned so wide she put Julia Roberts to shame. "Nope. I'm good. I think I'm going to start making some cider cupcakes for the coffee shop."

Kenny rankled a little more. He dropped into the seat opposite Aunt Ginny. "Alright. Let's get it over with."

Joanne did a little butt dance while she measured the gluten-free flour.

I unfolded the college transcript and placed it in front of Kenny. The blood drained from his face leaving red splotches on his cheeks like he'd been slapped. "I thought you didn't know Simon Beck."

Kenny flicked his eyes up to mine. "I know this looks bad."

Aunt Ginny smacked the table and the salt and pepper jumped. "'Bad' is an understatement, buddy."

I put my hand over hers. "I don't know what's

going on, but you've been lying to me from day one. You ran from the cops, and you disappeared out of here the moment this arrived. You look guilty as sin. Give me one good reason not to call Amber and tell her to come back here and arrest you."

Aunt Ginny chimed in—either to make up for her earlier faulty judgment or purely for her love of interrogation. "The cops already think you're suspicious because they found the stevia bottle buried in the ficus where you could have stuck it after everyone went to bed."

Kenny's eyes were pleading with Aunt Ginny. "Exactly. I could have planted that anywhere. I've taken out the trash three times since Simon Beck's murder. If I killed him, why would I hide the murder weapon in our house and leave it there?"

That's a good point. I tapped his name on the paper. "Right now, I want to know what this is all about."

Kenny dropped his head to his hands and sighed. "Do you remember the movie *Ghost*?"

"The pottery one with Patrick Swayze?"

Kenny nodded.

Aunt Ginny leaned back against the vinyl bench seat. "Mmm. That Patrick Swayze sure could razz my berries."

Joanne started to cough and sputter like she'd swallowed Listerine.

Either my cheeks flamed, or Kenny was generating a serious heat wave. We both looked in shock at Aunt Ginny, who was staring dreamily into the air. "Whoa! Settle down, lady. That's not daytime kitchen talk."

Aunt Ginny threw me some side-eye. "I've done a lot of things in this kitchen that you don't know about."

Kenny fanned himself with a napkin. "Anyway. I saw *Ghost* in the theater twenty-six times when it came out. I was so enamored by the thought of talking to spirits and helping lost souls cross over that I just knew I wanted to do that for the rest of my life. So, as soon as I graduated, I found a college offering paranormal studies and signed up for a whole new life."

Joanne snorted and flicked on the teakettle as if she wasn't hanging on every word.

Kenny threw her a scowl before continuing. "Paranormal studies was a hot new field because of the *Ghostbusters* movie a few years earlier. Problem was, it wasn't a real job. Very few colleges offered classes for it. A handsome guy like me who wanted to banish poltergeists had a scanty few options. The best program in the country, at that time, was at Staunton University because of—you-know-who."

"Simon Beck," I said.

Kenny's eyes grew very round, and he tilted his head dramatically. "I signed up for Paranormal Studies One-Oh-One . . . and that . . . was where it all went wrong."

Joanne started the grinder and the room filled with the smell of fresh roasted coffee. I gave her a look of exasperation. "You gotta do that right now?"

She held up the teakettle. "I need something after that raspberry comment."

"Fair enough."

Aunt Ginny moved to the edge of the bench seat and tapped Kenny's arm. "What happened?"

Kenny blushed like a sunburn. "After a couple weeks in Professor Beck's class, he said I was wasting my and—more importantly—*his* time. I had absolutely no psychic gift. I was a waste of skin. And I was fooling myself if I thought I'd ever be good enough to get a paranormal degree or a job. And I should give up and go flip burgers somewhere."

"Aww. That's so mean."

Kenny looked out the window and shrugged. "It's no big deal. But transferring meant I had to switch majors because Professor Beck ran the only Paranormal Department at SU. My dreams of being a Ghostbuster had to die."

"What about Felicity Van Smoot? Couldn't you take her class?"

Kenny puckered his lips and shook his head. "She wasn't a professor. She was just a PhD student who graded papers and smacked your butt when you passed her desk. Besides, I realized I didn't really want to communicate with ghosts like Bill Murray. I wanted to act in movies about communicating with ghosts like Bill Murray. So, I dropped the paranormal studies major and took up drama."

Joanne brought over a cup of coffee and set it before me. Then she pushed against me until I scooched down the bench seat and she could take my place and drink the coffee. "At least you can fall back on your successful movie star career. Oh—wait."

Geez, Joanne! "Are you sharing that coffee?"

She gave me an insincere grin. "Let me get you some." Then she pointed across the room. "It's over there."

I turned my attention back to the possible murderer—who was still only the third most frustrating person in the room. "I gotta be honest with you, Kenny. All of that just confirms that you had a really good motive to murder Simon Beck."

Kenny shook his head like Princess trying to get her eyeballs even. "I didn't murder him. I had to go to therapy because of him, but his failure as a teacher—and a decent human being—changed the course of my life for the better. I'd rather be doing what I'm doing now."

Joanne shook her pointy white spikes. "Uh-uh. I don't buy it. You'd rather be a forty-year-old chambermaid failing to break into community theater than have a career trapping ghosts—if that even is a thing."

Kenny's eyebrows shot to his forehead like a vampire flicking his cape. "I beg your pardon! First of all, it's 'manservant.' And second, I'm still in the thirty to thirty-nine age range and holding. And yes, I like where I am. I'm chasing my dreams to be onstage. I have a mentor."

Aunt Ginny slid Joanne's coffee over to herself and blew on it. "Royce said no."

Kenny didn't miss a beat. "I'm getting a mentor. I didn't need to kill Professor Beck, because I've risen above it."

"Then why'd you freak out when you saw him in the library the night of the tour?"

Kenny swallowed hard. "I thought he recognized me. He looked right at me and tried to throw himself over the couch out of disgust. It was humiliating. It was every nightmare I've ever had about facing him."

"I don't think that reaction was because of you. I think it was for Verna Fox. She'd just come in the door."

Kenny crossed his arms over the table. "She did stay on him like white on rice all night. And I think he filed a restraining order against her. He said one of the tour members shouldn't be in the same room with him *legally*."

"Yeah. Amber is waiting to receive confirmation on the restraining order. At least she was. I dunno. The information doesn't always flow both ways with her."

Joanne watched Aunt Ginny drink her stolen coffee and sighed. She got up from the table and took down another mug. "That doesn't answer why you been ducking the police this whole time, Dipwad."

Kenny looked me in the eye. "I was scared Frisky Van Smoot would tell the police about what happened when I was in the professor's class. She saw the whole thing. Then I'd be their prime suspect. Especially after Joanne blabbed that I put something in his drink—which I did—but it was just sugar. I'm just like Humphrey Bogart in *Dark Passage*, but without the wife."

I considered his words, and especially the fact that he could have hidden the stevia bottle a million places better than the ficus. "I believe you. *Mostly.*" *It's hard to put unwavering confidence in someone who's already lied to you.*

Kenny heaved a sigh of relief. "Good. I don't even use eye drops. I mean, the only one who could have planned ahead to bring poison along to kill him was someone who knew he was gonna be here and that was his girlfriend, right? And she didn't strike me as having enough interest in him to kill him. That May to September romance was only lasting as long as September was footing the bill. Whoever killed him committed a crime of passion. So, they must have just happened to have the eye drops with them the night of the murder. Although Professor Beck may not have even been their intended victim. After all, it was his girlfriend's stevia. Maybe he was just un-lucky."

Alarm bells were going off in my head. "Say that again."

"What? He was unlucky?"

"Before that."

"It was his girlfriend's stevia."

"I have to call Amber. What if we've been looking at this all wrong?"

CHAPTER 42

I knocked on the door of Gladys's suite. "Miss Philippot. I know you're in there. I just saw you run up the stairs."

"Go away!"

"I just want to check on you."

"Liar. Don't try to outsnoop a snoop."

"Fine. Don't you want to give me your side of the story?"

The door cracked open. "I'll tell you what. I'll answer your questions if you give me an exclusive."

God help me. "An exclusive on what?"

"How ya keep finding murder victims. Do you have a sixth sense?"

Please. "Answer my questions and I'll tell you."

She threw the door open. My beautiful Swallowtail Suite was covered in papers and notebooks. Two laptops were set up on the antique desk and a recorder was paused next to them. "Ask."

I took a step into the room. "Tell me about the lawsuit."

"Every word I printed was the truth. But there's no

quantifiable proof for paranormal activity, which means there's no quantifiable proof that it's fake. So, Dr. Beck sued me for defamation of character."

"Couldn't *Newsweek*'s lawyers fight that under freedom of the press or something?"

"They did. And they won. And then they suggested I maybe don't write for them anymore. It's not like I broke the Watergate scandal or uncovered a political coup. It was a human-interest story and not worth the legal fees it cost them."

"Simon Beck cost you your job."

"That pompous horse's end sure did."

"What'd you think when you saw him on the ghost tour?"

"I couldn't believe my luck. All those university people goin' at each other. Between them weirdos, Owen Rodney doing the Dr. Dolittle on the cat, and you being on fraud watch, I've had my hands full. I haven't stopped workin' since I got here."

"Seeing Dr. Beck in the house would have been a good opportunity to get revenge for what he cost you with *Newsweek*."

Gladys rolled her big eyes. "I don't need to kill him to get revenge. I was writing up the story about him being a philanderer. It's obvious he uses that class he teaches as his own personal dating service. I did some digging, and the guy's got a list of broken hearts as long as his arm. A friend a mine's got a lead for one a his castoffs who was so destroyed they had to move away. He's gonna see if he can get me an interview. Now let me ask you something."

"Okay."

"How you keep finding these bodies?"

Aunt Ginny called me from the bottom of the steps, "Poppy. Amber's here. She needs to talk to you!"

"I'm sorry, Gladys. The police are here again. I have to talk to them."

"What about my question?"

"I hate to tell you this. But it's just bad luck. There is no story."

"That's what you think. I work for a tabloid now. They believe in a more flexible view of the facts."

CHAPTER 43

"I don't want to go on a walking tour of Cape May, Amber."

The blond cop folded her arms across her chest. She'd only been gone a few hours, but any goodwill I'd earned finding that video of Sable and Jax had already evaporated. "Come on. You can walk from one side of Cape May to the other in forty minutes. It's less than two miles wide. The scavenger hunt is only a few blocks, and it's the last event your group has on their tour."

"Believe it or not, I'm busy running a failing bed and breakfast while I get harangued daily to give interviews for a tabloid that wants to expose me as a weirdo murder magnet and possible serial killer. Why can't you send Officer Simmons to do it? This sounds right up his alley."

"The tour group already knows you."

"They're already irritated with me."

Amber grinned. "In my experience, those things always go hand in hand. Look, the new information you turned in has us considering Brooklyn as the intended victim. If that's the case, my gut says focus on the ladies. Who was clearly in love with Simon Beck and had the greatest motive to want *the wife* out of the way? It would really help if you could get one of them to admit they poisoned Simon Beck by accident."

"Why don't I just arrest them for you too? I don't know how you think I'm going to accomplish all that on a nighttime scavenger hunt."

"You'd be surprised what people think they're getting away with under the cover of darkness."

I looked through the front door while I put my hair in a ponytail and pulled on a sweater, considering the darkening sky. "And Sable and Jax? You sure that angle won't work?"

Amber removed her sunglasses and tucked them into her shirt. "They insist they just wanted to scare him on camera and didn't get the chance to face him before he died because of what they called 'the dumpster fire of a ghost tour.' We haven't been able to question them in depth. Chief is at the station waiting for the girl's representation to arrive from New York. It's the only reason I was able to escape his grasp to come over by myself. They were ready for us and lawyered up before we had them in the squad car."

That's probably my fault. I shouldn't have been so helpful earlier. I waved my finger at the little blonde. "Tonight has to be it. I have plans with Henry and Gia tomorrow for trick or treating. I want my kitchen back. And let's just say I'm doing you this favor in exchange for a favor from you at a future date."

She cocked an eyebrow. "Future favor for what?"

"I don't know yet, but it involves Aunt Ginny and maybe some traumatized kids."

Amber gave me a silent stare.

"I've said too much."

"Okay, McAllister. Just get me the intel I need, and we'll revisit this soon, I'm sure."

Probably sooner than you realize. Amber returned to her patrol car while I stood in the foyer considering whether or not I'd need a coat. A soft thud sounded, and the sitting room door opened of its own accord. Then a gray floofy head followed and Figaro pushed through to the hallway and meowed.

"What are you up to?"

A yip sounded in the library and Fig trotted across the hall and shoved his fluffy gray paw under the door and pulled it open. Princess barked a little tirade before Owen told her Figaro just wanted to see what she was doing.

I grabbed my jacket from the coat tree by the front door and hollered down the hall, "I'll be back soon!"

I stepped outside and a cool breeze shook some of the orange and scarlet leaves free from the autumn tree's light grasp. I closed my eyes and tipped my face to the sky, enveloped in a swirling leaf shower. The leaves clattered to the ground and skittered in swirling pools as I walked over to the Inn of Cape May where the scavenger hunt began. The smell of woodsmoke mingled with damp earth and coaxed my shoulders down from around my ears where they shot up every time Amber sent me on one of her half-baked cop missions.

Linda was standing in front of the awning wrapped in a purple ankle-length sweater, handing out packets to the various tour groups. I'd seen some of these people arriving and departing my house throughout the week. Then of course, there was the handful of

familiar whackadoos who got me stuck on this tour
in the first place clustered on the porch by the Barefoot Bar.

Linda put her arm out to pull me into a side hug.
"Heya, Hunny Bunny. I hear you're going on the
haunted scavenger hunt with . . ."—she lowered her
voice to a whisper—"the other murder suspects."

"What do you mean, other? I'm not a suspect."

Linda laughed uncomfortably and handed a flyer
to a man in a red jacket. "Of course you aren't. Not
this time. Anyway."

Linda raised her voice and climbed a couple of
steps to address the waiting participants. "Everyone
is teamed up with the group they've been with all week.
There are twenty haunted locations on the tour and
every team has to collect clues at each stop. Except
for one location. The clues will tell you where your
next stop is."

Eli Lush kept his eyes on mine the entire walk
down the steps to get our packet, which he snatched
from Linda with a frown, and joined the three ladies.

Linda pretended not to notice. "You're all starting
at different locations and have the same two hours,
so you don't need to rush. Come back to the Inn
when you're finished, and we'll do the drawing for
the grand prize. Find your group and good luck,
everyone."

My people were having a moment of silent, seething anger. They started out a group of seven. One of
them had been murdered, and so far four of them
had been taken in for questioning. Instead of looking at each other with an appropriate amount of well-
deserved suspicion, all their eyes were on me like it
was my fault.

I pointed to the manila envelope in Eli's hand. "Where do we begin?"

Brooklyn crossed her arms like sharp swords and stared at the sidewalk. Felicity puckered her lips and gazed out at the ocean looking for all the world like she was thinking of making a run for it.

Verna removed her glasses and rubbed her eyes. "Haven't you done enough?"

"What did I do?"

"Every time you're around, one of us gets arrested."

"Because one of you killed Simon Beck! My proximity has nothing to do with it!" *You nutjob.*

Felicity grabbed Verna's arm. "Stop it. You know she's cursed. The cops probably have her wired at all times."

"They most certainly do not." *Do they?* I pulled out my cell phone and googled how to tell if you're bugged. *I'll read that later.* I shoved my phone back in my pocket.

Eli pulled a five-by-seven card from the packet. "Let's just get this over with. I'm only here so I can win back what I spent on this waste of time."

Brooklyn snatched the card from his hands and read, "'Begin your tour where the ghost of a woman holds her baby and watches the ocean, waiting for her husband to return home.'"

Felicity gasped. "The cupola. At the green-and-white hotel. Which one was that?"

"The Chalfonte." I pointed down the road. "It's that way and two blocks to the right."

Felicity looked hesitant, like she thought I was luring her into a trap.

"Use your GPS if you don't believe me."

"Found it." Eli was scrolling on his smart phone. "Down that way and to the right."

Exactly what I just said.

Eli started marching down the sidewalk with Felicity at his side. I had Verna and Brooklyn flanking me. Kinda hard to ask one if she tried to kill the other. Things could get awkward really fast.

"So, Verna. There is no way you all just happened to be on the same tour with Simon Beck and his . . . Brooklyn. You arranged it, right? You watched his schedule and set up all Dr. Van Smoot's travel around where Simon would be so you could follow him."

Brooklyn leaned across me to look at Verna.

Verna sighed. "You're just not going to let that go, are you? You got me. I followed Simon Beck's travel plans like a dumb teenager trying hopelessly to get a chance encounter with him because I'm a fool. Are you happy?"

Not at the moment.

Felicity stopped walking and turned around. "You what?"

Verna's shoulders slumped. "They were all really good locations, though."

Felicity's eyes rolled up to her wispy honey bangs. "I've been accusing Simon of stalking me for months. And you let me go on about it like an idiot."

A tear rolled down Verna's cheek. "I know. I'm sorry. I thought if I could get time alone with him, I could get him to see we belong together and that I'd wait for him. I tried to tell him during that ridiculous ghost tour, but he blew me off and said we 'agreed on some space.'"

"I told you he wasn't worth it and to focus on your dissertation."

Verna's voice broke. "I don't think you understand how badly I want a baby. Simon promised me we would start a family as soon as he was free to be mine."

Felicity huffed. "It was a lie, Verna. My God, when will you learn? Simon was a master at saying whatever he had to so he could end the relationship quietly and move to his next victim."

Verna crossed her arms and glared at her professor. "Maybe he did that with you, but it was different with me."

Brooklyn kicked through some leaves on the sidewalk. "If he meant to start a family with you, why was he playing house with me?"

Eli stopped walking a few yards ahead of us. "You're lagging behind. The other groups are going to beat us."

Like the other three ladies, I ignored his order, and instead asked a question. "If Verna was setting up Dr. Van Smoot's travel based on where Simon Beck would be, then why are you always with them?"

Eli cast his eyes towards Felicity and frowned. "Don't you say a word."

We started moving again to catch up with pouty Mr. Lush. "Were you following Simon Beck's itinerary like Verna? Or are you stalking Felicity? I know this isn't the first time you've traveled together."

Felicity marched on in silent vigil.

Verna breathed out a sigh as frustrated as a dieter working in a donut shop. "Just tell her so she'll leave us alone. It's not like she's going to report you to the university."

Felicity glanced over her shoulder at me with a stony expression. "I invited Eli to join me. We've been in a secret relationship for six months. He isn't a killer. He didn't even know Simon would be here.

Neither of us did." She threw some shade Verna's way.

Eli reached down and grabbed Felicity's hand. "It's asinine that relationships between honest grad students and their professors are forbidden at Staunton University. And it's all because Simon Beck's bedroom had a revolving door. Now everyone has to suffer."

Verna and Felicity both shot a look at Brooklyn.

We rounded the last corner to The Chalfonte, and I knew we might run into another tour group since we'd been lolling behind. "So, chalk that up to another reason why you were so angry with him."

Eli made a noise from deep in his throat like he was trying to laugh and hold back a cough at the same time. "I'm the only one in this contrary little group who has never been deceived by that square jaw and his boyish good looks."

Felicity murmured, "I said that one time. When are you going to let it go?"

I thought I'd point out the painfully obvious. "Except for when you confided in him with what you were working on and he stole it."

Eli scowled. "I had zero motive to kill Simon. I'd much rather get my revenge with a Nobel Prize, and show him, and the world, that he wasn't as smart as he thought he was. He didn't know it, but my next paper is being published ahead of schedule. It debunks an earlier discovery of his about the brain's ability to tap into hidden potential. I was expecting a publication announcement in this month's university newsletter. But, once again, the great Dr. Simon Beck takes center stage with the report of his untimely passing."

"At least you know it's the last time he'll scoop you."

We stopped in front of The Chalfonte, and Eli gave me a look that had me worried Amber had let him go by mistake.

Brooklyn chuckled. "No wonder Simon thought you all were following him. You actually were. I tried to convince him he was imagining things."

Verna cast her a hateful look. "Which one of us was imagining they were in a real relationship with Simon?"

Brooklyn shot her a sneer back. "We both were. But you were the only one desperate enough to stalk him like a psycho."

Eli let go of Felicity's hand. "I'll go get the clue. You lot stay here."

He left to go up to the cupola, and a chunky older woman with swiffy white hair fast walked down the steps waving an index card over her head. "Bahaha!"

She passed us and joined her group of seven as they huddled around the card.

I turned back to Verna. "How'd you get into a relationship with Professor Beck in the first place?"

"Okay, first of all, it's 'Dr. Beck.' Simon said that 'Doctor' was a title. Professor was a job. You were only allowed to call Simon Professor if you were his student, which you were not. And second, I started out as his research assistant about eighteen months ago when I began my doctorate studies."

Felicity reapplied her lipstick while she waited for Eli. "That's how most of them start."

Verna's voice grew a bitter edge. "I didn't start out looking to date my professor. I was attracted to his mind before his looks. Simon was brilliant. All the girls were throwing themselves at him. I tried to keep our relationship professional. But Simon was a man who went after what he wanted, and he swept me off my feet."

Brooklyn's tone was bitter. "He was like that with me too. I held him off for weeks because I didn't want a new relationship, but he was a charmer, and I eventually caved to those blue eyes and went out with him."

Verna's expression softened. "He said he loved me and he wanted to marry me and start a family, but he had a sick wife at home and had to wait until he was free from his obligation."

Felicity rolled her lips together and made popping sounds. "He's been using that sick wife story on girls for fifteen years."

"Verna, did Simon have you transferred to Felicity's department because you were stalking him?"

Verna pushed her glasses back with one jagged red fingernail. "I wasn't stalking him. At least not that he knew about. Besides, you don't just transfer to another department and go on like nothing happened. You either change majors like Felicity or change schools like Eli. And a professor doesn't have the power to make you switch majors against your will. I terminated my mentorship agreement with Simon because the pain of being around him every day was just too much to bear. I told Dr. Van Smoot everything he'd put me through, and she took me under her wing and said she'd be my mentor in the PhD program while I pursued independent study in the field."

"So, Simon didn't have to get a restraining order against you?"

"Where did you hear that? Of course not. Besides,

I plan to be on staff at Staunton University one day. I'd never show my emotional pain on the outside."

Alright, delusion—table for one.

Felicity dug around in her purse and pulled out a compact to check her reflection. "You don't have to take her word for it. Call the Dean. She should have all that in Simon's file. Not that she should divulge any of that to you. But hey, tell her about your curse and maybe you'll get special insider information."

Your sarcasm is not appreciated, lady.

Eli appeared on the front porch with an index card and ran down the steps. He lowered the card and Verna grabbed it from his hand. "It's my turn. While you've been off playing Sherlock, I've been getting interrogated."

"I hardly think asking a couple of innocent questions is an interrogation." *I could take you to Aunt Ginny's cross-examination on the porch swing if you want to see a real interrogation.*

Verna pushed her glasses back to her forehead and read the card. "'Al the handyman still haunts this Painted Lady.' The Painted Lady? Was that the big pink one?"

They all looked to me. "The Painted Ladies are the Stockton Row Cottages. This one would be the Belvidere." *I hope. Unless Mrs. Davis forgot to mention her house was haunted.* "Keep going that way around the block. You'll know them when you see them."

The ladies took off down the block in the direction I'd pointed. It was getting very chilly, but the look Eli gave me was what sent shivers across my neck. "Are you satisfied now that you've heard our secrets? Will you leave us alone?"

I shoved my hands in my pockets. "I'm not who

you have to worry about. I'm just a local B and B owner. But I'm sure the police are going to want to talk to you all again. For one thing, they haven't questioned Felicity about getting revenge against Simon for destroying her chances at tenure."

Felicity stopped short and spun around to face me. "Wait a minute. Stop right there. Simon didn't destroy my chances. He delayed them. Let's get that straight."

Verna latched onto Felicity to provide really mediocre backup. "Yeah! And she had to start over from scratch! Now it's fifteen years later and she almost has it in middle age, so back off."

Felicity frowned and lines appeared around her eyes. "Excuse me? Middle age?"

Brooklyn gave her a deadpan stare. "Are you planning to live to a hundred? Because that's the only way you're not middle-aged. And Simon said you switched departments because you were no good at paranormal investigation."

Eli marched on. "I'm going to get the clue."

We all started moving after him.

Felicity's eyes glittered with anger. "I was brilliant at paranormal investigation."

Brooklyn smiled sweetly. "He said you butchered your thesis and he had to rewrite it for you."

"He lied. Duh. That's what Simon did. I wrote a brilliant thesis and Simon wanted to put his name on it and send it to a peer review journal as his solo work. He said it was too important a discovery to come from an unknown woman who didn't have a PhD. When I wouldn't agree to that, he accused me of plagiarizing him."

"There's a motive for murder."

Felicity ran her hand through her honey hair. "I

didn't. I was about to eclipse him at the university as the foremost knowledgeable PhD in parapsychology ethics. It took me a long time to come this far, but I did it. And he knew his time at the top was over. He was on his second round of academic suspension for being involved with a student in two years. I wanted him alive to wallow in that fact."

"Oh-kay." We turned the corner heading towards the Stockton Row Cottages. I could see Mrs. Davis's house before me. All her lights were out. *Is it bingo night or salsa dance class?* I picked up the pace a bit trying to warm my feet. *I should have worn my UGGs.* The swiffy-haired woman's group passed us and waved three cards.

Eli put his arm around Felicity. "Everything Simon Beck touched was tainted with his greed and selfishness. If he didn't already have tenure, the university would probably have fired him instead of just suspending him again."

Felicity smiled and reached to hold Eli's hand on her shoulder. "Simon was a vain and jealous man, and he knew I was smarter than him. It's why he blocked my application for tenure. The Dean was very generous to keep me on staff after Simon tried to blackball me. Partly because the university wanted to avoid a sexual harassment lawsuit—I mean . . . an unlawful termination lawsuit. I've worked very hard in the Philosophy Department, and they allowed me to reapply for tenure. My probation is almost finished, and when I go before the tenure committee in a couple of months Simon won't be on it this time." Her eyes bugged and she quickly looked at me. "It wasn't me! Stop looking at me like that! Why aren't you cross-examining your waiter? You have to know Kenny Love was in Simon's class at SU."

"So, I gather you're the one who sent me his transcript?"

"You bet I did. I doubt Simon Beck would have had the same pull with the head of admissions." Felicity tossed her hair and pointed her nose to the sky. "I knew I recognized that boy from somewhere. You don't know the things that I know. If you did. You wouldn't be wasting your time harassing us."

"Why'd you send that to me instead of the police?"

"I don't want to get involved with the cops. I just want you to stop harassing the rest of us."

We reached the front of the Belvidere and Brooklyn accepted the card from the owner. "Tell me this: Why would you stay at Staunton University in Simon Beck's shadow after all he did to you? Couldn't you just go to another university since you had to start over anyway?"

All three of the university people looked at me like I was speaking pig Latin.

Felicity's voice took on a singsongy condescension. "We're not talking about a liberal arts degree, darling. This is parapsychology. There are very few remaining universities that have parapsychology departments in the US. Most of them ceased their paranormal programs in the eighties. If you want to work in this field, your options are very limited."

"I know. I checked days ago." I pulled out my cell phone and ran the search again. The list was very small. So small, in fact, that colleges I'd expected to see weren't even on the list.

Verna scowled. "Then why aren't you looking beyond us three?" she muttered angrily. "There's a whole world of possibilities out there. That's why I'm thinking about transferring my degree to the Koestler Parapsychology Unit in Edinburgh."

Eli's eyes lit up. "Oh, that's a good school. And you can come back to the States for work once you get your PhD. Everyone in the paranormal field knows everyone else. No matter what school you go to, eventually all our paths cross."

Verna nodded. "I just have to go somewhere else and get away from the broken promises of Simon Beck."

My stomach bottomed out twice. The first time was when I realized Figaro had been giving me hints about the killer all along and I'd missed them. And the second time was when Brooklyn read the next clue.

"'For your next house, be on the lookout for victims as you make your way to the home of the Cape May Murder Magnet.'"

CHAPTER 44

I'm going to have words with Linda at the Inn. I want to know what this nonsense about a clue card at my house is all about. I fired off a text of questions to Amber and told her we needed to talk ASAP. I was having some wild thoughts about Simon's killer, and I didn't like where they were taking me.

The rest of my tour group chatted amongst themselves, having aligned together against me. We arrived in front of my house in tense silence. One of the other groups from the Inn came around the corner and paused in front of the yard, whispering. Eli pointed to the garden gnome holding a ceramic bowl full of index cards. The leader took a card and they moved on after taking a few pictures.

I stared absently at my front porch, thinking over the events from the past few days. I turned to the four members of my scavenger hunt, "Go on without me. I have something to take care of here at home."

Verna waved the others on. "I'll catch up." She removed her cat-eye glasses and cleaned them on the corner of her sweater. "Can I use your bathroom?"

My phone buzzed in my pocket. Amber's reply had come in. "Sure."

Verna disappeared into the house while I checked the message:

You were right. Ethics committee at SU had this reprimand flagged in Simon's file. No restraining order on file at Uni.

A photo of the student involved in the reprimand was attached. *Well, crap.* I looked into the house.

Ritchie came out of the front door with a coil of cables for the TV equipment. He dropped the stack on the front step.

"Can I talk to you for a minute?"

He placed his headphones on the chair. "Sure. What do you need?"

"I need to see some footage from the night Simon Beck died."

"Okay. What are you looking for?"

"Something to prove me wrong."

Sometimes the most obvious answers are the hardest to come by. I should have paid closer attention to who was in the room when Simon Beck nearly fell over the couch that night.

Ritchie capped the thumb drive and handed it to me. We'd watched three hours of B-roll footage from the night of Simon's murder in about fifteen minutes. "That's not our best work. I couldn't find anything usable from that—that's why it was deleted."

I slid the device into my pocket. "It's what's *not* there that's the problem."

Ritchie shrugged. "I don't really understand, but I hope it helps."

Verna was waiting to catch a ride back with tonight's ghost tour guests. They'd finished their dessert and coffee and were waiting for the Victorian hearse to pick them up.

With a heavy sigh, I went up the stairs and knocked on the door of the Purple Emperor Suite.

The door cracked open, and Paisley blinked one eye at me.

"Hi, Poppy. What's up?"

"Can we talk?"

The door swung fully open. She was in her Berkeley sweats and hadn't applied her bright red lipstick or put on her glasses yet.

Harper was sitting on a tufted walnut chair. "What's going on?"

"Can I talk to Paisley alone for a minute?"

"Yeah, sure." Harper left the room and pulled the door closed behind her.

I crossed the room to sit on the chair she'd vacated and looked at the beautiful raven-haired woman. "How well did you know Simon Beck?"

Paisley sat gingerly on the bed. "Not at all. I just met Professor Beck here at your house the night of the tour. Why?"

"Did Harper get you those sweats? Or do you just visit UC Berkeley for the gift shop?"

She looked at the college name printed down her pant leg but didn't give me an answer.

"UC Berkeley doesn't offer a parapsychology degree. You transferred from Staunton University to the Berkeley Psychic Institute two years ago."

Paisley pulled her knees to her chest and hugged them. "That's not right. I never went to SU."

I took my phone out and pulled up the photo Amber had sent me. "According to their admissions office you did. There was a note in Simon's file about a reprimand he received involving you." I turned it to show Paisley the SU picture of her younger self without the glasses. "You normally wear contacts, don't you? Did you have to switch to your backup glasses recently because your eyes were bothering you? When I first met you, you were rubbing them a lot."

Paisley's eyes filled with tears. "You've got it wrong."

"Then tell me how to get it right. Because Ritchie fished the footage from your camera the night of the tour out of the recycle bin on your computer and it's two hours of Simon and Brooklyn except for five minutes when you paused the video in the middle of the ghost tour."

Paisley wiped her eyes. "Here. I'll show you." She got off the bed and walked calmly over to her suitcase by the door. I was ready to hurl myself into her and drag her to the floor if she pulled out a weapon. A person can only fall for that so many times. She unzipped the bag down one side, then opened the door and fled from the room.

Crap on a cracker! I was so startled I stared at the empty door. I ran out behind her, but Figaro was standing on the top step waiting to trip someone, and I had to dodge him. Paisley ran down the steps, through the departing tour group of eight getting their coats on in the foyer, and leapt through the open door.

"Excuse me." I jumped through the middle of the group out behind her, but forty years on the knees and eighty extra pounds everywhere else didn't fly as fast as a twenty-something-year-old.

I lumbered down the steps, past the carriage driver, regretting all the yoga I'd skipped.

Paisley jumped onto the Victorian hearse and the horses snorted and stomped.

The driver shouted from my porch where he was talking on his cell phone, "Hey! Get off of there!"

Paisley shook the reins, but the horses stood fast, giving me time to catch up and grab some of the black bunting hanging from the wagon. "Paisley, stop!"

She whimpered, "I can't go to jail. It was an accident. It was supposed to be her." She made lots of noises clicking and clucking her cheeks trying to get the horses to move, but they wouldn't budge.

I climbed into the back of the hearse and inched forward when Paisley suddenly figured out the magic horse word for *run like Seabiscuit*. She cracked the reins against a rump and those horses took off at a gallop, flinging me backwards into the wagonette.

"Paisley, pull the reins towards you!"

"No! Let me go!"

Up until this moment, the only horse interaction I'd ever had was at my sixth birthday party when Chester of the Shore Pony Ride circuit bit me on the stomach. My affection for the majestic equine had been forever tainted because of the lingering smell of Mr. Bubbles that Chester had mistakenly interpreted as that of a chubby apple. I can't say my second occasion was going much better.

The horses rounded the corner onto Washington. "Paisley, we're on an island. Where exactly do you think you're gonna go? I know you were trying to kill Brooklyn and killed Simon by mistake."

She cracked the horses on the rear again and they both took off, throwing me backwards. "I wasn't trying to kill her. I was just trying to make her sick. Simon said he loved me, but he couldn't commit because his wife was terminal. He wouldn't leave her, so we had to wait until after she died. He told me if I transferred to a school in California and waited for him that he'd be with me soon. I've seen pictures of his wife. She was old and emaciated. Then he showed up here with that actress who wasn't sick at all; I thought he'd gotten remarried to someone else."

We jerked to a stop in front of the Southern Mansion and the horses restlessly marched in place. I clutched my way forward trying to get the reins from the crazy woman who just this week had already proven that she was a stalker and a murderer. I reached for Paisley's shoulder, but she cracked the reins and the wagonette lurched forward. I lost my footing and landed hard on my butt. "She wasn't really his wife."

We turned the corner again and Paisley sobbed. "I didn't know that at the time, though, did I? I just wanted to punish her and Simon. He said I was the only woman he ever loved and getting married to her so young was a mistake. He never really loved her. Then she got sick and he couldn't leave her. I let him take credit for one of my papers. I should have won an Outstanding Contribution Award, but that jerk took all the credit and I let him. He said the next one we published would be all mine. Then he had the university threaten to expel me for stalking him. And still, I've been waiting for him, like a fool."

The horses zigzagged through the streets and ground to a stop in front of The Chalfonte. I struggled to my feet, and pulled myself forward inch by inch along the bench seats. "I know. I get it. He used you. He did that a lot. So, you swapped out Brooklyn's stevia for your Visine."

Paisley's voice was raw. She cracked the reins, and the horses gave her a sharp whinny before jerking away from the curb and causing me to drop to my knees. "It was just supposed to make her sick. How was I supposed to know she wouldn't touch it all night? And then Simon kept drinking more and more of that iced tea. He only drank Scotch when we were together. He would never have switched to iced tea for me."

I tried to stand, but the horses made a sharp turn onto the next street. They only knew one route. They'd walked it every night, and that route's next stop was The Hotel Macomber. *This is the worst get-away ever.*

Paisley shook the reins in frustration. "Come on, you dumb horses! Where's the bridge?!"

Where is Owen Rodney, Pet Psychic, when you need him? I grasped the front of the wagon. "You're not doing yourself any favors by running. By now the cops have probably found out that Simon had a restraining order against you."

Paisley shook her head and cried. "That was a misunderstanding. He said his wife was in the hospital. I only went to his house to surprise him for Valentine's Day. I thought waiting for him in bed covered in rose petals would be romantic."

"Oh, Paisley. You didn't."

"I really believed Simon was going to call me any day and let me know his wife had passed away and we could finally be together. He said he only wanted me gone because it was too painful to see me when he couldn't have me. Then I saw that Brooklyn sitting next to him. I was so angry and confused. No one was supposed to die."

"But why'd you hide the stevia bottle in the ficus? You could have just left it on the table and the cops would have assumed Brooklyn was the killer."

"I don't know. I was in shock. When the lights came back on, I knew Simon's death was my fault. All I could think was *hide the evidence*. I was going to go back later to throw it away somewhere else, but Clark would not stop filming in the dining room trying to reach Simon's ghost. And that pet psychic was in there with Figaro every single day when I came down. I've been waiting to be with Simon for two years. She was supposed to be sick. He deserved her being sick."

"I know." I had planned on taking the reins at that point and calmly letting the horses rest. Then a tourist shouted, "Look! It's the cursed lady!" and a blinding flash went off right in front of the horses' faces.

They were already spooked and lathered. This was more than they could handle. The wagonette pitched forward again. I held on to the back of the seat for dear life. Paisley had given up the will to fight and was lying on the bench, boneless. I was afraid she'd slide right off and get trampled.

"Stay with me, Paisley. Why'd you move the name cards to put Verna next to Simon?"

Paisley's voice was flat, and I could barely hear her over the sound of the horses' hooves and the creak of the wagonette. "I wanted to see how Simon would react to another woman in his wife's seat. He took out a restraining order on me just for wearing her lingerie. Now I realize he didn't really love me at all."

We rounded the corner and stopped in front of the Inn of Cape May, and I fell to the wagon bed. Two cop cars were sitting at the curb, their lights and sirens off. A crowd had gathered to see what was so exciting. The Victorian hearse driver was waiting calmly under the purple awning. He snatched the reins from Paisley. Then he patted the first horse on the neck and spoke to calm it down.

I clutched the side of the wagon and tried to pull myself upright. My hair had come out of its ponytail, and I was covered in dirt and sand from being tossed around in the back.

A light went off in my face and Gladys Philippot laughed. "That's a beauty."

Amber pulled her handcuffs off her belt. "Sorry. She followed us here with the carriage driver." Amber approached the driver's seat. "Paisley Bordeaux. I'm placing you under arrest for the murder of Simon Beck."

While Amber cuffed the pitiful young woman, she gave me a long look. "You, okay?"

"I guess." I noticed Linda watching me from the sidewalk. "Please take this as my official notice that the Butterfly Wings will not be continuing on with the Haunted Dinner Tour."

CHAPTER 45

"I'm fine. Really."

It had been a long night. Chief Kieran insisted I go to the police station to deliver my statement to him personally while he fact-checked every detail as to how I came across each piece of information. Paisley had confessed everything. Including that the empty Visine bottle was floating in the tank of my hall toilet.

In between dodging Kieran's barbs of irritation that I'd solved another crime before one of his officers, I also had to talk Gia off the ledge. "I'm not hurt. And I don't think I was ever in any real danger. The murder wasn't premeditated. I think Paisley was just overcome with grief when she realized she'd lost so much of her life waiting for a man who would never be who she wanted him to be. She's made a horrific mistake."

Gia's voice was tight and strained when he pulled me into his arms. "I need to keep you close, *cara mia*. Then if someone wants to hurt you, they have to go through me first."

"What happens if they want to hurt you?"

"Then they have to go through you, and may God have mercy on them."

Gia had restlessly binged his way through two rows of the entire vending machine lineup when Amber finally announced we were free to go.

We parked back at La Dolce Vita and walked the rest of the way to my house. As we rounded the corner, the wind picked up, sending dried leaves scuttling down the sidewalk like crabs. Thunder sounded in the distance. I looked at the almost full moon, but there weren't any clouds in the sky. *Is it supposed to rain?*

Gia slowed his pace. "What is going on in your yard?"

I looked closely and spotted four ninjas moving through the leaves. Three of them were tossing toilet paper in the air and one of them was putting together a headless scarecrow by the mailbox. My house was completely dark even though there should have been guests about. "Shh. It's the kids who've been pranking us all week. I want to see just who these punks are."

I watched for a few more seconds, and the ninjas were beginning to look a little more like brown bears lumbering around and struggling to get the toilet paper over the branches.

The wind picked up from out of nowhere, and an eerie glow lit from within the crown of the tree. The leaves came alive and began to moan. The bears stopped moving and were looking around wildly and pointing in every direction.

A rumble of thunder rolled over us. My yard filled with fog creeping out of the earth below like the Michael Jackson "Thriller" video. I wanted to call the police, but I was frozen in place, betrayed by my hands and feet.

Gia said something, but I couldn't hear him over the pounding of my blood in my ears.

A violent screech pierced the night as a white witch with bright red eyes and flowing gray rags flew out of the tree at the bears and headed straight for us in a sweeping arc. "Eeeeyahh!"

The bears all slammed into each other and fell in a heap.

The witch flew back to a high branch and flapped her cape at the bears.

I ripped my phone from my pocket and with a shaking hand tried to turn on the screen, but I fumbled and dropped it in the grass.

The witch made another sweep, only this time laughing so hard she snorted. She spun back and forth a couple of times getting slower and lower until she landed on the porch. She stood about four feet nine and I realized the scariest sight I'd ever witnessed in my life looked a lot like Aunt Ginny in a Stevie Nicks wig.

"That'll teach you to prank my yard!" She reached for one of the bears and ripped the ski mask off Mrs. Davis's face.

"Darn it, Ginny! You made me pee and I'm not wearing my Depends!"

"Serves you right, you hooligan."

The other two Biddies took off their masks in a fit of grumbles that Aunt Ginny had ruined their prank. "We've been working on this all month to get you back for signing us up for the pie-throwing contest at the Labor Day picnic."

Aunt Ginny wiped tears from her eyes. "I said I was sorry. I didn't know you were going to be the targets."

Mrs. Dodson wiped the mud from her knees. "That didn't affect your aim any, though. Did it?"

The yard filled with laughter from inside the fog. I still didn't have my breath back and I didn't recognize the voices. I also noticed for the first time the faces watching us through every available window. Joanne and Sawyer were in the library. Upstairs with Royce were several of the neighbors. They all began to applaud and whistle.

Figaro peered through the sitting room window in between Owen Rodney and Jennifer Beck. Princess's big eye and one of her ears appeared, then disappeared every few seconds until Jennifer placed her in the window next to Fig.

I stepped into the fog. "Aunt Ginny?"

The white witch was bent over laughing and holding her side. "Ow. Ow. It hurts. The way you all started running into each other."

Mrs. Dodson struggled to her feet with her cane. "I just want to know how you came flying out of that tree, Virginia. You scared the living daylights out of me!"

Mother Gibson pulled herself up by the porch railing. "I thought for sure I'd missed the rapture and you was a demon."

Most of the fog had lifted, and the Senior Center director waved to me from across the yard where he was coiling a long extension cord that led to what looked like a canister vacuum.

Aunt Ginny pointed in his direction and said through her laughter, "Neil set up the fog machine and the harness and pulleys for the flying. And Bebe did my costume and makeup."

Bebe pranced onto the porch dressed head to toe in black, but with fuchsia pink hair, lips, and nails.

She reached for Aunt Ginny's waist and removed a carabiner that was strapped to a white body harness. "Hey girl. Did you see your aunt fly?"

The wires were so obvious now that I was standing under the lights. They went from the roof to the trees. "I don't think I'll ever be able to unsee it."

Neil wound his cord up to the porch. "It's a good thing I've been planning the Senior Center production of *Phantom* for the spring. I hope you're all going to come try out for that." He put his hand down and helped Mrs. Dodson straighten herself to upright.

She smacked at him. "I can't believe you've been helping her! Shame on you!"

I looked across the yard where the fourth bear was trying to escape. "Who is that?"

Gia reached out and grabbed the bear's arm. The bear pulled away from Gia in an attempt to run, but Gia held it fast. I pulled the mask away and looked into the eyes of Georgina.

"You traitor!"

Georgina's cheeks turned as pink as the Biddies jacket I saw peeking out of her costume. "The gals called and asked me to help them with their strategic strikes. What was I supposed to say?"

Mrs. Davis came to the aide of my former mother-in-law. "You leave Gina alone. She's one heck of a getaway driver."

Mother Gibson added, "And child, you should see her carve a pumpkin."

I gazed at Aunt Ginny under her giant Stevie Nicks white wig and red reflective glasses. "How is it you can organize an entire production like this in less than twenty-four hours, but you can't remember to put gas in the car when you go to the Acme?"

Bebe lifted a pale cape from Aunt Ginny's shoulders. "It's all about the motivation, dahling."

Kenny crawled out of the lattice gate under the porch wearing headphones and dragging wires.

"What were you doing under there?"

Kenny grinned. "Sound and lights." He held up a square device with buttons. "I put the wind machine by the garage on remote control. Did it feel really windy to you?"

"Yeah."

"Cool."

Aunt Ginny shrugged out of her harness. "Where have you been?"

"Police station."

"What for?"

"I was kidnapped and dragged around town by wild horses while Paisley tried to escape capture because she murdered Simon Beck."

Aunt Ginny blinked at me. "Did you get bit on the tummy again?"

"No."

"Well, that's progress."

I nodded, glumly. "Can I have a peanut butter sandwich like last time?"

Aunt Ginny put her hand on my back. "Come on, baby. I'll make you a sammich and we'll change the sign for 'Days without being threatened by a murderer' back to zero."

CHAPTER 46

Gia gave me a final kiss good night and returned home to Henry. I wanted to go with him, but I had to sit in my kitchen while everyone fussed over me like I was a child.

"Oh, the insane hoops a desperate woman will jump through for a man." Aunt Ginny clicked her tongue. Then she spit on a paper towel and wiped it across the bridge of my nose.

"Eww. I'm not five anymore. And I rather think the dirt from the wagon was more sanitary."

Kenny handed me a hot cocoa. "I can't believe Paisley was the killer. She was so sweet."

I blew across the top of the mug. "I know. I really liked her."

Joanne grunted. "Well, you're a terrible judge of character."

Figaro jumped on the table and bonked his head against my hand. Either he was trying to comfort me, or he felt he was due some of the attention I was getting. He flopped on the table and started to purr, so it was probably the latter.

"All that stuff Owen Rodney said about Figaro trying to warn everybody, saying it was the water bowl and something had been moved. And him stealing Paisley's things and shushing her. That was all just a coincidence, right?"

Everyone chuckled nervously.

"Of course."

"Absolutely."

"No duh."

The room grew awkwardly silent.

Aunt Ginny showed me an Instagram account on her iPad. It was Paisley holding a gray cat with white feet. "She does have a cat and his name is Mittens."

"I don't want to talk about it."

Joanne grumbled. "I guess your kitchen is officially open again. So, since you don't need me anymore, I'll be off."

"Thanks, Joanne. You were a great help."

Aunt Ginny pinched my arm.

"Ow! What?"

Joanne grabbed her fanny pack off the hook and strapped it on. "Fine." She left the kitchen, but her voice cracked a bit as she said, "Later days, Buttface."

Is she upset? No. I'm imagining things. I've had a rough night.

Kenny watched her disappear around the corner. "Phew. I really thought she was gunning for my job. I am way more fun than she is, but I'm not gonna lie. Compared to her pastries, some of my dishes are not even appealing to me. And that shepherd's pie was way too spicy."

Aunt Ginny glared at me, waiting for me to figure something out on my own.

"What do you want from me? I was just dragged around town by a killer on wild horses."

Kenny laughed, then choked it back. "Sorry."

"There's nothing I can say to get her out of her lousy mood."

Aunt Ginny changed her usual glare to a new improved menacing glare.

I took a gulp of my cocoa and stared back at her. "Fine!" I set my cocoa on the table with a loud clunk. "I'll go talk to her."

The front door was closing, so I hollered, "Joanne, wait!"

It paused, then slammed shut.

I trucked down the hall double time. *Don't make me chase you. I think I have hay down the back of my jeans.*

The three remaining Paranormal Pathfinders were huddled in the library around the fire with Jennifer Beck, Owen, and Gladys. They silently watched me as I grabbed the handle and flung the door wide.

Joanne was fast walking to her truck.

"Slow down. I need to talk to you."

She stopped but didn't turn around. "What do you want, Moron? I have to go."

"Is there something going on that I'm missing?"

She wouldn't look at me. "Forget it."

"Forget what? I'm really in the dark here, Joanne. What is wrong?"

She turned and I saw her eyes were glassy and red. "Are you crying?"

"No, you stupid cow. I have allergies."

"Sudden Mischief Night hay fever allergies?"

"Maybe."

I stepped closer. "So, what's going on?"

Joanne bit her lip and rolled her eyes to mine. "Geez. You're such an idiot. I like it here, okay?"

I waited quietly, giving her room to say more.

"You're my only friends—you know, since you killed Barbie."

Friends? How long have we been friends? "I had nothing to do with Barbie's murder. That whack job is in jail."

"Whatever."

"You've been saying for months that you were only working for me—"

"With you."

"—to do Aunt Ginny a favor and you didn't want to be here."

Joanne stared at the sidewalk.

"Are you telling me now you want to stay?"

The wind picked up and I almost missed Joanne's answer over the flapping of Mrs. Pritchard's *It's Fall Y'all* flag. "This is the best job I've ever had."

I took a deep breath and let it out. "Well, heck, Joanne. Of course you can stay. You can work for me—"

"With you."

"—as long as you like."

Joanne rolled her eyes. "I get it. Stop begging."

"Very funny."

"I'm the head cook, though."

"Of course."

"And I don't take orders from you or Kenny."

"So, business as usual."

"Exactly."

"Okay. You think you can stop calling me Butt-face?"

"Don't push it."

"Okay. Baby steps." I put out my hand to her.

She cautiously raised hers to mine. "I should probably tell you, though. I put the tablespoon of cayenne pepper in Kenny's shepherd's pie."

"Oof. That's not cool, Joanne. That burned all the way through."

Aunt Ginny and Kenny were waiting for me in the kitchen. "Well?"

I sat back down and picked up my cocoa. "She's staying."

Kenny's orange eyebrows slid down his face like two caterpillars falling off a tree. "I'll go pack my things."

"You can stay too if you're ready to tell me what you were arrested for."

Kenny bit the inside of his cheek. "I was hoping you forgot about that. You can't even remember what you ate for breakfast without checking the dishes."

"I can't deny that. But fair is fair. You know my secrets."

Aunt Ginny helped. "You know she's a murder magnet."

"Yes, Aunt Ginny. Thank you. I almost forgot about that for a minute."

Kenny's look softened. "Oh, you are not. And I think you get pulled into these things because Amber is in awe of how clever you are."

"Flattery won't get you out of this."

Kenny dropped to the seat across from me and sent a look of defeat to Aunt Ginny. "Okay, but don't laugh."

Aunt Ginny shook her head. "I can't promise that."

"When I was in college, I spent a night in jail for stealing a goat."

I set my cocoa down. "What?"

"After I transferred into drama at SU, we were doing a production of *Fiddler* with livestock." Kenny lowered his head with his voice. "I thought it was inhumane to keep the goat locked up, so I stole it. I was going to set it free on an area farm, but before I got off campus it started to scream. And then it fainted."

Aunt Ginny laughed so hard that she hiccupped.

Kenny's voice dropped even lower, and his head bobbed as he spoke. "Campus security heard the goat's screams and jumped to the very wrong conclusion. They caught me in the parking lot, trying to strap a seat belt on the stiff goat, but I couldn't get it around its legs because they were all sticking straight out like a zombie."

Aunt Ginny was holding her sides with tears streaming down her cheeks.

Kenny looked from her to me to see how much he was going to be judged.

A snicker tried to escape, but I locked it down. "I think it's admirable that you were trying to save the goat."

Kenny's eyebrows relaxed.

"I'm also willing to bet money that Aunt Ginny spent time in jail for being naked and protesting something in the sixties."

Aunt Ginny stopped laughing. "How did you get that information? Those records are sealed."

"Lucky guess."

She frowned and took a swig of her Fresca.

Kenny stood and stretched. "Well, that's a relief. I'm going up to my room. *Plan 9 from Outer Space* is on tonight and I don't want to miss Criswell."

"Okay, and by the way . . ."

He paused at the pantry door.

"Joanne's in charge of all the food."

"What?" He grumbled for a bit. "Then we need to get her to make us those blintzes again."

"I'm way ahead of you. I've conveniently placed the compote where she can't miss it."

Kenny disappeared up the steps and Aunt Ginny cocked an eyebrow. "So, how'd it really go with Joanne?"

"She was crying."

"I tried to tell you."

"You didn't tell me anything. You pinched me."

"You hurt her feelings when you told her you didn't need her anymore."

"I thought she wanted to go. She's always so mean to me."

"She lashes out. People lash out because they're hurt and protecting themselves."

"Am I supposed to just let her treat me that way?"

"No. Of course not. But try to look beyond her actions to what lies beneath. Fear. Pain. Resentment. Misplaced anger. What do you think causes Joanne's behavior?"

"I dunno. Rage? She's a bully. So, meanness."

Aunt Ginny folded her arms across the table. "Yes, but why?"

I could feel forty years of being hurt by people like Joanne rising to the surface and my anger threatened to ignite like a rocket. "I don't know. Why do I have to be her punching bag while she figures it out?"

"You've had more advantages in life than she's had."

Are you insane, lady? "How? Where? I wasn't popular in high school. My husband is dead. I'm running a struggling B&B. I gain ten pounds by walking past a piece of cake. My boyfriend's mother hates me. What advantages do I have that are so special?"

Aunt Ginny stood and picked up her empty glass. "You have me."

In a moment, my anger and frustration rolled away like the retreating tide, and I was left with a rosy warmth that I still had this wonderful example who'd been there for me my entire life. "Well, that is more than anyone could wish for."

She hugged me. "And it wasn't the sixties. It was the nineties."

CHAPTER 47

In honor of my kitchen getting reopened and being allowed to keep abusing me with verbal wedgies, Joanne made a special Halloween breakfast of pumpkin cheesecake French toast and blackberry Pop-Tarts in the shape of bats. She even served prune juice in little cocktail glasses, but I'm not sure anyone drank it other than Aunt Ginny.

Clark and his *Paranormal Pathfinders* team were leaving right after breakfast. They were all shaken by the discovery that one of their own was a killer. Not even a successful taping could make up for their disappointment.

Clark put his hand out to mine. "Thank you for letting us stay. It's going to be one of our best episodes ever. It's not often we find an entity linked so directly to the homeowner."

I suspected the link had more to do with faulty wiring in my hundred-and-fifty-year-old house, and Figaro's ability to paw open doors. "Thank you for not telling everyone I'm cursed and calling me a weirdo on camera."

"Our loyal viewers are very open-minded. You'd be surprised with how sympathetic they can be."

"Isn't Elaine Grabstein one of your loyal viewers?"

"That's right, she is."

I'll need to start screening my calls.

Ritchie took my hand next. "It was a pleasure. Our production manager will let you know when the episode is going to air."

Harper gave me a tired smile. "I finished the diary last night. I think your entity is your great-great-grandfather, Callum McAllister. A few months after he bought the house, he had an argument with the next-door neighbor, and she said she put a curse on him and his children's children."

"Get out of here!"

Harper smiled. "It was hard-core. I marked the page with a Post-it for you. We tried to get the entity to confirm he was Callum last night after you went to bed, but he wouldn't cooperate without you there."

That's because Kenny was finished blow-drying his hair.

We said goodbye and they promised they'd come back if I ever needed them again.

Figaro had spent the morning zooming back and forth like he was possessed. Aunt Ginny tried to give him some tuna to calm him down, but he went right back to zooming after daintily choking it down.

Amber arrived late morning to let me know that Paisley was charged. "Confirmation on that restraining order finally came through this morning."

I offered her a cup of coffee. "Well, that was timely."

She dumped a couple of tablespoons of sugar into her cup. "Don't tell him I told you this, but Kieran mucked the request up because he only requested information about Verna Fox. He didn't include any other suspects in the search."

"Oh my gosh. And here he wouldn't let me use my kitchen for a week because he suspected Kenny."

"Well, your housekeeper didn't do himself any favors by running."

I stirred my coffee and considered my words carefully. "Why do you suppose Kenny's arrest record didn't come up in my background check?"

Amber snorted. "You probably only searched for felonies. Kidnapping a goat with intent to set it free is a misdemeanor."

"You could have told me that when you said he had a record."

She grinned. "Not my place. Besides, I didn't want you making a fuss about it."

"When do I ever make a fuss?"

Amber laughed. "Right. I'll remember that for the next time."

"No. No way. There isn't going to be a next time."

"I give you three months before I'm sitting here again taking your statement."

I made a face at her. "Are you sure you want to make that long of a prediction? I hear I'm the Cape May Murder Magnet."

Amber nodded slowly. "Let's make it six weeks."

I ran to the store and bought several bags of candy. I stuck the candy for the trick or treaters in a giant bowl and hid it in the dryer, and I placed the decoy bag of peanut butter cups in the kitchen drawer with a note that said, "Don't Eat." That would ensure that Aunt Ginny would blow through them before dinner. Then I unwrapped several bars of Snickers to make some candy bar brownies for La Dolce Vita.

The last pan was coming out of the oven when Kenny stuck his head in the kitchen. "Gladys Philippot is checking out and she says she needs to see you."

She was waiting in the hall with her suitcase and a folder tucked under her arm. Figaro galloped across the hall and disappeared into the sitting room. He came right back out again being chased by Princess, who was about half his size and running sideways dragging her pink leash behind her. They disappeared together into the library.

"Yeah, so. Before I go, I thought I oughtta let ya know this is comin' out on Sunday." She pulled two glossy pages from the folder and set them on the desk in front of me.

One was her article titled "B-and-B Owner: Cosmically Cursed or Carelessly Curious?" It speculated as to whether I had an ancient curse on me in way of reckoning for the sins committed in my past, or if I was just a nosy old lady with a police scanner in the kitchen.

The other was a black-and-white photo of me crawling from the Victorian hearse like a zombie clawing out of the grave. My hair wild around me, dirt was smudged on my cheek, and I clearly had the memory of Chester nipping me on the stomach playing across my face. "So, I gather you're moving ahead with your tabloid story even though I never claimed to be anything other than unlucky?"

"Hey, at least we're not printing that you're a fraud or a serial killer. You're just a regular freak like the guy who lives in a locker under Union Station. Plus, you made the cover, kid. Look for this at every supermarket and convenience store register west of

Choccolocco." Gladys tapped the photo. "You can keep this one. I have the file."

Figaro leapt to the top of my desk with his ears flattened and immediately threw up on the photo.

"Who's a good boy?" I ran my hand down Fig's cottony coat. Then I folded the picture in half and dumped it into the trash. "Have a lovely trip home to New York, Miss Philippot."

I picked Figaro up and carried him upstairs for some belly rubs before I prepped for the evening festivities.

Aunt Ginny's annual Halloween party had become an infamous social event on the Cape May Senior circuit. I had spent the afternoon baking finger foods that looked like actual fingers. Cream cheese stuffed-pepper mummies wrapped in pastry dough, deviled egg eyeballs, and sausage puffs that looked like spiders. Joanne had made mini pumpkin hand pies in the shape of ghosts just to make fun of me.

My thoughts drifted to Paisley off and on all day. Paisley got caught up in a moment of passion and it went too far. I understood firsthand the crazy things women do when they're in love. They've been known to drive hundreds of miles in diapers to confront the other woman. Or pour themselves into red leotards with black satin hot pants to make a five-year-old boy and his father happy.

I pulled on thigh-high black boots and a black Zorro mask and thought that Paisley and I weren't all that different. This plan was equally insane. I just got a better man.

Gia texted me:

What is this costume? Do I have to wear the tights? I look ridiculous.

I texted him back:

Trust me.

I teased out my hair and headed down the stairs to get Joanne's making fun of me out of the way.

Kenny met me in the foyer dressed like Han Solo. "Oh. My. Gawd. You look fab! You need to stop wearing those baggy shirts like yesterday!"

I giggled. "Do these hot pants look okay? It was not easy to find this costume in my size."

"Shut up! You look amazing. Gia is going to go nuts."

Both Kenny and my cell phones chimed one after the other.

I pulled mine out and checked the screen. "It's a Google alert."

Kenny's eyes went wide. "Oh no. The Underworld Warriors tagged you in a video."

We followed the link to YouTube, where Sable and Jax were standing in front of the house earlier in the afternoon.

"Justice was served this week when one of the biggest offenders in spirit disturbance was finally silenced. This is the bed and breakfast where Dr. Simon Beck was killed. We never got the chance to question him like we planned or to make him answer for his crimes, but the spirits had their own plans. Ironically, he was killed while giving a lecture to the owner about bringing a curse upon herself. In order to protect her identity, we won't tell you the name of the innkeeper, who was really cool for an old lady."

The video ended and Kenny started to laugh. "An old lady."

"They'd better be talking about Aunt Ginny."

The doorbell rang and Figaro galloped to the door dressed like a cowboy. He tried to flop, but the hat was throwing off his mojo and he threw himself in a corkscrew.

I opened the door to find the Biddies out of their balaclavas. They came in giggling and gave me twirls to show off their costumes.

Mother Gibson was dressed in a plus-sized leopard print catsuit and had covered her tight fade with a curly long wig. Mrs. Dodson had on a white satin tracksuit with pink stripes running down the legs and Nike high-tops. And Mrs. Davis had on pink shorts, a pink halter top, and a blond wig with long pigtails.

"Wow! Look at you, Poppy. Do you know who *we* are?"

"Uh. Is Mother Gibson Donna Summer?"

The ladies giggled. "Nope."

"Mrs. Dodson is a rapper?"

She tapped her cane that was decorated as a hockey stick. "Don't be ridiculous."

"And Mrs. Davis. Actually, I think I've seen you wear that outfit to bingo."

Mrs. Davis tittered. "I have."

"We're the Spice Girls, silly." Aunt Ginny had sneaked up behind me with Royce by her side. She was wearing a sequined minidress that looked like the Union Jack and had on a long red wig. "I'm Ginger. Lila's Scary, Edith's Sporty, and Thelma's Baby. I can't believe you didn't know that."

"Well, I think you're missing one."

Aunt Ginny patted Royce's arm. He was dressed like Thurston Howell III from *Gilligan's Island*. "Royce is our fifth."

"Who are you supposed to be?"

Royce grinned and doffed his captain's hat. "Old Spice."

Joanne brought in a punch bowl filled with something lime green and set it over a bowl of dry ice, so it appeared to sit in a bank of fog. She adjusted her pink taffeta skirt and picked up her magic wand. "What?"

"Nothing. I just didn't peg you as the Glinda the Good Witch type."

"There's a lot you don't know about me." She threw her nose in the air and flounced back to the kitchen.

You got that right.

There was another knock on the front door, and Figaro galloped to the foyer again. This time he miscalculated the weight of his lasso and slid into the umbrella stand.

"Well, that was embarrassing." I picked him up and gave him a head bonk. He swatted at my mask. It wasn't fooling him for a second.

I opened the door to find my sexy Italian dressed in an identical red-and-black leotard over a muscle suit, and a five-year-old mini me who hopped up and down giggling. "Yay! You did it. Look, Daddy. Poppy's the mommy, and you're the daddy, and I'm Dash! We're the Incredibles! Get it, Daddy?"

Gia's eyes were taking a slow journey from my Zorro mask to my thigh-high boots. I could see his face lose all color even behind the black velvet. "Yes, Piccolo. I see that."

Aunt Ginny took Henry's hand. "Why don't you come with me, and I'll introduce you to Pop Rocks while Daddy catches his breath."

"Ooh, what are Pop Rocks?"

Aunt Ginny led Henry into the party, and I stepped closer to Gia and smoothed the logo on his costume. "You look great. It's from a kids' movie. Are you okay with the tights?"

He pulled me against him and kissed me like I'd been away to war. *"Mi sono innamorato di te, mia cara."*

"What does that mean?"

"'I have fallen so in love with you.'" He kissed my hand and whispered something in my ear that made me heat up until I was in danger of melting the Incredibles logo on my chest.

"What's going to happen to Mia Famiglia? Are Marco and the guys out of work for the rest of the year?"

"We have decided to move to weekends only for next two months. Once it was announced on the website, reservations poured in, and they are just about full till Christmas."

"That's good."

"Everyone want to try the new manicotti."

"Oh."

Gia grinned. "I told Momma she need to apologize and accept you if she ever want your help again."

"What'd she say to that?"

"She put herself in a time-out with a bottle of Chianti."

"Oh dear. Well, one day I'll pass my secrets on to Henry. She'll have to wait until then to get her hands on the recipe."

Gia grinned and pulled me into another kiss.

Aunt Ginny marched Henry back to the foyer. He looked a little stunned and concerned.

"What's wrong?"

Aunt Ginny was a little sheepish. "He didn't love the Pop Rocks."

I put my hand on Henry's back. "No?"

He shook his head. He hadn't swallowed yet. "It's a mouthful of bees."

"Oh, baby. You want to spit it out?"

He nodded.

I grabbed a napkin from the table. He spit absolutely nothing into my hand because they had dissolved. "Okay. Let's go trick or treating and get that memory of the bees behind you."

Aunt Ginny walked us out to the porch. Kids in costume were running up and down the sidewalk. Mr. Winston was giving out candy to two of the Avengers. He lifted his hand and waved.

Owen Rodney and Jennifer Beck sat side by side in the rocking chairs. Owen had on his formal metal colander for special occasions, Princess sat on his lap, and Jennifer held the bowl of candy bars to give out.

She oohed over our costumes. "You guys look so cute."

Owen adjusted his colander and ran his hand over Princess's good ear. "You go and have fun. I'll keep an eye on Sir Figaro Newton to make sure he doesn't start that turf war with the raccoons."

"Thank you, Owen. We'll be back in a little while."

We got to the mailbox, and I had to stop. "Aunt Ginny?"

"Yeah?"

"Did you tell Owen Figaro's whole name?"

"No, why?"

"Neither did I."

EPILOGUE

Aunt Ginny had falsely reported that our loved ones had obligations with their other families and it would be just the two of us for Thanksgiving. We decided to have a simple affair instead of putting on a big to-do. I was a little put out that Gia and Henry were having dinner with Mussolini, but I agreed to Aunt Ginny's plan and bought two Cornish hens for dinner.

Then we discovered Gia, Henry, and Royce were in fact not going with the rest of their clans, they were always planning to have dinner with us, and Aunt Ginny wasn't to be trusted with passing messages anymore. Aunt Ginny said we would have a nice little family gathering. I bought a frozen turkey breast.

Kenny had a moment of hysteria that he couldn't go home for the holidays because Mother was spending the four-day weekend in Aruba with her slutty new boyfriend—unnaturally tan Chuck—and no one else loved him but us.

Then Sawyer asked if she could join us and bring Officer Ben since his mother lives in Ohio and he had to work on Friday and couldn't travel. I bought a ten-pound turkey.

Joanne found out about Kenny and got her hairnet in a bunch that we were having a "work thing" with everyone but her and made herself a martyr by offering to make a few pies so there would be some decent desserts for such a large group of friends and family before she sat at home eating her Hungry-Man turkey dinner for one. *For the love of God.*

I thought, *Heck. I can make do with what I have. I'll carve everything in the kitchen.*

Then Aunt Ginny *may* have let it slip to the Biddies that I was catering a free Thanksgiving buffet—price of entry: one mandarin orange Jell-O salad. And that was all before my former mother-in-law showed up to give the gift of passive aggression that keeps on giving—aka *Georgina time*—and she invited her "little Smitty" to join her for a homemade Thanksgiving dinner.

In my home. Made by me. For fourteen people.

A simple affair.

Now it's Thanksgiving Day I have a twenty-six-pound turkey, a ten-pound turkey, two frozen turkey breasts, two Cornish game hens, twenty pounds of potatoes and yams, four boxes of stuffing, a vat of gravy, one bag of frozen peas that will ease my conscience, but no one else will touch, and six martyr pies.

"Come and eat!"

Gia sneaked his arm around my waist and nuzzled my neck. "Everything smells delicious."

Smitty took the bowl of mashed potatoes out of my hand with a small amount of indignation. "Hey. Wise guy. You can make out after dinner. I didn't wear my lucky sweatpants to scrape these spuds off the tablecloth."

Georgina linked her arm in his. "Quit distracting Poppy and let her get the food on the table. You got my cranberries, didn't you?"

I picked up a bowl of Harry & David spiced chutney. "Right here. Along with Joanne's homemade cranberry sauce and this blob shaped like a can that Kenny had to have."

Kenny took the jiggly blob and moved it closer to his plate. "I'll have you know this is a tradition in my family."

This explains a lot of Kenny's recipe choices.

Everyone found their seat around the two tables in the dining room, and we were about to say grace and carve up the glorious golden brown and crispy turkey when the doorbell rang.

Royce narrowed his eyes and loudly whispered to Aunt Ginny, "Am I doing the ghost tour tonight? Because I didn't bring my cummerbund."

Aunt Ginny patted his hand. "No, dear. That's all over. It's probably the police have found a body."

She gave me a prim smile like she hadn't just thrown me under the funeral bus.

I excused myself and went to answer the door, Figaro taking immediate occupancy of my chair in the dining room. *It's not the cops. Why would it be?* I opened the door to Amber and Officer Birkwell, both in uniform. *Nuts.*

"Are we late?" Shane grinned.

Late for what? I blinked and tried to keep my face blank. "No. Not at all. Come on in."

I led them to the dining room while scanning the faces around the tables looking for someone who wouldn't make eye contact with me. I'd found the weakest link and her name was Sawyer.

Aunt Ginny popped up from her seat and added two place settings next to her and Royce with the Biddies. "Oh good. You made it before someone died for a change." She gave me a sideways look and I glanced towards Sawyer, who was very focused on her gravy.

I brought them each a glass. "You're always welcome. We just started."

Henry giggled and I turned to see Figaro sitting in his lap, eating a bite of turkey off Henry's fork.

Gia snapped his fingers at the naughty feline and Figaro glared at him with some side-eye without pausing to go in for bite number two.

I picked him up around the middle and he started to squirm in resistance. "Oh no you don't. Taking advantage of the small child who still thinks you're cute and not a little glutton. Your turkey is in the kitchen, friend." I placed him on the floor and took my seat next to my best little man.

Three days of cooking, and everyone was stuffed in twenty minutes. Except for Figaro, who split his begging time between Henry, who offered up most of his turkey, and Aunt Ginny, who dropped most of hers.

I made everyone to-go containers of leftovers while Kenny and Georgina cleared and did the first wave of dishes. Well, Georgina cleared her own plate, then hid in the bathroom until Kenny and Gia were finished with the dishes. Then we spent the evening playing charades and Pictionary and eating a second round of dessert. Other than Figaro stealing a swipe of whipped cream off of my pie while I was distracted by Gia trying to act out *Die Hard*, we had a blissful holiday with no meltdowns and no murders.

Thank God. I hate surprises.

The last guests were departing, and Joanne was obsessing. "Are you sure you can handle those dishes? I don't want to find a mess in that kitchen when I come back on Monday."

I put my hand on her shoulder and gently spun her towards the door while Sawyer tucked her into her jacket. "Don't worry. We'll finish the dishes, and the kitchen will be spotless when you come back to work. Go home and put your feet up. Everything was fabulous."

"It's just that I know you don't know how—"

Sawyer was closing the door as Joanne tried to fire off one final insult. Even though she spent the whole evening perfecting her natural scowl, I think she was afraid we'd have fun without her.

Kenny passed me in the foyer on his way up the stairs with a plate of cranberry pear pie. "Don't judge me. I'm so past it. I'm going to watch an old movie in bed. I'll see you for pajama pancakes in the morning. Spoiler alert—I plan on eating my weight in bacon after all the calories I burnt off acting out *Wizard of Oz* tonight."

Pajama pancakes was one of our new traditions Kenny had started for mornings where the bed and breakfast wasn't booked with guests. We still had Christmas reservation requests coming in via email, so we had to make the most out of the opportunities we were given.

I headed into the library to join Sawyer and Aunt Ginny and found Georgina lying on the couch groaning with her hand over her eyes. "I've never worked so hard in all my life as I did cleaning up from dinner."

That was probably true.

Aunt Ginny poured them each a tiny sherry. "Poppy, you outdid yourself. And those pies were out of this world. What was in that one with the pears and the crumble on top?"

"Figs."

Speaking of Figs. Figaro came flying into the room playing soccer with his new contraband and it bounced off of Sawyer's foot. She reached for it and held up a small blue velvet box in the palm of her hand.

The air was sucked from the room as four women who could recognize a ring box in a pitch-black cave underground gasped as one.

Aunt Ginny sputtered, "Is that what I think it is?"

Georgina sprang upright, suddenly getting her second wind. "Is there a name on it? Who's it for?"

Sawyer looked from the box to me. Her hand trembling. "There's nothing."

I picked up the cat who was trying to swat the box out of her hand. "Where did Figaro get that?"

Aunt Ginny inched forward on her chair. "That cat's a little thief. Now that he has a taste of klepto-mania, he can't give it up."

Georgina waved her hands in front of her face. "Stop talking and open it!"

I put my free hand over the box. "We can't. We don't know who it's for and it hasn't actually been given to anyone yet."

Aunt Ginny smacked my hand away and snatched the box from Sawyer. She looked at us one by one. No one tried to stop her. Slowly she lifted the lid.

The box creaked like the hinges had never been moved. It sounded like Bride of Frankenstein emerging from her casket. We all leaned in to get a look at what treasure was waiting on the little silk liner.

Inside was a stunning one-carat diamond set in a halo of smaller diamonds in a platinum setting. It was definitely an engagement ring.

With no name on it.

And all of our men had been here.

RECIPES

Pecan Pie Muffins

Yield: 12 muffins

Ingredients
1½ cup packed light brown sugar
¾ cup gluten-free flour
3 cups chopped pecans
1 cup butter, softened
3 eggs, beaten
1 teaspoon xanthan gum if not included in your
   flour
1 teaspoon salt
1 tablespoon vanilla extract

Preheat oven to 350 degrees F. Grease mini or regular muffin cups generously. Grease them well or they will stick. In medium bowl, stir together brown sugar, flour, and pecans. In a separate bowl, beat the butter and eggs together. Add the vanilla. Stir in dry ingredients just until combined.

Spoon batter into muffin cups about ⅔ full. Bake for 15–17 minutes for regular-size muffins. Run a knife around the edge of each muffin and pop it out.

Georgina won't stay out of these.

Harvest Fruit Muffins

Yield: 12 muffins

Ingredients

Filling
½ cup chopped dates (about 8)
½ cup chopped dried figs (about 8)
2 cups peeled and cored diced apples (about 2
    apples)
1 tablespoon butter
¼ cup sugar
1 teaspoon apple pie spice (or cinnamon)

Topping
½ cup packed brown sugar
⅓ cup all-purpose flour
1 teaspoon apple pie spice (or cinnamon)
½ cup toasted chopped hazelnuts
4 tablespoons butter, melted

Batter
2¼ cups gluten-free flour
½ teaspoon xanthan gum if not included in your
    flour
1 teaspoon baking soda
½ teaspoon salt
1 teaspoon apple pie spice (or cinnamon)
1 egg
1 cup buttermilk
½ cup butter, melted
1 teaspoon vanilla extract
1¼ cups packed brown sugar

Preheat the oven to 375 degrees F. Grease a 12-cup muffin tin or line with paper muffin cups.

Prepare the Fruit

If your dates and figs are too dry, place them in a microwavable bowl. Cover them with water (or apple-jack brandy—I'm not judging you), then cover the bowl with plastic wrap and microwave for 2 minutes. Let them sit and hydrate while you peel and chop your apples.

Melt 1 tablespoon butter in a frying pan over medium heat. Cook chopped apples, figs, and dates until the apples have softened and are starting to brown. Sprinkle on ½ cup brown sugar and 1 teaspoon apple pie spice. Set aside to cool.

Make the Topping

In a small bowl, stir together ½ cup brown sugar, ⅓ cup flour, apple pie spice, and hazelnuts. Drizzle in 4 tablespoons of melted butter while tossing with a fork until well blended.

Make the Batter

In a large bowl, stir together 2¼ cups flour, xanthan gum if necessary, baking soda, salt, and apple pie spice.

In a separate smaller bowl, mix together the egg, buttermilk, ½ cup melted butter, vanilla, and 1¼ cups brown sugar until sugar has dissolved. Pour into the flour mixture, then add the cooled fruit. Stir everything until blended. Spoon into the prepared muffin tin, filling the cups to the top.

Assemble the Muffins

Sprinkle topping over the tops of the muffins. Gently press into the batter.

Bake for 20 minutes in the preheated oven, or until the tops of the muffins spring back when lightly pressed.

Maple Cardamom Breakfast Cake

Yield: 1 loaf—about 12 slices

Cake Ingredients
2 egg whites beaten to soft peaks
1 cup unsalted butter, at room temperature
1 cup granulated sugar
4 large eggs at room temperature, beaten
1 teaspoon vanilla extract
1¼ cup gluten-free flour
½ teaspoon xanthan gum if not included in your
    flour
1 teaspoon kosher salt
1½ teaspoons cardamom
2 tablespoons sour cream

Maple Cardamom Glaze
½ cup powdered sugar
1 teaspoon cardamom
2 tablespoons maple syrup
1 tablespoon milk

Preheat your oven to 325 degrees F. Grease 9x5 loaf pan and set it aside.

In the bowl of a stand mixer fitted with the whisk attachment or a large bowl with a handheld mixer, whip 2 egg whites until they form soft peaks. Set aside.

In the bowl of a stand mixer fitted with the paddle attachment cream the butter on medium-high speed until it is light and fluffy. Add the sugar and beat until fluffy. Then add the whole eggs and vanilla on low speed, scraping down the sides of the bowl from time to time until well combined. Turn the mixer speed up to medium-high and beat until smooth.

In a small bowl, place the flour blend, xanthan gum if needed, salt, and cardamom. Whisk to combine. Add the flour mixture, about ¼ cup at a time, to the mixer bowl with the wet ingredients, and mix until just combined. Now add the sour cream and blend well. Fold in the egg whites and mix well until the batter is smooth. Spoon the batter into the prepared loaf pan and smooth the top.

Bake in the center of the preheated oven until lightly golden brown all over—about 50 minutes or until a toothpick inserted in the center comes out clean. Remove from the oven and let cool in the pan for at least 30 minutes. Remove from the pan and drizzle with maple cardamom glaze while still warm. Let cool completely.

Maple Cardamom Glaze

Combine all ingredients and mix well until a thick glaze forms. If it's too runny add a little powdered sugar. If glaze is too thick like a paste, add a very tiny amount of milk by the ¼ teaspoon until it's thin enough to run off a spoon easily.

Cassata Cupcakes

Yield: 12 cakes

Cupcake Batter
2¼ cups gluten-free flour blend
1 teaspoon xanthan gum if not included in your
   blend
½ teaspoon baking soda
2 teaspoons baking powder
½ teaspoon kosher salt
1 whole egg plus 4 egg whites at room temperature
1⅓ cups buttermilk at room temperature
2 teaspoons pure vanilla extract
10 tablespoons unsalted butter at room temperature
1½ cups granulated sugar

Cassata Filling
15 oz. whole-milk ricotta
¼ cup chopped cherries (sweet cherries or
   maraschino)
¼ cup chopped pistachios
¼ cup finely chopped candied orange peel
8 oz. mascarpone cheese
½ cup powdered sugar
1 teaspoon cinnamon
½ cup mini chocolate chips

Rum Syrup
⅓ cup water
⅓ cup sugar
¼ cup rum, preferably white

Optional
Sweetened chocolate powder, marzipan, or pow-
    dered sugar

Preheat your oven to 350 degrees F. Grease a cupcake pan or line with papers.

Into a medium bowl, sift the gluten-free flour blend,
xanthan gum if necessary, baking soda, baking powder, and salt. Whisk to combine. Set the dry ingredients aside.

In another medium-size bowl, place the whole egg,
egg whites, buttermilk, and vanilla. Whisk to combine.
Set the wet ingredients aside.

In the bowl of a stand mixer fitted with the paddle
attachment or a large bowl with a handheld mixer,
beat the butter and sugar on medium-high speed until
very light and fluffy. Add the dry ingredients in 3 equal
portions, alternating with the liquid ingredients. Mix
well to combine in between additions.

Beat for another minute on medium speed until
you have a smooth batter. Spoon into prepared pans.

Place the pans in the center of the preheated oven
and bake for 20 minutes or until the tops are lightly
browned and spring back when pressed. Allow to cool
completely before filling.

Make the Filling
Drain the ricotta of excess liquid.
Drain the cherries and pat dry.
Chop the cherries, pistachios, and candied peel.
Combine all ingredients in a mixing bowl and fold
together until well combined. Return to the refriger-
ator until ready to fill the cupcakes.

Make the Rum Syrup

Add water and sugar to a saucepan Place over medium heat and bring to a boil, stirring occasionally to dissolve the sugar. Remove the pan from the heat, stir in the rum, and allow the syrup to cool. (I've made this with Grand Marnier too and it's just as delicious)

Assemble the Cupcakes

Cut each cupcake in half horizontally. Brush the rum glaze over the cut half. Fill the cake with cassata filling and replace the top half. Brush the top half with run syrup.

At this point you can sprinkle the top with either sweetened chocolate powder (equal parts cocoa powder mixed with powdered sugar), a little disc of flattened marzipan, or powdered sugar.

Sicilian Lemon Earl Grey Tiramisu

Yield: 9 servings

1½ cup boiling water
6 Earl Grey tea bags
6 large egg yolks
1 cup granulated sugar (superfine if possible)
1¼ cup mascarpone cheese, softened
1¾ cup heavy whipped cream
Zest of 1 lemon
½ cup bergamot liqueur
1 package Schär Gluten Free Italian
    ladyfingers (about 30)
1 15-oz. jar lemon curd
¼ cup white chocolate powder (or powdered
    sugar) for dusting

Make a strong Earl Grey tea using the boiling water and 6 tea bags. Set aside to cool completely. Once you remove the tea bags you'll only have about 1 cup of tea.

Make the Sabayon

In the top of a double boiler over simmering water, add the egg yolks and sugar to a mixing bowl. Whisk them constantly for about 10 minutes until they double in size and get thick and lemony. Remove the bowl from the heat and continue to whip sabayon until it cools. If you're in a hurry you can put the bowl in a bowl full of ice water, making sure not to get any ice water in the sabayon.

Add softened mascarpone to the whipped yolks;

mix until well combined. Don't overmix; this can cause curdling.

In a separate bowl, or the bowl of your stand mixer, whip the cream to stiff peaks. Gently fold the whipped cream and the lemon zest into the mascarpone-sabayon mixture and refrigerate until you are ready to assemble the tiramisu.

Mix the 1 cup of cold Earl Grey tea with the bergamot liqueur.

Arrange half the ladyfingers in the bottom of a 9-inch square baking dish or casserole.

Brush the ladyfingers generously with half the Earl Grey / bergamot mixture. (Don't dip them, as gluten-free ladyfingers will disintegrate very fast if they soak up too much liquid.)

Spoon half the mascarpone cream filling over the ladyfingers.

Spread half the jar of lemon curd over the mascarpone cream.

Repeat process with another layer of ladyfingers.

Brush on the rest of the Earl Grey / bergamot mixture.

Top with the rest of the lemon curd. Then the rest of the mascarpone cream.

Refrigerate at least 4 hours. Overnight is best.

Dust with white chocolate powder or powdered sugar before serving.

Gluten-Free Focaccia

Yield: 1 loaf

3 cups gluten-free flour
½ teaspoon xanthan gum if not included in your
   flour
1½ teaspoons baking powder
1 tablespoon salt
1 tablespoon sugar
1½ cups warm water
2 tablespoons olive oil
Sprigs rosemary
Olive oil for drizzling over the top
1 teaspoon flaked sea salt for the top

In the bowl of your stand mixer, whisk together flour, xanthan gum if necessary, baking powder, salt, and sugar. Add the water and 2 tablespoons olive oil and mix with the paddle attachment until a smooth dough forms. If it's too sticky, add a little more flour a tablespoon at a time until the dough pulls away from the sides of the bowl.

Line a baking sheet with parchment paper. Pat your focaccia dough down to a flat disc about ¾ inch thick. Create wells with your knuckles all over the top of the dough. Stick a small tuft of rosemary in each well. Cover and let rise in a warm place for about an hour.

Preheat the oven to 425 degrees F. Drizzle the top of the dough with olive oil and sprinkle with flaked sea salt. Bake in the center of the oven for about 40 minutes or until the crust is golden brown. Allow to cool twenty minutes before cutting. You can wrap pieces in foil and rewarm them in the oven before serving.

Poppy's Chicken, Spinach, and Artichoke Manicotti

Yield: 6 servings

Ingredients
2 chicken breasts
1 box gluten-free manicotti noodles—about 14
    tubes
1 package frozen chopped spinach, thawed and
    drained
16 oz. cream cheese, softened
5 oz. shredded Parmesan cheese
10 oz. artichoke hearts, chopped
1 cup mayo
1 teaspoon garlic powder
½ teaspoon salt
½ teaspoon pepper
1 jar Alfredo sauce (or you can make about 2
    cups béchamel sauce on your own.)
8 oz. shredded mozzarella cheese

Cook, and shred (or finely chop) your chicken breasts. Set aside.

Cook your manicotti noodles for about 9 minutes. You don't want to cook them all the way according to package directions, but you can't stuff them dry either. There isn't enough moisture in the ingredients to finish cooking them. Drain them and set them aside.

Mix together the cooled shredded chicken, spinach, cheeses, chopped artichokes, mayo, garlic powder, salt, and pepper. Set aside.

Spoon about one cup of the Alfredo sauce in the bottom of a 9x13 casserole dish.

Stuff your cooled manicotti tubes with the chicken and cheese mixture. Make sure to stuff from both ends to fill them completely—but don't overstuff them and cause the pasta to split.

Line the stuffed tubes down the center of the casserole dish. You can top the first layer with a little Alfredo sauce, then build a second layer.

Top the finished rows with the rest of the Alfredo sauce and sprinkle on the mozzarella cheese.

Cover with a piece of buttered foil, shiny side down.

Bake in a preheated 350-degree F oven for about 30 minutes until you see the cheese is melted and the sauce is bubbly.

You can take the foil off for the last few minutes of baking if you like the cheese a little more browned.

ACKNOWLEDGMENTS

My sincere thanks to The Chalfonte, The Hotel Macomber, Southern Mansion, and the Inn of Cape May. You each have beautiful properties, and the information about your ghost tours was supremely helpful. Everything about the Haunted Homes Tour that Poppy got rooked into was completely fictional. Dillon, Charlotte, Crystal, Denise, Dawn, and Linda were all lovely and never once asked me to do the dishes. Also know that at the time of printing the Union Park Dining Room in The Hotel Macomber was a BYOB restaurant and would not have the bar that I described. Any errors in description are mine alone. No horses were harmed in the Victorian hearse scenes.

Another thanks goes to my writers group for their fabulous critiques of the rough draft. And my team of editors, who put all the punctuation in the right places.

Please come find me online at libbykleinbooks.com and sign up for my newsletter to get all my goings on plus gluten free recipes and Figaro's advice column.

Visit our website at
KensingtonBooks.com
to sign up for our newsletters, read
more from your favorite authors, see
books by series, view reading group
guides, and more!

Become a Part of Our
Between the Chapters Book Club
Community and Join the Conversation

Submit your book review for a chance to win exclusive
Between the Chapters swag you can't get anywhere else!
https://www.kensingtonbooks.com/pages/review/